Acclaim for Haruki Murakami's

Kafka on the Shore

"Anyone can tell a story that resembles a dream, it's the rare artist, like this one, who can make us feel that we are dreaming it ourselves."
— *The New York Times Book Review*

"An excellent demonstration of why [Murakami is] deservedly famous [for] postmodern fiction that's actually fun to read."
— *The Washington Post Book World*

"[A] fabulous trail through identity, mythology, philosophy, and dreams. . . . Murakami's power to imagine is breathtaking and the empathy infusing *Kafka on the Shore* makes it a responsible book, one that is adult, wise, and forgiving."
— *The Boston Globe*

"Gay and severe, tender and horrifying, with the monstrous confrontations and violent jump-cuts of Kabuki and the introspective tremors of a Salingeresque adolescent. . . . [Murakami] addresses the fantastic and the natural, each with the same mix of gravity and lightness."
— *Los Angeles Times Book Review*

"Murakami has set out to have serious fun, capturing history, myth, hearsay, and the pulse of modern Japanese life in the fish-eye lens of his own protean vision."
— *Elle*

"Remorselessly compelling [with a] nearly throwaway touch of poetry. . . . Is this a real Japan, or is it simply the vision of a great novelist?"
— *The New York Observer*

"An epic work that blends the sprawling designs of *Wind-Up Bird* with the psychological ruminations of *Hard-Boiled Wonderland* and the emotional sensitivity of *Norwegian Wood*. . . . The most ambitious and lucid account thus far of Murakami's wide-ranging and deftly entwined thematic concerns."
—*San Francisco Chronicle*

"*Kafka on the Shore* defies time and linearity. . . . Time blurs, identities are fractured and reconstructed, cats talk, fish fall from the sky— and what survives is the metaphor."
—*LA Weekly*

"I never so willingly suspend disbelief as when I enter Murakami's world. . . . A shade of noir mystery, a slice of everyday Stephen King– like horror, an ill-fated love story, a fairy tale, the search for an allegorical correspondence between dream life and the real world—all of it driven by a riveting narrative . . . Murakami's whimsical, inquisitive and generous spirit encompasses all. . . . A distinctive and influential voice in a new global literature." —Vernon Peterson, *The Oregonian*

"*Kafka on the Shore* is Murakami's biggest novel in a decade and the most fun to read. . . . A story about the fuzzy boundary between what happens in our minds and what happens in the real world—and how easily one can pass between the two."
—*The Orlando Sentinel*

"Unlike a lot of contemporary fiction, *Kafka on the Shore* risks much: it attempts to tap into the same fevered dream-logic as Franz Kafka's novels and stories, but unlike those metaphysical dead-ends, Murakami's narratives offer his characters a way out. (Though never a way back.) . . . [He] understands the ease with which we confuse our inside world with our outside world, our dreams with our waking life."
—*Austin American-Statesman*

Haruki Murakami

Kafka on the Shore

Haruki Murakami was born in Kyoto in 1949 and now lives near Tokyo. His work has been translated into more than fifty languages, and the most recent of his many international honors is the Jerusalem Prize, whose previous recipients include J. M. Coetzee, Milan Kundera, and V. S. Naipaul.

www.harukimurakami.com

INTERNATIONAL

Books by Haruki Murakami

Fiction

1Q84

After Dark

After the Quake

Blind Willow, Sleeping Woman

Colorless Tsukuru Tazaki and His Years of Pilgrimage

Dance Dance Dance

The Elephant Vanishes

Hard-Boiled Wonderland and the End of the World

Kafka on the Shore

Norwegian Wood

South of the Border, West of the Sun

Sputnik Sweetheart

The Strange Library

A Wild Sheep Chase

The Wind-Up Bird Chronicle

Nonfiction

Underground: The Tokyo Gas Attack and the Japanese Psyche

What I Talk About When I Talk About Running: A Memoir

Kafka on the Shore

Haruki Murakami

Kafka on the Shore

Translated from the Japanese by Philip Gabriel

VINTAGE INTERNATIONAL

Vintage Books   A Division of Random House, Inc.   New York

FIRST VINTAGE INTERNATIONAL EDITION, JANUARY 2006

Copyright © 2005 by Haruki Murakami

All rights reserved. Published in the United States by Vintage Books, a division of Random House, Inc., New York, and in Canada by Random House of Canada Limited, Toronto. Originally published in Japan in two volumes as *Umibe no Kafuka* by Shinchosha, Tokyo, in 2002. This translation originally published in hardcover in the United States by Alfred A. Knopf, a division of Random House, Inc., New York, in 2005.

Excerpt from *Elektra* is from Paul Roche's translation of the play.

The Library of Congress has cataloged the Knopf edition as follows:
Murakami, Haruki, [date]
[Umibe no Kafuka. English]
Kafka on the shore / by Haruki Murakami ; translated by Philip Gabriel.
p. cm.
1. Gabriel, J. Philip. II. Title.
PL856.U673U48   2005
895.6'35—dc22
2004048907

Vintage ISBN-10: 1-4000-7927-6
Vintage ISBN-13: 978-1-4000-7927-8

Book design by Iris Weinstein
Title page art: Kumamoto © 2004 by Iris Weinstein

www.vintagebooks.com

Printed in the United States of America
35   34   33   32   31

Kafka on the Shore

The Boy Named Crow

So you're all set for money, then?" the boy named Crow asks in his typical sluggish voice. The kind of voice like when you've just woken up and your mouth still feels heavy and dull. But he's just pretending. He's totally awake. As always.

I nod.

"How much?"

I review the numbers in my head. "Close to thirty-five hundred in cash, plus some money I can get from an ATM. I know it's not a lot, but it should be enough. For the time being."

"Not bad," the boy named Crow says. *"For the time being."*

I give him another nod.

"I'm guessing this isn't Christmas money from Santa Claus."

"Yeah, you're right," I reply.

Crow smirks and looks around. "I imagine you've started by rifling drawers, am I right?"

I don't say anything. He knows whose money we're talking about, so there's no need for any long-winded interrogations. He's just giving me a hard time.

"No matter," Crow says. "You really need this money and you're going to get it—beg, borrow, or steal. It's your father's money, so who cares, right? Get your hands on that much and you should be able to make it. *For the time being.* But what's the plan after it's all gone? Money isn't like mushrooms in a forest—it doesn't just pop up on its own, you know. You'll need to eat, a place to sleep. One day you're going to run out."

"I'll think about that when the time comes," I say.

"When the time comes," Crow repeats, as if weighing these words in his hand.

I nod.

3

"Like by getting a job or something?"

"Maybe," I say.

Crow shakes his head. "You know, you've got a lot to learn about the world. Listen—what kind of job could a fifteen-year-old kid get in some far-off place he's never been to before? You haven't even finished junior high. Who do you think's going to hire you?"

I blush a little. It doesn't take much to make me blush.

"Forget it," he says. "You're just getting started and I shouldn't lay all this depressing stuff on you. You've already decided what you're going to do, and all that's left is to set the wheels in motion. I mean, it's *your* life. Basically you gotta go with what you think is right."

That's right. When all is said and done, it *is* my life.

"I'll tell you one thing, though. You're going to have to get a lot tougher if you want to make it."

"I'm trying my best," I say.

"I'm sure you are," Crow says. "These last few years you've gotten a whole lot stronger. I've got to hand it to you."

I nod again.

"But let's face it—you're only fifteen," Crow goes on. "Your life's just begun and there's a ton of things out in the world you've never laid eyes on. Things you never could imagine."

As always, we're sitting beside each other on the old sofa in my father's study. Crow loves the study and all the little objects scattered around there. Now he's toying with a bee-shaped glass paperweight. If my father was at home, you can bet Crow would never go anywhere near it.

"But I have to get out of here," I tell him. "No two ways around it."

"Yeah, I guess you're right." He places the paperweight back on the table and links his hands behind his head. "Not that running away's going to solve everything. I don't want to rain on your parade or anything, but I wouldn't count on escaping this place if I were you. No matter how far you run. Distance might not solve anything."

The boy named Crow lets out a sigh, then rests a fingertip on each of his closed eyelids and speaks to me from the darkness within.

"How about we play our game?" he says.

"All right," I say. I close my eyes and quietly take a deep breath.

"Okay, picture a terrible sandstorm," he says. "Get everything else out of your head."

I do what he says, get everything else out of my head. I forget who I

4

am, even. I'm a total blank. Then things start to surface. Things that—as we sit here on the old leather sofa in my father's study—both of us can see.

"Sometimes fate is like a small sandstorm that keeps changing directions," Crow says.

Sometimes fate is like a small sandstorm that keeps changing directions. You change direction but the sandstorm chases you. You turn again, but the storm adjusts. Over and over you play this out, like some ominous dance with death just before dawn. Why? Because this storm isn't something that blew in from far away, something that has nothing to do with you. This storm is you. Something *inside* of you. So all you can do is give in to it, step right inside the storm, closing your eyes and plugging up your ears so the sand doesn't get in, and walk through it, step by step. There's no sun there, no moon, no direction, no sense of time. Just fine white sand swirling up into the sky like pulverized bones. That's the kind of sandstorm you need to imagine.

And that's exactly what I do. I imagine a white funnel stretching up vertically like a thick rope. My eyes are closed tight, hands cupped over my ears, so those fine grains of sand can't blow inside me. The sandstorm draws steadily closer. I can feel the air pressing on my skin. It really *is* going to swallow me up.

The boy called Crow softly rests a hand on my shoulder, and with that the storm vanishes.

"From now on—no matter what—you've got to be the world's toughest fifteen-year-old. That's the only way you're going to survive. And in order to do that, you've got to figure out what it means to be tough. You following me?"

I keep my eyes closed and don't reply. I just want to sink off into sleep like this, his hand on my shoulder. I hear the faint flutter of wings.

"You're going to be the world's toughest fifteen-year-old," Crow whispers as I try to fall asleep. Like he was carving the words in a deep blue tattoo on my heart.

And you really will have to make it through that violent, metaphysical, symbolic storm. No matter how metaphysical or symbolic it might be, make no mistake about it: it will cut through flesh like a thousand razor blades. People will bleed there, and *you* will bleed

too. Hot, red blood. You'll catch that blood in your hands, your own blood and the blood of others.

And once the storm is over you won't remember how you made it through, how you managed to survive. You won't even be sure, in fact, whether the storm is really over. But one thing is certain. When you come out of the storm you won't be the same person who walked in. That's what this storm's all about.

On my fifteenth birthday I'll run away from home, journey to a far-off town, and live in a corner of a small library. It'd take a week to go into the whole thing, all the details. So I'll just give the main point. **On my fifteenth birthday I'll run away from home, journey to a far-off town, and live in a corner of a small library.**

It sounds a little like a fairy tale. But it's no fairy tale, believe me. No matter what sort of spin you put on it.

Chapter 1

Cash isn't the only thing I take from my father's study when I leave home. I take a small, old gold lighter—I like the design and feel of it—and a folding knife with a really sharp blade. Made to skin deer, it has a five-inch blade and a nice heft. Probably something he bought on one of his trips abroad. I also take a sturdy, bright pocket flashlight out of a drawer. Plus sky blue Revo sunglasses to disguise my age.

I think about taking my father's favorite Sea-Dweller Oyster Rolex. It's a beautiful watch, but something flashy will only attract attention. My cheap plastic Casio watch with an alarm and stopwatch will do just fine, and might actually be more useful. Reluctantly, I return the Rolex to its drawer.

From the back of another drawer I take out a photo of me and my older sister when we were little, the two of us on a beach somewhere with grins plastered across our faces. My sister's looking off to the side so half her face is in shadow and her smile is neatly cut in half. It's like one of those Greek tragedy masks in a textbook that's half one idea and half the opposite. Light and dark. Hope and despair. Laughter and sadness. Trust and loneliness. For my part I'm staring straight ahead, undaunted, at the camera. Nobody else is there at the beach. My sister and I have on swimsuits—hers a red floral-print one-piece, mine some baggy old blue trunks. I'm holding a plastic stick in my hand. White foam is washing over our feet.

Who took this, and where and when, I have no clue. And how could I have looked so happy? And why did my father keep just that one photo? The whole thing is a total mystery. I must have been three, my sister nine. Did we ever really get along that well? I have no memory of ever going to the beach with my family. No memory of going *anywhere* with them. No matter, though—there is no way I'm going to

7

leave that photo with my father, so I put it in my wallet. I don't have any photos of my mother. My father threw them all away.

After giving it some thought I decide to take the cell phone with me. Once he finds out I've taken it, my father will probably get the phone company to cut off service. Still, I toss it into my backpack, along with the adapter. Doesn't add much weight, so why not. When it doesn't work anymore I'll just chuck it.

Just the bare necessities, that's all I need. Choosing which clothes to take is the hardest thing. I'll need a couple sweaters and pairs of underwear. But what about shirts and trousers? Gloves, mufflers, shorts, a coat? There's no end to it. One thing I do know, though. I don't want to wander around some strange place with a huge backpack that screams out, *Hey, everybody, check out the runaway!* Do that and someone is sure to sit up and take notice. Next thing you know the police will haul me in and I'll be sent straight home. If I don't wind up in some gang first.

Any place cold is definitely out, I decide. Easy enough, just choose the opposite—a *warm* place. Then I can leave the coat and gloves behind, and get by with half the clothes. I pick out wash-and-wear-type things, the lightest ones I have, fold them neatly, and stuff them in my backpack. I also pack a three-season sleeping bag, the kind that rolls up nice and tight, toilet stuff, a rain poncho, notebook and pen, a Walkman and ten discs—got to have my music—along with a spare rechargeable battery. That's about it. No need for any cooking gear, which is too heavy and takes up too much room, since I can buy food at the local convenience store.

It takes a while but I'm able to subtract a lot of things from my list. I add things, cross them off, then add a whole other bunch and cross them off, too.

My fifteenth birthday is the ideal time to run away from home. Any earlier and it'd be too soon. Any later and I would have missed my chance.

During my first two years in junior high, I'd worked out, training myself for this day. I started practicing judo in the first couple years of grade school, and still went sometimes in junior high. But I didn't join any school teams. Whenever I had the time I'd jog around the school grounds, swim, or go to the local gym. The young trainers there gave me free lessons, showing me the best kind of stretching exercises and how to use the fitness machines to bulk up. They taught me which muscles you use every day and which ones can only be built up with machines, even the correct way to do a bench press. I'm pretty tall to begin with, and with all this exercise I've developed pretty broad shoulders and pecs. Most strangers would take me for seventeen. If I ran away looking my actual age, you can imagine all the problems that would cause.

Other than the trainers at the gym and the housekeeper who comes to our house every other day—and of course the bare minimum required to get by at school—I barely talk to anyone. For a long time my father and I have avoided seeing each other. We live under the same roof, but our schedules are totally different. He spends most of his time in his studio, far away, and I do my best to avoid him.

The school I'm going to is a private junior high for kids who are upper-class, or at least rich. It's the kind of school where, unless you really blow it, you're automatically promoted to the high school on the same campus. All the students dress neatly, have nice straight teeth, and are boring as hell. Naturally I have zero friends. I've built a wall around me, never letting anybody inside and trying not to venture outside myself. Who could like somebody like that? They all keep an eye on me, from a distance. They might hate me, or even be afraid of me, but I'm just glad they didn't bother me. Because I had tons of things to take care of, including spending a lot of my free time devouring books in the school library.

I always paid close attention to what was said in class, though. Just like the boy named Crow suggested.

The facts and techniques or whatever they teach you in class isn't going to be very useful in the real world, that's for sure. Let's face it, teachers are basically a bunch of morons. But you've got to remember this: you're running away from home. You probably won't have any chance to go to school anymore, so like it or not you'd better absorb whatever you can while you've got the chance. Become like a sheet of blotting paper and soak it all in. Later on you can figure out what to keep and what to unload.

I did what he said, like I almost always do. My brain like a sponge, I focused on every word said in class and let it all sink in, figured out what it meant, and committed everything to memory. Thanks to this, I barely had to study outside of class, but always came out near the top on exams.

My muscles were getting hard as steel, even as I grew more withdrawn and quiet. I tried hard to keep my emotions from showing so that no one—classmates and teachers alike—had a clue what I was thinking. Soon I'd be launched into the rough adult world, and I knew I'd have to be tougher than anybody if I wanted to survive.

My eyes in the mirror are cold as a lizard's, my expression fixed and unreadable. I can't remember the last time I laughed or even showed a hint of a smile to other people. Even to myself.

I'm not trying to imply I can keep up this silent, isolated facade all the time. Sometimes the wall I've erected around me comes crumbling down. It doesn't happen very often, but sometimes, before I even realize what's going on, there I am—naked and defenseless and totally confused. At times like that I always feel an omen calling out to me, like a dark, omnipresent pool of water.

A dark, omnipresent pool of water.

It was probably always there, hidden away somewhere. But when the time comes it silently rushes out, chilling every cell in your body. You drown in that cruel flood, gasping for breath. You cling to a vent near the ceiling, struggling, but the air you manage to breathe is dry and burns your throat. Water and thirst, cold and heat—these supposedly opposite elements combine to assault you.

The world is a huge space, but the space that will take you in—and it doesn't have to be very big—is nowhere to be found. You seek a voice, but what do you get? Silence. You look for silence, but guess what? All you hear over and over and over is the voice of this omen. And sometimes this prophetic voice pushes a secret switch hidden deep inside your brain.

Your heart is like a great river after a long spell of rain, spilling over its banks. All signposts that once stood on the ground are gone, inundated and carried away by that rush of water. And still the rain beats down on the surface of the river. Every time you see a flood like that on the news you tell yourself: That's it. That's my heart.

Before running away from home I wash my hands and face, trim my nails, swab out my ears, and brush my teeth. I take my time, making sure my whole body's well scrubbed. Being really clean is sometimes the most important thing there is. I gaze carefully at my face in the mirror. Genes I'd gotten from my father and mother—not that I have any recollection of what she looked like—created this face. I can do my best to not let any emotions show, keep my eyes from revealing anything, bulk up my muscles, but there's not much I can do about my looks. I'm stuck with my father's long, thick eyebrows and the deep lines between them. I could probably kill him if I wanted to—I'm sure strong enough—and I can erase my mother from my memory. But there's no way to erase the DNA they passed down to me. If I wanted to drive that away I'd have to get rid of *me*.

There's an omen contained in that. A mechanism buried inside of me.

A mechanism buried inside of you.

I switch off the light and leave the bathroom. A heavy, damp stillness lies over the house. The whispers of people who don't exist, the breath of the dead. I look around, standing stock-still, and take a deep breath. The clock shows three p.m., the two hands cold and distant. They're pretending to be noncommittal, but I know they're not on my side. It's nearly time for me to say good-bye. I pick up my backpack and slip it over my shoulders. I've carried it any number of times, but now it feels so much heavier.

Shikoku, I decide. That's where I'll go. There's no particular reason it has to be Shikoku, only that studying the map I got the feeling that's where I should head. The more I look at the map—actually every time I study it—the more I feel Shikoku tugging at me. It's far south of Tokyo, separated from the mainland by water, with a warm climate. I've never been there, have no friends or relatives there, so if somebody started looking for me—which I kind of doubt—Shikoku would be the last place they'd think of.

I pick up the ticket I'd reserved at the counter and climb aboard the night bus. This is the cheapest way to get to Takamatsu—just a shade over ninety bucks. Nobody pays me any attention, asks how old I am, or gives me a second look. The bus driver mechanically checks my ticket.

Only a third of the seats are taken. Most passengers are traveling alone, like me, and the bus is strangely silent. It's a long trip to Takamatsu, ten hours according to the schedule, and we'll be arriving early in the morning. But I don't mind. I've got plenty of time. The bus pulls out of the station at eight, and I push my seat back. No sooner do I settle down than my consciousness, like a battery that's lost its charge, starts to fade away, and I fall asleep.

Sometime in the middle of the night a hard rain begins to fall. I wake up every once in a while, part the chintzy curtain at the window, and gaze out at the highway rushing by. Raindrops beat against the glass, blurring streetlights alongside the road that stretch off into the distance at identical intervals like they were set down to measure the earth. A new light rushes up close and in an instant fades off behind us. I check my watch and see it's past midnight. Automatically shoved to the front, my fifteenth birthday makes its appearance.

"Hey, happy birthday," the boy named Crow says.

"Thanks," I reply.

The omen is still with me, though, like a shadow. I check to make sure the wall around me is still in place. Then I close the curtain and fall back asleep.

Chapter 2

The following document, classified Top Secret by the U.S. Department of Defense, was released to the public in 1986 through the Freedom of Information Act. The document is now kept in the National Archives in Washington, D.C., and can be accessed there.

The investigations recorded here were carried out under the direction of Major James P. Warren from March to April 1946. The field investigation in [name deleted] County, Yamanashi Prefecture, was conducted by Second Lieutenant Robert O'Connor and Master Sergeant Harold Katayama. The interrogator in all interviews was Lt. O'Connor. Sgt. Katayama handled the Japanese interpreting, and Private William Cohen prepared the documents.

Interviews were conducted over a twelve-day period in the reception room of the [name deleted] Town town hall in Yamanashi Prefecture. The following witnesses responded individually to Lt. O'Connor's questions: a female teacher at the [deleted] Town [deleted] County public school, a doctor residing in the same town, two patrolmen assigned to the local police precinct, and six children.

The appended 1:10,000 and 1:2,000 maps of the area in question were provided by the Topographic Institute of the Ministry of Home Affairs.

U.S. ARMY INTELLIGENCE SECTION (MIS) REPORT
Dated: May 12, 1946
Title: Report on the Rice Bowl Hill Incident, 1944
Document Number: PTYX-722-8936745-42213-WWN

The following is a taped interview with Setsuko Okamochi (26), teacher in charge of the fourth-grade B class at the public school in [deleted] Town, [deleted] County. Materials related to the interview can be accessed using application number PTYX-722-SQ-118.

Impressions of the interviewer, Lt. Robert O'Connor: Setsuko Okamochi is an attractive, petite woman. Intelligent and responsible, she responded to the questions accurately and honestly. She still seems slightly in shock, though, from the incident. As she searched her memory she grew very tense at times, and whenever this happened she had a tendency to speak more slowly.

I think it must have been just after ten in the morning when I saw a silver light far up in the sky. A brilliant flash of silver. That's right, it was definitely light reflecting off something metal. That light moved very slowly in the sky from east to west. We all thought it had to be a B-29. It was directly above us, so to see it we had to look straight up. It was a clear blue sky, and the light was so bright all we could see was that silver, duralumin-like object.

But we couldn't make out the shape, since it was too far up. I assumed that they couldn't see us either, so we weren't afraid of being attacked or having bombs suddenly rain down on us. Dropping bombs in the mountains here would be pretty pointless anyway. I figured the plane was on its way to bomb some large city somewhere, or maybe on its way back from a raid. So we kept on walking. All I thought was how that light had a strange beauty to it.

—According to military records no U.S. bombers or any other kind of aircraft were flying over that region at the time, that is, around ten a.m. on November 7, 1944.

But I saw it clearly, and so did the sixteen children in my class. All of us thought it had to be a B-29. We'd all seen many formations of B-29s, and those are the only kind of planes that could possibly fly that high. There was a small airbase in our prefecture, and I'd occasionally seen Japanese planes flying, but they were all small and could never fly as high as what I saw. Besides, the way duralumin reflects light is different from other types of metal, and the only planes made out of that are

B-29s. I did think it was a little strange, though, that it was a solo plane flying all by itself, not part of a formation.

—Were you born in this region?

No, I was born in Hiroshima. I got married in 1941, and that's when I came here. My husband was a music teacher in a junior high school in this prefecture. He was called up in 1943 and died fighting in Luzon in June of 1945. From what I heard later, he was guarding an ammunition dump just outside Manila when it was hit by American shells and blew up, killing him. We have no children.

—Speaking of children, how many were you in charge of on that outing?

Sixteen all together, boys and girls. Two were out sick, but other than that it was the entire class. Eight boys and eight girls. Five of them were children who'd been evacuated from Tokyo.

We set out from the school at nine in the morning. It was a typical school outing, so everyone carried canteens and lunches with them. We had nothing in particular we were planning to study; we were just going up into the hills to gather mushrooms and edible wild plants. The area around where we lived was farmland, so we weren't that badly off in terms of food—which isn't to say we had plenty to eat. There was a strict rationing system in place and most of us were hungry all the time.

So the children were encouraged to hunt for food wherever they could find it. The country was at war, after all, and food took priority over studying. Everyone went on this kind of school outing—*outdoor study sessions*, as they were called. Since our school was surrounded by hills and woods, there were a lot of nice spots we used to go to. I think we were blessed in that sense. People in cities were all starving. Supply routes from Taiwan and the continent had been cut off by this time and urban areas were suffering terribly from a lack of food and fuel.

—You mentioned that five of your pupils had been evacuated from Tokyo. Did they get along well with the local children?

In my class at least they did. The environments the two groups grew up in, of course, were completely different—one way out in the country, the other in the heart of Tokyo. They spoke differently, even dressed differently. Most of the local kids were from poor farming families, while the majority of the Tokyo children had fathers who worked for companies or in the civil service. So I couldn't say they really understood each other.

Especially in the beginning you could sense some tension between the two groups. I'm not saying they bullied each other or got into fights, because they didn't. What I mean is one group didn't seem to understand what the other group was thinking. So they tended to keep to themselves, the local kids with other local kids, the Tokyo children in their own little group. This was only the first two months, though. After that they got along well. You know how it is. When kids start playing together and get completely absorbed by whatever they're doing, they don't care about things like that anymore.

—I'd like you to describe, in as much detail as you can, the spot where you took your class that day.

It was a hill we often went to on outings. It was a round hill shaped like an upside-down bowl. We usually called it "Owan yama." [Note: "Rice Bowl Hill."] It was a short walk to the west of the school and wasn't steep at all, so anybody could climb it. At the children's pace it took somewhere around two hours to get to the top. Along the way they'd search the woods for mushrooms and we'd have a simple lunch. The children, naturally, enjoyed going on these outdoor sessions much more than staying in our classroom studying.

The glittering airplane we saw way up in the sky reminded us for a moment of the war, but just for a short time, and we were all in a good mood. There wasn't a cloud in the sky, no wind, and everything was quiet around us—all we could hear were birds chirping in the woods. The war seemed like something in a faraway land that had nothing to do with us. We sang songs as we hiked up the hill, sometimes imitating the birds we heard. Except for the fact that the war was still going on, it was a perfect morning.

—It was soon after you observed the airplane-like object that you went into the woods, correct?

That's correct. I'd say it was less than five minutes later that we went into the woods. We left the main trail up the hill and went along a trampled-down path that went up the slope of the woods. It was pretty steep. After we'd hiked for about ten minutes we came to a clearing, a broad area as flat as a tabletop. Once we'd entered the woods it was completely still, and with the sun blocked out it was chilly, but when we stepped into that clearing it was like we were in a miniature town square, with the sky bright above us. My class often stopped by this spot whenever we climbed Owan yama. The place had a calming effect, and somehow made us all feel nice and cozy.

We took a break once we reached this "square," putting down our packs, and then the children went into the woods in groups of three or four in search of mushrooms. I insisted that they never lose sight of one another. Before they set out, I gathered them all together and made sure they understood this. We knew the place well, but it was a woods, after all, and if any of them got separated and lost we'd have a hard time finding them. Still, you have to remember these are small children, and once they start hunting mushrooms they tend to forget this rule. So I always made sure that as I looked for mushrooms myself I kept an eye on them, and a running head count.

It was about ten minutes or so after we began hunting mushrooms that the children started to collapse.

When I first spotted a group of three of them collapsed on the ground I was sure they'd eaten poisonous mushrooms. There are a lot of highly toxic mushrooms around here, even ones that can be fatal. The local kids know which ones not to pick, but a few varieties are hard to distinguish. That's why I always warned the children never to put any in their mouths until we got back to school and had an expert check them. But you can't always expect kids to listen, can you?

I raced over to the spot and lifted up the children who'd fallen to the ground. Their bodies were limp, like rubber that's been left out in the sun. It was like carrying empty shells—the strength was completely drained from them. But they were breathing fine. Their pulses were normal, and none of them had a temperature. They looked calm, not at all like they were in any pain. I ruled out things like bee stings or snakebites. The children were simply unconscious.

The strangest thing was their eyes. Their bodies were so limp it was like they were in a coma, yet their eyes were open as if they were looking at something. They'd blink every once in a while, so it wasn't like they were asleep. And their eyes moved very slowly from side to side like they were scanning a distant horizon. Their eyes at least were conscious. But they weren't actually looking at anything, or at least nothing visible. I waved my hand a few times in front of their faces, but got no reaction.

I picked up each of the three children in turn, and they were all exactly the same. All of them were unconscious, their eyes slowly moving from side to side. It was the weirdest thing I'd ever seen.

—Describe the group that first collapsed.

It was a group of girls. Three girls who were all good friends. I called out their names and slapped them on the cheek, pretty hard, in fact, but there was no reaction. They didn't feel a thing. It was a strange feeling, like touching a void.

My first thought was to send somebody running back to the school for help. There was no way I could carry three unconscious children down by myself. So I started looking for the fastest runner in the class, one of the boys. But when I stood up and looked around I saw that *all* the children had collapsed. All sixteen of them had fallen to the ground and lost consciousness. The only one still conscious and standing was me. It was like . . . a *battlefield*.

—Did you notice anything unusual at the scene? Any strange smell or sound—or a light?

[Thinks about it for a while.] No, as I already said, it was very quiet and peaceful. No unusual sounds or light or smells. The only thing unusual was that every single pupil in my class had collapsed and was lying there unconscious. I felt utterly alone, like I was the last person alive on Earth. I can't describe that feeling of total loneliness. I just wanted to disappear into thin air and not think about anything.

Of course I couldn't do that—I had my duty as a teacher. I pulled myself together and raced down the slope as fast as my legs would carry me, to get help at the school.

Chapter 3

It's nearly dawn when I wake up. I draw the curtain back and take a look. It must have just stopped raining, since everything is still wet and drippy. Clouds to the east are sharply etched against the sky, each one framed by light. The sky looks ominous one minute, inviting the next. It all depends on the angle.

The bus plows down the highway at a set speed, the tires humming along, never getting any louder or softer. Same with the engine, its monotonous sound like a mortar smoothly grinding down time and the consciousness of the people on board. The other passengers are all sunk back in their seats, asleep, their curtains drawn tight. The driver and I are the only ones awake. We're being carried, efficiently and numbly, toward our destination.

Feeling thirsty, I take a bottle of mineral water from the pocket of my backpack and drink some of the lukewarm water. From the same pocket I pull out a box of soda crackers and munch a few, enjoying that familiar dry taste. According to my watch it's 4:32. I check the date and day of the week, just to be on the safe side. Thirteen hours since I left home. Time hasn't leaped ahead more than it should or done an unexpected about-face. It's still my birthday, still the first day of my brand-new life. I shut my eyes, open them again, again checking the time and date on my watch. Then I switch on the reading light, take out a paperback book, and start reading.

Just after five, without warning, the bus pulls off the highway and comes to a stop in a corner of a roadside rest area. The front door of the bus opens with an airy hiss, lights blink on inside, and the bus driver makes a brief announcement. "Good morning, everybody. Hope you had a good rest. We're on schedule and should arrive in our final stop at Takamatsu Station in about an hour. But we're stopping here for a twenty-minute break. We'll be leaving again at five-thirty, so please be sure to be back on board by then."

The announcement wakes up most of the passengers, and they silently struggle to their feet, yawning as they stumble out of the bus. This is where people make themselves presentable before arriving in Takamatsu. I get off too, take a couple of deep breaths, and do some simple stretching exercises in the fresh morning air. I walk over to the men's room and splash some water on my face. I'm wondering where the heck we are. I go outside and look around. Nothing special, just the typical roadside scenery you find next to a highway. Maybe I'm just imagining things, but the shape of the hills and the color of the trees seem different from those back in Tokyo.

I'm inside the cafeteria sipping a free cup of hot tea when this young girl comes over and plunks herself down on the plastic seat next to me. In her right hand she has a paper cup of hot coffee she bought from a vending machine, the steam rising up from it, and in her left hand she's holding a small container with sandwiches inside—another bit of vending-machine gourmet fare, by the looks of it.

She's kind of funny looking. Her face is out of balance—broad forehead, button nose, freckled cheeks, and pointy ears. A slammed-together, rough sort of face you can't ignore. Still, the whole package isn't so bad. For all I know maybe she's not so wild about her own looks, but she seems comfortable with who she is, and that's the important thing. There's something childish about her that has a calming effect, at least on me. She isn't very tall, but has good-looking legs and a nice bust for such a slim body.

Her thin metal earrings sparkle like duralumin. She wears her dark brown, almost reddish dyed hair down to her shoulders, and has on a long-sleeved crewneck shirt with wide stripes. A small leather backpack hangs from one shoulder, and a light sweater's tied around her neck. A cream-colored miniskirt completes her outfit, with no stockings. She's evidently washed her face, since a few strands of hair, like the thin roots of a plant, are plastered to her broad forehead. Strangely enough, those loose strands of hair draw me to her.

"You were on the bus, weren't you?" she asks me, her voice a little husky.

"Yeah, that's right."

She frowns as she takes a sip of the coffee. "How old are you?"

"Seventeen," I lie.

"So you're in high school."

I nod.

"Where're you headed?"

"Takamatsu."

"Same with me," she says. "Are you visiting, or do you live there?"

"Visiting," I reply.

"Me too. I have a friend there. A girlfriend of mine. How about you?"

"Relatives."

I see, her nod says. No more questions. "I've got a younger brother the same age as you," she suddenly tells me, as if she'd just remembered. "Things happened, and we haven't seen each other for a long time. . . . You know something? You look a lot like that *guy*. Anybody ever tell you that?"

"*What* guy?"

"You know, the guy who sings in that band! As soon as I saw you in the bus I thought you looked like him, but I just can't come up with his name. I must have busted a hole in my brain trying to remember. That happens sometimes, right? It's on the tip of your tongue, but you just can't think of it. Hasn't anybody said that to you before—that you remind them of somebody?"

I shake my head. Nobody's ever said that to me. She's still staring at me, eyes narrowed intently. "What kind of person do you mean?" I ask.

"A TV guy."

"A guy who's on TV?"

"Right," she says, picking up her ham sandwich and taking an uninspired bite, washing it down with a sip of coffee. "A guy who sings in some band. *Darn*—I can't think of the band's name, either. This tall guy who has a Kansai accent. You don't have any idea who I mean?"

"Sorry, I don't watch TV."

The girl frowns and gives me a hard look. "You don't watch at all?"

I shake my head silently. Wait a sec—should I nod or shake my head here? I go with the nod.

"Not very talkative, are you? One line at a time seems your style. Are you always so quiet?"

I blush. I'm sort of a quiet type to begin with, but part of the reason I don't want to say much is that my voice hasn't changed completely. Most of the time I've got kind of a low voice, but all of a sudden it turns on me and lets out a squeak. So I try to keep whatever I say short and sweet.

"Anyway," she goes on, "what I'm trying to say is you look a lot like that singer with the Kansai accent. Not that you have a Kansai accent or anything. It's just—I don't know, there's something about you that's a lot like him. He seems like a real nice guy, that's all."

Her smile steps offstage for a moment, then does an encore, all while I'm dealing with my blushing face. "You'd resemble him even more if you changed your hair," she says. "Let it grow out a little, use some gel to make it flip up a bit. I'd love to give it a try. You'd definitely look good like that. Actually, I'm a hairdresser."

I nod and sip my tea. The cafeteria is dead silent. None of the usual background music, nobody else talking besides the two of us.

"Maybe you don't like talking?" she says, resting her head in one hand and giving me a serious look.

I shake my head. "No, that's not it."

"You think it's a pain to talk to people?"

One more shake of my head.

She picks up her other sandwich with strawberry jam instead of ham, then frowns and gives me this look of disbelief. "Would you eat this for me? I hate strawberry-jam sandwiches more than anything. Ever since I was a kid."

I take it from her. Strawberry-jam sandwiches aren't exactly on my top-ten list either, but I don't say a word and start eating.

From across the table she watches until I finish every last crumb. "Could you do me a favor?" she says.

"A favor?"

"Can I sit next to you until we get to Takamatsu? I just can't relax when I sit by myself. I always feel like some weird person's going to plop himself down next to me, and then I can't get to sleep. When I bought my ticket they told me they were all single seats, but when I got on I saw they're all doubles. I just want to catch a few winks before we arrive, and you seem like a nice guy. Do you mind?"

"No problem."

"Thanks," she says. " 'In traveling, a companion,' as the saying goes."

I nod. Nod, nod, nod—that's all I seem capable of. But what should I say?

"How does that end?" she asks.

"How does what end?"

"After *a companion*, how does it go? I can't remember. I never was very good at Japanese."

" 'In life, compassion,' " I say.

" 'In traveling, a companion, in life, compassion,' " she repeats, making sure of it. If she had paper and pencil, it wouldn't surprise me if she wrote it down. "So what does that really mean? In simple terms."

I think it over. It takes me a while to gather my thoughts, but she waits patiently.

"I think it means," I say, "that chance encounters are what keep us going. In simple terms."

She mulls that over for a while, then slowly brings her hands together on top of the table and rests them there lightly. "I think you're right about that—that chance encounters keep us going."

I glance at my watch. It's five-thirty already. "Maybe we better be getting back."

"Yeah, I guess so. Let's go," she says, making no move, though, to get up.

"By the way, where are we?" I ask.

"I have no idea," she says. She cranes her neck and sweeps the place with her eyes. Her earrings jiggle back and forth like two precarious pieces of ripe fruit ready to fall. "From the time I'm guessing we're near Kurashiki, not that it matters. A rest area on a highway is just a place you pass through. To get from here to there." She holds up her right index finger and her left index finger, about twelve inches apart.

"What does it matter what it's called?" she continues. "You've got your restrooms and your food. Your fluorescent lights and your plastic chairs. Crappy coffee. Strawberry-jam sandwiches. It's all pointless— assuming you try to find a point to it. We're coming from somewhere, heading somewhere else. That's all you need to know, right?"

I nod. And nod. And nod.

When we get back to the bus the other passengers are already aboard, with just us holding things up. The driver's a young guy with this intense look that reminds me of some stern watchman. He turns a reproachful gaze on the two of us but doesn't say anything, and the girl shoots him an innocent sorry-we're-late smile. He reaches out to push a lever and the door hisses closed. The girl lugs her little suitcase over and sits down beside me—a nothing kind of suitcase she must've picked up at some discount place—and I pick it up for her and store it away in the overhead rack. Pretty heavy for its size. She thanks me, then reclines her seat and fades off to sleep. Like it can barely wait to get going, the bus starts to roll the instant we get settled. I pull out my paperback and pick up where I'd left off.

The girl's soon fast asleep, and as the bus sways through each curve her head leans against my shoulder, finally coming to a rest there. Mouth closed, she's breathing quietly through her nose, the breath grazing my shoulder at regular beats. I look down and catch a glimpse of her bra strap through the collar of her crewneck shirt, a thin, cream-colored strap. I picture the delicate fabric at the end of that strap. The soft breasts beneath. The pink nipples taut under my fingertips. Not that I'm trying to imagine all this, but I can't help it. And—no surprise—I get a massive hard-on. So rigid it makes me wonder how any part of your body could ever get so rock hard.

Just then a thought hits me. Maybe—just maybe—this girl's my sister. She's about the right age. Her odd looks aren't at all like the girl in the photo, but you can't always count on that. Depending on how they're taken people sometimes look totally different. She said she has a brother my age who she hasn't seen in ages. Couldn't that brother be *me*—in theory, at least?

I stare at her chest. As she breathes, the rounded peaks move up and down like the swell of waves, somehow reminding me of rain falling softly on a broad stretch of sea. I'm the lonely voyager standing on deck, and she's the sea. The sky is a blanket of gray, merging with the gray sea off on the horizon. It's hard to tell the difference between sea and sky. Between voyager and sea. Between reality and the workings of the heart.

The girl wears two rings on her fingers, neither of which is a wedding or engagement ring, just cheap things you find at those little boutiques girls shop at. Her fingers are long and thin but look strong, the nails are short and nicely trimmed with a light pink polish. Her hands are resting lightly on the knees thrust out from her miniskirt. I want to touch those hands, but of course I don't. Asleep, she looks like a young child. One pointy ear peeks out from the strands of hair like a little mushroom, looking strangely fragile.

I shut my book and look for a while at the passing scenery. But very soon, before I realize it, I fall asleep myself.

Chapter 4

U.S. ARMY INTELLIGENCE SECTION (MIS) REPORT
Dated: May 12, 1946
Title: Report on the Rice Bowl Hill Incident, 1944
Document Number: PTYX-722-8936745-42216-WWN

The following is a taped interview with Doctor Juichi Nakazawa (53), who ran an internal medicine clinic in [name deleted] Town at the time of the incident. Materials related to the interview can be accessed using application number PTYX-722-SQ-162 to 183.

Impressions of the interviewer, Lt. Robert O'Connor: Doctor Nakazawa is so big boned and dark skinned he looks more like a farm foreman than a doctor. He has a calm manner but is very brisk and concise and says exactly what's on his mind. Behind his glasses his eyes have a very sharp, alert look, and his memory seems reliable.

That's correct—at eleven a.m. on November 7, 1944, I received a phone call from the assistant principal at the local elementary school. I used to be the school doctor, or something close to it, so that's why they contacted me first.

The assistant principal was terribly upset. He told me that an entire class had lost consciousness while on an outing in the hills to pick mushrooms. According to him they were totally unconscious. Only the teacher in charge had remained conscious, and she'd run back to school for help just then. She was so flustered I couldn't grasp the whole situation, though one fact did come through loud and clear: sixteen children had collapsed in the woods.

The kids were out picking mushrooms, so of course my first thought was that they'd eaten some poisonous ones and been paralyzed. If that were the case it'd be difficult to treat. Different varieties of mushrooms have different toxicity levels, and the treatments vary. The most we could do at the moment would be to pump out their stomachs. In the case of highly toxic varieties, though, the poison might enter the bloodstream quickly and we might be too late. Around here, several people a year die from poison mushrooms.

I stuffed some emergency medicine in my bag and rode my bike over to the school as fast as I could. The police had been contacted and two policemen were already there. We knew we had to get the unconscious kids back to town and would need all the help we could get. Most of the young men were away at war, though, so we set off with the best we had—myself, the two policemen, an elderly male teacher, the assistant principal and principal, the school janitor. And of course the homeroom teacher who'd been with the kids. We grabbed whatever bicycles we could find, but there weren't enough, so some of us rode two to a bike.

—What time did you arrive at the site?

It was 11:55. I remember since I happened to glance at my watch when we got there. We rode our bicycles to the bottom of the hill, as far as we could go, then climbed the rest of the way on foot.

By the time I arrived several children had partially regained consciousness. Three or four of them, as I recall. But they weren't fully conscious—sort of dizzily on all fours. The rest of the children were still collapsed. After a while some of the others began to come around, their bodies undulating like so many big worms. It was a very strange sight. The children had collapsed in an odd, flat, open space in the woods where it looked like all the trees had been neatly removed, with autumn sunlight shining down brightly. And here you had, in this spot or at the edges of it, sixteen elementary school kids scattered about prostrate on the ground, some of them starting to move, some of them completely still. The whole thing reminded me of some weird avant-garde play.

For a moment I forgot that I was supposed to treat the kids and just

26

stood there, frozen, staring at the scene. Not just myself—everyone in the rescue group reacted the same, paralyzed for a while by what they saw. This might be a strange way of putting it, perhaps, but it was like some mistake had occurred that allowed us to see a sight people should never see. It was wartime, and I was always mentally prepared, as a physician, to deal with whatever came, in the remote possibility that something awful would occur way out here in the country. Prepared as a citizen of Japan to calmly do my duty if the need arose. But when I saw this scene in the woods I literally froze.

I soon snapped out of it, and picked up one of the children, a little girl. Her body had no strength in it at all and was limp as a rag doll. Her breathing was steady but she was still unconscious. Her eyes, though, were open, tracking something back and forth. I pulled a small flashlight out of my bag and shined it on her pupils. Completely unreactive. Her eyes were functioning, watching something, yet showed no response to light. I picked up several other children and examined them and they were all exactly the same, unresponsive. I found this quite odd.

I next checked their pulse and temperature. Their pulses were between 50 and 55, and all of them had temperatures just below 97 degrees. Somewhere around 96 degrees or thereabouts, as I recall. That's correct—for children of that age this pulse rate is well below normal, the body temperature over one degree below average. I smelled their breath, but there was nothing out of the ordinary. Likewise with their throats and tongues.

I immediately ascertained these weren't the symptoms of food poisoning. Nobody had vomited or suffered diarrhea, and none of them seemed to be in any pain. If the children had eaten something bad you could expect—with this much time having elapsed—the onset of at least one of these symptoms. I heaved a sigh of relief that it wasn't food poisoning. But then I was stumped, since I hadn't a clue what was wrong with them.

The symptoms were similar to sunstroke. Kids often collapse from this in the summer. It's like it's contagious—once one of them collapses their friends all do the same, one after the other. But this was November, in a cool woods, no less. One or two getting sunstroke is one thing, but sixteen children simultaneously coming down with it was out of the question.

My next thought was some kind of poison gas or nerve gas, either naturally occurring or man-made. But how in the world could gas appear in the middle of the woods in such a remote part of the country? I couldn't account for it. Poison gas, though, would logically explain what I saw that day. Everyone breathed it in, went unconscious, and collapsed on the spot. The homeroom teacher didn't collapse because the concentration of gas wasn't strong enough to affect an adult.

But when it came to treating the children, I was totally lost. I'm just a simple country doctor and have no special expertise in poison gasses, so I was out of my league. We were out in this remote town and I couldn't very well ring up a specialist. Very gradually, in fact, some of the children were getting better, and I figured that perhaps with time they would all regain consciousness. I know it's an overly optimistic view, but at the time I couldn't think of anything else to do. So I suggested that we just let them lie there quietly for a while and see what developed.

—Was there anything unusual in the air?

I was concerned about that myself, so I took several deep breaths to see if I could detect any unusual odor. But it was just the ordinary smell of a woods in the hills. It was a bracing scent, the fragrance of trees. Nothing unusual about the plants and flowers around there, either. Nothing had changed shape or been discolored.

One by one I examined the mushrooms the children had been picking. There weren't all that many, which led me to conclude that they'd collapsed not long after they began picking them. All of them were typical edible mushrooms. I've been a doctor here for some time and am quite familiar with the different varieties. Of course to be on the safe side I collected them all and took them back and had a specialist examine them. But as far as I could tell, they were all ordinary, edible mushrooms.

—You said the unconscious children's eyes moved back and forth, but did you notice any other unusual symptoms or reactions? For instance, the size of their pupils, the color of the whites of their eyes, the frequency of their blinking?

No. Other than their eyes moving back and forth like a searchlight, there was nothing out of the ordinary. All other functions were completely normal. The children were looking at something. To put a finer point on it, the children weren't looking at what *we* could see, but something we *couldn't*. It was more like they were *observing* something rather than just looking at it. They were essentially expressionless, but overall they seemed calm, not afraid or in any pain. That's also one of the reasons I decided to just let them lie there and see how things played out. I decided if they're not in any pain, then just let them be for a while.

—Did anyone mention the idea that the children had been gassed?

Yes, they did. But like me they couldn't figure out how it was possible. I mean, no one had ever heard of somebody going on a hike in the woods and ending up getting gassed. Then one of the people there—the assistant principal, I believe it was—said it might have been gas dropped by the Americans. They must have dropped a bomb with poison gas, he said. The homeroom teacher recalled seeing what looked like a B-29 in the sky just before they started up the hill, flying right overhead. That's it! everyone said, some new poison gas bomb the Americans developed. Rumors about the Americans developing a new kind of bomb had even reached our neck of the woods. But why would the Americans drop their newest weapon in such an out-of-the-way place? That we couldn't explain. But mistakes are part of life, and some things we aren't meant to understand, I suppose.

—After this, then, the children gradually recovered on their own?

They did. I can't tell you how relieved I was. At first they started squirming around, then they sat up unsteadily, gradually regaining consciousness. No one complained of any pain during this process. It was all very quiet, like they were waking up from a deep sleep. And as they regained consciousness their eye movements became normal again. They showed normal reactions to light when I shined a flashlight in their eyes. It took some time, though, for them to be able to speak again—just like you are when you first wake up.

We asked each of the children what had happened, but they looked dumbfounded, like we were asking about something they didn't remember taking place. Going up the hill, starting to gather mushrooms—that much they recalled. Everything after that was a total blank. They had no sense of any time passing between then and now. They start gathering mushrooms, then the curtain falls, and here they are lying on the ground, surrounded by all these adults. The children couldn't figure out why we were all upset, staring at them with these worried looks on our faces. They seemed more afraid of us than anything else.

Sadly, there was one child, a boy, who didn't regain consciousness. One of the children evacuated from Tokyo. Satoru Nakata, I believe his name was. A small, pale little boy. He was the only one who remained unconscious. He just lay there on the ground, his eyes moving back and forth. We had to carry him back down the hill. The other children walked back down like nothing had happened.

—Other than this boy, Nakata, none of the other children showed any symptoms later on?

As far as any outward signs at least, no, they displayed no unusual symptoms. No one complained of pain or discomfort. As soon as we got back to the school I brought the children into the nurse's room one by one and examined them—took their temperature, listened to their heart with a stethoscope, checked their vision. Whatever I was able to do at the time I did. I had them solve some simple arithmetic problems, stand on one foot with their eyes closed, things like that. Physically they were fine. They didn't seem tired and had healthy appetites. They'd missed lunch so they all said they were hungry. We gave them rice balls to eat, and they gobbled them up.

A few days later I stopped by the school to observe how the children were doing. I called a few of them into the nurse's room and questioned them. Again, though, everything seemed fine. No traces remained, physically or emotionally, from their strange experience. They couldn't even remember that it had happened. Their lives were completely back to normal, unaffected by the incident. They attended class as usual, sang songs, played outside during recess, everything normal kids did. Their homeroom teacher, however, was a different story: she still seemed in shock.

But that one boy, Nakata, didn't regain consciousness, so the following day he was taken to the university hospital in Kofu. After that he was transferred to a military hospital, and never came back to our town again. I never heard what became of him.

This incident never made the newspapers. My guess is the authorities decided it would only cause unrest, so they banned any mention of it. You have to remember that during the war the military tried to squelch whatever they saw as groundless rumors. The war wasn't going well, with the military retreating on the southern front, suicide attacks one after the other, air raids on cities getting worse all the time. The military was especially afraid of any antiwar or pacifist sentiment cropping up among the populace. A few days after the incident the police came calling and warned us that under no circumstances were we to talk about what we'd seen.

The whole thing was an odd, unpleasant affair. Even to this day it's like a weight pressing down on me.

Chapter 5

I'm asleep when our bus drives across the huge new bridge over the Inland Sea. I'd seen the bridge only on maps and had been looking forward to seeing it for real. Somebody gently taps me on the shoulder and I wake up.

"Hey, we're here," the girl says.

I stretch, rub my eyes with the back of my hand, and look out the window. Sure enough, the bus is just pulling into what looks like the square in front of a station. Fresh morning sunlight lights up the scene. Almost blinding, but gentle somehow, the light is different from what I was used to in Tokyo. I glance at my watch. 6:32.

"Gosh, what a long trip," she says tiredly. "I thought my lower back was going to give out. And my neck's killing me. You aren't going to catch me on an all-night bus again. I'm taking the plane from now on, even if it's more expensive. Turbulence, hijackings—I don't care. Give me a plane any day."

I lower her suitcase and my backpack from the overhead rack. "What's your name?" I ask.

"My name?"

"Yeah."

"Sakura," she says. "What about you?"

"Kafka Tamura," I reply.

"Kafka Tamura," she muses. "Weird name. Easy to remember, though."

I nod. Becoming a different person might be hard, but taking on a different name is a cinch.

She gets off the bus, sets her suitcase on the ground, and plunks herself down on top, then pulls a notebook from a pocket in her small backpack, scribbles down something, rips the page out, and hands it to me. A phone number, by the looks of it.

"My cell phone number," she says with a wry expression. "I'm staying at my friend's place for a while, but if you ever feel like seeing somebody, give me a call. We can go out for a bite or whatever. Don't be a stranger, okay? 'Even chance meetings' . . . how does the rest of that go?"

"'Are the result of karma.'"

"Right, right," she says. "But what does it mean?"

"That things in life are fated by our previous lives. That even in the smallest events there's no such thing as coincidence."

She sits there on her yellow suitcase, notebook in hand, giving it some thought. "Hmm . . . that's a kind of philosophy, isn't it. Not such a bad way of thinking about life. Sort of a reincarnation, New Age kind of thing. But, Kafka, remember this, okay? I don't go around giving my cell phone number to just anybody. You know what I mean?"

I appreciate it, I tell her. I fold up the piece of paper and stick it in the pocket of my windbreaker. Thinking better of it, I transfer it to my wallet.

"So how long'll you be in Takamatsu?" Sakura asks.

"I don't know yet," I say. "It depends on how things go."

She gazes intently at me, her head tilted slightly to one side. *Okay, whatever*, she might be thinking. She climbs into a cab, gives a little wave, and takes off.

Once again I'm all alone. *Sakura*, I think—not my sister's name. But names are changed easily enough. Especially when you're trying to try to run away from somebody.

I have a reservation at a business hotel in Takamatsu. The YMCA in Tokyo had told me about the place, and through them I got a discount on the room. But that's only for the first three days, then it goes back to the normal room rate.

If I really wanted to save money, I could just sack out on a bench in front of the station, or since it's still warm out, I could sleep in my sleeping bag in a park somewhere. But then the cops will come and card me—the one thing I have to avoid at all costs. That's why I went for the hotel reservation, at least for three days. After that I'll figure something out.

At the station I pop into the first little diner that catches my eye, and eat my fill of udon. Born and raised in Tokyo, I haven't had much udon in my life. But now I'm in Udon Central—Shikoku—and confronted with noodles like nothing I've ever seen. They're chewy and fresh, and the soup smells great, really fragrant. And talk about cheap. It all tastes so good I order seconds, and for the first time in who knows how long, I'm happily stuffed. Afterward I plop myself down on a bench in the plaza next to the station and gaze up at the sunny sky. *I'm free*, I remind myself. Like the clouds floating across the sky, I'm all by myself, totally free.

I decide to kill time till evening at a library. Ever since I was little I've loved to spend time in the reading rooms of libraries, so I've come to Takamatsu armed with info on all the libraries in and around the city. Think about it—a little kid who doesn't want to go home doesn't have many places he *can* go. Coffee shops and movie theaters are off-limits. That leaves only libraries, and they're perfect—no entrance fee, nobody getting all hot and bothered if a kid comes in. You just sit down and read whatever you want. I always rode my bike to the local public library after school. Even on holidays that's where you'd find me. I'd devour anything and everything—novels, biographies, histories, whatever was lying around. Once I'd gone through all the children's books, I went on to the general stacks and books for adults. I might not always get much out of them, but I forged on to the very last page. When I got tired of reading I'd go into one of those listening booths with headphones and enjoy some music. I had no idea about music so I just went down the row of CDs they had there, giving them all a listen. That's how I got to know about Duke Ellington, the Beatles, and Led Zeppelin.

The library was like a second home. Or maybe more like a real home, more than the place I lived in. By going every day I got to know all the lady librarians who worked there. They knew my name and always said hi. I was painfully shy, though, and could barely reply.

Before coming to Takamatsu I found out some wealthy man from an old family in the suburbs had renovated his personal library into a private library open to the public. The place has a lot of rare books, and I heard that the building itself and the surrounding garden were worth checking out. I saw a photo of the place once in *Taiyo* magazine. It's a large, Japanese-style house with this really elegant reading room that looks more like a parlor, where people are sitting with their books on comfortable-looking sofas. For some reason that photo really stayed with me, and I wanted to see this in person if someday the chance came along. The Komura Memorial Library, the place was called.

I go over to the tourist information booth at the station and ask how to get there. A pleasant middle-aged lady marks the spot on a tourist map and gives me instructions on which train to take. It's about a twenty-minute ride, she explains. I thank her and study the schedule posted inside the station. Trains run about every twenty minutes. I have some time, so I pick up a takeout lunch at one of the little shops.

The train is just two little cars coupled together. The tracks cut through a high-rise shopping district, then past a mix of small shops and houses, factories and warehouses. Next comes a park and an apartment building under construction. I press my face against the window, drinking in the unfamiliar sights. I've hardly ever been outside of Tokyo, and everything looks fresh and new. The train I'm on, going out of town, is nearly empty this time of the morning, but the platforms on the other side are packed with junior and senior high school kids in summer uniforms, schoolbags slung across their shoulders. All heading to school. Not me, though. I'm alone, going in the opposite direction. We're on different tracks in more ways than one. All of a sudden the air feels thin and something heavy is bearing down on my chest. Am I really doing the right thing? The thought makes me feel helpless, isolated. I turn my back on the schoolkids and try not to look at them anymore.

The train runs along the sea for a time, then cuts inland. We pass tall fields of corn, grapevines, tangerine trees growing on terraced hills. An occasional irrigation pond sparkles in the sunlight. A river winding through a flat stretch of land looks cool and inviting, an empty lot is overgrown with summer grasses. At one point we pass a dog standing by the tracks, staring vacantly at the train rushing by. Watching this scenery makes me feel warm and calm all over again. *You're going to be okay*, I tell myself, taking a deep breath. All you can do is forge on ahead.

At the station I follow the map and walk north past rows of old stores and houses. Both sides of the street are lined with walls around people's homes. I've never seen so many different kinds—black walls made out of boards, white walls, granite block walls, stone walls with hedges on top. The whole place is still and silent, with no one else on the street. Hardly any cars pass by. The air smells like the sea, which must be nearby. I listen carefully but can't hear any waves. Far off, though, I hear the faint bee-like buzz of an electric saw, maybe from a construction site. Small signs with arrows pointing toward the library line the road from the station, so I can't get lost.

Right in front of the Komura Memorial Library's imposing front gate stand two neatly trimmed plum trees. Inside the gate a gravel path winds past other beautifully manicured bushes and trees—pines and magnolias, kerria and azaleas—with not a fallen leaf in sight. A couple of stone lanterns peek out between the trees, as does a small pond. Finally I get to the intricately designed entrance. I come to a halt in front of the open front door, hesitating for a moment about going inside. This place doesn't look like any library I've ever seen. But having come all this way I might as well take the plunge. Just inside the entrance a young man is sitting behind a counter where you check your bags. I slough off my backpack, then take off my sunglasses and cap.

"Is this your first visit?" he asks me in a relaxed, quiet voice. It's slightly high-pitched, but smooth and soothing.

I nod, but the words don't come. The question takes me by surprise and makes me kind of tense.

A long, freshly sharpened pencil between his fingers, the young man gazes intently at my face for a while. The pencil is yellow, with an eraser at the end. The man's face is on the small side, his features regular. Pretty, rather than handsome, might describe him best. He's wearing a button-down white cotton shirt and olive green chinos, with not a single wrinkle on either. When he looks down his longish hair falls over his brow, and occasionally he notices this and fingers it back. His sleeves are rolled up to the elbows, revealing slender white wrists. Delicately framed glasses nicely complement his features. The small plastic name tag pinned to his chest says *Oshima*. Not exactly the type of librarian I'm used to.

"Feel free to use the stacks," he tells me, "and if you find a book you'd like to read, just bring it to the reading room. Rare books have a red seal on them, and for those you'll need to fill out a request card. Over there to the right is the reference room. There's a card index and a computer you can use to search for material. We don't allow any books to be checked out. We don't carry any magazines or newspapers. No cameras are allowed. And neither is making copies of anything. All food and beverages should be consumed outside on the benches. And we close at five." He lays his pencil on the desk and adds, "Are you in high school?"

"Yes, I am," I say after taking a deep breath.

"This library is a little different from the ones you're probably used to," he says. "We specialize in certain genres of books, mainly old books by tanka and haiku poets. Naturally, we have a selection of general books as well. Most of the people who ride the train all the way out here are doing research in those fields. No one comes here to read the latest Stephen King novel. We might get the occasional graduate student, but very seldom someone your age. So—are you researching tanka or haiku, then?"

"No," I answer.

"That's what I thought."

"Is it still okay for me to use the library?" I ask timidly, trying to keep my voice from cracking.

"Of course." He smiles and places both hands on the desk. "This is a library, and anybody who wants to read is welcome. This can be our little secret, but I'm not particularly fond of tanka or haiku myself."

"It's a really beautiful building," I say.

He nods. "The Komura family's been a major sake producer since the Edo period," he explains, "and the previous head of the family was quite a bibliophile, nationally famous for scouring the country in search of books. His father was himself a tanka poet, and many writers used to stop by here when they came to Shikoku. Wakayama Bokusui, for instance, or Ishikawa Takuboku, and Shiga Naoya. Some of them must have found it quite comfortable here, because they stayed a long time. All in all, the family spared no expense when it came to the literary arts. What usually happens with a family like that is eventually a descendant squanders the inheritance, but fortunately the Komuras avoided that fate. They enjoyed their hobby, in its place, but made sure the family business did well."

"So they were rich," I say, stating the obvious.

"Very much so." His lips curve ever so slightly. "They aren't as rich now as they were before the war, but they're still pretty wealthy. Which is why they can maintain such a wonderful library. Of course making it a foundation helps lower their inheritance tax, but that's another story. If you're really interested in this building I suggest you take the little tour at two. It's only once a week, on Tuesdays, which happens to be today. There's a rather unique collection of paintings and drawings on the second floor, and the building itself is, architecturally, quite fascinating. I know you'll enjoy it."

"Thank you," I say.

You're quite welcome, his smile suggests. He picks his pencil up again and starts tapping the eraser end on the desk like he's gently encouraging me.

"Are you the one who does the tour?"

Oshima smiles. "No, I'm just a lowly assistant, I'm afraid. A lady named Miss Saeki is in charge here—my boss. She's related to the Komuras and does the tour herself. I know you'll like her. She's a wonderful person."

I go into the high-ceilinged stacks and wander among the shelves, searching for a book that looks interesting. Magnificent thick beams run across the ceiling of the room, and gentle early-summer sunlight is shining through the open window, the chatter of birds in the garden filtering in. The books in the shelves in front of me, sure enough, are just like Oshima said, mainly books of Japanese poetry. Tanka and haiku, essays on poetry, biographies of various poets. There are also a lot of books on local history. A shelf farther back contains general humanities—collections of Japanese literature, world literature, and individual writers, classics, philosophy, drama, art history, sociology, history, biography, geography. . . . When I open them, most of the books have the smell of an earlier time leaking out between the pages—a special odor of the knowledge and emotions that for ages have been calmly resting between the covers. Breathing it in, I glance through a few pages before returning each book to its shelf.

Finally I decide on a multivolume set, with beautiful covers, of the Burton translation of *The Arabian Nights*, pick out one volume, and take it back to the reading room. I've been meaning to read this book. Since the library has just opened for the day, there's no one else there and I have the elegant reading room all to myself. It's exactly like in the photo in the magazine—roomy and comfortable, with a high ceiling. Every once in a while a gentle breeze blows in through the open window, the white curtain rustling softly in air that has a hint of the sea. And I love the comfortable sofa. An old upright piano stands in a corner, and the whole place makes me feel like I'm in some friend's home.

As I relax on the sofa and gaze around the room a thought hits me: This is exactly the place I've been looking for forever. A little hideaway in some sinkhole somewhere. I'd always thought of it as a secret, imaginary place, and can barely believe that it *actually exists*. I close my eyes and take a breath, and like a gentle cloud the wonder of it all settles over me. I slowly stroke the creamish cover of the sofa, then stand up and walk over to the piano and lift the cover, laying all ten fingers down on the slightly yellowed keys. I shut the cover and walk across the faded grape-patterned carpet to the window and test the antique handle that opens and closes it. I switch the floor lamp on and off, then check out all the paintings hanging on the walls. Finally I plop back down on the sofa and pick up reading where I left off, focusing on *The Arabian Nights* for a while.

At noon I take my bottle of mineral water and box lunch out to the veranda that faces the garden and sit down to eat. Different kinds of birds fly overhead, fluttering from one tree to the next or flying down to the pond to drink and groom themselves. There are some I've never seen before. A large brown cat makes an appearance, which is their signal to clear out of there, even though the cat looks like he couldn't care less about birds. All he wants is to stretch out on the stepping-stones and enjoy the warm sunlight.

"Is your school closed today?" Oshima asks when I drop off my backpack on my way back to the reading room.

"No," I reply, carefully choosing my words, "I just decided to take some time off."

"Refusing to go to school," he says.

"I guess so."

Oshima looks at me with great interest. "You guess so."

"I'm not refusing to go to school. I just decided not to."

"Very calmly, all on your own, you stopped going to school?"

I merely nod. I have no idea how to reply.

"According to Aristophanes in Plato's *Symposium*, in the ancient world of myth there were three types of people," Oshima says. "Have you heard about this?"

"No."

"In ancient times people weren't just male or female, but one of three types: male/male, male/female, or female/female. In other words, each person was made out of the components of two people. Everyone was happy with this arrangement and never really gave it much thought. But then God took a knife and cut everybody in half, right down the middle. So after that the world was divided just into male and female, the upshot being that people spend their time running around trying to locate their missing other half."

"Why did God do that?"

"Divide people into two? You got me. God works in mysterious ways. There's that whole wrath-of-God thing, all that excessive idealism and so on. My guess is it was punishment for something. Like in the Bible. Adam and Eve and the Fall and so forth."

"Original sin," I say.

"That's right, original sin." Oshima holds his pencil between his middle and index fingers, twirling it ever so slightly as if testing the balance. "Anyway, my point is that it's really hard for people to live their lives alone."

Back in the reading room I return to "The Tale of Abu-l-Hasan, the Wag," but my mind wanders away from the book. *Male/male, male/female, and female/female?*

At two o'clock I lay down my book and get up from the sofa to join the tour of the building. Miss Saeki, leading the tour, is a slim woman I'd guess is in her mid-forties. She's a little on the tall side for someone of her generation. She's wearing a blue half-sleeved dress and a cream-colored cardigan, and has excellent posture. Her long hair is loosely tied back, her face very refined and intelligent looking, with beautiful eyes and a shadowy smile playing over her lips, a smile whose sense of completeness is indescribable. It reminds me of a small, sunny spot, the special patch of sunlight you find only in some remote, secluded place. My house back in Tokyo has one just like that in the garden, and ever since I was little I loved that bright little spot.

She makes a strong impression on me, making me feel wistful and nostalgic. Wouldn't it be great if this were my mother? But I think the same thing every time I run across a charming, middle-aged woman. The chances that Miss Saeki's actually my mother are close to zero, I realize. Still, since I have no idea what my mother looks like, or even her name, the possibility *does* exist, right? There's nothing that rules it out completely.

The only other people taking the tour are a middle-aged couple from Osaka. The wife is short and pudgy with glasses as thick as a Coke bottle. The husband's a skinny guy with hair so stiff I bet he needs a wire brush to tame it. With narrow eyes and a broad forehead, he reminds me of some statue on a southern island, eyes fixed on the horizon. The wife keeps up a one-sided conversation, her husband just grunting out a monosyllable every once in a while to let her know he's still alive. Other than that, he gives the occasional nod to show he's properly impressed or else mutters some fragmentary comment I can't catch. Both of them are dressed more for mountain climbing than for visiting a library, each wearing a waterproof vest with a million pockets, sturdy lace-up boots, and hiking hats. Maybe this is how they always dress when they go on a trip, who knows. They seem okay—not that I'd want them as parents or anything—and I'm relieved not to be the only one taking the tour.

Miss Saeki begins by explaining the library's history—basically the same story Oshima told me. How they opened to the public the books and paintings the umpteenth head of the family had collected, devoting the library to the region's cultural development. A foundation was set up based on the Komura fortune and now managed the library and occasionally sponsored lectures, chamber music concerts, and the like. The building itself dated from the early Meiji period, when it was built to serve double duty as the family library and guesthouse. In the Taisho period it was completely renovated as a two-story building, with the addition of magnificent guest rooms for visiting writers and artists. From the Taisho to the early Showa period, many famous artists visited the Komuras, leaving behind mementos—poems, sketches, and paintings—in gratitude for having been allowed to stay here.

"You'll be able to view some selected items from this valuable collection in the second-floor gallery," Miss Saeki adds. "Before World War II, a vibrant local culture was established less through the efforts of local government than those of wealthy connoisseurs such as the Komura family. They were, in short, patrons of the arts. Kagawa Prefecture has produced quite a number of talented tanka and haiku poets, and one reason for this was the dedication with which the Komura family founded and supported the local art scene. Quite a number of books, essays, and reminiscences have been published on the history of these fascinating artistic circles, all of which are in our reading room. I hope you'll take the opportunity to look at them.

"The heads of the Komura family down through the years have been well versed in the arts, with an especially refined appreciation of the truly excellent. This might have run in the blood. They were very discerning patrons of the arts, supporting artists with the highest aims who produced the most outstanding works. But as you're surely aware, in the arts there is no such thing as an absolutely perfect eye.

Unfortunately, some exceptional artists did not win their favor or were not received by them as they deserved to be. One of these was the haiku poet Taneda Santoka. According to the guestbook, Santoka stayed here on numerous occasions, each time leaving behind poems and drawings. The head of the family, however, called him a 'beggar and a braggart,' wouldn't have much to do with him, and in fact threw away most of these works."

"What a terrible waste," the lady from Osaka says, apparently truly sorry to hear this. "Nowadays Santoka fetches a hefty price."

"You're exactly right," Miss Saeki says, beaming. "But at the time, he was an unknown, so perhaps it couldn't be helped. There are many things we only see clearly in retrospect."

"You got that right," the husband pipes in.

After this Miss Saeki guides us around the first floor, showing us the stacks, the reading room, the rare-books collection.

"When he built this library, the head of the family decided not to follow the simple and elegant style favored by artists in Kyoto, instead choosing a design more like a rustic dwelling. Still, as you can see, in contrast to the bold structure of the building, the furnishings and picture frames are quite elaborate and luxurious. The carving of these wooden panels, for instance, is very elegant. All the finest master craftsmen in Shikoku were assembled to work on the construction."

Our little group starts upstairs, a vaulted ceiling soaring over the staircase. The ebony railing's so highly polished it looks like you'll leave a mark if you touch it. On a stained-glass window next to the landing, a deer stretches out its neck to nibble at some grapes. There are two parlors on the second floor, as well as a spacious hall that in the past was probably lined with tatami for banquets and gatherings. Now the floor is plain wood, and the walls are covered with framed calligraphy, hanging scrolls, and Japanese-style paintings. In the center, a glass case displays various mementos and the story behind each. One parlor is in the Japanese style, the other Western. The Western-style room contains a large writing desk and a swivel chair that look like someone's still using. There's a line of pines outside the window behind the desk, and the horizon's faintly visible between the trees.

The couple from Osaka walks around the parlor, inspecting all the items, reading the explanations in the pamphlet. Every time the wife makes a comment, the husband chimes in to second her opinion. A lucky couple that agrees on everything. The things on display don't do much for me, so I check out the details of the building's construction. While I'm nosing around the Western parlor Miss Saeki comes up to me and says, "You can sit in that chair, if you'd like to. Shiga Naoya and Tanizaki both sat there at one time or another. Not that this is the same chair, of course."

I sit down on the swivel chair and quietly rest my hands on the desk.

"How is it? Feel like you could write something?"

I blush a little and shake my head. Miss Saeki laughs and goes back to the couple. From the chair I watch how she carries herself, every motion natural and elegant. I can't express it well, but there's definitely something *special* about it, as if her retreating figure is trying to tell me something she couldn't express while facing me. But *what* this is, I haven't a clue. Face it, I remind myself—there're tons of things you don't have a clue about.

Still seated, I give the room a once-over. On the wall is an oil painting, apparently of the seashore nearby. It's done in an old-fashioned style, but the colors are fresh and alive. On top of the desk is a large ashtray and a lamp with a green lampshade. I push the switch and, sure enough, the light comes on. A black clock hangs on the opposite wall, an antique by the looks of it, though the hands tell the right time. There are round spots worn here and there into the wooden floor, and it creaks slightly when you walk on it.

At the end of the tour the Osaka couple thanks Miss Saeki and disappears. It turns out they're members of a tanka circle in the Kansai region. I wonder what kind of poems they compose—the husband, especially. Grunts and nods don't add up to poetry. But maybe writing poetry brings out some hidden talent in the guy.

I return to the reading room and pick up where I'd left off in my book. Over the afternoon a few other readers filter in, most of them with those reading glasses old people wear and that everybody looks the same in. Time passes slowly. Nobody says a word, everyone lost in quiet reading. One person sits at a desk jotting down notes, but the rest are sitting there silently, not moving, totally absorbed. Just like me.

At five o'clock I shut my book and put it back on the shelf. At the exit I ask, "What time do you open in the morning?"

"Eleven," Oshima replies. "Planning on coming back tomorrow?"

"If it's no bother."

Oshima narrows his eyes as he looks at me. "Of course not. A library's a place for people who want to read. I'd be happy if you came back. I hope you don't mind my asking, but do you always carry that backpack with you? It looks pretty heavy. What in the world could be inside? A stack of Krugerrands, perhaps?"

I blush.

"Don't worry—I'm not really trying to find out." Oshima presses the eraser end of his pencil against his right temple. "Well, see you tomorrow."

"Bye," I say.

Instead of raising his hand, he lifts his pencil in farewell.

I take the train back to Takamatsu Station. For dinner I stop inside a cheap diner near the station and order chicken cutlet and a salad. I have a second helping of rice and a glass of warm milk after the meal. At a mini-mart outside I buy a bottle of mineral water and two rice balls in case I get hungry in the middle of the night, then start for my hotel. I walk not too fast or too slow, at an ordinary pace just like everybody else, so no one notices me.

The hotel is pretty large, a typical second-rate business hotel. I fill in the register at the front desk, giving Kafka instead of my real first name, a phony address and age, and pay for one night. I'm a little nervous, but none of the clerks seem suspicious. Nobody yells out, *Hey, we can see right through your ruse, you little fifteen-year-old runaway!* Everything goes smooth as silk, business as usual.

The elevator clanks ominously to the sixth floor. The room is minuscule, outfitted with an uninviting bed, a rock-hard pillow, a miniature excuse for a desk, a tiny TV, sun-bleached curtains. The bathroom is barely the size of a closet, with none of those little complimentary shampoo or conditioner bottles. The view out the window is of the wall of the building next door. I shouldn't complain, though, since I have a roof over my head and hot water coming out of the tap. I plunk my backpack on the floor, sit down on the chair, and try to acclimatize myself to the surroundings.

I'm free, I think. I shut my eyes and think hard and deep about how free I am, but I can't really understand what it means. All I know is I'm totally alone. All alone in an unfamiliar place, like some solitary explorer who's lost his compass and his map. Is this what it means to be free? I don't know, and I give up thinking about it.

I take a long, hot bath and carefully brush my teeth in front of the sink. I flop down in bed and read, and when I get tired of that I watch the news on TV. Compared to everything I've gone through that day, though, the news seems stale and boring. I switch off the TV and get under the covers. It's ten p.m., but I can't get to sleep. A new day in a brand-new place. And my fifteenth birthday, besides—most of which I spent in that charming, offbeat library. I met a few new people. Sakura. Oshima. Miss Saeki. Nobody threatening, thank God. A good omen?

I think about my home back in Nogata, in Tokyo, and my father. How did he feel when he found I'd suddenly disappeared? Relieved, maybe? Confused? Or maybe nothing at all. I'm betting he hasn't even noticed I'm gone.

I suddenly remember my father's cell phone and take it out of my backpack. I switch it on and dial my home number. It starts ringing, 450 miles away, as clearly as if I were calling the room next door. Startled by this, I hang up after two rings. My heart won't stop pounding. The phone still works, which means my father hasn't canceled the contract. Maybe he hasn't noticed the phone's missing from his desk. I shove the phone back in the pocket of my backpack, turn off the light, and close my eyes. I don't dream. Come to think of it, I haven't had any dreams in a long time.

Chapter 6

"Hello there," the old man called out.

The large, elderly black tomcat raised its head a fraction and wearily returned the greeting in a low voice.

"A very nice spell of weather we're having."

"Um," the cat said.

"Not a cloud in the sky."

". . . for the time being."

"Is the weather going to take a turn for the worse, then?"

"It feels like it'll cloud up toward evening." The black cat slowly stretched out a leg, then narrowed its eyes and gave the old man another good long look.

With a big grin on his face, the man stared right back. The cat hesitated for a time, then plunged ahead and spoke. "Hmm . . . so you're able to speak."

"That's right," the old man said bashfully. To show his respect, he took off his threadbare cotton hiking hat. "Not that I can speak to every cat I meet, but if things go well I can. Like right now."

"Interesting," the cat said simply.

"Do you mind if I sit down here for a while? Nakata's a little tired from walking."

The black cat languidly rose to its feet, whiskers atwitch, and yawned so tremendously its jaw looked almost unhinged. "I don't mind. Or perhaps I should say it's not up to me. You can sit anywhere you like. Nobody's going to bother you for that."

"Thank you kindly," the man said, lowering himself down beside the cat. "Boy oh boy, I've been walking since six this morning."

"Um . . . I take it, then, that you're Mr. Nakata?"

"That's right. Nakata's the name. And you would be?"

"I forget my name," the cat said. "I had one, I know I did, but somewhere along the line I didn't need it anymore. So it's slipped my mind."

"I know. It's easy to forget things you don't need anymore. Nakata's exactly the same way," the man said, scratching his head. "So what you're saying, Mr. Cat, is that you don't belong to some family somewhere?"

"A long time ago I did. But not anymore. Some families in the neighborhood give me food to eat now and then, but none of them own me."

Nakata nodded and was silent for a time, then said, "Would you mind very much, then, if I called you Otsuka?"

"Otsuka?" the cat said, looking at him in surprise. "What are you talking about? Why do I have to be Otsuka?"

"No special reason. The name just came to me. Nakata just picked one out of a hat. It makes things a lot easier for me if you have a name. That way somebody like me, who isn't very bright, can organize things better. For instance, I can say, *On this day of this month I spoke with the black cat Otsuka in a vacant lot in the 2-chome neighborhood*. It helps me remember."

"Interesting," the cat said. "Not that I totally follow you. Cats can get by without names. We go by smell, shape, things of this nature. As long as we know these things, there're no worries for us."

"Nakata understands completely. But you know, Mr. Otsuka, people don't work that way. We need dates and names to remember all kinds of things."

The cat gave a snort. "Sounds like a pain to me."

"You're absolutely right. There's so much we have to remember, it *is* a pain. Nakata has to remember the name of the Governor, bus numbers. Still, you don't mind if I call you Otsuka? Maybe it's a little unpleasant for you?"

"Well, now that you mention it, I suppose it isn't all that pleasant. . . . Not that it's particularly *un*pleasant, you understand. So I guess I don't really mind. You want to call me Otsuka, be my guest. I'll admit, though, that it doesn't sound right when you call me that."

"Nakata's very happy to hear you say that. Thank you so much, Mr. Otsuka."

"I must say that for a human you have an odd way of talking," Otsuka commented.

"Yes, everybody tells me that. But this is the only way Nakata can speak. I try to talk normally but this is what happens. Nakata's not very bright, you see. I wasn't always this way, but when I was little I was in an accident and I've been dumb ever since. Nakata can't write. Or read a book or a newspaper."

"Not to boast or anything, but I can't write either," the cat said, licking the pads of his right paw. "I'd say my mind is average, though, so I've never found it inconvenient."

"In the cat world that's to be expected," Nakata said. "But in the human world if you can't read or write you're considered dumb. Nakata's father—he passed away a long time ago—was a famous professor in a university. His specialty was something called *theery of fine ants*. I have two younger brothers, and they're both very bright. One of them works at a company, and he's a *depart mint chief*. My other brother works at a place called the *minis tree of trade and indus tree*. They both live in huge houses and eat eel. Nakata's the only one who isn't bright."

"But you're able to talk with cats."

"That's correct," Nakata said.

"Then you're not so dumb after all."

"Yes. No . . . I mean, Nakata doesn't really know about that, but ever since I was little people said, *You're dumb, you're dumb*, so I suppose I must be. I can't read the names of stations so I can't buy a ticket and take a train. If I show my *handycap* pass, though, they let me ride the city bus."

"Interesting . . . ," Otsuka said without much interest.

"If you can't read or write you can't find a job."

"Then how do you make a living?"

"I get a *sub city*."

"*Sub city?*"

"The Governor gives me money. I live in a little room in an apartment in Nogata called the *Shoeiso*. And I eat three meals a day."

"Sounds like a pretty good life. To me, at least."

"You're right. It *is* a pretty good life. Nakata can keep out of the wind and rain, and I have everything I need. And sometimes, like now, people ask me to help them find cats. They give me a present when I do. But I've got to keep this a secret from the Governor, so don't tell anybody. They might cut down my *sub city* if they find out I have some extra money coming in. It's never a lot, but thanks to it I can eat eel every once in a while. Nakata loves eel."

"I like eel too. Though I only had it once, a long time ago, and can't really recall what it tastes like."

"Eel is quite a treat. There's something different about it, compared to other food. Certain foods can take the place of others, but as far as I know, nothing can take the place of eel."

On the road in front of the empty lot a young man walked by with a large Labrador retriever with a red bandanna tied around its neck. It glanced over at Otsuka but walked on by. The old man and the cat sat there in the lot, silently waiting for the dog and his master to disappear.

"You said you look for cats?" Otsuka asked.

"That's correct. I search for lost cats. I can speak with cats a little, so I go all over tracking down ones that have gone missing. People hear that Nakata's good at this, so they come and ask me to look for their lost cats. These days I spend more days than not out searching for cats. I don't like to go too far away, so I just look for them inside Nakano Ward. Otherwise I'll be the one lost and they'll be out looking for *me*."

"So right now you're searching for a lost cat?"

"Yes, that's correct. Nakata's looking for a one-year-old tortoiseshell cat named Goma. Here's a photo of her." Nakata pulled a color copy out of his canvas shoulder bag and showed it to Otsuka. "She's wearing a brown flea collar."

Otsuka stretched out to gaze at the photograph, then shook his head.

"No, 'fraid I've never run across this one. I know most of the cats around here, but this one I don't know. Never seen, or heard, anything about her."

"Is that right?"

"Have you been looking for her for a long time?"

"Well, today is, let me see . . . one, two, three . . . the third day."

Otsuka sat there thinking for a time. "I assume you're aware of this, but cats are creatures of habit. Usually they live very ordered lives, and unless something extraordinary happens they generally try to keep to their routine. What might disrupt this is either sex or an accident—one of the two."

"Nakata's thinking the same thing."

"If it's sex, then you just have to wait till they get it out of their system and they'll be back. You do understand what I mean by sex?"

"I haven't done it myself, but I think I understand. It has to do with your weenie, right?"

49

"That's right. It's all about the weenie." Otsuka nodded, a serious look on his face. "But if we're talking about an accident, you might never see her again."

"That's true."

"Also, sometimes when a cat's on the prowl for sex it might wander off and have trouble finding its way back home again."

"If Nakata went out of Nakano Ward, finding my way home wouldn't be easy."

"That's happened to me a few times. Course that was a long time ago, when I was much younger," Otsuka said, eyes narrowed as he searched his memory. "Once you're lost, you panic. You're in total despair, not knowing what to do. I hate it when that happens. Sex can be a real pain that way, course when you get in the mood all you can think about is what's right under your nose—that's sex, all right. So that cat—what was her name? The one that's lost?"

"Do you mean Goma?"

"Yes, of course. *Goma.* I'd like to do what I can to help you find her. A young tortoiseshell cat like that, with some nice family taking care of her, wouldn't know the first thing about making her way in the world. Wouldn't be able to fight off anybody or fend for herself, the poor thing. Unfortunately, however, I've never seen her. I think you might want to search somewhere else."

"Well, then, I suppose I should follow your advice and go to some other place to look. Nakata's very sorry to have interrupted your nap. I'm sure I'll stop by here again sometime, so if you spot Goma in the meantime, please let me know. I'd like to give you something for your help."

"No need—I enjoyed talking with you. Feel free to drop by again. On sunny days this is where you'll mostly find me. When it rains I'm generally in that shrine over there where the steps go down."

"Well, thank you very much. Nakata was very happy, too, to be able to talk with you, Mr. Otsuka. I can't always speak so easily to every cat I meet. Sometimes when I try the cat is on his guard and runs away without saying a word. When all I ever said was hello."

"I can well imagine. There're all sorts of cats—just like there're all sorts of people."

"That's exactly right. Nakata feels the same way. There are all kinds of people in the world, and all kinds of cats."

Otsuka stretched and looked up at the sky. Golden sunlight filled the vacant lot but the air held a hint of rain, something Otsuka was able to sense. "Didn't you say that when you were little you had an accident, and that's why you're not so smart?"

"Yes, that's right. That's exactly what Nakata said. I had an accident when I was nine years old."

"What sort of accident?"

"Nakata can't really remember. They don't know why, but I had a high fever for about three weeks. I was unconscious the whole time. I was asleep in a bed in a hospital, they told me, with an *intra venus* in me. And when I finally woke up, I couldn't remember a thing. I'd forgotten my father's face, my mother's face, how to read, how to add, what my house looked like inside. Even my own name. My head was completely empty, like a bathtub after you pull the plug. They tell me before the accident Nakata always got good grades. But once I collapsed and woke up I was dumb. My mother died a long time ago, but she used to cry about this a lot. Because I got stupid. My father never cried, but he was always angry."

"Instead of being smart, though, you found yourself able to talk with cats."

"That's correct."

"Interesting. . . ."

"Besides that, I'm always healthy and haven't been sick once. I don't have any cavities, and don't have to wear glasses."

"As far as I can tell, you seem fairly intelligent."

"Is that so?" Nakata said, inclining his head. "Nakata's well past sixty now, Mr. Otsuka. Once I got past sixty I was quite used to being dumb, and people not having anything to do with me. You can survive without riding trains. Father's dead, so nobody hits me anymore. Mother's dead too, so she doesn't cry. So actually, if you say I'm pretty smart, it's a bit upsetting. You see, if I'm not dumb then the Governor won't give me a *sub city* anymore, and no more special bus pass. If the Governor says, *You're not dumb after all*, then Nakata doesn't know what to say. So this is fine, being dumb."

"What I'm trying to say is your problem isn't that you're dumb," Otsuka said, an earnest look on his face.

"Really?"

"Your problem is that your *shadow* is a bit—how should I put it? *Faint*. I thought this the first time I laid eyes on you, that the shadow you cast on the ground is only half as dark as that of ordinary people."

"I see. . . ."

"I ran across another person like that once."

Mouth slightly ajar, Nakata stared at Otsuka. "You mean you saw somebody like Nakata?"

"Yes, I did. That's why I wasn't so surprised that you could talk to cats."

"When was that?"

"A long time ago, when I was still a youngster. But I can't remember the details—the person's face or name or where and when we met. As I said before, cats don't have that sort of memory."

"I see."

"That person's shadow, too, looked like half of it had gotten separated from him. It was as faint as yours."

"I see."

"What I think is this: You should give up looking for lost cats and start searching for the other half of your shadow."

Nakata tugged a few times at the bill of his hat in his hands. "To tell the truth, Nakata's had that feeling before. That my shadow is weak. Other people might not notice, but I do."

"That's good, then," the cat said.

"But I'm already old, and may not live much longer. Mother's already dead. Father's already dead. Whether you're smart or dumb, can read or can't, whether you've got a shadow or not, once the time comes, everybody passes on. You die and they cremate you. You turn into ashes and they bury you at a place called Karasuyama. Karasuyama's in Setagaya Ward. Once they bury you there, though, you probably can't think about anything anymore. And if you can't think, then you can't get confused. So isn't the way I am now just fine? What I *can* do, while I'm alive, is never go out of Nakano Ward. But when I die, I'll have to go to Karasuyama. That can't be helped."

"What you think about it is entirely up to you, of course," Otsuka said, and again began licking the pads of his paw. "Though you should consider how your shadow feels about it. It might have a bit of an inferiority complex—as a shadow, that is. If I were a shadow, I know I wouldn't like to be half of what I should be."

"I understand," Nakata said. "You may well be right. Nakata's never thought about it. I'll think about it more after I get home."

"An excellent idea."

The two of them were silent for a while. Nakata quietly stood up, carefully brushing away stray bits of grass from his trousers, and put on his threadbare hat. He adjusted it a few times, until he got the angle just right. He shouldered his canvas bag and said, "Thank you very kindly. Nakata really values your opinions, Mr. Otsuka. I hope you stay happy and well."

"You too."

After Nakata left, Otsuka lay down again in the grass and closed his eyes. There was still some time before the clouds would come and the rain would start. His mind a blank, he fell asleep for a short nap.

Chapter 7

At seven-fifteen I eat breakfast in the restaurant next to the lobby—toast, hot milk, ham and eggs. But this free hotel breakfast doesn't come close to filling me up. The food's all gone before I realize it, and I'm still hungry. I look around, and seconds on toast don't seem likely to materialize. I let out a big sigh.

"Well, what are you gonna do?" the boy named Crow says.

He's sitting right across from me.

"You're not back home anymore, where you can stuff yourself with whatever you like," he says. "I mean, you've run away from home, right? Get that through your head. You're used to getting up early and eating a huge breakfast, but those days are long gone, my friend. You'll have to scrape by on what they give you. You know what they say about how the size of your stomach can adjust to the amount of food you eat? Well, you're about to see if that's really true. Your stomach's gonna get smaller, though that'll take some time. Think you can handle it?"

"Yeah, I can handle it," I reply.

"Good," Crow tells me. "You're supposed to be the toughest fifteen-year-old on the planet, remember?"

I give him a nod.

"Well, then, how about you stop staring at your empty plate and get a move on?"

Following this advice, I stand up and go to the front desk to negotiate over the price of my room. I explain I'm a student at a private high school in Tokyo and have come here to write my graduation paper. (Which isn't a total lie, since the high school affiliated with my school has this kind of setup.) I add that I'm collecting materials for the paper at the Komura Memorial Library. There's much more to research than I'd imagined, so I'll have to stay at least a week in Takamatsu. But since I'm on a budget, would the discounted room rate be possible not just for three days, but for the whole time I'm here? I offer to pay each day in advance, and promise not to cause any trouble.

I stand there in front of the girl in charge, trying to do my best imitation of a nice, well-brought-up young man who's in a tight spot. No dyed hair for me, no piercings. I have on a clean white Ralph Lauren polo shirt, chinos, and a pair of brand-new Topsiders. My teeth are gleaming and I smell like soap and shampoo. I know how to speak politely. When I feel like it, I'm pretty good at impressing people older than me.

The girl listens silently, nodding, her lips slightly twisted up. She's petite, and wearing a green uniform blazer over a white blouse. She looks a little sleepy, but goes about her morning duties briskly. She's about the same age as my sister.

"I understand," she says, "but I have to clear it with the manager. We should have an answer for you by noon." Her tone is businesslike, but I can tell that in her book, I pass. She notes down my name and room number. I have no idea whether this negotiating will get me anywhere. It might blow up in my face—if the manager demands to see my student ID, say, or tries to get in touch with my parents. (Of course I gave a phony home phone number when I registered.) But seeing as how my funds are limited, I figure it's worth the risk.

I check the Yellow Pages and call a public gym and ask about their weight machines. They have most of what I need, and it only costs five bucks a day. I get directions from the station, thank them, and hang up.

I go back to my room for my backpack, then hit the streets. I could just leave my stuff in the room, or in the hotel safe, but I feel better carrying it all with me. It's like it's a part of me already, and I can't let go.

On the bus from the terminal in front of the station to the gym, I can feel my face tighten up, I'm so nervous. Suppose somebody asks why a kid my age is traipsing off to the gym in the middle of the day? I don't know this town and have no idea what these people are thinking. But no one gives me a second glance. I'm starting to feel like the Invisible Man or something. I pay the entrance fee at the desk, no questions asked, and get a key to a locker. After changing into shorts and a T-shirt in the locker room, I do some stretching exercises. As my muscles relax, so do I. I'm safe inside this container called *me*. With a little click, the outlines of this being—*me*—fit right inside and are locked neatly away. Just the way I like it. I'm where I belong.

I start on my circuit training. With Prince blasting away on my

Walkman, I put in a good hour of training, making my usual round of the seven machines. I thought for sure a gym in such a small town would be full of dated machines, but these are the latest models, with the metallic smell of brand-new steel. The first round I do with light weights, then increase the weight for the second circuit. I know exactly how much weight and how many reps work for me. Pretty soon I start to sweat and stop every once in a while to take a swig from the bottle and a bite out of a lemon I bought on the way over.

Once I finish training I take a hot shower using the soap and shampoo I've brought along. I do a good job of washing my cock, not too many years out of its foreskin, and under my arms, balls, and butt. I weigh myself and flex my muscles a bit in front of a mirror. Finally I rinse out my sweaty shorts and T-shirt in the sink, wring them out, and stow them away in a plastic bag.

I take a bus back to the station and have a steaming bowl of udon in the same diner as the day before. I take my time, gazing out the window as I eat. The station's packed with people streaming in and out, all of them dressed in their favorite clothes, bags or briefcases in hand, each one dashing off to take care of some pressing business. I stare at this ceaseless, rushing crowd and imagine a time a hundred years from now. In a hundred years everybody here—me included—will have disappeared from the face of the earth and turned into ashes or dust. A weird thought, but everything in front of me starts to seem unreal, like a gust of wind could blow it all away.

I spread my hands out in front of me and take a good hard look at them. What am I always so tense about? Why this desperate struggle just to survive? I shake my head, turn from the window, clear my mind of thoughts of a hundred years away. I'll just think about *now*. About books waiting to be read in the library, machines in the gym I haven't worked out on. Thinking about anything else isn't going to get me anywhere.

"That's the ticket," Crow tells me. "Remember, you're supposed to be the toughest fifteen-year-old on the planet."

Like the day before, I buy a box lunch at the station and take the train, arriving at the Komura Library at eleven-thirty. And sure enough, Oshima's there at the counter. Today he's wearing a blue rayon shirt buttoned to the neck, white jeans, and white tennis shoes. He's sitting at his desk, absorbed in some massive book, with the same yellow pencil, I guess, lying beside him. His bangs are all over his face. When I come in he looks up, smiles, and takes my backpack from me.

"Still not going back to school, I see."

"I'm never going back," I confess.

"A library's a pretty good alternative, then," he says. He turns around to check the time on the clock behind him, then goes back to his reading.

I head off to the reading room and back to *Arabian Nights*. Like always, once I settle down and start flipping pages, I can't stop. The Burton edition has all the stories I remember reading as a child, but they're longer, with more episodes and plot twists, and so much more absorbing that it's hard to believe they're the same. They're full of obscene, violent, sexual, basically outrageous scenes. Like the genie in the bottle they have this sort of vital, living sense of play, of freedom, that common sense can't keep bottled up. I love it and can't let go. Compared to those faceless hordes of people rushing through the train station, these crazy, preposterous stories of a thousand years ago are, at least to me, much more real. How that's possible, I don't know. It's pretty weird.

At one o'clock I go out to the garden again, sit on the porch, and eat my lunch. I'm about halfway done when Oshima comes over and says I have a phone call.

"A phone call?" I say, at a loss for words. "For me?"

"As long as your name's Kafka Tamura."

I blush, get to my feet, and take the cordless phone from him.

It's the girl at the front desk at the hotel, most likely checking to see if I'm really doing research at the library. She sounds relieved to find out I hadn't lied to her. "I talked with the manager," she says, "and he said they've never done this before, but seeing as how you're young and there are special circumstances, he'll make an exception and let you stay at the rate the YMCA arranged for you. We're not so busy right now, he said, so we can bend the rules a bit. He also said that library's supposed to be really nice, so he hopes you'll be able to take your time and do as much research as you need to."

I breathe a sigh of relief and thank her. I feel a little bad about lying, but there's not much I can do about it. I've got to bend some rules myself if I want to survive. I hang up and hand the phone back to Oshima.

"You're the only high school student who comes here, so I figured it must be for you," he says. "I told her you're here from morning till night, your nose stuck in a book. Which is true."

"Thanks," I tell him.

"Kafka Tamura?"

"That's my name."

"Kind of strange."

"Well, that's my name," I insist.

"I assume you've read some of Kafka's stories?"

I nod. *The Castle,* and *The Trial,* 'The Metamorphosis,' plus that weird story about an execution device."

"'In the Penal Colony,'" Oshima says. "I love that story. Only Kafka could have written that."

"That's my favorite of his short stories."

"No kidding?"

I nod.

"Why's that?"

It takes me a while to gather my thoughts. "I think what Kafka does is give a purely mechanical explanation of that complex machine in the story, as sort of a substitute for explaining the situation we're in. What I mean is . . ." I have to give it some more thought. "What I mean is, that's his own device for explaining the kind of lives we lead. Not by talking about our situation, but by talking about the details of the machine."

"That makes sense," Oshima says and lays a hand on my shoulder, the gesture natural, and friendly. "I imagine Franz Kafka would agree with you."

He takes the cordless phone and disappears back into the building. I stay on the veranda for a while, finishing my lunch, drinking my mineral water, watching the birds in the garden. For all I know they're the same birds from yesterday. The sky's covered with clouds, not a speck of blue in sight.

Oshima most likely found my explanation of the Kafka story convincing. To some extent at least. But what I really wanted to say didn't get across. I wasn't just giving some general theory of Kafka's fiction, I was talking about something very real. Kafka's complex, mysterious execution device wasn't some metaphor or allegory—it's actually *here,* all around me. But I don't think anybody would get that. Not Oshima. Not anybody.

I go back to the reading room, where I sink down in the sofa and into the world of *The Arabian Nights*. Slowly, like a movie fadeout, the real world evaporates. I'm alone, inside the world of the story. My favorite feeling in the world.

When at five I'm about to leave Oshima's still behind the counter, reading the same book, his shirt still without a single wrinkle. Like always, a couple strands of hair have fallen across his face. The hands of the electric clock on the wall behind him soundlessly tick forward. Everything around him is silent and clean. I doubt the guy ever sweats or hiccups. He looks up and hands me my backpack. He frowns a bit, like it's too heavy for him. "Do you take the train here from town?"

I nod.

"If you're going to come every day, you should have this." He hands me a sheet of paper, the train schedule, it turns out, between Taka-matsu Station and the station where I get off for the library. "They usually run on time."

"Thanks," I say, slipping the sheet in my backpack.

"Kafka—I don't have any idea where you came from, or what your plans are, but you can't stay in a hotel forever, right?" he says, choosing his words carefully. With the fingers of his left hand he checks the tips of his pencils. Not that it's necessary, since they're all as sharp as can be.

I don't say anything.

"I'm not trying to butt in, believe me. I just thought I might as well ask. A boy your age in a place you've never been before—I can't imagine it's easy going."

I nod again.

"Are you headed someplace else after here? Or are you going to be here for a while?"

"I haven't decided yet, but I think I'll be here for a while. No other place to go," I admit.

Maybe I should tell Oshima everything. I'm pretty sure he won't put me down, give me a lecture, or try to force some common sense on me. But right now I'm trying to keep my words to a minimum. Plus I'm not exactly used to telling people how I feel.

"For the time being, then, you think you can manage?" Oshima asks.

I give a short nod.

"Good luck, then," he says.

Except for a few minor details, I spend the next seven days in the same way. (Except for Monday, of course, when the library's closed, and I spend the day at a big public library.) The alarm clock gets me up at six-thirty every morning, and I gulp down the hotel's pseudo-breakfast. If the chestnut-haired girl's behind the front desk, I give her a little wave. She always nods and repays me with a smile. I think she likes me, and I kind of like her, too. Could *she* be my sister? The thought does cross my mind.

Every morning I do some easy stretching exercises in my room, and when the time rolls around I go to the gym and run through the usual circuit training. Always the same amount of weight, the same number of reps. No more, no less. I take a shower and wash every inch of me. I weigh myself, to make sure my weight's staying steady. Before noon I take the train to the Komura Library. Exchange a few words with Oshima when I give him my backpack, and when I pick it up. Eat lunch out on the veranda. And read. When I finish *The Arabian Nights* I tackle the complete works of Natsume Soseki—there're still a couple of his novels I haven't read yet. At five I exit the library. So most of the day I'm in the gym or the library. As long as I'm in one of those two, nobody seems to worry about me. Chances are pretty slim a kid skipping school would hang out in either one. I eat dinner at the diner in front of the station. I try to eat as many vegetables as I can, and occasionally buy fruit from a stand and peel it using the knife I took from my father's desk. I buy cucumbers and celery, wash them in the sink at the hotel, and eat them with mayonnaise. Sometimes I pick up a container of milk from the mini-mart and have a bowl of cereal.

Back in my room I jot down what I did that day in my diary, listen to Radiohead on my Walkman, read a little, and then it's lights out at eleven. Sometimes I masturbate before going to sleep. I think about the girl at the front desk, putting any thoughts of her potentially being my sister out of my head, for the time being. I hardly watch any TV or read any newspapers.

But on the evening of the eighth day—as had to happen sooner or later—this simple, centripetal life is blown to bits.

Chapter 8

U.S. ARMY INTELLIGENCE SECTION (MIS) REPORT
Dated: May 12, 1946
Title: Report on the Rice Bowl Hill Incident, 1944
Document Number: PTYX-722-8936745-42216-WWN

The following is a taped interview with Doctor Shigenori Tsukayama (52), professor in the Department of Psychiatry in the School of Medicine, Tokyo Imperial University, which took place over a three-hour span at the GHQ of the Supreme Commander for the Allied Powers. Documentation related to the interview can be accessed using application number PTYX-722-SQ-267 to 291. [Note: Documents 271 and 278 are missing.]

Impressions of the interviewer, Lt. Robert O'Connor: Professor Tsukayama was quite calm and relaxed throughout the interview, as one might expect of an expert of his caliber. He is one of the leading psychiatrists in Japan and has published a number of outstanding books on the subject. Unlike most Japanese, he avoids vague statements, drawing a sharp distinction between facts and conjecture. Before the war he was an exchange scholar at Stanford, and is quite fluent in English. He is surely well liked and respected by many.

We were ordered by the military to immediately undertake an examination of the children in question. It was the middle of November 1944. It was quite unusual for us to receive requests or orders from the military. The military, of course, had its own extensive medical branch, and being a self-contained entity that put a high priority on secrecy, they usually preferred to handle matters internally. Apart from the rare times when they needed the special knowledge and techniques that only outside researchers or physicians had, they seldom appealed to civilian doctors or researchers.

Thus when they broached this we immediately surmised that something extraordinary had occurred. Frankly, I didn't like to work under military directions. In most cases their goals were strictly utilitarian, with no interest in pursuing truth in an academic sense, only arriving at conclusions that accorded with their preconceptions. They weren't the type of people swayed by logic. But it was wartime and we couldn't very well say no. We had to keep quiet and do exactly as we were told.

We'd been continuing our research despite the American air raids. Most of our undergrads and grad students, though, had been drafted. Students in psychiatry weren't exempt from the draft, unfortunately. When the order came from the military we dropped everything and took a train to [name deleted] in Yamanashi Prefecture. There were three of us—myself and a colleague from the Psychiatry Department, as well as a research physician from the Department of Neurosurgery with whom we'd been conducting research.

As soon as we got there they warned us that what they were about to reveal was a military secret we could never divulge. Then they told us about the incident that had occurred at the beginning of the month. How sixteen schoolchildren had lost consciousness in the hills and fifteen of them had regained consciousness thereafter, with no memory of what had taken place. One boy, they told us, hadn't regained consciousness and was still in a military hospital in Tokyo.

The military doctor who'd examined the children right after the incident, an internal medicine specialist named Major Toyama, gave us a detailed explanation about what had transpired. Many army doctors are more like bureaucrats concerned with protecting their own little preserve than with medicine, but fortunately Major Toyama wasn't one of them. He was honest and straightforward, and obviously a talented physician. He never tried to use the fact that we were civilians to lord it over us or conceal anything from us, as some might do. He provided all the details we needed, in a very professional manner, and showed us medical records that had been kept on the children. He wanted to get to the bottom of this as much as anybody. We were all quite impressed by him.

The most important fact we gleaned from the records was that, medically speaking, the incident had caused no lasting impact on the children. From right after the event to the present day, the examinations and tests consistently indicated no internal or external abnormalities. The children were leading healthy lives, just as they had before the incident. Detailed examinations revealed that several of the children had parasites, but nothing out of the ordinary. Otherwise they were completely asymptomatic—no headaches, nausea, pain, loss of appetite, insomnia, listlessness, diarrhea, nightmares. Nothing.

The one notable thing was that the two-hour span during which the children had been unconscious in the hills was erased from their memory. As if that part had been extracted in toto. Rather than a memory loss, it was more a memory *lack*. These aren't medical terms, and I'm using them for the sake of convenience, but there's a big difference between *loss* and *lack*. I suppose it's like—well, imagine a train steaming down a track. The freight's disappeared from one of the cars. A car that's empty inside—that's *loss*. When the whole car itself has vanished, that's *lack*.

We discussed the possibility that the children had breathed in poison gas. Dr. Toyama said that naturally they'd considered this. *That's why the military is involved,* he told us, *but it seems a remote possibility.* He then told us, *Now this is a military secret, so you can't tell anyone. The army is definitely developing poison gas and biological weapons, but this is carried out mainly by a special unit on the Chinese mainland, not in Japan itself. It's too dangerous a project to attempt in a place as densely populated as Japan. I can't tell you whether or not these sorts of weapons are stored anywhere in Japan, though I can assure you most definitely that they are not kept anywhere in Yamanashi Prefecture.*

—So he categorically denied that special weapons, including poison gas, were being stored in the prefecture?

Correct. He was very clear about that. We basically had no choice except to believe him, but he sounded believable. We also concluded that it was highly unlikely that poison gas had been dropped from a B-29. If the Americans had actually developed such a weapon and decided to use it, they'd drop it on some large city where the effects would be massive. Dropping a canister or two on such a remote place wouldn't allow them to ascertain what effects the weapon had. Besides, even if you accepted the premise that a poison gas had been dropped on the spot, any gas that makes children fall unconscious for two hours with no other lasting effects would be worthless as military arsenal.

Also we knew that no poison gas, whether man-made or naturally occurring, would act like this, leaving no aftereffects whatsoever. Especially when you're dealing with children, who are more sensitive and have a more delicate immune system than adults, there would have to be some aftereffects, particularly in the eyes or mucous membranes. We crossed off food poisoning for the same reason.

So what we were left with were psychological problems, or problems dealing with brain function. In a case like that, standard medical methodology wouldn't help at all in isolating the cause. The effects would be invisible, something you couldn't quantify. We finally understood why we had been called here by the military to consult.

We interviewed every child involved in the incident, as well as the homeroom teacher and attending physician. Major Toyama also participated. But these interviews yielded almost nothing new—we merely confirmed what the major had already told us. The children had no memory whatsoever of the event. They saw what looked like a plane glinting high up in the sky, climbed up Owan yama, and began hunting mushrooms. Then there's a gap in time and the next thing they recall is lying on the ground, surrounded by a group of worried-looking teachers and policemen. They felt fine, without any pain, discomfort, or nausea. Their minds just felt a bit blank, as you do when you first wake up in the morning. That was all. Each child gave the same exact response.

After conducting these interviews we concluded that this was a case of mass hypnosis. From the symptoms the homeroom teacher and school doctor observed at the scene, this hypothesis made the most sense. The regular movement of the eyes, the slight lowering of respiration, heartbeat, and temperature, the lack of memory—it all fit. The teacher alone didn't lose consciousness because for whatever reason what produced this mass hypnosis didn't affect adults.

We weren't able to pinpoint the cause, however. Generally speaking, though, mass hypnotism requires two elements. First, the group must be close-knit and homogeneous, and placed in restricted circumstances. Secondly, something has to trigger the reaction, something that acts simultaneously on everyone. In this case it might have been the glint of that airplane they saw. This is just a hypothesis, mind you—we weren't able to find any other candidates—and there may very well have been some other trigger that set it off. I broached the idea of it being a case of mass hypnosis with Major Toyama, making it clear this was merely a conjecture. My two colleagues generally concurred. Coincidentally, this also happened to be indirectly related to a research topic we were investigating ourselves.

"That does seem to fit the evidence," Major Toyama said after giving it some thought. "This is not my field, but it would appear to be the likeliest explanation. But there's one thing I don't understand—what made them snap out of this mass hypnosis? There'd have to be some sort of *reverse* triggering mechanism."

I really don't know, I admitted. All I could do was speculate. My hypothesis was this: There is a system in place which, after a certain amount of time passes, automatically breaks the spell. Our bodies have strong defense mechanisms in place, and if an outside system takes over momentarily, once a certain amount of time has passed it's like an alarm bell goes off, activating an emergency system that deprograms this foreign object that blocks our built-in defenses—in this case the effects of mass hypnosis—and eliminates it.

Unfortunately, I don't have the materials in front of me, so I can't quote the exact figures, but as I told Major Toyama, there have been reports of similar incidents occurring abroad. All of them are considered mysteries with no logical explanation. A large number of children lose consciousness at the same time, and several hours later wake up without any memory of what happened.

This incident is quite unusual, in other words, but not without precedent. One strange instance took place around 1930, in the outskirts of a small village in Devonshire, England. For no apparent reason, a group of thirty junior high students walking down a country path fell to the ground, one after the other, and lost consciousness. Several hours later, as if nothing had happened, they regained consciousness and walked back to school under their own steam. A physician examined them right away but could find nothing medically wrong. Not one of them could recall what had taken place.

At the end of the last century, a similar incident occurred in Australia. Outside of Adelaide fifteen teenage girls from a private girls' school were on an outing when all of them lost consciousness, and then regained it. Again there were no injuries, no aftereffects. It ended up classified as a case of heatstroke, but all of them had lost consciousness and recovered it at nearly the same time, and nobody showed symptoms of heatstroke, so the real cause remains a mystery. Besides, it wasn't a particularly hot day when it occurred. Probably there was no other accounting for what had taken place, so they decided this was the best explanation.

These cases share several things in common: they took place among a group of either young boys or girls, somewhat distant from their school, all of whom lost consciousness essentially simultaneously and then regained it about the same time, with no one displaying any aftereffects. It's reported that some of the adults who happened to be with the children also lost consciousness, and some did not. Each case was different in that regard.

There are other similar incidents, but these two are the best documented, and thus are representative cases in the literature of this phenomenon. This recent instance in Yamanashi Prefecture, however, contains one element that differentiates it from the rest: namely that one boy did *not* regain consciousness. This child is the key to unlocking the truth to this whole event. We returned to Tokyo after our interviews in Yamanashi and went straight to the army hospital where the boy was being cared for.

—The army, then, was only interested in this incident because they suspected it may have been caused by poison gas?

That's my understanding. But Major Toyama would know more about this, and I suggest you ask him directly.

—Major Toyama was killed in Tokyo in March 1945, in the line of duty, during an air raid.

I'm very sorry to hear that. We lost so many promising people in the war.

—Eventually, though, the army concluded that this was not caused by any chemical weapons. They couldn't determine the cause, but they decided, didn't they, that it was unrelated to the war?

Yes, I believe that's true. At this point they'd concluded their investigation into the matter. But the boy, Nakata, was allowed to remain in the military hospital, since Major Toyama was personally interested in the case and had some connections there. Thus we were able to go to the military hospital every day, and take turns staying overnight to investigate this unconscious boy's case further, from a number of angles.

Though unconscious, the boy's bodily functions nevertheless continued normally. He was given nutrients intravenously and discharged urine at regular intervals. He shut his eyes at night and went to sleep when we turned out the lights, then opened them again in the morning. Other than being unconscious, he appeared completely healthy. He was in a coma, but didn't dream, apparently. When people dream they exhibit characteristic eye movements and facial expressions. Your heart rate goes up as you react to experiences in your dreams. But with the Nakata boy we couldn't detect any of these indicators. His heart rate, breathing, and temperature were still slightly on the low side, but surprisingly stable.

It might sound strange to put it this way, but it seemed like the real Nakata had gone off somewhere, leaving behind for a time the fleshly container, which in his absence kept all his bodily functions going at the minimum level needed to preserve itself. The term "spirit projection" sprang to mind. Are you familiar with it? Japanese folktales are full of this sort of thing, where the soul temporarily leaves the body and goes off a great distance to take care of some vital task and then returns to reunite with the body. The sort of vengeful spirits that populate *The Tale of Genji* may be something similar. The notion of the soul not just leaving the body at death but—assuming the will is strong enough—also being able to separate from the body of the living is probably an idea that took root in Japan in ancient times. Of course there's no scientific proof of this, and I hesitate to even raise the idea.

The practical problem that faced us was how to wake this boy from his coma, and restore him to consciousness. Struggling to find a reverse trigger to undo the hypnosis, we tried everything. We brought his parents there, had them shout out his name. We tried that for several days, but there was no reaction. We tried every trick in the book as far as hypnosis goes—clapping our hands in different ways right in front of his face. We played music he knew, read his schoolbooks aloud to him, let him catch a whiff of his favorite foods. We even brought in his cat from home, one he was particularly fond of. We used every method we could think of to bring him back to reality, but nothing worked.

About two weeks into this, when we'd run out of ideas and were exhausted and discouraged, the boy woke up on his own. Not because of anything we'd done. Without warning, as if the time for this had been decided in advance, he came to.

—Did anything out of the ordinary take place that day?

Nothing worth mentioning. It was a day like any other. At ten a.m. the nurse came to draw a blood sample. Right after that he choked a bit, and some of the blood spilled on the sheets. Not much, and they changed the sheets right away. That was about the only thing different that day. The boy woke up about a half hour after that. Out of the blue he sat up in bed, stretched, and looked around the room. He had regained consciousness, and medically he was perfectly fine. Soon, though, we realized he'd lost his entire memory. He couldn't even remember his own name. The place he lived in, his school, his parents' faces—it was all gone. He couldn't read, and wasn't even aware this was Japan or the Earth. He couldn't even fathom the concept of Japan or the Earth. He'd returned to this world with his mind wiped clean. The proverbial blank slate.

Chapter 9

When I come to I'm in thick brush, lying there on the damp ground like some log. I can't see a thing, it's so dark.

My head propped up by prickly brambles, I take a deep breath and smell plants, and dirt, and, mixed in, a faint whiff of dog crap. I can see the night sky through the tree branches. There's no moon or stars, but the sky is strangely bright. The clouds act as a screen, reflecting all the light from below. An ambulance wails off in the distance, grows closer, then fades away. By listening closely, I can barely catch the rumble of tires from traffic. I figure I must be in some corner of the city.

I try to pull myself together and pick up the scattered jigsaw puzzle pieces of *me* lying all around. *This is a first,* I think. Or is it? I had this feeling somewhere before. But when? I search my memory, but that fragile thread snaps. I close my eyes and let time pass by.

With a jolt of panic I remember my backpack. Where could I have left it? No way can I lose it—everything I own's inside. But how am I going to find it in the dark? I try to get to my feet, but my fingers have lost all their strength.

I struggle to raise my left hand—why is it so heavy all of a sudden?—and bring my watch close to my face, fixing my eyes on it. The digital numbers read 11:26. May 28. I think of my diary. *May 28 . . .* good—so I haven't lost a day. I haven't been lying here, out cold, for days. At most my consciousness and I parted company for a few hours. Maybe four hours, I figure.

May 28 . . . a day like any other, the same exact routine. Nothing out of the ordinary. I went to the gym, then to the Komura Library. Did my usual workout on the machines, read Soseki on the same sofa. Had dinner near the station. The fish dinner, as I recall. Salmon, with a second helping of rice, some miso soup, and salad. After that . . . after that I don't know what happened.

My left shoulder aches a little. As my senses return, so does the pain. I must have bumped into something pretty hard. I rub that part with my right hand. There's no wound, or swelling. Did I get hit by a car, maybe? But my clothes aren't ripped, and the only place that hurts is that spot in my left shoulder. Probably just a bruise.

I fumble around in the bushes, but all I touch are branches, hard and twisted like the hearts of bullied little animals. No backpack. I go through my pant pockets. My wallet's there, thank God. Some cash is in it, the hotel key card, a phone card. Besides this I've got a coin purse, a handkerchief, a ballpoint pen. As far as I can tell in the dark, nothing's missing. I'm wearing cream-colored chinos, a white V-neck T-shirt under a long-sleeved dungaree shirt. Plus my navy blue Topsiders. My cap's vanished, my New York Yankees baseball cap. I know I had it on when I left the hotel, but not now. I must have dropped it, or left it someplace. No big deal. Those are a dime a dozen.

Finally I locate my backpack, leaning up against the trunk of a pine tree. Why in the world would I leave it there and then scramble into this thicket, only to collapse? *Where the hell am I, anyway?* My memory's frozen shut. Anyway, the important thing is that I found it. I take out my mini flashlight from a side pocket and check out the contents. Nothing seems to be missing. Thank God the sack with all my cash's there.

I shoulder the backpack and step over bushes, brushing branches out of the way, until I reach a small clearing. There's a narrow path there, and I follow the beam of my flashlight into a place where there're some lights. It appears to be the grounds of a Shinto shrine. I'd lost consciousness in a small woods behind the main shrine building.

A mercury lamp on a high pole illuminates the extensive grounds, casting a kind of cold light on the inner shrine, the offering box, the votive tablets. My shadow looks weirdly long on the gravel. I find the shrine's name on the bulletin board and commit it to memory. Nobody else is around. I see a restroom nearby and go inside and it turns out to be fairly clean. I take off my backpack and wash my face, then check out my reflection in the blurry mirror over the sink. I prepare myself for the worst, and I'm not disappointed—I look like hell. A pale face with sunken cheeks stares back at me, my neck all muddy, hair sticking out in all directions.

I notice something dark on the front of my white T-shirt, shaped sort of like a huge butterfly with wings spread. I try brushing it away, but it won't come off. I touch it and my hands come away all sticky. I need to calm down, so consciously taking my time I slowly take off both my shirts. Under the flickering fluorescent light I realize what this is—darkish blood that's seeped into the fabric. The blood's still fresh, wet, and there's lots of it. I bring it close for a sniff, but there's no smell. Some blood's been spattered on the dungaree shirt as well, but only a little, and it doesn't stand out on the dark blue material. The blood on the T-shirt is another story—against the white background there's no mistaking that.

I wash the T-shirt in the sink. The blood mixes with the water, dyeing the porcelain sink red, though no matter how hard I scrub the stain won't come out. I'm about to toss the shirt into the garbage can, then decide against it. If I throw it away, some other place would be better. I wring out the shirt and stow it in the plastic bag with my other rinsed-out clothes, and stuff the whole thing into my backpack. I wet my hair and try to get some of the tangles out. Then I take some soap out of my toilet kit and wash my hands. They're still trembling a little, but I take my time, carefully washing between my fingers and under my fingernails. With a damp towel I wipe away the blood that's seeped onto my bare chest. Then I put on my dungaree shirt, button it up to my neck, and tuck it into my pants. I don't want people looking at me, so I've got to look at least halfway normal.

But I'm scared, and my teeth won't stop chattering. Try as I might I can't get them to stop. I stretch out my hands and look at them. Both are shaking a bit. They look like somebody else's hands, not my own. Like a pair of little animals with a life all their own. My palms sting, like I grabbed onto a hot metal bar.

I rest my hands against the sink and lean forward, my head shoved against the mirror. I feel like crying, but even if I do, nobody's going to come to my rescue. Nobody . . .

Man alive, how'd you get all that blood all over you? What the hell were you doing? But you don't remember a thing, do you. No wounds on you, though, that's a relief. No real pain, either—except for that throbbing in your left shoulder. So the blood's gotta be from somebody else, not you. Somebody else's blood.

Anyway, you can't stay here forever. If a patrol car happens to spot you here, covered with blood, you're up a creek, my friend.

Course going back to the hotel might not be a good idea. You don't know who might be lying in wait, ready to jump you. You can't be too careful. Looks like you've been involved in some crime, something you don't remember. Maybe *you* were the perp. Who knows?

Lucky thing you got all your stuff with you. You were always careful enough to lug everything you own around in that heavy backpack. Good choice. You did what's right, so don't worry. Don't be afraid. Everything's going to work out. 'Cause remember— you're the toughest fifteen-year-old on the planet, right? Get ahold of yourself! Take some deep breaths and start using your head. Things'll be fine. But you gotta be very careful. That's real blood we're talking about—somebody else's blood. And we're not just talking a drop or two. As we speak I'll bet somebody's trying to track you down.

Better get a move on. There's only one thing to do, one place you gotta go to. And you know where that is.

I take a couple of deep breaths to calm down, then pick up my pack and get out of the restroom. I crunch along the gravel, the mercury light beating down on me, and try to get my brain in gear. Throw the switch, turn the crank, get the old thought process up and running. But it's no go—not enough juice in the battery to get the engine to turn over. I need someplace that's safe and warm. That I can escape to for a while and pull myself together. But *where*? The only place that comes to mind is the library. But the Komura Library's shut until tomorrow at eleven, and I need somewhere to lie low till then.

I come up with an alternative. I sit down where nobody can spot me and take the cell phone from my backpack. I check to see it's still connected, then take Sakura's phone number from my wallet and punch in the numbers. My fingers still aren't working well, and it takes a few times before I get the whole number right. I don't get her voice mail, thank God. Twelve rings later she answers. I tell her my name.

"Kafka Tamura," she repeats, not exactly thrilled. "Do you have any idea how late it is? I've got to get up early tomorrow."

"I know, I'm sorry to call so late," I tell her. My voice sounds tense. "But I had no choice. I'm sort of in trouble, and you're the only one I could think of."

No response on the other end. Seems like she's checking my tone of voice, weighing it in her mind.

"Is it something . . . serious?" she finally asks.

"I can't tell you right now, but I think so. You've got to help me. Just this once. I promise I won't be a bother."

She gives it some thought. Not like she's confused or anything, just thinking it over. "So where are you?"

I tell her the name of the shrine.

"Is that in Takamatsu City?"

"I'm not totally sure, but I think so."

"You don't even know where you are?" she says, dumbfounded.

"It's a long story."

She lets out a sigh. "Grab a cab and come to the Lawson's convenience store on the corner near my apartment. They have a big sign and you can't miss it." She gives me the directions. "Do you have money for a cab?"

"I'm good," I say.

"All right," she says and hangs up.

I go out the torii gate at the entrance to the shrine and head for the main road to flag down a cab. It doesn't take long. I ask the driver if he knows the Lawson's on that corner, and he says he does. When I ask if it's far, he says no, about a ten-dollar ride.

The cab stops outside the Lawson's and I pay the driver, my hands still unsteady. I pick up my backpack and go inside the store. I got there so fast Sakura hasn't arrived yet. I buy a small carton of milk, heat it up in the microwave, and sip it slowly. The warm milk slips down my throat and calms my stomach a little. When I went inside the store the clerk glanced at my backpack, keeping an eye out for shoplifters, but after that nobody pays any attention to me. I stand at the magazine rack, pretending to be picking one out, and check out my reflection in the window. Though my hair's still a bit of a mess, you can barely see the blood on my dungaree shirt. If anybody noticed it they'd think it was just a stain. Now all I have to do is stop trembling.

Ten minutes later Sakura strolls in. It's nearly one a.m. She has on a plain gray sweatshirt and faded jeans. Her hair's in a ponytail and she's wearing a navy blue New Balance cap. The moment I spot her, my teeth finally stop chattering. She sidles up beside me and looks me over carefully, like she's checking out the teeth of some dog she's about to buy. She lets out a sound halfway between a sigh and actual words, then lightly pats me twice on the shoulder. "Come on," she says.

Her apartment's two blocks from the Lawson's. A tacky, two-story building. She walks upstairs, takes the keys out of her pocket, and opens the green paneled door. The apartment consists of two rooms plus a kitchen and a bathroom. The walls are thin, the floors creak, and probably the only natural light the place gets during the day is when the blinding sunset shines in. I hear a toilet flush in some other unit, the scrape of a cabinet being shut somewhere. Seedy, all right, but at least it has the feel of real people living real lives. Dishes piled up in the kitchen sink, empty plastic bottles, half-read magazines, past-their-prime potted tulips, a shopping list taped to the fridge, stockings hanging over the back of a chair, newspaper on the table opened to the TV schedule, an ashtray, a thin box of Virginia Slims. For some strange reason this scene relaxes me.

"This is my friend's apartment," she explains. "She used to work with me at a salon in Tokyo, but last year she had to come back to Takamatsu, where she's from. But then she said she wanted to travel to India for a month and asked me to watch the place. I'm taking over her job while she's gone. She's a hairdresser too. I figured it's a good change of pace to get out of Tokyo for a while. She's one of those New Age types, so I doubt she'll be able to pull herself away from India in a month."

She has me sit down at the dining table, and brings me a can of Pepsi from the fridge. No glass, though. Normally I don't drink colas — way too sweet and bad for your teeth. But I'm dying of thirst and down the whole can.

"You want anything to eat? All I've got is Cup Noodle, if that'll do."
I'm okay, I tell her.
"You look awful. You know that?"
I nod.
"So what happened?"
"I wish I knew."
"You have no idea what happened. You didn't even know where you were. And it's a long story," she says, pinning down the facts. "But you're definitely in trouble?"
"Definitely," I reply. I hope that, at least, gets through.

Silence. All the while, she's bathing me in a deep frown. "You don't really have any relatives in Takamatsu, do you? You ran away from home."

Again I nod.

"Once, when I was your age, I ran away from home. I think I understand what you're going through. That's why I gave you my cell phone number. I figured it might come in handy."

"I really appreciate it," I say.

"I lived in Ichikawa, in Chiba. I never got along with my parents and hated school, so I stole some money from my folks and took off, trying to get as far away as I could. I was sixteen. I got as far as Abashiri, up in Hokkaido. I stopped by a farm I happened to see and asked them to let me work there. I'll do anything, I told them, and I'll work hard. I don't need any pay, as long as there's a roof over my head and you feed me. The lady there was nice to me, had me sit down and have some tea. Just wait here, she said. The next thing I knew a patrol car pulled up outside and the police were hauling me back home. This wasn't the first time the lady had gone through this sort of thing. The thought hit me hard then that I had to learn a trade, so no matter where I went I could always find work. So I quit high school, went to a trade school, and became a hairdresser." The edges of her lips rise a bit in a faint smile. "A pretty sound approach to things, don't you think?"

I agree with her.

"Hey, would you tell me the whole story, from the beginning?" she says, pulling out a cigarette and lighting it. "I don't think I'm going to get much more sleep tonight, so I might as well hear it all."

I explain everything to her, from the time I left home. I leave out the omen part, though. That, I know, I can't tell just anyone.

Chapter 10

Is it all right, then, if Nakata calls you Kawamura?" He repeated the question to the striped brown cat, enunciating his words slowly, making it as easy to understand as he could.

This particular cat had said he thought he had run across Goma, the missing one-year-old tortoiseshell, in this vicinity. But from Nakata's viewpoint, he spoke very strangely. The feeling was mutual, for the cat seemed to be having its own problems following him. Their conversation was at cross purposes.

"I don't mind at all, the tallest of heads."

"Pardon me, but Nakata doesn't understand what you're saying. Forgive me, but I'm not so bright."

"It's a tuna, to the very end."

"Are you perhaps saying you'd like to eat a tuna?"

"No. The hands tied up, before."

Nakata never went into these conversations with cats expecting to be able to easily communicate everything. You have to anticipate a few problems when cats and humans try to speak to each other. And there was another factor to consider: Nakata's own basic problems with talking—not just with cats, but also with people. His easy conversation with Otsuka the previous week was more the exception than the rule, for invariably getting across even a simple message took a great deal of effort. On bad days it was more like two people on the opposite shores of a canal yelling to each other on a windy day. And today was one of those days.

He wasn't sure why, but striped brown cats were the hardest to get on the same wavelength with. With black cats things mostly went well. Communicating with Siamese cats was the easiest of all, but unfortunately there weren't too many stray Siamese wandering the streets, so the chance didn't present itself often. Siamese were mainly kept at home, well taken care of. And for some reason striped brown cats made up the bulk of the strays.

Even knowing what to expect, Nakata found Kawamura impossible to decipher. He enunciated his words poorly, and Nakata couldn't catch what each one meant, or the connection between them. What the cat said came off sounding more like riddles than sentences. Still, Nakata was infinitely patient, and had plenty of time on his hands. He repeated the same question, over and over, having the cat repeat his responses. The two of them were seated on a boundary stone marking a little park for children in a residential area. They'd been talking for nearly an hour, going round and round in circles.

"*Kawamura* is just a name I'll call you. It doesn't mean anything. Nakata gives names to each cat so it's easy to remember. It won't cause you any problems, I guarantee it. I'd just like to call you that, if you don't mind."

In response Kawamura kept muttering something incomprehensible, and seeing as how this wasn't likely to stop anytime soon Nakata interrupted, trying to move their talk along by showing Kawamura the photo of Goma once more.

"Mr. Kawamura, this is Goma. The cat that Nakata is looking for. A one-year-old tortoiseshell cat. She's owned by the Koizumis of the 3-chome neighborhood in Nogata, who lost track of her a while back. Mrs. Koizumi opened a window and the cat leaped out and ran away. So once more I'd like to ask you, have you seen this cat?"

Kawamura gazed at the photograph again and nodded.

"If it's tuna, Kwa'mura tied. Tied up, try to find."

"I'm sorry, but as I said a moment ago, Nakata is not very bright, and can't understand very well what you're getting at. Would you mind repeating that?"

"If it's tuna, Kwa'mura tries. Try to find and tied it up."

"By *tuna*, you mean the fish?"

"Tries the tuna, tie it, Kwa'mura."

Nakata rubbed his closely cropped, salt-and-pepper hair and puzzled this over. What could he possibly do to solve this tuna riddle and escape from the maze the conversation had become? No matter how much he put his mind to it, however, he was clueless. Puzzling things out logically, after all, wasn't exactly his forte. Totally blithe to it all, Kawamura lifted a rear leg and gave the spot just below his chin a good scratch.

Just then Nakata thought he heard a small laugh behind him. He turned and saw, seated on a low concrete wall next to a house, a lovely, slim Siamese looking at him with narrowed eyes.

"Excuse me, but would you by chance be Mr. Nakata?" the Siamese purred.

"Yes, that's correct. My name's Nakata. It's very nice to meet you."

"Likewise, I'm sure," the Siamese replied.

"It's been cloudy since this morning, but I don't expect we'll be seeing any rain soon," Nakata said.

"I do hope the rain holds off."

The Siamese was a female, just approaching middle age. She proudly held her tail up straight, and had a collar with a name tag. She had pleasant features and was slim, with not an ounce of extra fat.

"Please call me Mimi. The Mimi from *La Bohème*. There's a song about it, too: 'Si, Mi Chiamano Mimi.' "

"I see," Nakata said, not really following.

"An opera by Puccini, you know. My owner happens to be a great fan of opera," Mimi said, and smiled amiably. "I'd sing it for you, but unfortunately I'm not much of a singer."

"Nakata's very happy to meet you, Mimi-san."

"Same for me, Mr. Nakata."

"Do you live near here?"

"Yes, in that two-story house over there. The Tanabes' house. You see it, right? The one with the cream-colored BMW 530 parked in front?"

"I see," Nakata repeated. He had no idea what a BMW was, but he did spot a cream-colored car. That must be what she meant.

"Mr. Nakata," Mimi said, "I'm known as self-reliant, or perhaps you'd say a very private sort of cat, and I don't normally interfere in others' affairs. But that youngster—the one I believe you're referring to as Kawamura?—is not what I would call the brightest kitty in the litter. When he was still young a child hit him with his bicycle, the poor thing, and he struck his head against some concrete. Ever since then he hasn't made much sense. So even if you are patient with him, as I see you've been, you won't get anywhere. I've been watching for a while, and I'm afraid I couldn't just sit idly by. I know it's forward of me to do so, but I had to say something."

"No, please don't think that. I'm very happy you told me. Nakata's as dumb as Kawamura, I'm afraid, and can't get by without other people's help. That's why I get a *sub city* from the Governor every month. So I'm very happy to hear your opinion, Mimi."

"I take it you're looking for a cat," Mimi said. "I wasn't eavesdropping, mind you, but just happened to overhear you as I was taking a nap here. Goma, I believe you said the name was?"

"Yes, that's correct."

"And Kawamura has seen Goma?"

"That's what he told me. But Nakata can't figure out what he said after that."

"If you wouldn't mind, Mr. Nakata, why don't I step in and try to talk with him? It's easier for two cats to communicate, and I'm fairly used to the way he talks. So why don't I sound him out, then summarize it for you?"

"That would be very helpful, I'm sure."

The Siamese nodded lightly, and like a ballet dancer nimbly leaped down from the concrete wall. Black tail held up high like a flagstaff, she leisurely walked over and sat down beside Kawamura. He immediately began to sniff Mimi's rump, but the Siamese gave him a swift blow to the cheek and the younger cat shrank back. With barely a pause Mimi dealt him another blow to the nose.

"Now pay attention, you brainless dingbat! You stinky good-for-nothing!" Mimi hissed, then turned to Nakata. "You've got to show him who's in charge up front or you'll never get anywhere. Otherwise he'll go all spacey on you, and all you get is drivel. It's not his fault he's this way, and I do feel sorry for him, but what are you going to do?"

"I see," Nakata said, not at all sure what he was agreeing to.

The two cats began conversing, but they spoke so quickly and softly that Nakata wasn't able to catch any of it. Mimi grilled Kawamura in a sharp tone, the younger cat replying timidly. Any hesitation got him another merciless slap to the face. This Siamese cat was clever, and educated too. Nakata had met many cats up till this point, but never before one who listened to opera and knew models of cars. Impressed, he watched as Mimi went about her business with a brisk efficiency.

Once Mimi had heard everything she wanted to, she chased the younger cat off. "Be on your way!" she said sharply, and he dejectedly slunk away.

Mimi affably nestled up into Nakata's lap. "I think I've got the gist of it."

"Much obliged," Nakata said.

"That cat—Kawamura, that is—said he's seen Goma several times in a grassy spot just down the road. It's an empty lot they were planning to build on. A real estate firm bought up a car company's parts warehouse and tore it down, planning to put up a high-class condo. A citizens' movement opposed the development, there was a legal battle, and the construction's been put on hold. The sort of thing that happens all the time these days. The lot's overgrown with grass and people hardly ever come there, so it's the perfect hangout for all the strays in the neighborhood. I don't keep company with many cats, and I don't want to get fleas, so I hardly ever go over there. As you're no doubt aware, fleas are like a bad habit—awfully hard to get rid of once you get them."

"I see," Nakata said.

"He told me the cat's just like the one in the photograph—a timid, pretty young tortoiseshell with a flea collar. Can't seem to speak that well, either. It's clear to anyone that it's a naive house cat that can't find its way back home."

"When was this, I wonder?"

"The last time he saw the cat seems to be three or four days ago. He's not very bright, so he's not even sure about days. But he did say it was the day after it rained, so I'm thinking it must have been Monday. I seem to recall it rained pretty hard on Sunday."

"Nakata doesn't know about the days of the week, but I think it did rain around then. He hasn't seen her since?"

"That was the last time. The other cats haven't seen her either, he says. He's a spacey, good-for-nothing cat, but I pressed him closely and believe most of what he says."

"I really want to thank you."

"No need—it was my pleasure. Most of the time I have only this worthless bunch of cats around here to talk to, and we never seem to agree on anything. I find it incredibly irritating. So it's a breath of fresh air to be able to talk with a sensible human such as yourself."

"I see," Nakata said. "There's one thing Nakata still doesn't understand. Mr. Kawamura kept going on about *tuna*, and I was wondering if he meant the fish?"

Mimi lithely lifted her left front leg, inspecting the pink flesh of the pad, and chuckled. "The youngster's terminology isn't very extensive, I'm afraid."

"*Termanolgy?*"

"The number of words he's familiar with is limited, is what I'm saying. So for him everything that's good to eat is *tuna*. For him tuna's the crème de la crème, as far as food goes. He doesn't know there are such things as sea bream, halibut, or yellowtail."

Nakata cleared his throat. "Actually, Nakata's very fond of tuna. Of course I like eel as well."

"I'm fond of eel myself. Though it's not the sort of thing you can eat all the time."

"That's true. You couldn't eat it all the time."

The two of them were silent for a time, eel musings filling the passing moments.

"Anyway, what that cat was getting at is this," Mimi said, as if suddenly remembering. "Not long after the neighborhood cats began hanging out at that vacant lot, a bad person showed up who catches cats. The other cats believe this man may have taken Goma away. The man lures them with something good to eat, then throws them inside a large sack. The man's quite skilled at catching cats, and a hungry, innocent cat like Goma would easily fall into his trap. Even the stray cats who live around here, normally a wary bunch, have lost a couple of their number to this man. It's simply hideous, because nothing could be worse for a cat than to be stuffed inside a bag."

"I see," Nakata said, and again rubbed his salt-and-pepper hair with his palm. "But what does this man do with the cats once he's caught them?"

"That I don't know. In the old days they used to make shamisens out of cat skin, but nowadays not too many people play the shamisen. And besides, I hear they mainly use plastic now. In some parts of the world people eat cats, though not in Japan, thank goodness. So I think we can exclude both of these as motives. Which leaves, let me see . . . people who use cats in scientific experiments. Cats are used a lot in experiments. One of my friends, in fact, was used in a psychology experiment at Tokyo University. A terrible thing, but it's a long story and I won't go into it now. There are also perverts—not many, mind you—who just enjoy tormenting cats. Catching a cat and chopping off its tail, for instance."

"What do they do after they chop it off?"

"Nothing. They just want to torment and hurt the cats. Makes them feel good for some reason. I'm afraid there are twisted people like that in the world."

Nakata gave this some thought. How could chopping off a cat's tail possibly be fun? "So what you're saying is that maybe this *twisted person* has taken Goma away?" he asked.

Mimi screwed up her long white whiskers and frowned. "I'd rather not think that, or even imagine it, but it *is* a possibility. Mr. Nakata, I haven't lived all that many years, but I've seen terrible things I never could have imagined. Most people look at cats and think *what a life*—all we do is lie around in the sun, never having to lift a finger. But cats' lives aren't that idyllic. Cats are powerless, weak little creatures that injure easily. We don't have shells like turtles, nor wings like birds. We can't burrow into the ground like moles or change colors like a chameleon. The world has no idea how many cats are injured every day, how many of us meet a miserable end. I happen to be lucky enough to live with the Tanabes in a warm and friendly family, the children treat me well, and I've got everything I need. But even my life isn't always easy. When it comes to strays, though, they have a very tough time of it."

"You're really smart, aren't you, Mimi?" Nakata said, impressed by the Siamese's eloquence.

"No, not really," Mimi replied, narrowing her eyes in embarrassment. "I just spend too much time lying in front of the TV and this is what happens—my head gets full of worthless facts. Do you ever watch TV, Mr. Nakata?"

"No, Nakata doesn't watch TV. The people on TV talk too fast, and I can't keep up with them. I'm dumb, so I can't read, and if you can't read TV doesn't make much sense. Sometimes I listen to the radio, but the words there are also too fast, and it tires me out. I much prefer doing this—enjoy talking with a cat outside, under the sky."

"Indeed," Mimi said.

"That's right," Nakata replied.

"I really hope that Goma is all right."

"Mimi, Nakata's going to have a look at that empty lot."

"According to the youngster, this man is very tall, and wears a strange tall hat and long leather boots. And he walks fast. He looks very unusual, so you'll recognize him right away, he told me. Whenever the cats that gather at the empty lot see him coming, they scatter in all directions. But a newcomer might not know enough to. . . ."

Nakata stored this information away in his head, carefully folding it all away in a front drawer so he wouldn't forget it. *The man is very tall, and wears a strange tall hat and long leather boots.* . . .

"I hope I've been of help," Mimi said.

"Nakata appreciates everything you've done. If you hadn't been kind enough to speak up I'd still be going round and round about tuna. I'm grateful."

"What I think," Mimi said, gazing up at Nakata with knit brows, "is that that man is *trouble*. A *lot* of trouble. He's more dangerous than you can ever imagine. If it were me I'd never go near that lot. But you're a human, and it's your job, after all, but I hope you'll take every precaution."

"Thank you very kindly. I'll be as careful as I can."

"Mr. Nakata, this world is a terribly violent place. And nobody can escape the violence. Please keep that in mind. You can't be too cautious. The same holds true for cats and human beings."

"I'll remember that," Nakata replied.

But he had no idea where and how the world could be violent. The world was full of things Nakata couldn't comprehend, and most things connected with violence fell into that category.

After saying good-bye to Mimi, he went to see the empty lot, which turned out to be about the size of a small playground. A tall plywood fence enclosed the lot, with a sign on it saying KEEP OUT: SITE OF FUTURE CONSTRUCTION (which Nakata, naturally, couldn't read). A heavy chain blocked the entrance, but around back was a gap in the fence, and he easily got inside. Someone must have pried it open.

All the warehouses that had originally stood there had been torn down, but the land hadn't been graded for construction and was covered with grass. Goldenrod grew as high as a child, a couple of butterflies flickering above it. Mounds of earth had hardened in the rain, in some places rising up in little hillocks. A perfect place for cats. People wouldn't come in, and there were all sorts of little creatures to catch and plenty of places to hide.

Kawamura was nowhere to be seen. Two scrawny cats with rough coats were there, but when Nakata called out a friendly greeting they just glanced at him coldly and disappeared into the weeds. Which made sense—none of them wanted to get caught and have his tail chopped off. Nakata himself certainly didn't want to have that happen to him, not that he had a tail. It was no wonder the cats were wary of him.

Nakata stood on higher ground and took a good look around. No one else was there, just the butterflies, searching for something, fluttering above the weeds. He found a good spot to sit down, lowered his canvas bag from his shoulder, took out two bean-jam buns, and had his usual lunch. He drank hot tea from a thermos, eyes narrowed as he quietly sipped. Just a quiet early afternoon. Everything was at rest, placid, harmonious. Nakata found it hard to believe that somebody might be lying in wait to torment and torture cats.

He rubbed his cropped salt-and-pepper hair as he chewed. If somebody else was with him he could explain—*Nakata's not very bright*—but unfortunately he was alone. All he could do was nod a few times to himself and continue chewing. Once he finished the buns he folded up the cellophane they'd been wrapped in into a compact square and put it in his bag. He screwed the lid back on the thermos tight and put it in his bag as well. The sky was covered with a layer of clouds, but from their color he could tell the sun was almost directly overhead.

The man is very tall, and wears a strange tall hat and long leather boots.

Nakata tried to picture this man, but had no idea what a strange tall hat and long leather boots looked like. In his whole life he'd never encountered any tall hats and long leather boots. Kawamura had told Mimi that you'd know him when you saw him. So, Nakata decided, I suppose I'll just have to wait until I see him. That's definitely the best plan. He stood up and relieved himself in the weeds—a long, honest pee—and then went over to a clump of weeds in a corner of the vacant lot, where he had the best chance of remaining hidden from sight, and sat out the rest of the afternoon, waiting for that strange man to show up.

Waiting was a boring task. He had no clue when the man might next appear—maybe tomorrow, maybe not for a week. Or maybe he'd never show up again—there was that possibility. But Nakata was used to aimless waiting and spending time alone, doing nothing. He wasn't bothered in the least.

Time wasn't the main issue for him. He didn't even own a watch. Nakata operated on his own sense of time. In the morning it got light, in the evening the sun set and it got dark. Once it got dark he'd go to the nearby public bath, and after coming home from his bath he'd go to sleep. The public bath was closed on certain days of the week, and when that happened he'd just give up and go back home. His stomach told him when it was time to eat, and when the time came for him to go pick up his *sub city* (somebody was always nice enough to tell him when that day was near) he knew another month had passed. The next day he'd always go for a haircut at the local barber shop. Every summer someone from the ward office would treat him to eel, and every New Year they'd bring him rice cakes.

Nakata let his body relax, switched off his mind, allowing things to flow through him. This was natural for him, something he'd done ever since he was a child, without a second thought. Before long the borders of his consciousness fluttered around, just like the butterflies. Beyond these borders lay a dark abyss. Occasionally his consciousness would fly over the border and hover over that dizzying, black crevass. But Nakata wasn't afraid of the darkness or how deep it was. And why should he be? That bottomless world of darkness, that weighty silence and chaos, was an old friend, a part of him already. Nakata understood this well. In that world there was no writing, no days of the week, no scary Governor, no opera, no BMWs. No scissors, no tall hats. On the other hand, there was also no delicious eel, no tasty bean-jam buns. *Everything* is there, but there are no *parts*. Since there are no parts, there's no need to replace one thing with another. No need to remove anything, or add anything. You don't have to think about difficult things, just let yourself soak it all in. For Nakata, nothing could be better.

Occasionally he dozed off. Even when he slept, though, his senses, ever vigilant, kept watch over the vacant lot. If something happened, if somebody came, he could wake up and do what needed to be done. The sky was covered with a flat line of gray clouds, but at least it wasn't going to rain. The cats all knew it. And so did Nakata.

Chapter 11

When I finish talking it's pretty late. Sakura listens intently the whole time, resting her head in her hands on the kitchen table. I tell her that I'm actually fifteen, in junior high, that I stole my father's money and ran away from my home in Nakano Ward in Tokyo. That I'm staying in a hotel in Takamatsu and spending my days reading at a library. That all of a sudden I found myself collapsed outside a shrine, covered with blood. Everything. Well, *almost* everything. Not the important stuff I can't talk about.

"So your mother left home with your older sister when you were just four. Leaving you and your father behind."

I take the photo of my sister and me at the shore from my wallet and show her. "This is my sister," I say. Sakura looks at the photo for a while, then hands it back without a word.

"I haven't seen her since then," I say. "Or my mom. She's never gotten in touch, and I have no idea where she is. I don't even remember what she looks like. There aren't any photos of her left. I remember her smell, her touch, but not her face."

"Hmm," Sakura says. Head still in her hands, she narrows her eyes and looks at me. "Must have been hard on you."

"Yeah, I guess. . . ."

She continues to gaze at me silently. "So you didn't get along with your dad?" she asks after a while.

Didn't get along? How am I supposed to answer that? I don't say anything, just shake my head.

"Dumb question—of course you didn't. Otherwise you wouldn't have run away," Sakura says. "So anyway, you left your home, and today you suddenly lost consciousness or your memory or something."

"Yeah."

"Did that ever happen before?"

"Sometimes," I tell her honestly. "I fly into a rage, and it's like I blow a fuse. Like somebody pushes a switch in my head and my body does its thing before my mind can catch up. It's like I'm here, but in a way it's not me."

"You lose control and do something violent, you mean?"

"It's happened a few times, yeah."

"Have you hurt anybody?"

I nod. "Twice I did. Nothing serious."

She thinks about this.

"Is that what happened this time?"

I shake my head. "This is the first time something this bad's happened. This time . . . I don't know how it started, and I can't remember at all what happened. It's like my memory was wiped clean. It never was this bad before."

She looks over the T-shirt I haul out of my backpack, carefully checking the blood I couldn't wash out. "So the last thing you remember is eating dinner, right? At a restaurant near the station?"

I nod.

"And everything after that's a blank. The next thing you knew, you were lying in the bushes behind that shrine. About four hours later. Your shirt covered in blood and your left shoulder aching?"

I give her another nod. She brings over a city map from somewhere and checks out the distance between the station and the shrine.

"It's not so far, but it would take a while to walk. But why would you have been over there in the first place? It's the opposite direction from your hotel. Have you ever gone there before?"

"Never."

"Take off your shirt for a minute," she says.

I strip bare to the waist, and she walks behind me and grabs my left shoulder hard. Her fingers dig into my flesh, and I can't help but gasp. This girl's pretty strong.

"Does it hurt?"

"You bet it does," I say.

"You hit something pretty hard. Or something hit you."

"I don't remember a thing."

"Anyway, nothing's broken," she says. She proceeds to prod around the sore spot, and aside from the pain, her fingers feel really nice. When I tell her so she smiles.

"I've always been good at giving massages. It's a useful skill for a hairdresser."

She keeps on massaging my shoulder. "Doesn't look like anything major. Give it a good night's sleep and you should feel better."

She picks up my T-shirt, puts it in a plastic bag, and tosses it in the garbage. My dungaree shirt she gives a once-over and throws in the washing machine. She rummages around in her dresser and comes up with a white T-shirt. She hands it to me, a brand-new white shirt that says *Maui Whale Watching Cruise* on it, with a picture of a fluke sticking out of the water.

"This is the biggest shirt I could find. It's not mine, but don't worry about it. It's just a souvenir from somebody. Might not be your style, but give it a try."

I tug the shirt on, and it fits perfectly.

"You can keep it if you want," she says.

I thank her.

"So you never had such a total memory loss before?" she asks.

I nod, then close my eyes, feeling the T-shirt, taking in its new smell. "Sakura, I'm really scared," I tell her. "I don't know what to do. I don't have any memory of hurting anybody. Whatever it was got me covered in blood, but I can't remember anything. If I committed a crime, I'm still legally responsible, right, whether I have a memory of it or not?"

"Maybe it was just a nosebleed. Somebody was walking down the street, bumped into a telephone pole, and got a bloody nose. And all you did was help them out. See? I understand why you're worried, but let's try not to think about worst-case scenarios, okay? At least not tonight. In the morning we can look in the paper, watch the news on TV. If something terrible really happened, we'll know about it. Then we can consider our options. There're plenty of reasons why someone might get bloody, and most of the time it's not nearly as bad as it looks. I'm a girl, so I'm used to seeing blood—I see that much every month. You know what I mean?"

I nod, and feel myself blushing a little. She scoops a little Nescafé into a big cup and heats up some water in a small pan. She smokes, waiting for the water to boil. She takes a couple of puffs, then extinguishes the cigarette with tap water. I catch a whiff of menthol.

"I don't mean to pry, but there's something I want to ask you. Do you mind?"

"I don't mind," I tell her.

"Your older sister was adopted. They got her from somewhere before you were born, right?"

"That's right," I reply. "I don't know why, but my parents adopted her. After that I was born. Not exactly what they had in mind, I imagine."

"So you're definitely the child of your mother and father."

"As far I know," I tell her.

"But when your mother left, she didn't take you, but took your sister, who's unrelated to her," Sakura says. "Not what you'd normally expect a woman to do."

I don't say anything.

"Why'd she do that?"

I shake my head. "I have no idea," I tell her. "I've asked myself the same question a million times."

"That must have hurt."

Did it? "I don't know. But if I get married someday I don't think I'll have any kids. I wouldn't have any idea how to get along with them if I did."

"My situation wasn't as complicated as yours," she says, "but I didn't get along with my folks for a long time, and I got mixed up in a lot of stupid things because of it. So I know how you feel. But it's not a good idea to make decisions so soon. There's no such thing as absolutes."

She stands in front of the kitchen stove and sips her Nescafé, steam rising from the large cup. The cup has a drawing of the Moomin cartoon characters on it. She doesn't say anything, and neither do I.

"Do you have anybody, relatives or someone, who can help?" she asks after a while.

"No," I say. "My father's parents died a long time ago, and he doesn't have any brothers, sisters, uncles, or aunts. Not a one. Not that I can prove this. But I do know he never had anything to do with any relatives. And I never heard anything about relatives on my mother's side. I mean, I don't even know my mother's name—so how was I supposed to know about her relatives?"

"Your father sounds like an alien from outer space or something," Sakura says. "Like he came from some far-off planet, took on human form, kidnapped an Earth woman, and then had you. Just so he could have more descendants. Your mother found out, got frightened, and ran away. Like in some film noir science fiction flick."

I have no idea what to say.

"All joking aside," she says, and smiles broadly to show that she means it, "my point is, in this whole wide world the only person you can depend on is *you*."

"I guess so."

She stands there leaning against the sink, drinking her coffee.

"I have to get some sleep," she says, as if suddenly remembering. It's past three. "I have to get up at seven-thirty so I won't get much, but a little's better than none. I hate going to work on no sleep at all. So what're you going to do?"

"I have my sleeping bag with me," I tell her, "so if it's no bother I'll just sack out in a corner." I take my tightly rolled-up sleeping bag out of my backpack, spread it out, and fluff it up.

She watches, impressed. "A regular Boy Scout," she says.

After she turns out the light and gets in bed, I climb into my sleeping bag, shut my eyes, and try to go to sleep. But I can't stop picturing that bloody white T-shirt. I still feel that burning sensation in my palm. I open my eyes and stare at the ceiling. A floor creaks somewhere. Somebody turns on a faucet. And again I hear an ambulance in the night, far off but echoing sharply in the darkness.

"Can't fall asleep?" she whispers in the dark.

"No," I say.

"Me neither. Shouldn't have had that coffee. That was dumb." She switches on her bedside light, checks the time, then turns the light off. "Don't get me wrong," she says, "but if you'd like to come over here you can. I can't get to sleep either."

I slip out of my sleeping bag and climb in bed with her. I'm wearing boxers and the T-shirt. She has on a pair of light pink pajamas.

"I have a steady boyfriend in Tokyo," she tells me. "He's not much to brag about, but he's my guy. So I don't have sex with anybody else. I might not look like it, but when it comes to sex I'm pretty straightlaced. Call me old-fashioned. I wasn't always that way—I used to be pretty wild—but I don't fool around anymore. So don't get any ideas, okay? Just think of us as brother and sister. You understand?"

"Gotcha," I tell her.

She puts her arms around me, hugs me close, and rests her cheek on my forehead. "You poor thing," she says.

I don't need to tell you that I get a hard-on right away. Big-time. And it couldn't help rubbing up against her thigh.

"My oh my!" she says.

"Sorry," I tell her. "I didn't mean to."

"It's okay," she says. "I know what an inconvenience it is. Nothing you can do to stop it."

I nod in the darkness.

She hesitates for a moment, then lowers my boxers, pulls out my rock-hard cock, and cradles it gently in her hand. Like she's making sure of something, the way a doctor takes a pulse. With her soft hand touching me, I feel something—a stray thought, maybe—spring up in my crotch.

"How old would your sister be now?"

"Twenty-one," I say. "Six years older than me."

She thinks about this for a while. "Do you want to see her?"

"Maybe," I say.

"*Maybe?*" Her hand grasps my cock a little harder. "What do you mean, *maybe?* You really don't want to see her that much?"

"I don't know what we'd talk about, and she might not want to see *me*. Same thing with my mother. Maybe neither one of them wants to have anything to do with me. No one's searching for me. I mean, they left and everything." *Without me*, I silently complete the thought.

She doesn't say anything. Her hand on my cock loosens a bit, then tightens. In time with this my cock relaxes, then gets even harder.

"You want to come?" she asks.

"Maybe," I say.

"Again with the *maybes?*"

"Very much," I correct myself.

She sighs lightly and slowly begins to move her hand. It feels out of this world. Not just an up-and-down motion, but more of an all-over massage. Her fingers gently stroke my cock and my balls. I close my eyes and let out a big sigh.

"You can't touch me. And when you're about to come let me know so you don't mess up the sheets."

"Okay," I say.

"How is it? I'm pretty good, huh?"

"Fantastic."

"Like I was telling you, I'm very nimble-fingered. But this isn't sex, okay? I'm just—helping you relax, is what it is. You've had a rough day, you're all tense, and you're not going to sleep well unless we do something about it. Got it?"

"Yeah, I get it," I say. "But I do have one request."

"What's that?"

"Is it okay if I imagine you naked?"

Her hand stops and she looks me in the eyes. "You want to imagine me naked while we're doing this?"

"Yeah. I've been trying to keep from imagining that, but I can't."

"Really?"

"It's like a TV you can't turn off."

She laughs. "I don't get it. You didn't have to tell me that! Why don't you just go ahead and imagine what you want? You don't need my permission. How can I know what's in your head?"

"I can't help it. Imagining something's very important, so I thought I'd better tell you. It has nothing to do with whether you know or not."

"You are some kind of polite boy, aren't you," she says, impressed. "I guess it's nice, though, that you wanted to let me know. All right, permission granted. Go ahead and picture me nude."

"Thanks," I say.

"How is it? Is my body nice?"

"It's amazing," I reply.

This languid sensation spreads over my lower half, like a liquid floating to the surface. When I tell her, she grabs some tissue from the bedside, and I come, over and over, like crazy. . . . A little while later she goes to the kitchen, tosses away the tissue paper, and rinses her hand.

"Sorry," I say.

"It's all right," she says, snuggling back into bed. "No need to apologize. It's just a part of your body. So—do you feel better?"

"Definitely."

"I'm glad." She thinks for a while, then says, "I was thinking how nice it'd be if I was your real sister."

"Me too," I say.

She lightly touches my hair. "I'm going to sleep now, so why don't you go back to your sleeping bag. I can't sleep well unless I'm alone, and I don't want your hard-on poking me all night, okay?"

I go back to my sleeping bag and close my eyes. This time I can get to sleep. A deep, deep sleep, maybe the deepest since I ran away from home. It's like I'm in some huge elevator that slowly, silently carries me deeper and deeper underground. Finally all light has disappeared, all sound faded away.

When I wake up, Sakura's gone off to work. It's nine a.m. My shoulder hardly aches at all anymore. Just like she said. On the kitchen table I find a folded-up morning paper, a note, and a key.

Her note says: *I watched the TV news at seven and looked through the entire paper, but there weren't any bloody incidents reported around here. So I don't think that blood was anything. Good news, huh? There isn't much in the fridge, but help yourself. And make use of whatever you need around the house. If you aren't planning to go anywhere, feel free to hang out here. Just put the key under the doormat if you go out.*

I grab a carton of milk from the fridge, check the expiration date, and pour it over some cornflakes, boil some water, and make a cup of Darjeeling tea. Toast two slices of bread, and eat them with some low-fat margarine. Then I open the newspaper and scan the local news. Like she said, no violent crimes in the headlines. I let out a sigh of relief, fold up the paper, and put it back where it was. At least I won't have to run all over trying to evade the cops. But I decide it's better not to go back to the hotel, just to play it safe. I still don't know what happened during those lost four hours.

I call the hotel. A man answers, and I don't recognize his voice. I tell him something's come up and I have to check out. I try my best to sound grown-up. I've paid in advance so that shouldn't be a problem. There are some personal effects in the room, I tell him, but they can be discarded. He checks the computer and sees that the bill's up-to-date. "Everything's in order, Mr. Tamura," he says. "You're all checked out." The key's a plastic card, so there's no need to return it. I thank him and hang up.

I take a shower. Sakura's underwear and stockings are drying out in the bathroom. I try not to look at them and concentrate on my usual job of thoroughly scrubbing myself. And I try my best not to think about last night. I brush my teeth and put on a pair of new shorts, roll up my sleeping bag and stuff it in my backpack, then wash my dirty clothes in the washer. There's no dryer, so after they go through the spin cycle I fold them up and put them in a plastic bag and into my pack. I can always dry them at a coin laundry later on.

I wash all the dishes piled up in the sink, let them drain, dry them, and place them back in the shelf. Then I straighten up the contents of the fridge and toss whatever's gone bad. Some of the food stinks— moldy broccoli, an ancient, rubbery cucumber, a pack of tofu well past its expiration date. I take whatever's still edible, transfer it to new containers, and wipe up some spilled sauce. I throw away all the cigarette butts, make a neat stack of the scattered old newspapers, and run a vacuum around the place. Sakura might be good at giving a massage, but when it comes to keeping house she's a disaster. I iron the shirts she's crammed in the dresser, and think about going shopping and making dinner. At home I tried to take care of household chores myself, so none of this is any trouble. But making dinner, I decide, might be going too far.

Finished with all that, I sit down at the kitchen table and look around the apartment. I know I can't stay here forever. I'd have a semipermanent hard-on, with semipermanent fantasies. Can't avoid looking at those tiny black panties hanging in the bathroom, can't keep asking her permission to let my imagination roam. But most of all I can't forget what she did for me last night.

I leave a note for Sakura, using the blunt pencil and the memo pad beside the phone. *Thanks. You really saved me. I'm sorry I woke you up so late last night. But you're the only one I could count on.* I stop for a moment to think what I should write next, and do a three-sixty of the room as I'm thinking. *Thanks for letting me stay over. I'm grateful you said I could stay here as long I liked. It would be nice if I could, but I don't think I should bother you anymore. There're all sorts of reasons I won't go into. I've got to make it on my own. I hope you'll still think kindly of me the next time I'm in a jam.*

I stop again. Someone in the neighborhood's got their TV on at full volume, one of those morning talk shows for housewives. The people on the show all yelling at each other, and commercials just as loud and obnoxious. I sit at the table, spinning the blunt pencil in my hand, pulling my thoughts together. *To tell the truth, though, I don't think I deserve your kindness. I'm trying my best to be a much better person, but things aren't going so well. The next time we meet I hope I'll have my act together. Whether that will happen or not, I don't know. Thanks for last night. It was wonderful.*

I slip the note under a cup, shoulder my backpack, and head out of the apartment, leaving the key under the doormat like she said. A black-and-white spotted cat's lying in the middle of the stairs, taking a nap. He must be used to people because he doesn't make a move to get up as I go down the stairs. I sit down beside him and stroke his large body for a while. The feel of his fur brings back memories. The cat narrows his eyes and starts to purr. We sit there on the stairs for a long time, each enjoying his own version of this intimate feeling. Finally I tell him good-bye and walk down the road. A fine rain's begun to fall.

Having checked out of the hotel and left Sakura's, I have no idea where I'll spend the night. Before the sun sets I've got to find a roof to sleep under, someplace safe. I don't know where to begin but decide to take the train out to the Komura Library. Once I get there, something will work out. I don't know why, but I just have a feeling it will.

Fate seems to be taking me in some even stranger directions.

Chapter 12

October 19, 1972

Dear Professor,

I'm sure you must be quite surprised to receive a letter from me, out of the blue. Please forgive me for being so forward. I imagine that you no longer remember my name, Professor, but I was at one time a teacher at a small elementary school in Yamanashi Prefecture. When you read this, you may recall something about me. I was the teacher in charge of the group of children on a field trip, the ones involved in the incident in which the children all lost consciousness. Afterward, as you may remember, I had the opportunity to speak with you and your colleagues from the university in Tokyo several times when you visited our town with people from the military to investigate.

In the years following I've often seen your name mentioned prominently in the press, and I have followed your career and achievements with the deepest admiration. At the same time, I have fond memories of when we met, especially your very businesslike, brisk way of speaking. I feel blessed, too, to have been able to read several of your books. I've always been impressed by your insights, and I find the worldview that runs through all of your publications very convincing—namely that as individuals each of us is extremely isolated, while at the same time we are all linked by a prototypical memory. There have been times in my own life that I felt exactly this way. From afar, then, I pray for your continued success.

After that incident I continued to teach at the same elementary school. A few years ago, however, I unexpectedly fell ill, was hospitalized for a long spell in Kofu General Hospital, and, after some time, submitted my resignation. For a year I was in and out of the hospital, but eventually I recovered, was discharged, and opened a small tutorial school in our town. My students were the children of my former pupils. It's a trite observation, perhaps, but it is true what they say—that time does fly—and I've found the passage of time to be incredibly swift.

During the war I lost both my husband and my father, then my mother as well in the confused period following the surrender. With my husband off to war soon after we married, we never had any children, so I've been all alone in the world. I wouldn't say my life has been happy, but it has been a great blessing to have been able to teach for so long and have the chance to work with so many children over the years. I thank God for this opportunity. If it hadn't been for teaching I don't think I'd have been able to survive.

I summoned up my courage today to write to you, Professor, because I've never been able to forget that incident in the woods in the fall of 1944. Twenty-eight years have passed, but to me it's as fresh in my mind as if it took place yesterday. Those memories are always with me, shadowing my every waking moment. I've spent countless sleepless nights pondering it all, and it's even haunted my dreams.

It's as if the aftershocks of that incident affect every aspect of my life. To give you an example, whenever I run across any of the children involved in the incident (half of whom still live here in town and are now in their mid-thirties) I always wonder what effects the incident had on them, and on myself. Something as traumatic as that you'd think would have to have some lingering physical or psychological impact on all of us. I can't believe otherwise. But when it comes to pinpointing what sort of effects these were, and how great an impact it all had, I'm at a loss.

As you're well aware, Professor, the military kept news of this incident from reaching the public. During the Occupation the American military conducted their own investigation behind closed doors. The military's always the same, whether Japanese or American. Even when censorship was lifted after the Occupation, no articles about the incident appeared in newspapers or magazines. Which I suppose is understandable, since it had taken place years before and no one had died.

Because of this, most people are unaware that such an incident ever took place. During the war there were so many horrific events, and millions of people lost their lives, so I don't suppose people would be very shocked by what happened in our little town. Even here not many people remember what happened, and those who do don't appear willing to talk about it. I'd say most people who recall the incident find it an unpleasant memory they'd prefer not to touch on.

Most things are forgotten over time. Even the war itself, the life-and-death struggle people went through, is now like something from the distant past. We're so caught up in our everyday lives that events of the past, like ancient stars that have burned out, are no longer in orbit around our minds. There are just too many things we have to think about every day, too many new things we have to learn. New styles, new information, new technology, new terminology . . . But still, no matter how much time passes, no matter what takes place in the interim, there are some things we can never assign to oblivion, memories we can never rub away. They remain with us forever, like a touchstone. And for me, what happened in the woods that day is one of these.

I realize there's nothing I can do about it now, and I would certainly understand if you are puzzled about why I'm bringing this up at this late date. But while I'm still alive there's something I have to get off my chest.

During the war, of course, we lived under strict censorship, and there were things we couldn't easily talk about. When I met you, Professor, there were military officers with us and I couldn't speak freely. Also, I didn't know anything about you then, or about your work, so I certainly didn't feel—as a young woman talking to a man she didn't know—I could be candid about any private matter. Thus I kept several facts to myself. In other words, in the official investigation I intentionally changed some of the facts about the incident. And when, after the war, the American military interviewed me, I stuck to my story. Out of fear and to keep up appearances, perhaps, I repeated the same lies I'd told you. This may well have made it more difficult for you to investigate the incident, and may have somewhat skewed your conclusions. No, I *know* it did. This has bothered me for years, and I'm ashamed of what I did.

I hope this explains why I've written this long letter to you. I realize you're a busy man and may not have time for this. If so, please feel free to treat it all as the ramblings of an old woman and toss the letter away. The thing is, I feel the need, while I'm still able, to confess all that really took place then, write it down, and pass it along to someone who should know. I recovered from my illness, but you never know when there might be a relapse. I hope you will take this into consideration.

The night before I took the children up into the hills, I had a dream about my husband, just before dawn. He had been drafted and was off at war. The dream was extremely realistic and sexually charged—one of those dreams that's so vivid it's hard to distinguish between dream and reality.

In the dream we were lying on a large flat rock having sex. It was a light gray rock near the top of a mountain. The whole thing was about the size of two tatami mats, the surface smooth and damp. It was cloudy and looked like it was about to storm, but there wasn't any wind. It seemed near twilight, and birds were hurrying off to their nests. So there the two of us were, under that cloudy sky, silently having intercourse. We hadn't been married long at this time, and the war had separated us. My body was burning for my husband.

I felt an indescribable pleasure. We tried all sorts of positions and did it over and over, climaxing again and again. It's strange, now that I think of it, for in real life the two of us were quiet, rather introverted people. We'd never given in to our passions like this or experienced such soaring pleasure. But in the dream, for the first time in our lives, we'd thrown away all restraints and were going at it like animals.

When I opened my eyes it was still dim outside and I felt very odd. My body felt heavy, and I could still feel my husband deep inside me. My heart was pounding and I found it hard to breathe. My vagina was wet, just like after intercourse. It felt as if I'd really made love and not just dreamed it. I'm embarrassed to say it, but I masturbated at this point. I was burning with lust and had to do something to calm down.

Afterward I rode my bike to school as usual and escorted the children on our field trip to Owan yama. As we walked up the mountain path I could still feel the lingering effects of sex. All I had to do was close my eyes and I could feel my husband coming inside me, his semen shooting against the wall of my womb. I'd clung to him for all I was worth, my legs spread as wide as possible, my ankles entangled with his thighs. I was, frankly, in a daze as I took the children up the hill. I felt like I was still in the middle of that realistic, erotic dream.

We climbed up the mountain, reached the spot we were aiming at, and just as the children were getting ready to fan out to hunt for mushrooms, my period suddenly started. It wasn't time for it. My last one had stopped only ten days before, and my periods were always regular. Perhaps this erotic dream had stirred something up inside me and set it off. Naturally I hadn't come prepared, and here we were in the hills far from town.

I instructed the children to take a short break, then I went off alone far into the woods and took care of myself as best I could with a couple of towels I'd brought along. There was a great deal of blood, and it made quite a mess, but I was sure I'd be able to manage until we made it back to school. My head was a complete blank, and I couldn't focus at all. I had a guilty conscience, I imagine—about that uninhibited dream, about masturbating, and about having sexual fantasies in front of the children. I was usually the type who suppressed those kinds of thoughts.

I had the children go off to gather their mushrooms, and was thinking we'd better make it a short trip and go back as soon as we could. Back at school I'd be able to clean up better. I sat down and watched the children as they hunted for mushrooms. I kept a head count, and made sure none of them were out of my sight.

After a while, though, I noticed one little boy walking toward me with something in his hands. It was the boy named Nakata—the same boy who didn't regain consciousness and was hospitalized. He was holding the bloody towels I'd used. I gasped and couldn't believe my eyes. I'd hidden them far away, out of sight, where the children wouldn't go. You have to understand that this is the most embarrassing thing for a woman, something you don't want anybody else to see. How he was able to unearth them I have no idea.

Before I realized what I was doing, I was slapping him. I grabbed him by the shoulders and was slapping him hard on the cheeks. I might have been yelling something, I don't recall. I was out of control, no longer in my right mind. I think the embarrassment must have been so great I was in shock. I'd never, *ever* struck one of the children before. But it wasn't me who was doing it.

Suddenly I noticed all the children there, staring at me. Some were standing, some sitting, all of them facing me. It was all right in front of them—me, pale, standing there, Nakata collapsed on the ground from all the blows, the bloody towels. It was a moment frozen in time. Nobody moved, nobody said a word. The children were expressionless, their faces like bronze masks. A deep silence descended on the woods. All you could hear were the birds chirping. I can't get that scene out of my mind.

I don't know how much time passed. Probably not so long, but it seemed like forever—time driving me to the very edge of the world. Finally I snapped out of it. Color had returned to the world around me. I hid the bloody towels behind me and lifted Nakata up from where he lay. I held him tight and apologized to him as best I could. I was wrong, please, please forgive me, I begged him. He looked like he was still in shock. His eyes were blank, and I don't think he could hear what I said. With him still in my arms I turned to the other children and told them to resume their mushroom hunting. They probably couldn't comprehend what had just taken place. It was all too strange, too sudden.

I stood there for a while, holding Nakata tight in my arms, feeling like I wanted to die or disappear. Just over the horizon the violence of war went on, with countless people dying. I no longer had any idea what was right and what was wrong. Was I really seeing the real world? Was the sound of birds I was hearing real? I found myself alone in the woods, totally confused, blood flowing freely from my womb. I was angry, afraid, embarrassed—all of these rolled into one. I cried quietly, without making a sound.

And that's when the children collapsed.

I wasn't about to tell the military people what had really happened. It was wartime, and we had to keep up appearances. So I left out the part about my period starting, about Nakata finding the bloody towels, and me hitting him. Again, I'm afraid this threw an obstacle in your path as you investigated the incident. You can't imagine how relieved I am to finally get it off my chest.

Strangely enough, none of the children had any memory of the incident. Nobody remembered the bloody towels or me beating Nakata. Those memories had fallen away completely from their minds. Later, soon after the incident, I was able to indirectly sound out each child and confirm that this was indeed the case. Perhaps the mass coma had already started by then.

I'd like to say a few things about young Nakata, as his former home-room teacher. What happened to him after the incident, I don't really know. When I was interviewed after the war the American officer told me he'd been taken to a hospital in Tokyo and finally regained consciousness. But he wouldn't tell me any details. I imagine that you know more about this than I do, Professor.

Nakata was one of the five children evacuated to our town from Tokyo, and of the five he was the brightest and had the best grades. He had very pleasant features and always dressed well. He was a gentle boy and never butted in where he didn't belong. Never once during class did he volunteer an answer, but when I called on him, he always gave the correct answer, and when I asked his opinion he'd give a logical reply. He caught on right away, no matter what the subject. Every class has a student like that, one who'll study what he needs to without supervision, who you know will one day attend a top college and get an excellent job. A child who's innately capable.

But as his teacher I will say there were a couple of things about him that bothered me. Every so often I felt a sense of resignation in him. Even when he did well on difficult assignments, he never seemed happy. He never struggled to succeed, never seemed to experience the pain of trial and error. He never sighed or cracked a smile. It was as if these were things he had to get through, so he just did them. He handled whatever came his way efficiently—like a factory worker, screwdriver in hand, working on a conveyor belt, tightening a screw on each part that comes down the line.

I've never met his parents so I can't say anything for certain, but there had to be a problem back home. I'd seen a number of cases like this. Adults constantly raise the bar on smart children, precisely because they're able to handle it. The children get overwhelmed by the tasks in front of them and gradually lose the sort of openness and sense of accomplishment they innately have. When they're treated like that, children start to crawl inside a shell and keep everything inside. It takes a lot of time and effort to get them to open up again. Kids' hearts are malleable, but once they gel it's hard to get them back the way they were. Next to impossible, in most cases. But maybe I shouldn't be giving my opinions on the matter—this is, after all, your area of expertise.

I also sensed a hint of violence in the boy's background. Sometimes there'd be a flash of fear in his eyes that seemed an instinctive reaction to long-term exposure to violence. What level of violence this was, I had no way of knowing. Nakata was a very self-disciplined child and good at hiding his fear. But there'd be the occasional involuntary flinch, ever so slight, that he couldn't cover up. I knew that something violent had taken place in his home. After you spend a lot of time with children, you pick up on these things.

Rural families can be pretty violent. Most of the parents are farmers, all of them struggling to make ends meet. They're exhausted, doing backbreaking work from morning to night, and when they have a bit to drink and get angry, they're liable to strike out physically. It's no secret this kind of thing goes on, and most of the time the farm kids take it in stride and survive with no emotional scars. But Nakata's father was a university professor, and his mother, from what I could gather from the letters she sent me, was a well-educated woman. An upper-middle-class urban family, in other words. If there was any violence taking place in a family like that, it was bound to be something more complicated and less direct than what farm kids experience. The kind of violence a child keeps wrapped up inside himself.

That's why I especially regretted hitting him on the mountain that day, whether I did it unconsciously or not. I should never have acted that way, and I've felt guilty and ashamed ever since. I regret it even more since Nakata—after being dragged away from his parents and placed in an unfamiliar environment—was finally on the verge of opening up to me before the incident.

The kind of violence I displayed then may very well have dealt a fatal blow to whatever feelings had been budding inside him. I was hoping for an opportunity to repair the harm I'd caused, but circumstances dictated otherwise. Still unconscious, Nakata was taken to the hospital in Tokyo, and I never saw him again. It's something I regret to this day. I can still see the look on his face as I was beating him. The tremendous fear and resignation he felt at that instant.

I'm sorry, I didn't plan to write such a long letter, but there is one more thing I have to mention. To tell the truth, when my husband died in the Philippines just before the end of the war, it wasn't that much of a shock. I didn't feel any despair or anger—just a deep sense of helplessness. I didn't cry at all. I already knew that somewhere, on some distant battlefield, my husband would lose his life. Ever since the year before, when all those things I just wrote about took place— that erotic dream, my period starting ahead of time, hitting Nakata, the children falling into that mysterious coma—I'd accepted my husband's death as inevitable, as something fated to be. So news of his death merely confirmed what I already knew. The whole experience on the hill was beyond anything I've ever experienced. I feel like I left a part of my soul in those woods.

In closing, I'd like to express my hope that your research will continue to flourish. Please take good care of yourself.

Sincerely yours,

Chapter 13

It's after twelve, and I'm eating lunch and gazing at the garden when Oshima comes over and sits down next to me. Today I've pretty much got the library to myself. As always my lunch is the cheapest box lunch from the little shop at the train station. We talk for a while, and Oshima urges half his sandwiches on me.

"I made extra today, just for you," he insists. "Don't take it the wrong way, but you look like you're not eating."

"I'm trying to make my stomach shrink," I explain.

"On purpose?" he asks.

I nod.

"You're doing that to save money?"

Again I nod.

"I can understand that, but at your age you need to eat, and fill up whenever you get the chance. You need your nutrition."

The sandwich he's offering me looks delicious. I thank him and start eating. Smoked salmon, watercress, and lettuce on soft white bread. The crust is nicely crunchy, and horseradish and butter complete the sandwich.

"Did you make this yourself?" I ask.

"No one's about to make it for me," he says.

He pours black coffee from his thermos into a mug, while I drink milk from a little carton.

"What are you reading these days?"

"Natsume Soseki's complete works," I say. "I still haven't read some of his novels, so this is a great chance to read them all."

"You like him enough to want to read everything he wrote?" Oshima asks.

I nod.

Steam's rising from the cup in his hand. It's dark and cloudy outside, but at least the rain's stopped.

"Which of his novels have you read since you came here?"

"I finished *The Miner*, and now I'm on *Poppies*."

"*The Miner*, huh?" Oshima says, apparently searching out a vague memory of the book. "That's the story of a college student from Tokyo who winds up working in a mine, right? And he goes through all these tough times with the other miners and finally returns to the world outside? A sort of medium-length novel, as I recall. I read it a long time ago. The plot isn't what you normally expect from Soseki, and the style's kind of unpolished, too. Not one of his best. What do you like about it?"

I try putting into words my impressions of the novel, but I need Crow's help—need him to show up from wherever he is, spread his wings wide, and search out the right words for me.

"The main character's from a rich family," I say, "but he has an affair that goes sour and he gets depressed and runs away from home. While he's sort of wandering around, this shady character comes up to him and asks him to work in a mine, and he just tags along after him and finds himself working in the Ashio Mine. He's way down underground, going through all kinds of experiences he never could have imagined. This innocent rich boy finds himself crawling around in the dregs of society."

I sip my milk and try to piece together the rest of what I want to say. It takes a while before Crow comes back, but Oshima waits patiently.

"Those are life-and-death-type experiences he goes through in the mines. Eventually he gets out and goes back to his old life. But nothing in the novel shows he learned anything from these experiences, that his life changed, that he thought deeply now about the meaning of life or started questioning society or anything. You don't get any sense, either, that he's matured. You have a strange feeling after you finish the book. It's like you wonder what Soseki was trying to say. It's like not really knowing what he's getting at is the part that stays with you. I can't explain it very well."

"So *The Miner*'s structured very differently from, say, Soseki's *Sanshiro*, your typical modern bildungsroman?"

I nod. "I don't know about that, but you might be right. Sanshiro grows up in the story. Runs into obstacles, ponders things, overcomes difficulties, right? But the hero of *The Miner*'s different. All he does is

106

watch things happen and accept it all. I mean, occasionally he gives his own opinions, but nothing very deep. Instead, he just broods over his love affair. He comes out of the mine about the same as when he went in. He has no sense that it was something he decided to do himself, or that he had a choice. He's like totally passive. But I think in real life people are like that. It's not so easy to make choices on your own."

"Do you see yourself as sort of like the hero of *The Miner*?"

I shake my head. "No, I never thought of it that way."

"But people need to cling to something," Oshima says. "They have to. You're doing the same, even though you don't realize it. It's like Goethe said: Everything's a metaphor."

I mull this over for a while.

Oshima takes a sip of coffee. "At any rate, that's an interesting take on *The Miner*. Especially since you're both runaways. Makes me want to read it again."

I finish the sandwich, crush the now empty milk carton, and toss it in the waste can. "Oshima," I say, deciding to come right out with it, "I'm sort of in a fix and you're the only one I can ask for advice."

He opens both hands wide with a go-right-ahead gesture.

"It's a long story, but I don't have anywhere to stay tonight. I've got a sleeping bag, so I don't need a futon or bed or anything. Just a roof over my head. Do you know of any place around here like that?"

"I'm guessing that you're not thinking of a hotel or inn?"

I shook my head. "Money's a factor. But I'm also hoping not to be too conspicuous."

"To the juvenile section of the police, I bet."

"Yeah."

Oshima thinks it over for a time and says, "Well, you could stay here."

"In the *library*?"

"Sure. It has a roof, and a vacant room, too, that nobody uses at night."

"But do you think it's all right?"

"Of course we'll have to make some arrangements first. But it is possible. Or not impossible, I should say. I'm sure I can manage it."

"How so?"

"You like to read good books, to figure things out on your own. You look like you're in good shape physically, and you're an independent kind of guy. You like to lead a well-regulated life and have a lot of willpower. I mean, even the willpower to make your stomach smaller, right? I'll talk with Miss Saeki about you becoming my assistant and staying in the empty room here at the library."

"You want me to be your assistant?"

"You won't have to do much," Oshima says. "Basically help me open and close the place. We hire professionals to do the heavy cleaning or to input things on the computer. Apart from this, there's not a whole lot to do. You can just read whatever you like. Sound good?"

"Yeah, of course it does. . . ." I'm not sure what to say. "But I don't think Miss Saeki's going to go for it. I'm only fifteen, and a runaway she doesn't know anything about."

"But Miss Saeki's . . . how should I put it?" Oshima begins, then uncharacteristically comes to a halt, searching for the right word. "A little different."

"Different?"

"She has a different take on things than other people."

I nod. A different take on things? What does *that* mean? "You mean she's an unusual person?"

Oshima shakes his head. "No, I wouldn't say that. If you're talking about unusual, that would be *me*. She just isn't bound by conventional ways of doing things."

I'm still trying to figure out the difference between *different* and *unusual*, but decide to hold off on any more questions. For the time being.

After a pause Oshima says, "Staying here tonight, though, is a problem. So I'll take you someplace else, where you can stay for a couple of days till we get things settled. You don't mind, do you? It's a little far away."

"No problem," I tell him.

"The library closes at five," Oshima says, "and I have to straighten things up, so we'll leave around five-thirty. I'll drive you there in my car. Nobody's staying there now. And not to worry—the place has a roof."

"I appreciate it."

"You can thank me after we get there. It might not be what you're imagining."

I go back to the reading room and pick up where I left off in *Poppies*. I'm not a fast reader. I like to linger over each sentence, enjoying the style. If I don't enjoy the writing, I stop. Just before five I finish the novel, put it back on the shelf, then sit back down on the sofa, close my eyes, and think about what happened last night. About Sakura. About her room. What she did to me. All the twists and turns as events take their course.

At five-thirty I'm standing outside the library waiting for Oshima. He leads me to the parking lot out around back and we get into his green sports car. A Mazda Miata with the top down. My backpack's too big for the little trunk, so we tie it down tight on the rear rack.

"It's a long drive, so we'll stop along the way for dinner," Oshima says. He turns the ignition key and starts up the engine.

"Where are we headed?"

"Kochi," he replies. "Ever been there?"

I shake my head. "How far is it?"

"It'll take us about two and a half hours to get where we're going. Toward the south, over the mountains."

"You don't mind going so far?"

"It's okay. It's a straight shot, and it's still light out. And I've got a full tank."

We drive through the twilit city streets, then get on the highway heading west. Oshima changes lanes smoothly, slipping in between other cars, effortlessly shifting gears. Each time the hum of the engine changes slightly. When he shifts gears and floors it, the little car's soon zipping along at over ninety.

"The car's specially tuned, so it's got a lot of pickup. This isn't your ordinary Miata. Do you know much about cars?"

I shake my head. Cars are definitely not my specialty. "Do you enjoy driving?" I ask.

"The doctor made me give up any risky sports. So instead I drive. Compensation."

"Is something wrong with you?"

"The medical name's kind of long, but it's a type of hemophilia," Oshima says casually. "Do you know what that is?"

"I think so," I say. I learned about it in biology class. "Once you start bleeding you can't stop. It's genetic, where the blood doesn't coagulate."

"That's right. There're all kinds of hemophilia, and the type I have is pretty rare. It's not such a bad type of the disease, but I have to be careful not to get injured. Once I start bleeding I have to go to the hospital. Besides, these days there're problems with the blood supply in hospitals. Dying a slow death from AIDS isn't an option for me. So I've made some connections in town to supply me with safe blood, just in case. Because of my disease I don't go on trips. Except for regular checkups at the university hospital in Hiroshima, I hardly ever leave town. It's not so bad, though—I never did like traveling or sports all that much anyway. I can't use a kitchen knife, so doing any real cooking's out, which is kind of a shame."

"Driving's a risky enough sport," I tell him.

"It's a different kind of risk. Whenever I drive I try to go as fast as I can. If I'm in an accident driving fast I won't just wind up getting a cut finger. If you lose a lot of blood, there's no difference between a hemophiliac and anybody else. It evens things out, since your chances of survival are the same. You don't have to worry about things like blood coagulation or anything, and can die without any regrets."

"I see."

"Don't worry," Oshima laughs. "I'm not going have an accident. I'm a careful driver and don't push it. I keep my car in top condition, too. Besides, when I die I want to die quietly, all by myself."

"Taking someone else with you, then, isn't an option either."

"You got it."

We pull into a rest stop restaurant for dinner. I have chicken and a salad, he orders the seafood curry and a salad. Just something to fill our stomachs, is the best you could say about it. Oshima pays the bill, and we climb into the car again. It's already gotten dark. He steps on the accelerator and the tachometer shoots way up.

"Do you mind if I put on some music?" Oshima asks.

"Of course not," I reply.

He pushes the CD's play button and some classical piano music starts. I listen for a while, figuring out the music. I know it's not Beethoven, and not Schumann. Probably somebody who came in between.

"Schubert?" I ask.

"Good guess," he replies. His hands at ten-and-two on the steering wheel, he glances over at me. "Do you like Schubert?"

"Not particularly," I tell him.

"When I drive I like to listen to Schubert's piano sonatas with the volume turned up. Do you know why?"

"I have no idea."

"Because playing Schubert's piano sonatas well is one of the hardest things in the world. Especially this, the Sonata in D Major. It's a tough piece to master. Some pianists can play one or maybe two of the movements perfectly, but if you listen to all four movements as a unified whole, no one has ever nailed it. A lot of famous pianists have tried to rise to the challenge, but it's like there's always something missing. There's never one where you can say, *Yes! He's got it!* Do you know why?"

"No," I reply.

"Because the sonata itself is imperfect. Robert Schumann understood Schubert's sonatas well, and he labeled this one 'Heavenly Tedious.'"

"If the composition's imperfect, why would so many pianists try to master it?"

"Good question," Oshima says, and pauses as music fills in the silence. "I have no great explanation for it, but one thing I can say. Works that have a certain imperfection to them have an appeal for that very reason—or at least they appeal to certain *types* of people. Just like you're attracted to Soseki's *The Miner*. There's something in it that draws you in, more than more fully realized novels like *Kokoro* or *Sanshiro*. You discover something about that work that tugs at your heart—or maybe we should say the work discovers *you*. Schubert's Sonata in D Major is sort of the same thing."

"To get back to the question," I say, "why do you listen to Schubert's sonatas? Especially when you're driving?"

"If you play Schubert's sonatas, especially this one straight through, it's not art. Like Schumann pointed out, it's too long and too pastoral, and technically too simplistic. Play it through the way it is and it's flat and tasteless, some dusty antique. Which is why every pianist who attempts it adds something of his own, something extra. Like this—hear how he articulates it there? Adding rubato. Adjusting the pace, modulation, whatever. Otherwise they can't hold it all together. They have to be careful, though, or else all those extra devices destroy the dignity of the piece. Then it's not Schubert's music anymore. Every single pianist who's played this sonata struggles with the same paradox."

He listens to the music, humming the melody, then continues.

"That's why I like to listen to Schubert while I'm driving. Like I said, it's because all the performances are imperfect. A dense, artistic kind of imperfection stimulates your consciousness, keeps you alert. If I listen to some utterly perfect performance of an utterly perfect piece while I'm driving, I might want to close my eyes and die right then and there. But listening to the D major, I can feel the limits of what humans are capable of—that a certain type of perfection can only be realized through a limitless accumulation of the imperfect. And personally, I find that encouraging. Do you know what I'm getting at?"

"Sort of. . . ."

"I'm sorry," Oshima says. "I tend to get carried away on the subject."

"But there's all kinds and degrees of imperfection, right?" I say.

"Sure, of course."

"*Comparatively* speaking, which performance of the D major sonata do you think's the best?"

"That's a tough one." Oshima gives it some thought. He shifts down, swings over to the passing lane, swiftly slips past a huge refrigerated eighteen-wheeler, shifts up, and steers back into our lane. "Not to frighten you, but a green Miata is one of the hardest vehicles to spot on the highway at night. It has such a low profile, plus the green tends to blend into the darkness. Truck drivers especially can't see it from up in their cabs. It can be a risky business, particularly in tunnels. Sports cars really should be red. Then they'd stand out. That's why most Ferraris are red. But I happen to like green, even if it makes things more dangerous. Green's the color of a forest. Red's the color of blood."

He glances at his watch and goes back to humming along with the music. "Generally I'd have to say Brendel and Ashkenazy give the best performances, though they don't do anything for me emotionally. Schubert's music challenges and shatters the ways of the world. That's the essence of Romanticism, and Schubert's music is the epitome of the Romantic."

I keep on listening to the sonata.

"What do you think? Kind of boring?" he asks.

"Kind of," I admit.

"You can appreciate Schubert if you train yourself. I was the same way when I first listened to him—it bored me silly. It's only natural for someone your age. In time you'll appreciate it. People soon get tired of things that aren't boring, but not of what *is* boring. Go figure. For me, I might have the leisure to be bored, but not to grow tired of something. Most people can't distinguish between the two."

"You said you're an unusual person. Do you mean because of the hemophilia?"

"That's part of it," he says, and gives this devilish sort of smile. "There's more to it than that."

Schubert's long "Heavenly" sonata finishes, and we don't listen to any more music. We fall silent, each of us filling in the silence with our own random thoughts. I gaze vacantly at the passing signs. At a junction we turn south and the road heads into the mountains, one long tunnel after another. Oshima concentrates hard each time he passes another vehicle. We go by a number of slow-moving trucks on the road, and every time there's this *whooshing* moan of air, like somebody's soul is being yanked out. Occasionally I look back to make sure my backpack's still tied down okay.

"The place we're headed is deep in the mountains, not the most pleasant dwelling in the world," Oshima says. "I doubt you'll see anybody else while you're there. There's no radio, TV, or phone. Sure you don't mind?"

"I don't," I reply.

"You're used to being alone," Oshima comments.

I nod.

"But solitude comes in different varieties. What's waiting for you might be a little unexpected."

"How so?"

Oshima pushes up the bridge of his glasses. "I can't really say. It might change, depending on you."

We get off the highway and start down a small regional roadway. Along a side road near the exit there's a small town. Oshima stops at a convenience store and buys almost more groceries than we can carry—vegetables and fruit, crackers, milk and mineral water, canned goods, bread, pouch-packed instant food, mostly things that don't require much cooking. I start to take out my wallet, but he shakes his head and pays for it all.

Back in the sports car, we head down the road. I'm holding the bags that wouldn't fit into the trunk. Once we leave the little town everything is dark around us. No houses, and only the occasional car, the road so narrow it's hard for two cars to pass each other. Oshima flips on the high beams and races ahead, braking, accelerating, shifting from second to third and back. His expression is fixed as he focuses on driving, lips tight, eyes riveted on a point up ahead in the darkness, right hand clutching the top of the wheel, left hand poised for action on the gearshift knob.

A sharp bluff appears on our left side. It looks like there's a mountain stream down below. The curves get sharper, the road more slippery, and a couple of times the rear end of the car spins, but I decide not to worry about it. As far as Oshima is concerned, having an accident here most likely *isn't an option*.

My watch shows a little before nine. I crack open my window and let the cold air rush in. Everything sounds different here. We're in the mountains, heading in deeper. I breathe a sigh of relief when the road finally cuts away from the bluffs and turns into a forest. Trees magically soar above us. Our headlights lick at the trunks, illuminating one after another. We've left the paved road behind, the tires squirting out pebbles that ricochet against the bottom of the car. The suspension dances up and down over the rough road. There's no moon out, no stars. A fine rain occasionally splashes against the windshield.

"Do you come here a lot?" I ask.

"I used to. Now, with the job and all, I can't come so often. My older brother's a surfer and lives on the shore in Kochi. He runs a surf shop there and makes surfboards. He comes here sometimes. Do you surf?"

"Never tried it," I tell him.

"If you have the chance, you should have my brother teach you. He's very good," Oshima says. "If you meet him you'll see he's not at all like me. He's big, tan, kind of quiet, not so sociable, and likes beer. And wouldn't know Schubert from Wagner. But we get along really well."

We continue down the road through thick woods, and finally turn off. Oshima stops the car and, leaving the engine running, climbs out and unlocks a kind of wire fence and pushes it open. We drive inside and proceed down another windy, bumpy road into a clearing where the road ends. Oshima stops the car, sighs heavily, and brushes his hair back with both hands, then kills the engine and sets the parking brake.

The fan still hums, cooling off the overheated engine as steam rises from the hood, but with the engine off a heavy stillness falls over us. I hear a small stream nearby, the faint sound of water. High above us the wind rustles symbolically. I open the door and step outside. Patches of chill hang in the air. I have on a yacht jacket over my T-shirt and zip it up to my neck.

There's a small building in front of us, a log cabin by the look of it, though it's too dark to see much. Just a dark outline floating against the background of the forest. The headlights still on, Oshima slowly approaches the cabin, flashlight in hand, walks up the porch steps, takes out a key, and unlocks the door. He goes inside, strikes a match, and lights a lamp. He then steps out onto the porch, holding the lamp, and announces, "Welcome to my house." It all looks like a drawing in an old storybook.

I walk up the steps and go inside. Oshima lights a larger lamp suspended from the ceiling. The cabin consists of a single big, boxy room. There's a small bed in the corner, a dining table and two wooden chairs, an old sofa, a hopelessly faded rug—a bunch of old furniture nobody wanted, it looks like, just thrown together. There's a cinder block and board shelf crammed full of books, their covers worn like they've been read a lot. There's also an old chest for storing clothes. And a simple kitchen with a counter, a small gas stove, and a sink but no running water. Instead, an aluminum pail I guess is for water. A pan and kettle on a shelf, plus a frying pan hanging from the wall. And in the middle of the room there's a black wood-burning stove.

"My brother built this cabin almost all by himself. He took the original rough lumberjack hut and remodeled it completely. He's good with his hands. I was still pretty little then and helped out a bit, making sure I didn't get cut or anything. It's pretty primitive. No electricity. No running water. No toilet. The only modern convenience is the propane gas." Oshima pours some mineral water into the kettle and sets it to boil.

"My grandfather originally owned this mountain. He was a pretty wealthy man in Kochi, with a lot of property. He passed away ten years ago, and my brother and I inherited almost the entire mountain. No other relatives wanted it. It's too far off the beaten track, and not worth much. If you were going to maintain it for harvesting trees, you'd have to hire people and it'd cost too much."

I open the curtain at the window. All I can see is a wall of total darkness.

"When I was just about your age," Oshima says, dipping chamomile tea bags into a pot, "I used to come here a lot and live on my own. Not see anybody else, not talk to anybody. My brother almost forced me to. Usually, with somebody who has a disease like mine, you wouldn't do that—too dangerous for them to be alone in some isolated spot. But my brother didn't mind." He leans back against the counter, waiting for the water to boil. "He wasn't trying to discipline me or anything, it's just what he believed I needed. Looking back on it, I can see it was a good experience, something I did need. I could read a lot, think things over. To tell the truth, after a certain period I hardly went to school. School and I had sort of a mutual hate relationship going. I was different from everybody else. Out of the kindness of their hearts they let me graduate from junior high, but after that I was on my own, basically. Just like you. Did I already tell you all this?"

I shake my head. "Is that why you're being so nice to me?"

"That's part of it," he says, then pauses. "But that's not the whole reason."

Oshima passes me a cup of tea and sips at his own. My nerves are tense after the long drive, and the chamomile is just what I need to calm down.

Oshima glances at his watch. "I'd better be going, so let me explain everything. There's a nice stream nearby you can use for water. It's spring fed so you can drink it as is. Much better than these bottles of mineral water. There's firewood stacked up in back so use the stove if you get cold. It gets pretty chilly here. I've even used it a few times in August. You can use the stove for simple cooking. If you need any other tools or anything, check the toolshed out back. And feel free to wear any old clothes of my brother's you find in the dresser. He doesn't care if somebody wears his things."

Oshima rests his hands on his hips and gives the cabin a once-over. "It's not some romantic getaway, that's for sure. But for simple living, it'll do. One thing I've got to warn you about—don't go very far into the woods. The forest is really dense, and there's not a good path through it. Always keep the cabin in sight. It's easy to get lost if you go any farther, and it's hard to find your way back. I had a terrible experience there once. I was only a couple hundred yards from here but spent half the day going in circles. You might think Japan's a small country, that there's no chance you could get lost in a forest. But once you get lost in these woods, believe me, you *stay* lost."

I file that away for future reference.

"And except for an emergency, I wouldn't come down off the mountain. It's too far to any other houses. Just wait here, and I'll be back in a couple of days to pick you up. You have enough food to see you through. By the way, do you have a cell phone?"

"I do," I tell him, pointing at my backpack.

He grins at me. "Keep it in your pack. It won't work here—you're out of range. And of course a radio won't work either. You're cut off from the world. You should be able to get a lot of reading done."

I suddenly think of a very practical question. "If there's no toilet, where should I go to the bathroom?"

Oshima spreads both hands wide. "The forest is all yours. It's up to you."

Chapter 14

Nakata visited the vacant lot for several days. One morning it rained heavily, so he spent the day doing simple woodworking in his room, but apart from that he spent his time seated in the weeds waiting for the missing tortoiseshell cat to show up, or the man in the strange hat. But no luck.

At the end of each day Nakata stopped by the home of the people who'd hired him and gave an update on his search—where he'd gone, what sort of information he'd managed to pick up. The cat's owner would pay him twenty dollars, his going rate. Nobody had ever officially set that fee, word just got around that there was a master cat-finder in the neighborhood and somehow he settled on that daily rate. People would always give him something extra besides the money, too—food, occasionally clothes. And a bonus of eighty dollars once he actually tracked down the missing cat.

Nakata wasn't constantly being asked to search for missing cats, so the fees he accumulated each month didn't add up to much. The older of his younger brothers paid his utilities out of the inheritance Nakata's parents had left him—which wasn't very much to begin with—and he lived on his meager savings and a municipal monthly subsidy for the elderly handicapped. He managed to get by on the subsidy alone, so he could spend his cat-finding fees as he wished, and for him it seemed like a substantial amount. Sometimes, though, he couldn't come up with any idea of how to spend it, other than enjoying his favorite grilled eel. Going to the bank or having a savings account at the post office involved filling out forms, so any leftover money he hid beneath the tatami in his room.

Being able to converse with cats was Nakata's little secret. Only he and the cats knew about it. People would think he was crazy if he mentioned it, so he never did. Everybody knew he wasn't very bright, but being dumb and being crazy were different matters altogether.

Sometimes people would walk by when he was deep in conversation with a cat, but they never seemed to care. It wasn't so unusual, after all, to see old folks talking to animals as if they were people. But if anyone did happen to comment on his abilities with cats and say something like, "Mr. Nakata, how are you able to know cats' habits so well? It's almost like you can talk with them," he'd just smile and let it pass. Nakata was always serious and well mannered, with a pleasant smile, and was a favorite among the housewives in the neighborhood. His neat appearance also helped. Poor though he was, Nakata enjoyed bathing and doing laundry, and the nearly brand-new clothes his clients often gave him only added to his clean-cut look. Some of the clothes—a salmon pink Jack Nicklaus golf shirt, for instance—didn't exactly suit him, but Nakata didn't mind as long as they were neat and clean.

Nakata was standing at the front door, giving a halting report to his present client, Mrs. Koizumi, on the search for her cat, Goma.

"Nakata finally got some information about little Goma," he began. "A person named Kawamura said that a few days ago he saw a cat resembling Goma over in the empty lot, the one with the wall around it, over in the 2-chome district. It's two big roads away from here, and he said the age, coat, and collar are all the same as Goma's. Nakata decided to keep a lookout at the empty lot, so I take a lunch and sit there every day, morning till sunset. No, don't worry about that—I have plenty of free time, so unless it's raining hard I don't mind at all. But if you think it's no longer necessary, ma'am, for me to be on the lookout, then please tell me. I will stop right away."

He didn't tell her that this Mr. Kawamura wasn't a person but a striped brown cat. That, he figured, would only complicate matters.

Mrs. Koizumi thanked him. Her two little daughters were in a gloomy mood after their beloved pet suddenly vanished, and had lost their appetite. Their mother couldn't just explain it away by telling them that cats tended to disappear every once in a while. But despite the shock to the girls, she didn't have the time to go around town looking for their cat. That made her all the more glad to find a person like Nakata who, for a mere twenty dollars per diem, would do his best to search for Goma. Nakata was a strange old man, and had a weird way of speaking, but people claimed he was an absolute genius when it came to locating cats. She knew she shouldn't think about it like this, but the old man didn't seem bright enough to deceive anyone. She handed him his fee in an envelope, as well as a Tupperware container with some vegetable rice and taro potatoes she'd just cooked.

Nakata bowed as he took the Tupperware, sniffed the food, and thanked her. "Thank you kindly. Taro is one of Nakata's favorites."

"I hope you enjoy it," Mrs. Koizumi replied.

A week had passed since he first staked out the empty lot, during which time Nakata had seen a lot of different cats come in and out. Kawamura, the striped brown cat, stopped by a couple of times each day to say hello. Nakata greeted him, and chatted about the weather and his *sub city*. He still couldn't follow a word the cat said.

"Crouch on pavement, Kawara's in trouble," Kawamura said. He seemed to want to convey something to Nakata, but the old man didn't have a clue and he said so.

The cat seemed perplexed by this, and repeated the same—*possibly* the same—thought in different words. "Kawara's shouting tied." Nakata was even more lost.

Too bad Mimi's not here to help out, he thought. Mimi'd give the cat a good slap on the cheek and get him to make some sense. A smart cat, that Mimi. But Mimi never showed up in a field like this, since she hated getting fleas from other cats.

Once he'd spilled out all these ideas Nakata couldn't follow, Kawamura left beaming.

Other cats filtered in and out. At first they were on their guard when they spotted Nakata, gazing at him from a distance in annoyance, but after they saw that he was simply sitting there, doing nothing, they forgot all about him. In his typical friendly way, Nakata tried to strike up conversations. He'd say hello and introduce himself, but most of the cats turned a deaf ear, pretending they couldn't hear him, or stare right through him. The cats here were particularly adept at giving someone the cold shoulder. They must have had some pretty awful experiences with humans, Nakata decided. He was in no position to demand anything of them, and didn't blame them for their coldness. He knew very well that in the world of cats he would always be an outsider.

"So you can talk, huh?" the cat, a black-and-white tabby with torn ears, said a bit hesitantly as it glanced around. The cat spoke gruffly but seemed nice enough.

"Yes, a little," Nakata replied.

"Impressive all the same," the tabby commented.

"My name's Nakata," Nakata said, introducing himself. "And your name would be?"

"Ain't got one," the tabby said brusquely.

"How about Okawa? Do you mind if I call you that?"

"Whatever."

"Well, then, Mr. Okawa," Nakata said, "as a token of our meeting each other, would you care for some dried sardines?"

"Sounds good. One of my favorites, sardines."

Nakata took a saran-wrapped sardine from his bag and opened it up for Okawa. He always had a few sardines with him, just in case. Okawa gobbled down the sardine, stripping it from head to tail, then cleaned his face.

"That hit the spot. Much obliged. I'd be happy to lick you somewhere, if you'd like."

"No, there's no need to. Nakata's grateful for the offer, but right now I don't need to be licked anywhere, thanks all the same. Actually, I've been asked by its owner to locate a missing cat. A female tortoiseshell by the name of Goma." Nakata took the color snapshot of Goma out of his bag and showed it to Okawa. "Someone told me this cat has been spotted in this vacant lot. So Nakata's been sitting here for several days waiting for Goma to show up. I was wondering if, by chance, you may have run across her."

Okawa glanced at the photo and made a gloomy face. Frown lines appeared between his eyebrows and he blinked in consternation several times. "I'm grateful for the sardine, don't get me wrong. But I can't talk about that. I'll be in hot water if I do."

Nakata was bewildered. "In hot water if you talk about it?"

"A dangerous, nasty business, it is. I think you'd better write that cat off. And if you know what's good for you, you'll stay away from this place. I don't want you to get in trouble. Sorry I couldn't be of more help, but just consider this warning my way of thanking you for the food." With this Okawa stood up, looked around, and disappeared into a thicket.

Nakata sighed, took out his thermos, and slowly sipped some tea.

Okawa had said it was dangerous to be here, but Nakata couldn't imagine how. All he was doing was looking for a lost little cat. What could possibly be dangerous about *that*? Maybe it was that cat-catcher with the strange hat Kawamura told him about who's dangerous. But Nakata was a person, not a cat. So why should he be afraid of a cat-catcher?

But the world was full of many things Nakata couldn't hope to fathom, so he gave up thinking about it. With a brain like his, the only result he got from thinking too much was a headache. Nakata sipped the last drop of his tea, screwed the cap on the thermos, and placed it back inside his bag.

After Okawa disappeared into the thicket, no other cats showed up for a long time. Just butterflies, silently fluttering above the weeds. A flock of sparrows flew into the lot, scattered in various directions, regrouped, and winged away. Nakata dozed off a few times, coming awake with a start. He knew approximately what time it was by the position of the sun.

It was nearly evening when the dog showed up in front of him.

A huge, black dog suddenly appeared from out of the thicket, silently lumbering forward. From where Nakata sat, the beast looked more like a calf than a dog. It had long legs, short hair, bulging, steely muscles, ears as sharp as knife points, and no collar. Nakata didn't know much about breeds of dogs, but one glance told him this was the vicious variety, or at least one that could turn mean if it had to. The kind of dog the military used in its K-9 corps.

The dog's eyes were totally expressionless and the skin around its mouth turned up, exposing wicked-looking fangs. Its teeth had blood stuck to them, and slimy bits of meat matted around its mouth. Its bright red tongue flicked out between its teeth like a flame. The dog fixed its glare on Nakata and stood there, unmoving, without a sound, for a long time. Nakata was silent too. He didn't know how to speak to dogs—only cats. The dog's eyes were as glazed and lifeless as glass beads congealed from swamp water.

Nakata breathed quietly, shallowly, but he wasn't afraid. He had a pretty good idea he was face-to-face with a hostile, aggressive animal. (*Why* this was, he had no idea.) But he didn't carry this thought one step further and see *himself* in imminent peril. The concept of death was beyond his powers of imagination. And pain was something he wasn't aware of until he actually felt it. As an abstract concept pain didn't mean a thing. The upshot of this was he wasn't afraid, even with this monstrous dog staring him down. He was merely perplexed.

Stand up! the dog said.

Nakata gulped. The dog was talking! Not really *talking*, since its mouth wasn't moving—but communicating through some means other than speech.

Stand up and follow me! the dog commanded.

Nakata did as he was told, clambering to his feet. He considered saying hello to the dog, then thought better of it. Even if they were able to converse, he didn't think it would be of much use. Besides, he didn't feel like talking with the dog, much less giving it a name. No amount of time would turn it into a friend.

A thought crossed Nakata's mind: Maybe this dog has some connection with the Governor, who found out he was getting money for finding cats and was going to take away his *sub city*! Wouldn't surprise me at all, he thought, if the Governor had this K-9 kind of dog. And if that's what's going on, I'm in big trouble!

Once Nakata got to his feet, the dog slowly started to walk away. Nakata shouldered his bag and set off after him. The dog had a short tail and, below its base, two large balls.

The dog cut straight across the vacant lot and slipped out between the wooden fence. Nakata followed, and the dog never looked back. No doubt he could tell by the sound of his footsteps that Nakata was behind him. As they drew closer to the shopping district the streets grew more crowded, mostly with housewives out shopping. Eyes fixed straight ahead, the dog walked on, his whole bearing overpowering. When people spied this giant, violent-looking beast, they leaped aside, a couple of bicyclists even getting off and crossing over to the other side of the street to avoid facing him.

Walking behind this monstrous dog made Nakata feel that people were getting out of *his* way. Maybe they thought he was walking the dog, minus a leash. And indeed some people shot him reproachful looks. This made him sad. I'm not doing this because I want to, he wanted to explain to them. Nakata's being led by this dog, he wanted to say. Nakata's not a strong person, but a *weak* one.

He followed the dog quite a distance. They passed a number of intersections and emerged from the shopping district. The dog ignored traffic signals at crosswalks. The roads weren't so wide, and the cars weren't going fast, so it wasn't all that dangerous to cross on red. The drivers slammed on their brakes when they saw this huge animal in front of them. For his part, the dog bared his fangs, glared at the drivers, and sauntered defiantly across the street. The dog knew full well what the traffic lights meant, Nakata could sense, but was willfully ignoring them. This dog was used to getting his way.

Nakata no longer knew where they were. At one point they passed a residential area in Nakano Ward he was familiar with, but then they turned a corner and he was no longer in familiar territory. Nakata felt anxious. What was he going to do if he got lost and couldn't find his way back? For all he knew they might not even be in Nakano Ward anymore. He craned his neck, trying to spot familiar landmarks, but no such luck. This was a part of the city he'd never seen before.

Unconcerned, the dog kept walking, keeping a pace he knew Nakata could keep up with, head up, ears perked, balls swaying like a pendulum.

"Say, is this still Nakano Ward?" Nakata called out.

The dog didn't respond or look around.

"Do you work for the Governor?"

Again no response.

"Nakata's just looking for a lost cat. A small tortoiseshell cat named Goma."

Nothing.

This was getting him nowhere, and he gave up.

They came to a corner in a quiet residential area with big houses but no passersby, and the dog boldly strode through an open old-fashioned double gate set into an old-style stone wall surrounding one of the houses. A large car was parked in a carport—big and black just like the dog, and shiny. The front door of the house was open as well. The dog went right inside, without hesitating. Before stepping into the house, Nakata took off his old sneakers and lined them up neatly at the entrance, stuffed his hiking hat inside his bag, and brushed grass blades off his trousers. The dog stood there, waiting for Nakata to make himself presentable, then went down the polished wooden corridor, leading him to what looked like either a sitting room or a library.

The room was dark. The sun had almost set and the heavy curtain at the window facing the garden was drawn. No lights were on. Farther back in the room was a large desk, and it looked like someone was sitting beside it. Nakata knew he'd have to wait until his eyes adjusted to say for sure. A black silhouette floated there indistinctly, like a paper cutout. As Nakata entered the room the silhouette slowly turned. Whoever was there sat in a swivel chair and had turned around to face him. His duty done, the dog came to a halt, plopped down on the floor, and closed his eyes.

"Hello," Nakata said to the dark outline.

The other person didn't say a thing.

"Sorry to bother you, but my name is Nakata. I'm not an intruder."

No reply.

"This dog told me to follow him, so here I am. Excuse me, but the dog just went right into your house and I came after him. If you don't mind terribly, I'll be leaving. . . ."

"Take a seat on the sofa, if you would," the man said in a soft but strong tone.

"All right, I'll do that," Nakata said, lowering himself onto the one-person sofa. Right next to him, the dog was still as a statue. "Are you . . . the Governor?"

"Something like that," the man said from the darkness. "If that makes it easier for you, then go ahead and think that. It doesn't matter."

The man turned around and tugged at a chain to turn on a floor lamp. A yellow, antiquish light snapped on, faint but sufficient for the room.

The man before him was tall, thin, and wearing a black silk hat. He was seated on a leather swivel chair, his legs crossed in front of him. He had on a formfitting red coat with long tails, a black vest, and long black boots. His trousers were as white as snow and fit him perfectly. One hand was raised to the brim of his hat, like he was tipping it politely to a lady. His left hand gripped a black walking stick by the round, gold knob. Looking at the hat, Nakata suddenly thought: *This must be the cat-catcher!*

The man's features weren't as unusual as his clothes. He was somewhere between young and old, handsome and ugly. His eyebrows were sharp and thick, and his cheeks had a healthy glow. His face was terribly smooth, with no whiskers at all. Below narrowed eyes, a cold smile played at his lips. The kind of face it was hard to remember, especially since it was his unusual clothes that caught the eye. Put another set of clothes on him and you might not even recognize the man.

"You know who I am, I assume?"

"No, sir, I'm afraid I don't," Nakata said.

The man looked a bit let down by this. "Are you sure?"

"Yes, I am. I forgot to mention it, but Nakata isn't very bright."

"You've never seen me before?" the man said, rising from the chair to stand sideways to Nakata, a leg raised as if he were walking. "Doesn't ring a bell?"

"No, I'm sorry. I don't recognize you."

"I see. Perhaps you're not a whisky drinker, then," the man said.

"That's right. Nakata doesn't drink or smoke. I'm poor enough to get a *sub city* so I can't afford that."

The man sat back down and crossed his legs. He picked up a glass on the desk and took a sip of whisky. Ice cubes clinked in the glass. "I hope you don't mind if I indulge?"

"No, I don't mind. Please feel free."

"Thank you," the man said, gazing intently at Nakata. "So you really don't know who I am."

"I'm sorry, but I'm afraid I don't."

The man's lips twisted slightly. For a brief moment a cold smile rose like a distorted ripple on the surface of water, vanished, then rose up again. "Anyone who enjoys whisky would recognize me right away, but never mind. My name is Johnnie Walker. *Johnnie Walker*. Most everyone knows who I am. Not to boast, but I'm famous all over the world. An iconic figure, you might say. I'm not the real Johnnie Walker, mind you. I have nothing to do with the British distilling company. I've just borrowed his appearance and name. A person's got to have an appearance and name, am I right?"

Silence descended on the room. Nakata had no idea what the man was talking about, though he did catch the name Johnnie Walker. "Are you a foreigner, Mr. Johnnie Walker?"

Johnnie Walker inclined his head. "Well, if that helps you understand me, feel free to think so. Or not. Because both are true."

Nakata was lost. He might as well be talking with Kawamura, the cat. "So you're a foreigner, but also not a foreigner. Is that what you mean?"

"That is correct."

Nakata didn't pursue the point. "Did you have this dog bring me here, then?"

"I did," Johnnie Walker replied simply.

"Which means . . . that maybe you have something you'd like to ask me?"

"It's more like *you* have something to ask *me*," Johnnie Walker replied, then took another sip of his whisky. "As I understand it, you've been waiting in that vacant lot for several days for me to show up."

"Yes, that's right. I completely forgot! Nakata's not too bright, and I forget things quickly. It's just like you said. I've been waiting for you in that vacant lot to ask you about a missing cat."

Johnnie Walker tapped his black walking stick smartly against the side of his black boots, and the dry click filled the room. The black dog's ears twitched. "The sun's setting, the tide's going out. So why don't we cut to the chase," Johnnie Walker said. "You wanted to see me because of this cat?"

"Yes, that's correct. Mrs. Koizumi asked Nakata to find her, and I've been looking all over for Goma for the past ten days or so. Do you know Goma?"

"I know her very well."

"And do you know where she might be?"

"I do indeed."

Lips slightly parted, Nakata stared at the silk hat, then back at his face. Johnnie Walker's thin lips were tightly closed, with a confident look.

"Is she nearby?"

Johnnie Walker nodded a few times. "Yes, very near."

Nakata gazed around the room, but couldn't see any cats. Only the writing desk, the swivel chair the man was seated on, the sofa he himself was on, two more chairs, the floor lamp, and a coffee table. "So can I take Goma home?" Nakata asked.

"That all depends on you."

"On Nakata?"

"Correct. It's all up to *you*," Johnnie Walker said, one eyebrow raised slightly. "If you make up your mind to do it, you can take Goma back home. And make Mrs. Koizumi and her daughters happy. Or you can never take her back, and break their hearts. You wouldn't want to do that, I imagine?"

"No, Nakata doesn't want to disappoint them."

"The same with me. I don't want to disappoint them either."

"So what should I do?"

Johnnie Walker twirled the walking stick. "I want you to do something for me."

"Is it something that Nakata can do?"

"I never ask the impossible. That's a colossal waste of time, don't you agree?"

Nakata gave it some thought. "I suppose so."

"Which means that what I'm asking you to do is something you're capable of doing."

Nakata pondered this. "Yes, I'd say that's true."

"As a rule, there's always counterevidence for every theory."

"Beg pardon?" Nakata said.

"For every theory there has to be counterevidence—otherwise science wouldn't progress," Johnnie Walker said, defiantly tapping his stick against his boots. The dog perked up his ears again. "Not at all."

Nakata kept quiet.

"Truth be told, I've been looking for someone like you for a long time," Johnnie Walker said. "But it wasn't easy to find the right person. The other day, though, I saw you talking to a cat and it hit me—this is the exact person I've been looking for. That's why I've had you come all this way. I feel bad about having you go to all the trouble, though."

"No trouble at all. Nakata has plenty of free time."

"I've prepared a couple of theories about you," Johnnie Walker said. "And of course several pieces of counterevidence. It's like a game, a mental game I play. But every game needs a winner and a loser. In this case, winning and losing involves determining which theory is correct and which theories aren't. But I don't imagine you understand what I'm talking about."

Silently, Nakata shook his head.

Johnnie Walker tapped his walking stick against his boots twice, a signal for the dog to stand up.

Chapter 15

Oshima climbs into his Miata and flips on the headlights. As he steps on the gas, pebbles shoot up, scraping the bottom of the car. He backs up, then turns around to face the road. He raises his hand in farewell, and I do the same. The brake lights are swallowed up in darkness, the sound of the engine fading. Then it's completely gone, and the silence of the forest takes over.

I go back into the cabin and bolt the door shut from the inside. Like it was lying in wait for me, silence wraps itself around me tightly once I'm alone. The night air's so cold it's hard to believe it's early summer, but it's too late to light the stove. All I can do is crawl inside my sleeping bag and get some sleep. My mind's a little spacey from lack of sleep and my muscles ache from bouncing around in the car so long. I turn down the light on the lamp. The room dims as the shadows that fill the corners grow more intense. It's too much trouble to change clothes, so I crawl into my sleeping bag with my jeans and yacht jacket on.

I close my eyes but can't fall asleep, my body dying for rest while my mind's wide awake. A bird occasionally breaks the silence of the night. Other sounds filter in too, things I can't identify. Something trampling on fallen leaves. Something heavy rustling the branches. The sound of a deep breath. The occasional ominous creak of floorboards on the porch. They sound like they're right near the cabin, an army of invisible creatures that populates the darkness and has me surrounded.

And I feel like somebody's watching me. My skin smarts with the sense of eyes boring in on me. My heart beats out a hollow thump. Several times from inside the sleeping bag I open my eyes a slit and peer around the dimly lit room just to be sure no one else is there. The front door's bolted with that heavy bolt, and the thick curtains at the windows are shut tight. So I'm okay, I tell myself. I'm alone in this room and no one's gazing in at me through the windows.

But still I can't shake the feeling that I'm being watched. My throat's parched and I'm having trouble breathing. I need to drink some water, but if I do I'll need to take a leak and that means going outside. I have to hold on till morning. Curled up in my sleeping bag, I give a small shake of my head.

Are you kidding me? You're like some scared little kid, afraid of the silence and the dark. You're not going to wimp out on me now, are you? You always thought you were tough, but when it hits the fan, you look like you're about to burst into tears. Look at you—I bet you're going to wet your bed!

Ignoring him, I close my eyes tight, zip the bag up to just below my nose, and clear my head. I don't open my eyes for anything—not when I hear an owl hooting, not when something lands with a thud on the ground outside. Not even when I sense something moving inside the cabin. *I'm being tested*, I tell myself. Oshima spent a few days alone here too, when he was about my age. He must have been scared out of his wits, same as me. That's what he meant by *solitude comes in different varieties*. Oshima knows exactly how I feel being here alone at night, because he's gone through the same thing, and felt the same emotions. This thought helps me relax a little. I feel like I can trace the shadows of the past that linger here and imagine myself as a part of it. I take a deep breath, and I fall asleep before I know it.

It's after six a.m. when I wake up. The air is filled with a shower of bird calls. The birds busily flit from branch to branch, calling out to each other in piercing chirps. Their message has none of the deep echo and hidden implications of those the night before. When I pull back the curtains, every bit of last night's darkness has disappeared from around the cabin. Everything sparkles in a newborn golden glow. I light the stove, boil some mineral water, and make a cup of chamomile tea, then open a box of crackers and have a few with cheese. After that I brush my teeth at the sink and wash my face.

I pull on a windbreaker over my yacht jacket and go outside. The morning light pours down through the tall trees onto the open space in front of the cabin, sunbeams everywhere and mist floating like freshly minted souls. The pure clean air pierces my lungs with each breath. I sit down on a porch step and watch the birds scudding from tree to tree, listening to their calls. Most of them move about in pairs, constantly checking to see where their partner is, screeching out to keep in touch.

I follow the sound of the water and find the stream right away, close by. Rocks form a kind of pool where the water flows in, swirling around in a maze of eddies before rushing back out to rejoin the stream. The water is clear and beautiful. I scoop some up to drink—it's cold and delicious—and then hold my hands in the current.

Back at the cabin I cook ham and eggs in the frying pan, make some toast using a metal net, and heat milk in a small pan to wash down my meal. After eating I haul a chair out to the porch, prop my legs up on the railing, and spend the morning reading. Oshima's bookshelf is crammed full of hundreds of books. Only a few are novels, chiefly classics. Mostly they're books on philosophy, sociology, history, geography, natural sciences, economics—a huge number of subjects, a random selection of fields. Oshima said he'd hardly attended school at all, so this must have been how he got his education.

I pick out a book on the trial of Adolf Eichmann. I have a vague notion of him as a Nazi war criminal, but no special interest in the guy. The book just happens to catch my eye, is all. I start to read and learn how this totally practical lieutenant colonel in the SS, with his metal-frame glasses and thinning hair, was, soon after the war started, assigned by Nazi headquarters to design a "final solution" for the Jews—extermination, that is—and how he investigated the best ways of actually carrying this out. Apparently it barely crossed his mind to question the morality of what he was doing. All he cared about was how best, in the shortest period of time and for the lowest possible cost, to dispose of the Jews. And we're talking about eleven million Jews he figured needed to be eliminated in Europe.

Eichmann studied how many Jews could be packed into each railroad car, what percentage would die of "natural" causes while being transported, the minimal number of people needed to keep this operation going. The cheapest method of disposing of the dead bodies—burning, or burying, or dissolving them. Seated at his desk Eichmann pored over all these numbers. Once he put it into operation, everything went pretty much according to plan. By the end of the war some six million Jews had been disposed of. Strangely, the guy never felt any remorse. Sitting in court in Tel Aviv, behind bulletproof glass, Eichmann looked like he couldn't for the life of him figure out why he was being tried, or why the eyes of the world were upon him. He was just a technician, he insisted, who'd found the most efficient solution to the problem assigned him. Wasn't he doing just what any good bureaucrat would do? So why was he being singled out and accused?

Sitting in the quiet woods with birds chirping all around me, I read the story of this practical guy. In the back of the book there's a penciled note Oshima had written. His handwriting's pretty easy to spot: *It's all a question of imagination. Our responsibility begins with the power to imagine. It's just like Yeats said:* In dreams begin responsibilities. *Flip this around and you could say that where there's no power to imagine, no responsibility can arise. Just like we see with Eichmann.*

I try to picture Oshima sitting in this chair, his usual nicely sharpened pencil in hand, looking back over this book and writing down his impressions. *In dreams begin responsibilities.* The words hit home.

I shut the book, lay it on my lap, and think about my own responsibility. I can't help it. My white T-shirt was soaked in fresh blood. I washed the blood away with these hands, so much blood the sink turned red. I imagine I'll be held responsible for all that blood. I try to picture myself being tried in a court, my accusers doggedly trying to pin the blame on me, angrily pointing fingers and glaring at me. I insist that you can't be held responsible for something you can't remember. I don't have any idea what really took place, I tell them. But they counter with this: "It doesn't matter whose dream it started out as, you have the same dream. So you're responsible for whatever happens in the dream. That dream crept inside you, right down the dark corridor of your soul."

Just like Adolf Eichmann, caught up—whether he liked it or not— in the twisted dreams of a man named Hitler.

I put the book down, stand up, and stretch. I have been reading for a long time and need to get up and move around a little. I take the aluminum pail by the sink and go to the stream to fill it. Next I take an armload of firewood from the shed in back and set it by the stove.

In a corner of the porch there's a faded nylon rope for hanging out laundry. I pull out my damp clothes from my backpack, smooth out all the wrinkles, and hang them up to dry. I take everything else out of the pack and lay it out on the bed, then sit down at the desk and fill in my diary for the last few days. I use a pen with a fine tip and write down in small letters everything that's happened to me. I don't know how long I'll remember all the details, so I better get them down as fast as I can. I search my memory. How I lost consciousness and came to in the woods behind a shrine. The darkness and my blood-soaked shirt. Phoning Sakura, spending the night at her place. How we talked, how she did *that* to me.

She'd said, I don't get it. You didn't have to tell me that! Why don't you just go ahead and imagine what you want? You don't need my permission. How can I know what's in your head?

But she got it wrong. What I imagine *is* perhaps very important. For the entire world.

That afternoon I decide to go into the woods. Oshima said that going too far into the forest is dangerous. *Always keep the cabin in sight*, he warned me. But I'll probably be here for a few days, and I should know something about this massive wall of a forest that surrounds me. Better to know a little, I figure, than nothing at all. Empty-handed, I say good-bye to the sunny lot and step into the gloomy sea of trees.

There's a kind of rough path trod down through the forest, mostly following the lay of the land, but improved here and there with a few flat rocks laid down like stepping-stones. Places prone to erosion have been neatly buttressed with wooden planks, so that even if the weeds grow over it you can still follow the path. Maybe Oshima's brother worked on the path little by little each time he stayed here. I follow it into the woods, uphill at first, then it goes down and skirts around a high boulder before climbing up again. Overall it's mostly uphill, but not a very tough climb. Tall trees line both sides, with dull-colored trunks, thick branches growing out every which way, dense leaves overhead. The ground is covered with undergrowth and ferns that have managed to soak up as much of the faint light as they can. In places where the sun doesn't reach, moss has silently covered the rocks.

Like someone excitedly relating a story only to find the words petering out, the path gets narrower the farther I go, the undergrowth taking over. Beyond a certain point it's hard to tell if it's really a path or something that just vaguely resembles one. Eventually it's completely swallowed up in a sea of ferns. Maybe the path does continue up ahead, but I decide to save that exploration for next time. I don't have on the right kind of clothes and haven't really prepared for that.

I come to a halt and turn around. Suddenly nothing looks familiar, there's nothing I can cling to. A tangle of tree trunks ominously blocks the view. It's dim, the air filled with a stagnant green, and not a bird to be heard.

I'm suddenly covered in goose bumps, but there's nothing to worry about, I tell myself. The path is right over there. As long as I don't lose sight of that I'll be able to return to the light. Eyes glued to the ground, I carefully retrace my steps and, after much longer than it took me to get here, finally arrive back in front of the cabin. The lot is filled with bright, early-summer sunlight, and the clear calls of birds echo as they search for food. Everything's exactly the same as I left it. Or at least I *think* it is. The chair I was sitting on is still on the porch. The book I was reading is facedown like I left it.

Now I know exactly how dangerous the forest can be. And I hope I never forget it. Just like Crow said, the world's filled with things I don't know about. All the plants and trees there, for instance. I'd never imagined that trees could be so weird and unearthly. I mean, the only plants I've ever really seen or touched till now are the city kind—neatly trimmed and cared-for bushes and trees. But the ones here—the ones *living* here—are totally different. They have a physical power, their breath grazing any humans who might chance by, their gaze zeroing in on the intruder like they've spotted their prey. Like they have some dark, prehistoric, magical powers. Like deep-sea creatures rule the ocean depths, in the forest trees reign supreme. If it wanted to, the forest could reject me—or swallow me up whole. A healthy amount of fear and respect might be a good idea.

I go back to the cabin, take my compass out of my backpack, and check that the needle's showing north. It might come in handy sometime, so I slip it in my pocket. I go sit on the porch, gaze at the woods, and listen to Cream and Duke Ellington on my Walkman, songs I recorded off a library's collection of CDs. I play "Crossroads" a couple of times. Music helps me calm down, but I can't listen for very long. There's no electricity here and no way to recharge the batteries, so once my extra batteries are dead the music's over for good.

I work out a bit before dinner. Push-ups, sit-ups, squats, handstands, different kinds of stretching exercises—a routine that keeps you in shape without any machines or equipment. Kind of boring, I'll admit, but you get a decent workout. A trainer at the gym taught me the routine. "Prisoners in solitary confinement like this best," he explained, calling it the "world's loneliest workout routine." I focus on what I'm doing and go through a couple of sets, my shirt getting sweaty in the process.

After a simple dinner I go out on the porch and gaze up at the stars twinkling above, the random scattering of millions of stars. Even in a planetarium you wouldn't find this many. Some of them look really big and distinct, like if you reached your hand out intently you could touch them. The whole thing is breathtaking.

Not just beautiful, though—the stars are like the trees in the forest, alive and breathing. And they're watching me. What I've done up till now, what I'm going to do—they know it all. Nothing gets past their watchful eyes. As I sit there under the shining night sky, again a violent fear takes hold of me. My heart's pounding a mile a minute, and I can barely breathe. All these millions of stars looking down on me, and I've never given them more than a passing thought before. Not just stars— how many other things haven't I noticed in the world, things I know nothing about? I suddenly feel helpless, completely powerless. And I know I'll never outrun that awful feeling.

Back inside the cabin, I carefully arrange some firewood in the stove, ball up a few sheets of an old newspaper, light it, and make sure the wood catches fire. In grade school I was sent to camp, and learned how to build a fire. I hated camp, but at least one good thing came out of it, I suppose. I open the damper to let the smoke out. It doesn't go well at first, but when a piece of kindling catches the fire spreads to the other sticks. I shut the door on the stove and scrape a chair over in front of it, set a lamp nearby, and pick up where I'd left off in the book. Once the fire's built up a bit I set a kettle of water on top to boil, and after a while the kettle burbles pleasantly.

Back to Eichmann. Of course his project didn't always go according to plan. Conditions at various sites slowed things down. When this happened he acted like a human being—at least a little. He got angry, is what I'm saying. He grew incensed at these uncertain elements that threw his elegant solution into disarray. Trains ran late. Bureaucratic red tape held things up. People in charge were replaced, and relations with their successors didn't go well. After the collapse of the Russian front, concentration camp guards were sent there to fight. There were heavy snowfalls. Power outages. Not enough poison gas to go around. Rail lines were bombed. Eichmann hated the war itself—that element of uncertainty that screwed up his plans.

At his trial he described all this, no emotion showing on his face. His recall was amazing. His life was entirely made up of these details.

At ten I put the book down, brush my teeth, and wash my face. The fire bathes the room in an orange glow, and the pleasant warmth calms my tension and fear. I snuggle into my sleeping bag dressed only in a T-shirt and boxers. Compared to last night I'm able to shut my eyes easily. Thoughts of Sakura cross my mind.

"I was thinking how nice it'd be if I was your real sister," she'd said.

None of that tonight. I've got to get some sleep. A log topples over in the stove, an owl hoots outside. And I topple down into an indistinct dream.

The next day's the same. Birds wake me up a little after six. I boil some water, make a cup of tea, and have breakfast. Read on the porch, listen to music, go fill up the water pail at the stream. And I walk down the path into the woods, this time carrying my compass, glancing at it every once in a while to get a general idea of where the cabin is. I found a hatchet in the shed and use it to chop simple hatch marks on trees. I clear out some of the underbrush to make the path easier to follow.

Just like yesterday the forest is dark and deep, the towering trees forming a thick wall on both sides. Something of the forest is hiding there, in the darkness between the trees, like some 3-D painting of an animal, watching my every move. But the fear that made me shudder isn't there anymore. I've made my own rules, and by following them I won't get lost. At least I hope not.

I come to the place where I stopped yesterday and forge on, stepping into the sea of ferns. After a while the path reemerges, and again I'm surrounded by a wall of trees, on whose trunks I hack out some markings as I go. Somewhere in the branches above me a huge bird flaps its wings, but looking up I can't spot it. My mouth is dry.

I walk on for a while and reach a round sort of clearing. Surrounded by tall trees, it looks like the bottom of a gigantic well. Sunlight shoots down through the branches like a spotlight illuminating the ground at my feet. The place feels special, somehow. I sit down in the sunlight and let the faint warmth wash over me, taking out a chocolate bar from my pocket and enjoying the sweet taste. Realizing all over again how important sunlight is to human beings, I appreciate each second of that precious light. The intense loneliness and helplessness I felt under those millions of stars has vanished. But as time passes, the sun's angle shifts and the light disappears. I stand up and retrace the path back to the cabin.

In the afternoon dark clouds suddenly color the sky a mysterious shade and it starts raining hard, pounding the roof and windows of the cabin. I strip naked and run outside, washing my face with soap and scrubbing myself all over. It feels wonderful. In my joy I shut my eyes and shout out meaningless words as the large raindrops strike me on the cheeks, the eyelids, chest, side, penis, legs, and butt—the stinging pain like a religious initiation or something. Along with the pain there's a feeling of closeness, like for once in my life the world's treating me fairly. I feel elated, as if all of a sudden I've been set free. I face the sky, hands held wide apart, open my mouth wide, and gulp down the falling rain.

Back inside the hut, I dry off with a towel, sit down on the bed, and look at my penis—a light-colored, healthy, youthful penis. The head still stings a little from the rain. For a long while I stare at this strange organ that, most of the time, has a mind of its own and contemplates thoughts not shared by my brain.

I wonder if Oshima, when he was my age and stayed here, struggled with sexual desire. He must have, but I can't picture him taking care of business on his own. He's too detached, too cool for that.

"I was different from everybody else," he'd said. I don't know what that means, but I'm sure he wasn't just spouting something off the top of his head. He didn't say it to be mysterious and coy, either.

I consider jerking off but think better of it. Being pummeled by the rain so hard made me feel strangely purified, and I want to hold on to that sensation a while longer. I pull on some boxers, take a few deep breaths, and start doing squats. A hundred squats later I do a hundred sit-ups. I focus on one muscle group at a time. Once my routine's done, my mind's clear. The rain's stopped, the sun's starting to shine through breaks in the clouds, and the birds have started chirping again.

But that calm won't last long, you know. It's like beasts that never tire, tracking you everywhere you go. They come out at you deep in the forest. They're tough, relentless, merciless, untiring, and they never give up. You might control yourself now, and not masturbate, but they'll get you in the end, as a wet dream. You might dream about raping your sister, your mother. It's not something you can control. It's a power beyond you—and all you can do is accept it.

You're afraid of imagination. And even more afraid of dreams. Afraid of the responsibility that begins in dreams. But you have to sleep, and dreams are a part of sleep. When you're awake you can suppress imagination. But you can't suppress dreams.

I lie down in bed and listen to Prince on my headphones, concentrating on this strangely unceasing music. The batteries run out in the middle of "Little Red Corvette," the music disappearing like it's been swallowed up by quicksand. I yank off my headphones and listen. Silence, I discover, is something you can actually *hear*.

Chapter 16

The black dog stood up and led Nakata out of the study and down the dark corridor to the kitchen, which had only a couple of windows and was dark. Though it was neat and clean, it had an inert feel, like a science lab in school. The dog stopped in front of the doors of a large refrigerator, turned around, and drilled Nakata with a cold look.

Open the left door, he said in a low voice. Nakata knew it wasn't the dog talking but Johnnie Walker, speaking to Nakata through him. Looking at Nakata through the dog's eyes.

Nakata did as he was told. The avocado green refrigerator was taller than he was, and when he opened the left door the thermostat came on with a thump, the motor groaning to life. White vapor, like fog, wafted out. This side of the refrigerator was a freezer, at a very low setting.

Inside was a row of about twenty round, fruit-like objects, neatly arranged. Nothing else. Nakata bent over and looked at them fixedly. When the vapor cleared he saw it wasn't fruit at all but the severed heads of cats. Cut-off heads of all colors and sizes, arranged on three shelves like oranges at a fruit stand. The cats' faces were frozen, facing forward. Nakata gulped.

Take a good look, the dog commanded. **Check with your own eyes whether Goma's in there or not.**

Nakata did this, examining the cats' heads one by one. He didn't feel afraid—his mind focused on finding the missing little cat. Nakata carefully checked each head, confirming that Goma's wasn't among them. No doubt about it—not a single tortoiseshell. The faces of the bodyless cats had a strangely vacant expression, not one of them appearing to have suffered. That, at least, brought Nakata a sigh of relief. A few of the cats had their eyes closed, but most were staring out blankly at a point in space.

"I don't see Goma here," Nakata said in a flat tone. He cleared his throat and shut the refrigerator door.

Are you absolutely sure?

"Yes, I'm sure."

The dog stood up and led Nakata back to the study. Johnnie Walker was still seated in the swivel chair, waiting for him. As Nakata entered, he touched the brim of his silk hat in greeting and smiled pleasantly. Then he clapped his hands loudly, twice, and the dog left the room.

"I'm the one who cut off all those cats' heads," he said. He lifted his glass of whisky and took a drink. "I'm collecting them."

"So you're the one who's been catching cats in that vacant lot and killing them."

"That's right. The infamous cat-killer Johnnie Walker, at your service."

"Nakata doesn't understand this so well, so do you mind if I ask a question?"

"Be my guest," Johnnie Walker said, lifting his glass. "Feel free to ask anything. To save time, though, if you don't mind, I can guess that the first thing you want to know is *why* I have to kill all these cats. Why I'm collecting their heads. Am I right?"

"Yes, that's right. That's what Nakata wants to know."

Johnnie Walker set his glass down on the desk and looked straight at Nakata. "This is an important secret I wouldn't tell just anybody. For you, Mr. Nakata, I'll make an exception, but I don't want you telling other people. Not that they'd believe you even if you did." He chuckled.

"Listen—I'm not killing cats just for the fun of it. I'm not so disturbed I find it amusing," he went on. "I'm not just some dilettante with time on his hands. It takes a lot of time and effort to gather and kill this many cats. I'm killing them to collect their souls, which I use to create a special kind of flute. And when I blow that flute it'll let me collect even larger souls. Then I collect larger souls and make an even bigger flute. Perhaps in the end I'll be able to make a flute so large it'll rival the universe. But first come the cats. Gathering their souls is the starting point of the whole project. There's an essential order you have to follow in everything. It's a way of showing respect, following everything in the correct order. It's what you need to do when you're dealing with other souls. It's not pineapples and melons I'm working with here, agreed?"

"Yes," Nakata replied. But actually he had no idea. A flute? Was he talking about a flute you held sideways? Or maybe a recorder? What sort of sound would it make? And what did he mean by cats' *souls*? All of this exceeded his limited powers of comprehension. But Nakata did understand one thing: he had to locate Goma and get her out of here.

"What you want to do is take Goma home," Johnnie Walker said, as though reading Nakata's mind.

"That's right. Nakata wants to take Goma back to her home."

"That's your mission," Johnnie Walker said. "We all follow our mission in life. That's natural. Now I imagine you've never heard a flute made out of cats' souls, have you?"

"No, I haven't."

"Of course you haven't. You can't hear it with your ears."

"It's a flute you can't hear?"

"Correct. *I* can hear it, of course," Johnnie Walker said. "If I don't hear it none of this would work. Ordinary people, though, can't detect it. Even if they do hear it, they don't realize it. They may have heard it in the past but don't remember. A very strange flute, for sure. But maybe — just maybe — *you* might be able to hear it, Mr. Nakata. If I had a flute on me right now we could try it, but I'm afraid I don't." Then, as if recalling something, he pointed one finger straight up. "Actually, I was about to cut off the heads of the cats I've rounded up. Harvest time. I've got all the cats that can be caught in that vacant lot, and it's time to move on. The cat you're looking for, Goma, is among them. Of course if I cut her head off, you wouldn't be able to take her home to the Koizumis, now would you?"

"That's right," Nakata said. He couldn't take back Goma's cut-off head to the Koizumis. If those two little girls saw that they might give up eating forever.

"I want to cut off Goma's head, but you don't want that to happen. Our two missions, our two interests, conflict. That happens a lot in the world. So I'll tell you what — we'll negotiate. What I mean is, if you do something for me, I'll return the favor and give you Goma safe and sound."

Nakata lifted a hand above his head and vigorously rubbed his salt-and-pepper hair, his habitual pose when puzzling over something. "Is it something I can do?"

"I thought we'd already settled that," Johnnie Walker said with a wry smile.

"Yes, we did," Nakata said, remembering. "That's correct. We did settle that already. Pardon me."

"We don't have a lot of time, so let me jump to the conclusion, if you don't mind. What you can do for me is *kill me*. Take my life, in other words."

Hand resting on the top of his head, Nakata stared at Johnnie Walker for a long time. "You want Nakata to kill you?"

"That's right," Johnnie Walker said. "Truthfully, I'm sick and tired of this life. I've lived a long, long time. I don't even remember how old I am. And I don't feel like living any longer. I'm sick and tired of killing cats, but as long as I live that's what I have to do—murder one cat after another and harvest their souls. Following things in the correct order, step one to step ten, then back to one again. An endless repetition. And I've *had* it! Nobody respects what I'm doing, it doesn't make anybody happy. But the whole thing's all fixed already. I can't just suddenly say I quit and stop what I'm doing. And taking my own life isn't an option. That's already been decided too. There're all sorts of rules involved. If I want to die, I have to get somebody else to kill me. That's where you come in. I want you to fear me, to hate me with a passion—and then terminate me. First you fear me. Then you hate me. And finally you kill me."

"But why—why ask *me*? Nakata's never ever killed anyone before. It's not the kind of thing I'm suited for."

"I know. You've never killed anyone, and don't want to. But listen to me—there are times in life when those kinds of excuses don't cut it anymore. Situations when nobody cares whether you're suited for the task at hand or not. I need you to understand that. For instance, it happens in war. Do you know what war is?"

"Yes, I do. There was a big war going on when Nakata was born. I heard about it."

"When a war starts people are forced to become soldiers. They carry guns and go to the front lines and have to kill soldiers on the other side. As many as they possibly can. Nobody cares whether you like killing other people or not. It's just something you have to do. Otherwise *you're* the one who gets killed." Johnnie Walker pointed his index finger at Nakata's chest. "Bang!" he said. "Human history in a nutshell."

"Is the Governor going to make Nakata a soldier and order me to kill people?"

"Yes, that's what the Governor will do. Tell you to kill somebody."

Nakata thought about this but couldn't quite figure it out. Why in the world would the Governor do that?

"You've got to look at it this way: this is *war*. You're a soldier, and you have to make a decision. Either I kill the cats or you kill me. One or the other. You need to make a choice right here and now. This might seem an outrageous choice, but consider this: most choices we make in life are equally outrageous." Johnnie Walker lightly touched his silk hat, as if making sure it was still in place.

"The one saving grace for you here—if indeed you need such a thing—is the fact that I *want* to die. I've *asked* you to kill me, so you don't need to suffer any pangs of conscience. You're doing exactly what I'm hoping for. It's not like you're killing somebody who doesn't want to die. In fact, you're doing a good deed."

Nakata wiped away the beads of sweat that had formed on his hairline. "But there's no way Nakata could do something like that. Even if you tell me to kill you, I don't know how to go about it."

"I hear you," Johnnie Walker said admiringly. "You've never killed anybody before, so you don't know how to go about it. All right then, let me explain. The knack to killing someone, Mr. Nakata, is not to hesitate. Focus your prejudice and execute it swiftly—that's the ticket when it comes to killing. I have an excellent example right here. It's not a person, but it might help you get the picture."

Johnnie Walker stood up and picked up a large leather case from the shadows below the desk. He placed it on the chair where he'd been sitting and opened it, whistling a cheery tune. As if performing a magic trick, he extracted a cat from out of the case. Nakata had never seen this cat before, a gray-striped male that had just reached adulthood. The cat was limp, but its eyes were open. It looked conscious, though only barely. Still whistling his merry tune—"Heigh-Ho" from Disney's *Snow White*, the one the Seven Dwarves sang—Johnnie Walker held up the cat like he was showing off a fish he'd just caught.

"I've got five cats inside this case, all from that vacant lot. A fresh batch. Just picked, fresh from the grove, so to speak. I've given them all injections to paralyze them. It's not an anesthetic—they're not asleep and they can feel pain, but they can't move their arms or legs. Or even their heads. I do this to keep them from thrashing about. What I'm going to do is slice open their chests with a knife, extract their still-beating hearts, and cut their heads off. Right in front of your eyes. There'll be lots of blood, and unimaginable pain. Imagine how much it'd hurt if somebody cut open your chest and pulled out *your* heart! Same thing holds true for cats—it's got to hurt. I feel sorry for the poor little things. I'm not some cold, cruel sadist, but there's nothing I can do about it. There has to be pain. That's the rule. Rules everywhere you look here." He winked at Nakata. "A job's a job. Got to accomplish your mission. I'm going to dispose of one cat after another, and finish off Goma last. So you still have some time to decide what you should do. Remember, now—it's either *I* kill the cats or *you* kill *me*. There's no other choice."

Johnnie Walker placed the limp cat on top of the desk, opened a drawer, and with both hands extracted a large black package. He carefully unwrapped it and spread out the contents on the desk. These included a small electric saw, scalpels of various sizes, and a very large knife, all of them gleaming like they'd just been sharpened. Johnnie Walker lovingly checked each and every blade as he lined them up on the desk. Next he got several metal trays from another drawer and arranged them, too, on the desk. Then he took a large black plastic bag from a drawer. All the while whistling "Heigh-Ho."

"As I mentioned, Mr. Nakata, in everything there's a proper order," Johnnie Walker said. "You can't look too far ahead. Do that and you'll lose sight of what you're doing and stumble. I'm not saying you should focus solely on details right in front of you, mind you. You've got to look ahead a bit or else you'll bump into something. You've got to follow the proper order and at the same time keep an eye out for what's ahead. That's critical, no matter what you're doing."

Johnnie Walker narrowed his eyes and gently stroked the cat's head. He ran the tip of his index finger up and down the cat's belly, then picked up a scalpel in his right hand and without any warning made an incision straight down the stomach. It all happened in an instant. The belly split wide open and reddish guts spilled out. The cat tried to scream but barely made any sound at all. His tongue, after all, was numb, and he could hardly open his mouth. But his eyes were contorted in terrible pain. And Nakata could well imagine how awful this pain was. A moment later blood gushed out, wetting Johnnie Walker's hands and running down his vest. But he didn't pay attention. Still to the accompaniment of "Heigh-Ho," he thrust his hand inside the cat's body and with a small scalpel skillfully cut loose the tiny heart.

He placed the gory lump on his palm and held it out for Nakata to see. "Take a peek. It's still beating."

Then, as if it were the most natural thing in the world, he popped the heart into his mouth and began chewing silently, leisurely savoring the taste. His eyes glistened like a child enjoying a pastry hot from the oven.

He wiped the blood from his mouth with the back of his hand and carefully licked his lips clean. "Fresh and warm. And still beating in my mouth."

Nakata stared at the scene before him without a word. He couldn't look away. The smell of fresh blood filled the room.

Still whistling his jolly tune, Johnnie Walker sawed the cat's head off. The teeth of the saw crunched through the bone and severed it. He seemed to know exactly what he was doing. The neck bone wasn't very thick, so the whole operation was quickly finished. But the sound had a strange weight to it. Johnnie Walker lovingly placed the severed head on the metal tray. As if relishing a work of art, he narrowed his eyes and gazed at it intently. He stopped whistling for a second, extracted something stuck between his teeth with a fingernail, popped it in his mouth and carefully tasted it, then smacked his lips, satisfied, and gulped it down. Next he opened the black plastic bag and casually tossed in the dead cat's body like some useless shell.

"One down," Johnnie Walker said, spreading his bloody hands in front of Nakata. "A bit of work, don't you think? You can enjoy a nice fresh heart, but look how bloody you get. *No, this my hand will rather the multitudinous seas incarnadine, making the green one red.* A line from *Macbeth*. This isn't as bad as *Macbeth*, but you wouldn't believe the dry-cleaning bills. This is a special outfit, after all. I should wear a surgical gown and gloves, but I can't. Another *rule*, I'm afraid."

Nakata didn't say a word, though something was beginning to stir in his mind. The room smelled of blood, and strains of "Heigh-Ho" rang in his ears.

Johnnie Walker pulled out the next cat from his bag, a white female, not so young, with the tip of her tail bent a little. As before, he stroked the cat's head for a while, then leisurely traced an invisible line down her stomach. He picked up a scalpel and again made a quick cut to open up the chest. The rest was the same as before. The silent scream, the convulsing body, guts spilling out. Pulling out the bloody heart, showing it to Nakata, popping it in his mouth, chewing it slowly. The satisfied smile. Wiping the blood away with the back of his hand. All with "Heigh-Ho" as background music.

Nakata sank back in his chair and closed his eyes. He held his head in his hands, the fingertips digging into his temples. Something was definitely rising up within him, a horrible confusion transforming his very being. He was breathing rapidly, and a sharp pain throbbed in his neck. His vision was changing drastically.

"Mr. Nakata," Johnnie Walker said brightly, "don't poop out on me yet. We're just getting to the main event. That was just the opening act, a mere warm-up. Now we're getting to the lineup you know. So open your eyes wide and take a good long look. This is the best part! I hope you'll appreciate how hard I've tried to make this entertaining for you."

Whistling his tune, he took out the next cat. Sunk in his chair, Nakata opened his eyes and looked at the next victim. His mind was a complete blank, and he couldn't even stand up.

"I believe you already know each other," Johnnie Walker said, "but I'll do the honors anyway. Mr. Nakata, this is Mr. Kawamura. Mr. Kawamura, Mr. Nakata." Johnnie Walker tipped his hat in a theatrical gesture, greeting first Nakata, then the paralyzed cat.

"Now that you've said hello, I'm afraid we move right into farewells. Hello, good-bye. Like flowers scattered in a storm, man's life is one long farewell, as they say." He gave Kawamura's soft stomach a gentle caress. "Now's the time to stop me if you're going to, Mr. Nakata. Time's ticking away, and I won't hesitate. In the dictionary of the infamous cat-killer Johnnie Walker, *hesitate* is one word you won't find."

And indeed without any hesitation at all he slit open Kawamura's belly. This time the scream was audible. Maybe the cat's tongue hadn't been fully paralyzed, or perhaps it was a special kind of scream that only Nakata could hear. An awful, bloodcurdling scream. Nakata closed his eyes and held his trembling head in his hands.

"You have to look!" Johnnie Walker commanded. "That's another one of our rules. Closing your eyes isn't going to change anything. Nothing's going to disappear just because you can't see what's going on. In fact, things will be even worse the next time you open your eyes. That's the kind of world we live in, Mr. Nakata. Keep your eyes wide open. Only a coward closes his eyes. Closing your eyes and plugging up your ears won't make time stand still."

Nakata did as he was told and opened his eyes.

Once he was sure they were open, Johnnie Walker made a show of devouring Kawamura's heart, taking more time than before to savor it. "It's soft and warm. Just like fresh eel liver," Johnnie Walker commented. He then lifted a bloody index finger to his mouth and sucked it. "Once you've acquired a taste for this, you get hooked. Especially the sticky blood."

He wiped the blood off the scalpel, whistling cheerily as always, and sawed off Kawamura's head. The fine teeth of the blade cut through the bone and blood spurted out everywhere.

"Please, Mr. Walker, Nakata can't stand it anymore!"

Johnnie Walker stopped whistling. He halted his work and scratched an earlobe. "That won't fly, Mr. Nakata. I'm sorry you feel bad, I really am, but I can't just say, *Okay, will do,* and call this off. I told you. This is *war.* It's hard to stop a war once it starts. Once the sword is drawn, blood's going to be spilled. This doesn't have anything to do with theory or logic, or even my ego. It's just a rule, pure and simple. If you don't want any more cats to be killed, you've got to kill me. Stand up, focus your hatred, and strike me down. And you've got to do it *now*. Do that and it's all over. End of story."

Johnnie Walker started whistling again. He finished cutting off Kawamura's head and tossed the headless body into the garbage bag. Now there were three heads lined up on the metal tray. They'd suffered such agony, yet their faces were as strangely vacant as those of the cats lined up in the freezer.

"Next comes the Siamese." Johnnie Walker said this and then extracted a limp Siamese from his bag—which of course turned out to be Mimi. "So now we come to little 'Mi Chiamano Mimi.' The Puccini opera. This little cat really does have that elegant coquetry, doesn't she? I'm a big Puccini fan, myself. Puccini's music is kind of—what should I call it?—eternally antagonistic to the times. Mere popular entertainment, you might argue, but it never gets old. Quite an artistic accomplishment."

He whistled a bar from "Mi Chiamano Mimi."

"But I have to tell you, Mr. Nakata, it took some doing to catch Mimi. She's clever and cautious, very quick on the draw. Not the type to get suckered into anything. One tough customer. But the cat that can elude Johnnie Walker, the matchless cat-killer, has yet to be born. Not that I'm bragging or anything, I'm just trying to convey how hard it was to nab her. . . . At any rate, *voilà*! Your friend Mimi! Siamese are my absolute favorites. You're not aware of this, but a Siamese cat's heart is a real gem. Sort of like truffles. It's okay, Mimi. Never fear— Johnnie Walker's here! Ready to enjoy your warm, cute little heart. Ah—you're trembling!"

"Johnnie Walker." From deep inside himself Nakata managed to force out the words in a low voice. *"Please*, stop it. If you don't, Nakata's going to go crazy. I don't feel like myself anymore."

Johnnie Walker laid Mimi down on the desk and as always let his fingers slowly crawl along her belly. "So you're no longer yourself," he said carefully and quietly. "That's very important, Mr. Nakata. A person not being himself anymore." He picked up a scapel he hadn't used yet and tested its sharpness with the tip of his finger. Then, as if doing a trial cut, he ran the blade along the back of his hand. A moment later blood oozed up, dripping onto the desk and Mimi's body. Johnnie Walker chuckled. "A person's not being himself anymore," he repeated. "You're no longer yourself. That's the ticket, Mr. Nakata. Wonderful! The most important thing of all. O, *full of scorpions is my mind! Macbeth* again."

Without a word, Nakata stood up. No one, not even Nakata himself, could stop him. With long strides he walked over to the desk and grabbed what looked like a steak knife. Grasping the wooden handle firmly, he plunged the blade into Johnnie Walker's stomach, piercing the black vest, then stabbed again in another spot. He could hear something, a loud sound, and at first didn't know what it was. But then he understood. Johnnie Walker was laughing. Stabbed in the stomach and chest, his blood spouting out, he continued to laugh.

"That's the stuff!" he yelled. "You didn't hesitate. Well done!" Laughing like it was the funniest joke he'd ever heard. Soon though, his laughter turned into a sob. The blood gurgling in his throat sounded like a drain coming unplugged. A terrible convulsion wracked his body, and blood gushed out of his mouth along with dark, slimy lumps—the hearts of the cats he'd eaten. The blood spewed over the desk, onto Nakata's golf shirt. Both men were drenched in blood. Mimi, too, lying on the desk, was soaked with it.

Johnnie Walker collapsed at Nakata's feet. He was on his side, curled up like a child on a cold night, and was unmistakably dead. His

148

left hand was pressed against his throat, his right thrust straight out as though reaching for something. The convulsions had ceased and, of course, the laughter. A faint sneer still showed on his lips. Blood puddled on the wooden floor, and the silk hat had rolled off into a corner. The hair on the back of Johnnie Walker's head was thin, the skin visible beneath. Without the hat he looked much older and more feeble.

Nakata dropped the knife and it clattered on the floor as loudly as the gear of some large machine clanking away in the distance. Nakata stood next to the body for a long time. Everything in the room had come to a standstill. Only the blood continued, silently, to flow, the puddle slowly spreading across the floor.

Finally, Nakata pulled himself together and gathered Mimi up from the desk. Warm and limp in his hands, she was covered in blood but apparently unharmed. Mimi looked up as if trying to tell him something, but the drug kept her mouth from moving.

Nakata then found Goma inside the case and lifted her out. He'd only seen photos of her, but felt a wave of nostalgia like he was meeting a long-lost friend. "Goma . . . ," he murmured. Holding the two cats, Nakata sat down on the sofa. "Let's go home," he told them, but he couldn't stand up.

The black dog had appeared from somewhere and sat down next to his dead master. He might have lapped at the pool of blood, but Nakata couldn't remember for sure. His head felt heavy and dim, and he took a deep breath and closed his eyes. His mind began to fade and, before he knew it, sank down into the darkness.

Chapter 17

It's my third night in the cabin. With each passing day I've gotten more used to the silence and how incredibly dark it is. The night doesn't scare me anymore—or at least not as much. I fill the stove with firewood, settle down in front of it, and read. When I get tired, I just space out and stare at the flames. I never grow tired of looking at them. They come in all shapes and colors, and move around like living things—they are born, connect up, part company, and die.

When it's not cloudy I go outside and gaze up at the sky. The stars don't seem as intimidating as before, and I'm starting to feel closer to them. Each one gives out its own special light. I identify certain stars and watch how they twinkle in the night. Every once in a while they blaze more brightly for a moment. The moon hangs there, pale and bright, and if I look closely it's like I can make out individual crags on the surface. I don't form any coherent thoughts, just gaze, enthralled, at the sky.

Having no music doesn't bother me as much as I thought it would. There're lots of other sounds that take its place—the chirping of birds, the cries of all sorts of insects, the gurgle of the brook, the rustling of leaves. Rain falls, something scrambles across the cabin roof, and sometimes I hear indescribable sounds I can't explain. I never knew the world was full of so many beautiful, natural sounds. I've ignored them my entire life, but not now. I sit on the porch for hours with my eyes closed, trying to be inconspicuous, picking up each and every sound around me.

The woods don't scare me as much as they used to, either, and I've started to feel a kind of closeness and respect. That said, I don't venture too far from the cabin, and stay on the path. As long as I follow these rules, it shouldn't get too precarious. That's the important thing— follow the rules and the woods will wordlessly accept me, sharing some of their peace and beauty. Cross the line, though, and beasts of silence lay in wait to maul me with razor-sharp claws.

I often lie down in the round little clearing and let the sunlight wash over me. Eyes closed tight, I give myself up to it, ears tuned to the wind whipping through the treetops. Wrapped in the deep fragrance of the forest, I listen to the flapping of birds' wings, to the stirring of the ferns. I'm freed from gravity and float up—just a little—from the ground and drift in the air. Of course I can't stay there forever. It's just a momentary sensation—open my eyes and it's gone. Still, it's an overwhelming experience. Being able to float in the air.

It rains hard a couple times, but doesn't last, and each time I run outside, naked, to wash myself. Sometimes I get all sweaty exercising, rip off my clothes, and sunbathe on the porch. I drink a lot of tea, and concentrate on reading, sitting on the porch or by the stove. Books on history, science, folklore, mythology, sociology, psychology, Shakespeare, you name it. Instead of racing straight through, I reread parts I think are most important till I understand them, to get something tangible out of them. All sorts of knowledge seeps, bit by bit, into my brain. I imagine how great it'd be to stay here as long as I wanted. There are lots of books on the shelf I'd like to read, still plenty of food. But I know I'm just passing through and will have to leave before long. This place is too calm, too natural—too complete. I don't deserve it. At least not yet.

On the fourth day Oshima shows up late in the morning. I'm stark naked, sprawled on the chair on the porch, dozing in the sun, and don't hear him approach. I don't hear the sound of his car. Shouldering a backpack, he's walked here up the road. He quietly steps up on the porch, sticks out his hand, and lightly brushes my head. Startled, I leap to my feet and scramble around for a towel. There isn't one handy.

"Don't sweat it," Oshima says. "When I stayed here I used to sunbathe nude all the time. It feels great, having the sun on places it never reaches."

Naked like this in front of him, I feel totally defenseless and vulnerable, my pubic hair, penis, balls all exposed. I have no idea what to do. It's a little too late to cover up. "Hey," I say, straining to sound casual. "So you walked up?"

"It's such a nice day I decided to," he says. "I left my car down by the gate." He takes a towel draped over the railing and hands it to me. I wrap it around my waist and can finally relax.

Singing a song in a low voice he boils water, then takes out flour, eggs, and milk from his pack and whips up some pancakes in the frying pan. Tops these with butter and syrup. He then takes out lettuce, tomatoes, and an onion. He's very careful with the kitchen knife as he chops up everything for a salad. We have all this for lunch.

"So how were your three days here?" he asks, cutting a piece of pancake.

I tell him what a wonderful time I had. I omit the part about going into the woods. Somehow, it's better not to talk about it.

"I'm glad," Oshima says. "I was hoping you'd like it here."

"But we're going back to the city now, aren't we?"

"That's right. It's time to go back."

Getting ready to leave, we briskly straighten up the cabin. Wash the dishes and put them away in the shelves, clean up the stove. Empty the water pail, shut the valve in the propane tank. Store the food that will last in the cupboard, throw the rest away. Sweep the floor, wipe off the tops of the tables and chairs. Dig a hole outside to bury the garbage.

As Oshima locks up the cabin, I turn to look one last time. Up till a minute ago it felt so real, but now it seems imaginary. Just a few steps is all it takes for everything associated with it to lose all sense of reality. And me—the person who was there until a moment ago—now I seem imaginary too. It takes thirty minutes to walk to where Oshima parked the car, and we hardly exchange a word as we go down the mountain road. Oshima's humming some melody. I let my mind wander.

At the bottom, the little green sports car blends into the background of the forest. Oshima closes the gate to discourage trespassers, wraps the chain around it twice, and locks the padlock. Like before, I secure my backpack to the rack on the back of the car. The top's down.

"Back to the city," Oshima says.

I nod.

"I'm sure you enjoyed living all alone with nature like that, but it's not easy to live there for a long time," Oshima says. He puts on sunglasses and fastens his seat belt.

I sit down beside him and snap on my seat belt.

"In theory it's not impossible to live like that, and of course there are people who do. But nature is actually kind of *un*natural, in a way. And relaxation can actually be threatening. It takes experience and preparation to really live with those contradictions. So we're going back to the city for the time being. Back to civilization."

Oshima steps on the gas and we start down the mountain road. This time he's in no hurry and drives at a leisurely pace, enjoying the scenery and the rush of wind that whips through his bangs. The unpaved road ends and we start down the narrow paved road, passing villages and fields.

"Speaking of contradictions," Oshima suddenly says, "when I first met you I felt a kind of contradiction in you. You're seeking something, but at the same time running away for all you're worth."

"What is it I'm seeking?"

Oshima shakes his head. He glances in the rearview mirror and frowns. "I have no idea. I'm just saying I got that impression."

I don't reply.

"From my own experience, when someone is trying very hard to get something, they don't. And when they're running away from something as hard as they can, it usually catches up with them. I'm generalizing, of course."

"If you generalize about me, then, what's in my future? If I'm seeking and running at the same time."

"That's a tough one," Oshima says, and smiles. A moment passes before he goes on. "If I had to say anything it'd be this: Whatever it is you're seeking won't come in the form you're expecting."

"Kind of an ominous prophecy."

"Like Cassandra."

"Cassandra?" I ask.

"The Greek tragedy. Cassandra was the princess of Troy who prophesied. She was a temple priestess, and Apollo gave her the power to predict fate. In return he tried to force her to sleep with him, but she refused and he put a curse on her. Greek gods are more mythological than religious figures. By that I mean they have the same character flaws humans do. They fly off the handle, get horny, jealous, forgetful. You name it."

He takes a small box of lemon drops out of the glove compartment and pops one in his mouth. He motions for me to take one, and I do.

"What kind of curse was it?"

"The curse on Cassandra?"

I nod.

"The curse Apollo laid on her was that all her prophecies would be true, but nobody would ever believe them. On top of that, her prophecies would all be unlucky ones—predictions of betrayals, accidents, deaths, the country falling into ruin. That sort of thing. People not only didn't believe her, they began to despise her. If you haven't read them yet, I really recommend the plays by Euripides or Aeschylus. They show a lot of the essential problems we struggle with even today. In *koros*."

"*Koros*? What's that?"

"That's what they called the chorus they used in Greek plays. It stands at the back of the stage and explains in unison the situation or what the characters are feeling deep down inside. Sometimes they even try to influence the characters. It's a very convenient device. Sometimes I wish I had my own chorus standing behind me."

"Are you able to prophesy?"

"No such luck." He smiles. "For better or for worse, I don't have that kind of power. If I sound like I'm always predicting ominous things, it's because I'm a pragmatist. I use deductive reasoning to generalize, and I suppose this sometimes winds up sounding like unlucky prophecies. You know why? Because reality's just the accumulation of ominous prophecies come to life. All you have to do is open a newspaper on any given day and weigh the good news versus the bad news, and you'll see what I mean."

Oshima carefully downshifts at each curve, the kind of practiced gear shifting you hardly notice. Only the change in the sound of the engine gives it away.

"There is one piece of good news, though," he says. "We've decided to take you in. You'll be a staff member of the Komura Memorial Library. Which I think you're qualified for."

Instinctively I glance at him. "You mean I'm going to be working at the library?"

"More precisely, from now on you'll be a *part* of the library. You're going to be staying in the library, living there. You'll open the doors when it's time for the library to open, shut them when it's time to close up. As I said before, you seem to be a pretty self-disciplined sort of person, and fairly strong, so I don't imagine the job will be very hard for you. Miss Saeki and I aren't all that strong physically, so it'll really help us out a lot. Other than that, you'll just help with small day-to-day things. Nothing to speak of, really. Making delicious coffee for me, going out shopping for us. We've prepared a room that's attached to the library for you to stay in. It's originally a guest room, but we don't have any guests staying over so it hasn't been used for a long time. That's where you'll live. It has its own shower, too. The best thing is you'll be in the library so you can read whatever you like."

"But why—" I begin to say, but can't finish.

"Why are we doing this? It's all based on a very simple principle. I understand *you*, and Miss Saeki understands *me*. I accept you, and she accepts me. So even if you're some unknown fifteen-year-old runaway, that's not a problem. So, what do you think?"

I give it some thought. "All I was looking for was a roof over my head. That's all that matters right now. I don't really know what it means to become *part* of the library, but if it means I can live there, I'm grateful. At least I won't have to commute anymore."

"Then it's settled," Oshima says. "Let's go to the library. So you can become a *part* of it."

We get on the highway and pass a number of towns, a giant billboard for a loan company, a gas station with gaudy decorations, a glass-enclosed restaurant, a love hotel made up to look like a European castle, an abandoned video store with only its sign left, a pachinko place with an enormous parking lot, a McDonald's, 7-Eleven, Yoshinoya, Denny's. . . . Noisy reality starts to surround us. The hiss of eighteen-wheelers' air brakes, horns, and exhaust. Everything near me until now—the fire in the stove, the twinkle of the stars, the stillness of the forest—has faded away. I find it hard to even imagine them.

"There are a couple of things you should know about Miss Saeki," Oshima says. "When she was little, my mother and Miss Saeki were classmates and very close. She says that Miss Saeki was a bright little girl. She got good grades, was good at composition, sports of all kinds, and could play the piano well, too. She was the best at whatever she tried. And beautiful. Of course she's still quite a stunning person."

I nod.

"When she was still in grade school she had a sweetheart. The eld-est son of the Komura family—a distant relative, actually. They were the same age and made a handsome couple, a regular Romeo and Juliet. They lived near each other and were never apart. And when they became adults they fell in love. They were like one body and spirit, according to my mother."

We're waiting at a red light, and Oshima looks up at the sky. When the signal turns green, he steps on the gas and we zoom out in front of a tanker truck. "Do you remember what I told you in the library? About how people are always wandering around, searching for their other half?"

"That part about male/male, female/female, and male/female?"

"Right. What Aristophanes said. How we stumble through our lives desperately fumbling for our other half. Miss Saeki and that young man never had to do that. They were born with their other half right there in front of them."

"They were lucky."

Oshima nods. "Absolutely. Up to a point."

He rubs his chin with his palm like he's checking out how well he shaved. There's no trace of a razor—his skin is as smooth as porcelain.

"When the young man was eighteen he went to Tokyo to go to college. He had good grades and a major he was interested in. He also wanted to see what the big city was like. She went to a local college and majored in piano. This is a conservative part of the country, and she came from an old-fashioned kind of family. She was an only child, and her parents didn't want her going off to Tokyo. So the two of them were separated for the first time in their lives. Just like God had cut them cleanly apart with a knife.

"Of course they wrote to each other every day. 'It might be good for us to try being apart like this,' he wrote her. 'Then we can really tell how much we mean to each other.' But she didn't believe that. She knew their relationship was real enough that they didn't need to go out of their way to test it. It was a one-in-a-million union, fated to be, something that could never be broken apart. She was absolutely sure of that. But *he* wasn't. Or maybe he was, but simply didn't accept it. So he went ahead and went to Tokyo, thinking that overcoming a few obstacles would strengthen their love for each other. Men are like that sometimes.

"When she was nineteen Miss Saeki wrote a poem, set it to music, and played the piano and sang it. It was a melancholy melody, innocent and lovely. The lyrics, on the other hand, were symbolic, contemplative, hard to figure out. The contrast gave the song a kind of spirit and immediacy. Of course the whole song, lyrics and melody, was her way of crying out to her boyfriend, so far away. She sang the song a few times in front of people. She was ordinarily shy, but she loved to sing and had even been in a folk music band in college. Someone was very impressed by the song, made a demo tape, and sent it to a friend of his who was a director at a record company. He loved the song and had her go to their studio in Tokyo and record it.

"It was her first time in Tokyo, and she was able to see her boyfriend. Between recording sessions they were able to love each other, as before. My mother said she thought they'd had a sexual relationship since they were around fourteen. Both were rather precocious, and like many precocious young people they found it hard to grow up. It was as if they were eternally fourteen or fifteen. They clung to each other and could again feel the intensity of their love. Neither one of them had ever been attracted to anyone else. Even while they were apart, no one else could ever come between them. Sorry—am I boring you with this fairy-tale romance?"

I shake my head. "I have a feeling you're about to come to a turning point."

"You're right," Oshima says. "That's how stories happen—with a turning point, an unexpected twist. There's only one kind of happiness, but misfortune comes in all shapes and sizes. It's like Tolstoy said. Happiness is an allegory, unhappiness a *story*. Anyway, the record went on sale and was a huge hit. It kept on selling—a million copies, two million, I'm not sure of the exact figure. At any rate it was a record-breaking number at the time. Her photo was on the record jacket, a picture of her seated at a grand piano in the studio, smiling at the camera.

"She hadn't prepared any other songs, so the B side of the single was an instrumental version of the same song. With a piano and an orchestra, she of course playing the piano. A beautiful performance. It was around 1970. The song was on all the radio stations at the time, my mother said. This was before I was born, so I don't know for sure. This was her one and only song as a professional singer. She didn't put out an LP or a follow-up single."

"I wonder if I've heard that song."

"Do you listen to the radio much?"

I shake my head. I hardly ever listen to the radio.

"You probably haven't heard it, then. Unless it's on some oldies station, chances are you haven't. But it's a wonderful song. I have it on a

CD and listen to it every once in a while. When Miss Saeki's not around, of course. She hates any mention of the song. She doesn't like anyone bringing up the past."

"What's the name of the song?"

"'Kafka on the Shore.'" Oshima says.

"'Kafka on the Shore'?"

"That's correct, Kafka Tamura. The same name as you. A strange coincidence, don't you think?"

"But Kafka isn't my real name. Tamura is, though."

"But you chose it yourself, right?"

I nod. I'd decided a long time ago that this was the right name for the new me.

"That's the point, I'd say," Oshima says.

Miss Saeki's boyfriend died when he was twenty, Oshima goes on. Right when "Kafka on the Shore" was a hit. His college was on strike during the period of student unrest and shut down. He went to bring supplies to a friend of his who was manning the barricades, just before ten one night. The students occupying the building mistook him for a leader of an opposing faction—he did resemble him a lot—and grabbed him, tied him to a chair, and interrogated him as a spy. He tried to explain that they'd made a mistake, but every time he did they smashed him with a steel pipe or baton. When he fell to the floor they'd kick him with their boots. By dawn he was dead. His skull was caved in, his ribs broken, his lungs ruptured. They tossed his corpse out on the street like a dead dog. Two days later the college asked the national guard to come in, and within a couple of hours the student revolt was put down and several of them were arrested and charged with murder. The students confessed what they'd done and were put on trial, but since it wasn't premeditated two of them were convicted of involuntary manslaughter and given short prison sentences. His death was totally pointless.

Miss Saeki never sang again. She locked herself in her room and wouldn't talk to anybody, even on the phone. She didn't go to his funeral, and dropped out of college. After a few months, people suddenly realized she was no longer in town. Nobody knows where she went or what she did. Her parents refused to discuss it. Maybe even they didn't know where she'd been. She vanished into thin air. Even her best friend, Oshima's mother, didn't have a clue. Rumors flew that she'd been committed to a mental hospital after a failed suicide attempt in the deep forests surrounding Mount Fuji. Others said a friend of a friend had spotted her on the streets of Tokyo. According to this person she was working in Tokyo as a writer or something. Other rumors had it she was married and had a child. All of these, though, were groundless, with nothing to back them up. Twenty years passed.

No matter where she was or what she was doing all this time, Miss Saeki didn't hurt for money. Her royalties for "Kafka on the Shore" were deposited in a bank account, and even after taxes still amounted to a substantial sum. She got royalties every time the song was played on the radio or included in an oldies compilation. So it was simple for her to live far away, out of the limelight. Besides, her family was rich and she was their only daughter.

Suddenly, twenty-five years later, Miss Saeki reappeared in Takamatsu. The ostensible reason was her mother's funeral. (Her father had died five years before, but she hadn't come to the funeral.) She held a small service for her mother and then, after things had quieted down, sold the house she'd been born and raised in. She moved into an apartment she'd purchased in a quiet part of the city and seemed to settle down again. After a time she had some talks with the Komura family. (The head of the family, after the death of the eldest son, was his younger brother, three years younger. It was just the two of them, and no one knows what they talked about, exactly.) The upshot was Miss Saeki became head of the Komura Library.

Even now she's slim and beautiful and has the same neat, smart look you see on the record jacket of "Kafka on the Shore." But there's one thing missing: that lovely, innocent smile. She still smiles from time to time, definitely a charming smile, but it's always limited somehow, a smile that never goes beyond the moment. A high, invisible wall surrounds her, holding people at arm's length. Every morning she drives her gray Volkswagen Golf to the library, and drives it back home in the evening.

Back in her hometown, she had very little to do with former friends and relatives. If they happen to meet she makes polite conversation, but this seldom goes beyond a few standard topics. If the past happens to come up—especially if it involves her—she makes a quick, smooth segue to another topic. She's always polite and kind, but her words lack the kind of curiosity and excitement you'd normally expect. Her true feelings—assuming such things exist—remain hidden away. Except for when a practical sort of decision has to be made, she never gives her personal opinion about anything. She seldom talks about herself, instead letting others talk, nodding warmly as she listens. But most people start to feel vaguely uneasy when talking with her, as if they suspect they're wasting her time, trampling on her private, graceful, dignified world. And that impression is, for the most part, correct.

So even after settling back into her hometown, she remained a cipher. A stylish woman wrapped in refined mystery. Something about her made it hard to approach her. Even her nominal employers, the Komura family, kept their distance.

Eventually Oshima became her assistant and started to work in the library. At the time Oshima wasn't working or going to school, just staying at home reading and listening to music. Except for a few people he exchanged e-mails with, he hardly had any friends. Because of his hemophilia, he spent a lot of time going to see a specialist at the hospital, riding around town in his Mazda Miata, and except for his regular appointments at the University Hospital in Hiroshima and the occasional stay at the cabin in the Kochi mountains, he never left town. Not to imply that he was unhappy with this life. One day Oshima's mother happened to introduce him to Miss Saeki, who took an instant liking to him. The feeling was mutual, and the notion of working in a library intrigued him. Oshima soon became the only person Miss Saeki normally dealt with or spoke to.

"Sounds to me like Miss Saeki came back here in order to become head of the library," I say.

"I'd have to agree. Her mother's funeral was just the opportunity that brought her back. Her hometown must be so full of bittersweet memories that I imagine it was a hard decision to return."

"Why was the library so important to her?"

"Her boyfriend used to live in a building that's part of the library now. He was the eldest Komura son, and a love of reading was in his blood, I suppose. He liked to be alone—another family trait. So when he went into junior high he insisted on living apart from the main house, in a separate building, and his parents gave their okay. The whole family loved reading, so they could understand where he was coming from. If you want to be surrounded by books, it's fine with us — that kind of thing. So he lived in that annex, with nobody bothering him, coming back to the main house only for meals. Miss Saeki went to see him there almost every day. The two of them studied together, listened to music, and talked forever. And most likely made love there. The place was their own bit of paradise."

Both hands resting on top of the steering wheel, Oshima looks over at me. "That's where you'll be living now, Kafka. In that room. As I said, the library's been renovated, but it's the very same room."

Silence on my part.

"Miss Saeki's life basically stopped at age twenty, when her lover died. No, maybe not age twenty, maybe much earlier. . . . I don't know the details, but you need to be aware of this. The hands of the clock buried inside her soul ground to a halt then. Time outside, of course, flows on as always, but she isn't affected by it. For her, what we consider normal time is essentially meaningless."

"Meaningless?"

Oshima nods. "Like it doesn't exist."

"What you're saying is Miss Saeki still lives in that frozen time?"

"Exactly. I'm not saying she's some living corpse or anything. When you get to know her better you'll understand."

Oshima reaches out and lays a hand on my knee in a totally natural gesture. "Kafka, in everybody's life there's a point of no return. And in a very few cases, a point where you can't go forward anymore. And when we reach that point, all we can do is quietly accept the fact. That's how we survive."

We're about to merge onto the main highway. Before we do, Oshima stops the car, puts up the top, and slips a Schubert sonata into the CD player.

"There's one other thing I'd like you to be aware of," he goes on. "Miss Saeki has a wounded heart. To some extent that's true of all of us, present company included. But Miss Saeki has a special *individual* wound that goes beyond the usual meaning of the term. Her soul moves in mysterious ways. I'm not saying she's dangerous — don't get me wrong. On a day-to-day level she's definitely got her act together, probably more than anybody else I know. She's charming, deep, intelligent. But just don't let it bother you if you notice something odd about her sometimes."

"Odd?" I can't help asking.

Oshima shakes his head. "I really like Miss Saeki, and respect her. I'm sure you'll come to feel the same way."

This doesn't really answer my question, but Oshima doesn't say anything. With perfect timing he shifts gears, steps on the gas, and passes a small van just before we enter a tunnel.

Chapter 18

Nakata found himself faceup in a clump of weeds. As he awakened he slowly opened his eyes. It was night, but he couldn't see any stars or the moon. Still, the sky was faintly light. He could smell the strong scent of summer grasses and hear insects buzzing around. Somehow he was back in the vacant lot he'd been staking out every day. Feeling something rough and warm brush against his face, he turned and saw two cats eagerly licking both his cheeks with their tiny tongues. It was Goma and Mimi. Nakata slowly sat up, reached out, and petted them. "Was Nakata asleep?" he asked.

The cats cried out like they were complaining about something, but Nakata couldn't catch the words. He had no idea what they were trying to tell him. They were just two cats meowing.

"I beg your pardon, but I can't understand what you're trying to say." He stood up and checked his body to make sure there was nothing out of the ordinary. He felt no pain, and his arms and legs were working fine. His eyes took some time to adjust to the darkness, but once they did he saw that there wasn't any blood on his arms or clothes. His clothes weren't rumpled or messed up, either, and looked the same as when he'd left his apartment. His canvas bag was right beside him, lunch and thermos inside, and his hat was inside his trouser pocket where it belonged. Everything was in order. Nakata couldn't figure out what was going on.

In order to save the two cats, he'd stabbed Johnnie Walker—the cat-killer—to death. That much he remembered all too clearly. He could still feel the knife in his hands. It wasn't a dream—blood had spurted out of Johnnie Walker and he'd collapsed to the floor, curled up, and died. Then Nakata had sunk back on the couch and lost consciousness. And the next thing he knew, here he was lying among the weeds in the vacant lot. But how did he get back here? He didn't even know the road back. And his clothes had no blood on them at all. Seeing Mimi and Goma beside him proved it wasn't a dream, but for some strange reason now he couldn't understand a word they said.

Nakata sighed. He couldn't think straight. But never mind—he'd figure it all out later. He slung the bag over his shoulder, picked up the two cats, and left the vacant lot. Once outside the fence, Mimi started to squirm as if she wanted to be let down.

Nakata lowered her to the ground. "Mimi, you can go back home on your own, I imagine. It's nearby."

That's right, Mimi's wagging tail seemed to say.

"Nakata doesn't understand what's happened, but for some reason I can't talk with you anymore. But I was able to find Goma, and I'd better take her back to the Koizumis. Everyone's waiting for her. Thank you so much for everything, Mimi."

Mimi meowed, wagged her tail again, then scurried off and disappeared around the corner. There was no blood on her, either. Nakata decided to remember that.

The Koizumis were overjoyed by Goma's return. It was past ten p.m. but the children were still up, brushing their teeth before bed. Their parents were drinking tea and watching the news on TV, and they welcomed Nakata warmly. The two little girls, in pajamas, jostled each other to be the first to hug their precious pet. They quickly gave Goma some milk and cat food, which she eagerly tucked into.

"My apologies for stopping by so late at night. It would be much better to come earlier, but Nakata couldn't help it."

"That's all right," Mrs. Koizumi said. "Please don't worry about it."

"Don't worry about the time," her husband said. "That cat is like a member of the family. I can't tell you how happy we are you could find her. How about coming in and having a cup of tea?"

"No thank you, Nakata must be going. I just wanted to get Goma back to you as soon as possible."

Mrs. Koizumi went to another room and returned with Nakata's pay in an envelope, which her husband handed to Nakata. "It's not much, but please accept this token for all you've done. We're very grateful."

"Thank you very much. Much obliged," Nakata said, and bowed.

"I'm surprised, though, you could find her in the dark like this."

"Yes, it's a long story. Nakata can't tell the whole thing. I'm not too bright, and not so good at giving long explanations."

"That's quite all right. We are so grateful to you, Mr. Nakata," Mrs. Koizumi said. "I'm sorry it's just leftovers, but we have some grilled egg-plant and vinegared cucumbers we'd like you to take home with you."

"I'd be happy to. Grilled eggplant and vinegared cucumbers are some of Nakata's favorites."

Nakata stowed the Tupperware container of food and the envelope in his bag. He walked quickly toward the station and went to a police box near the shopping district. A young officer was seated at a desk inside, intently working on some paperwork. His hat was on top of the desk.

Nakata slid the glass door open. "Good evening. Sorry to bother you," he said.

"Good evening," the policeman replied. He looked up from the paperwork and gave Nakata a once-over. Basically a nice, harmless old man, was his professional assessment, most likely stopping by to ask directions.

Standing at the entrance, Nakata removed his hat and stuffed it in his pocket, then took a handkerchief from the other pocket and blew his nose. He folded up the handkerchief and put it back.

"Is there something I can do for you?" the policeman asked.

"Yes, there is. Nakata just murdered somebody."

The policeman dropped his pen on the desk and stared open-mouthed at the old man. For a moment he was speechless. What the—?

"Here, why don't you sit down," he said dubiously, pointing to a chair opposite him. He reached out and checked that he had his pistol, baton, and handcuffs on him.

"Thank you," Nakata said, and sat down. Back held straight, hands resting in his lap, he looked straight at the officer.

"So what you're saying is . . . you killed somebody?"

"Yes. Nakata killed a person with a knife. Just a little while ago," Nakata admitted frankly.

The young officer took out a form, glanced at the clock on the wall, and noted down the time and the statement about a knifing. "I'll need your name and address."

"My name is Satoru Nakata, and my address is—"

"Just a moment. What characters do you write your name with?"

"I don't know about characters. I'm sorry, but I can't write. Or read, either."

The officer frowned. "You're telling me you can't read at all? You can't even write your name?"

"That's right. Until I was nine I could read and write, but then there was an accident and after that I can't. Nakata's not too bright."

The officer sighed and laid down his pen. "I can't fill out the form if I don't know how your name is written."

"I apologize."

"Do you have any family?"

"Nakata's all alone. I have no family. And no job. I live on a *sub city* from the Governor."

"It's pretty late, and I suggest you go on home. Go home and get a good night's sleep, and then tomorrow if you remember something come and see me again. We can talk then."

The policeman was nearing the end of his shift and wanted to finish up all his paperwork before he went off duty. He'd promised to meet a fellow officer for a drink at a nearby bar when he got off, so the last thing he wanted to do was waste time talking to some crazy old coot.

But Nakata gave him a harsh look and shook his head. "No, sir, Nakata wants to tell everything while he still remembers it. If I wait until tomorrow I might forget something important. Nakata was in the empty lot in the 2-chome section. The Koizumis had asked me to find their missing cat, Goma. Then a huge black dog suddenly appeared and took me to a house. A big house with a big gate and a black car. I don't know the address. I've never been to that part of town before. But I'm pretty sure it's in Nakano Ward. Inside the house was a man named Johnnie Walker who had on a funny kind of black hat. A very high sort of hat. Inside the refrigerator in the kitchen there were rows of cats' heads. About twenty or so, I'd say. He collects cats, cuts off their heads with a saw, and eats their hearts. He's collecting the cats' souls to make a special kind of flute. And then he's going to use that flute to collect people's souls. Right in front of Nakata, Johnnie Walker killed Mr. Kawamura with a knife. And several other cats. He cut open their stomachs with a knife. He was going to kill Goma and Mimi, too. But then Nakata used a knife to kill Johnnie Walker.

"Johnnie Walker said he wanted Nakata to kill him. But I didn't plan to kill him. I've never killed anybody before. I just wanted to stop

Johnnie Walker from killing any more cats. But my body wouldn't listen. It did what it wanted. I picked up one of the knives there and stabbed Johnnie Walker two times. Johnnie Walker fell down, all covered with blood, and died. Nakata got all bloody then, too. I sat down over on the sofa and must have fallen asleep. When I woke up it was the middle of the night and I was back in the empty lot. Mimi and Goma were beside me. That was just a little while ago. Nakata took Goma back, got some grilled eggplant and vinegared cucumbers from Mrs. Koizumi, and came directly here. And I thought I'd better report to the Governor right away. Tell him what happened."

Nakata sat up straight through this whole recitation, and when he'd finished he took a deep breath. He'd never spoken this much in one spurt in his life. He felt completely drained. "So please report this to the Governor," he added.

The young policeman had listened to the entire story with a vacant look, and didn't understand much of what the old man was getting at. Goma? *Johnnie Walker?* "I understand," he replied. "I'll make sure the Governor hears of this."

"I hope he doesn't cut off my *sub city*."

Looking displeased, the policeman pretended to fill out a form. "I understand. I'll write it down just like that: *The person in question desires that his subsidy not be cut off.* Is that all right then?"

"Yes, that's fine. Much obliged. Sorry to take your time. And please say hello to the Governor for me."

"Will do. So don't worry, and just take it easy today, okay?" the policeman said. He couldn't help adding a personal aside: "You know, your clothes look pretty clean for having killed someone and gotten all bloody. There's not a spot on you."

"Yes, you're entirely correct. To tell the truth, Nakata finds it very strange too. It doesn't make any sense. I should be covered in blood, but when I looked it had all disappeared. It's very strange."

"It certainly is," the policeman said, his voice tinged with an entire day's worth of exhaustion.

Nakata slid the door open and was about to leave when he stopped and turned around. "Excuse me, sir, but will you be in this area tomorrow evening?"

"Yes, I will," the policeman replied cautiously. "I'm on duty here tomorrow evening. Why do you ask?"

"Even if it's sunny, I suggest you bring an umbrella."

The policeman nodded. He turned and looked at the clock. His colleague should be phoning any minute now. "Okay, I'll be sure to bring one."

"There will be fish falling from the sky, just like rain. A lot of fish. Mostly sardines, I believe. With a few mackerel mixed in."

"Sardines and mackerel, huh?" the policeman laughed. "Better turn the umbrella upside down, then, and catch a few. Could vinegar some for a meal."

"Vinegared mackerel's one of Nakata's favorites," Nakata said with a serious look. "But by that time tomorrow I believe I'll be gone."

The next day when—sure enough—sardines and mackerel rained down on a section of Nakano Ward, the young policeman turned white as a sheet. With no warning whatsoever some two thousand sardines and mackerel plunged to earth from the clouds. Most of the fish were crushed to a pulp as they slammed into the ground, but a few survived and flopped around on the road in front of the shopping district. The fish were fresh, still with a smell of the sea about them. The fish struck people, cars, and roofs, but not, apparently, from a great height, so no serious injuries resulted. It was more shocking than anything else. A huge number of fish falling like hail from the sky—it was positively apocalyptic.

The police investigated the matter but could come up with no good explanation for how it happened. No fish market or fishing boat reported any large number of sardines and mackerel missing. No planes or helicopters were flying overhead at the time. Neither were there any reports of tornados. They dismissed the possibility it was some elaborate practical joke—who would possibly do something so utterly bizarre? At the request of the police, the Nakano Ward Health Office collected some of the fish and examined them, but found nothing unusual. They were just ordinary sardines and mackerel. Fresh—and good to eat, by the looks of them. Still, the police, afraid these mystery fish might contain some dangerous substance, sent out a loudspeaker truck around the neighborhood warning people not to eat any.

This was the kind of story TV news shows lapped up, and crews rushed to the scene. Reporters crowded around the shopping district and sent out their reports on this curious event across the nation. The reporters scooped up fish with their shovels to illustrate what had happened. They also interviewed a housewife who had been struck on the head by one of the falling mackerel, the dorsal fin cutting her cheek.

"I'm just glad it wasn't a tuna," she said, pressing a handkerchief to her cheek. That made sense, but still viewers chuckled. One of the more adventuresome reporters grilled some of the fish on the spot. "Delicious," he told viewers proudly. "Very fresh, with just the right amount of fat. Too bad I don't have any grated radish and hot rice to round out the meal."

The policeman was baffled. The strange old codger—what was his name again?—had predicted all these fish raining down from the sky. Sardines and mackerel, just like he'd said. . . . But I just laughed it off, the policeman thought, and didn't even get his name and address. Should he tell his boss about it? He supposed so, but then again what good would it do now? Nobody really got hurt, and there wasn't any proof that a crime was involved. Just a sudden squall of fish, raining from the sky.

But who's to say my boss would even believe me? he asked himself. Say I told him the whole story—that the day before this happened a weird old guy stopped by the police box and predicted there'd be a shower of fish. He'd think I've completely lost it. And the story would make the rounds of the precinct, getting fishier with each retelling, and end up as a running joke with him as the butt of it.

One more thing, the policeman thought. That old man had come to report that he'd murdered somebody. To give himself up, in other words. And I never took him seriously. Didn't even note it in the logbook. This was definitely against regulations, and I could be brought up on charges. But the old man's story was so *preposterous*. No policeman would ever take it seriously. It's a madhouse working the police box sometimes, with paperwork up to here. The world's filled with people with a screw loose, and, as if by agreement, at one time or another they all seem to find their way into police boxes to blab out some nonsense. If you bother yourself with every one of these nutcases, you'll go nuts yourself!

But that prediction about fish raining from the sky, a lunatic statement if there ever was one, actually did happen, so maybe—just maybe—that story he told about knifing somebody to death—Johnnie Walker, as he put it—might actually be true. Assuming it was, this was a major problem, for he'd turned away someone confessing to murder and didn't even write up a report on it.

Finally a garbage truck came and cleaned up all the mounds of fish. The young policeman directed traffic, blocking off the entrance to the shopping district so cars couldn't come in. Fish scales were stuck to the street in front of the shops and wouldn't come off no matter how much they were hosed down. The street remained wet for some time, causing a couple of housewives on bicycles to slip and fall. The place reeked of fish for days afterward, getting the neighborhood cats all worked up. The policeman was kept busy with the cleanup and didn't have time to think any more about the strange old man.

The day after it rained fish, though, the policeman gulped in shock when the body of a man, stabbed to death, was discovered nearby. The dead man was a famous sculptor, and his body was discovered by the cleaning woman who came every other day. The body was naked, lying in a pool of blood. Estimated time of death was in the evening two days previous, the murder weapon a steak knife from the kitchen. To his dismay, the young policeman finally believed what the old man had told him. My *God*, he thought, what a complete mess I've gotten myself into! I should have called up the precinct and taken the old man in. He confessed to murder, so I should've handed him over to the higher-ups and let *them* decide if he's crazy or not. But I shirked my duty. Now that it's come to this, the young policeman decided, the best thing to do is to just clam up and pretend it never happened.

But by this time, Nakata was no longer in town.

Chapter 19

It's Monday and the library's closed. The library is quiet enough most of the time, but on a day like this when it's closed it's like the land that time forgot. Or more like a place that's holding its breath, hoping time won't stumble upon it.

Down the corridor from the reading room, past a STAFF ONLY sign, there's a sink area where you can make coffee or tea, and there's a microwave oven, too. Just past this is the door to the guest room, which includes a bare-bones bathroom and closet. Next to the single bed is a nightstand outfitted with a reading lamp and alarm clock. There's also a little writing desk with a lamp on it. Plus an old-fashioned set of chairs, covered in white cloth, for receiving guests, and a chest for clothes. On top of a small, bachelor-size refrigerator are some dishes and a small shelf for stowing them away. If you feel like making a simple meal, the sink area's right outside. The bathroom's outfitted with a shower, soap and shampoo, a hair dryer, and towels. Everything you need for a comfortable short stay. Through a west-facing window you can see the trees in the garden. It's getting close to evening, and the sinking sun glints past the cedar branches.

"I've stayed here a couple of times when it was too much trouble to go home," Oshima says. "But nobody else uses the room. As far as I know, Miss Saeki never uses it. It's not going to put anybody out, your staying here, is what I'm trying to say."

I set my backpack on the floor and look around my new lodgings.

"There's a clean set of sheets, and enough in the fridge to tide you over. Milk, some fruit, vegetables, butter, ham, cheese . . . Not enough for a decent meal, but enough for a sandwich or salad at least. If you want something more, I suggest takeout, or going out to eat. For laundry you'll have to make do with rinsing things out in the bathroom, I'm afraid. Let's see, have I forgotten anything?"

"Where does Miss Saeki usually work?"

Oshima points to the ceiling. "You remember that room on the second floor you saw on the tour? She's always there, writing. If I have to go out for a while she sometimes comes downstairs and takes over at the counter. But unless she's got something to do on the first floor, that's where you'll find her."

I nod.

"I'll be here tomorrow before ten to run through what your job involves. Until then, just relax and take it easy."

"Thanks for everything," I tell him.

"My pleasure," he replies.

After he leaves I unload my backpack. Arrange my meager assortment of clothes in the dresser, hang up my shirts and jacket, line up my notebook and pens on the desk, put my toiletries in the bathroom, and finally stow the pack itself in the closet.

The room doesn't have any decorations at all, except for a small oil painting, a realistic portrait of a young boy by the shore. Not bad, I decide—maybe done by somebody famous? The boy looks about twelve or so, and he's wearing a white sunhat and sitting on a small deck chair. His elbow's on one of the arms of the chair, his chin resting in his hand. He looks a little sad, but kind of pleased, too. A black German shepherd sits next to the boy, like he's guarding him. In the background is the sea and a couple of other people, but they're too far away to make out their faces. A small island's visible, and a few fist-shaped clouds float over the water. Most definitely a summer scene. I sit down at the desk and gaze at the painting for a while. I start to feel like I can hear the crash of waves, the salty smell of the sea.

The boy in the painting might be the boy who used to live in this room, the young man Miss Saeki loved. The one who got caught up in the student movement clashes and was pointlessly beaten to death. There's no saying for sure, but I'm betting that's who it is. The scenery looks a lot like what you see around here, for one thing. If that's the case, then it must be from about forty years ago—an eternity to somebody like me. I try imagining myself in forty years, but it's like trying to picture what lies beyond the universe.

The next morning Oshima arrives and shows me what I'm supposed to do to get the library ready to open. First I have to unlock and open the windows to air out the rooms, make a quick pass with the vacuum cleaner, wipe the desktops, change the flowers in the vases, turn on the lights, occasionally sprinkle water in the garden to keep down the dust, and, when the time comes, open the door. At closing time it's the same procedure in reverse—lock the windows, wipe the desktops again, turn off the lights, and close the front door.

"There's not much for anybody to steal here, so maybe we don't need to be so worried about always locking the door," Oshima tells me. "But Miss Saeki and I don't like things done sloppily. So we try to do things by the book. This is *our house*, so we treat it with respect. And I hope you'll do the same."

I nod.

Next he shows me what to do at the reception desk, how to help out people coming to use the library.

"For the time being you should just sit next to me and watch what I do. It's not all that hard. If something ever comes up you can't handle, just go upstairs and ask Miss Saeki. She'll take care of it."

Miss Saeki shows up just before eleven. Her Volkswagen Golf makes a distinctive roar as it pulls up, and I can tell right away it's her. She parks, comes in through the back door, and greets the two of us. "Morning," she says. "Good morning," we answer back. That's the extent of our conversation. Miss Saeki has on a navy blue short-sleeved dress, a cotton coat in her arms, a shoulder bag. Nothing you could call an accessory, and hardly a hint of makeup. Still, there's something about her that's dazzling. She glances at me standing next to Oshima and looks for a moment like she wants to say something, but doesn't. She merely beams a slight smile in my direction and walks up to her office on the second floor.

"Not to worry," Oshima assures me. "She has no problem with your being here. She just doesn't go in for a lot of small talk, that's all."

At eleven Oshima and I open up the main door, but nobody comes for a while. During the interval he shows me how to use the computers to search for books. They're typical library PCs I'm already familiar with. Next he shows me how to arrange all the catalog cards. Every day the library receives copies of newly published books, and one of the other tasks is to log in these new arrivals by hand.

Around eleven-thirty two women come in together, wearing identical jeans. The shorter of the two has cropped hair like a swimmer, while the taller woman wears her hair pulled back. Both of them have on jogging shoes, one a pair of Nikes, the other Asics. The tall one looks around forty or so, with glasses and a checked shirt, the shorter woman, a decade younger, is wearing a white blouse. Both have little daypacks on, and expressions as gloomy as a cloudy day. Neither one says very much. Oshima relieves them of their packs at the entrance, and the women, looking displeased, extract notebooks and pens before leaving them.

The women go through the library, checking the stacks one by one, earnestly flipping through the card catalog, occasionally taking notes. They don't read anything or sit down. They act less like people using a library than inspectors from the tax office checking a company's inventory. Oshima and I can't figure out who they are or what they could possibly be up to. He gives me a significant look and shrugs. To put it mildly, I don't have a good feeling about this.

At noon, while Oshima goes out to the garden to eat his lunch, I fill in for him behind the counter.

"Excuse me, but I have a question," one of the women comes over and says. The tall one. Her tone of voice is hard and unyielding, like a loaf of bread someone forgot on the back of a shelf.

"Yes, what can I do for you?"

She frowns and looks at me like I'm some off-kilter picture frame. "Aren't you a high school student?"

"Yes, that's right. I'm a trainee," I answer.

"Is there one of your superiors I could talk to?"

I go out to the garden to get Oshima. He slowly takes a sip of coffee to dissolve the bite of food in his mouth, brushes the crumbs from his lap, and comes inside.

"Yes, may I help you?" Oshima asks her amiably.

"Just to let you know, we're investigating public cultural facilities in the entire country from a woman's point of view, looking at ease of use, fair access, and other issues," she says. "Our group is doing a year-long investigation and plans to publish a public report on our findings. A large number of women are involved in this project, and the two of us happen to be in charge of this region."

"If you don't mind," Oshima says, "would you tell me the name of this organization?"

The woman whips out a business card and passes it to him.

His expression unchanged, Oshima reads it carefully, places it on the counter, then looks up with a blazing smile and gazes intently at the woman. A first-class smile guaranteed to make any red-blooded woman blush.

This woman, strangely enough, doesn't react, not even a twitch of an eyebrow. "What we've concluded is that, unfortunately, this library has several issues that need to be addressed."

"From the viewpoint of women, is what you're saying," Oshima commented.

"Correct, *from the viewpoint of women*," the woman answers. She clears her throat. "And we'd like to bring this up with your administration and hear their response, so if you don't mind?"

"We don't have something as fancy as an administration, but I would be happy to listen to you."

"Well, first of all you have no restroom set aside for women. That's correct, isn't it?"

"Yes, that's right. There's no women's restroom in this library. We have one restroom for both men and women."

"Even if you are a private facility, since you're open to the public don't you think—in principle—that you should provide separate restrooms for men and women?"

"In principle?" Oshima says.

"Correct. Shared facilities give rise to all sorts of harassment. According to our survey, the majority of women are reluctant to use shared bathrooms. This is a clear case of neglect of your female patrons."

"Neglect . . . ," Oshima says, and makes a face like he's swallowed something bitter by mistake. He doesn't much like the sound of the word, it would seem.

"An intentional oversight."

"Intentional oversight," he repeats, and gives some thought to this clumsy phrase.

"So what is your reaction to all this?" the woman asks, barely containing her irritation.

"As you can see," Oshima says, "we're a very small library. And unfortunately we don't have the space for separate restrooms. Naturally it would be better to have separate facilities, but none of our patrons have ever complained. For better or for worse, our library doesn't get very crowded. If you'd like to pursue this issue of separate restrooms further, I suggest you go to the Boeing headquarters in Seattle and address the issue of restrooms on 747s. A 747's much bigger than our little library, and much more crowded. As far as I'm aware, all restrooms on passenger jets are shared by men and women."

The tall woman frowns at him severely, her cheekbones jutting forward and her glasses riding up her nose. "We are not investigating airplanes. 747s are beside the point."

"Wouldn't restrooms in both jets and in our library—in principle— give rise to the same sorts of problems?"

"We are investigating, one by one, public facilities. We're not here to argue over principles."

Oshima's supple smile never fades during this exchange. "Is that so? I could have sworn that *principles* were exactly what we were discussing."

The woman realizes she's blown it. She blushes a bit, though not because of Oshima's sex appeal. She tries a different tack. "At any rate, jumbo jets are irrelevant here. Don't try to confuse the issue."

"Understood. No more airplanes," Oshima promises. "We'll bring things down to earth."

The woman glares at him and, after taking a breath, forges on. "One other issue I'd like to raise is how you have authors here separated by sex."

"Yes, that's right. The person who was in charge before us cataloged these and for whatever reason divided them into male and female. We were thinking of recataloging all of them, but haven't been able to as of yet."

"We're not criticizing you for this," she says.

Oshima tilts his head slightly.

"The problem, though, is that in all categories male authors are listed before female authors," she says. "To our way of thinking this violates the principle of sexual equality and is totally unfair."

Oshima picks up her business card again, runs his eyes over it, then lays it back down on the counter. "Ms. Soga," he begins, "when they called the role in school your name would have come before Ms. Tanaka, and after Ms. Sekine. Did you file a complaint about that? Did you object, asking them to reverse the order? Does G get angry because it follows F in the alphabet? Does page 68 in a book start a revolution just because it follows 67?"

"That's not the point," she says angrily. "You're intentionally trying to confuse the issue."

Hearing this, the shorter woman, who'd been standing in front of a stack taking notes, races over.

"*Intentionally trying to confuse the issue*," Oshima repeats, like he's underlining the woman's words.

"Are you denying it?"

"That's a red herring," Oshima replies.

The woman named Soga stands there, mouth slightly ajar, not saying a word.

"In English there's this expression *red herring*. Something that's very interesting but leads you astray from the main topic. I'm afraid I haven't looked into why they use that kind of expression, though."

"Herrings or mackerel or whatever, you're dodging the issue."

"Actually what I'm doing is shifting the *analogy*," Oshima says. "One of the most effective methods of argument, according to Aristotle. The citizens of ancient Athens enjoyed using this kind of intellectual trick very much. It's a shame, though, that at the time women weren't included in the definition of 'citizen.'"

"Are you making fun of us?"

Oshima shakes his head. "Look, what I'm trying to get across is this: I'm sure there are many more effective ways of making sure that Japanese women's rights are guaranteed than sniffing around a small library in a little town and complaining about the restrooms and the card catalog. We're doing our level best to see that this modest library of ours helps the community. We've assembled an outstanding collection for people who love books. And we do our utmost to put a human face on all our dealings with the public. You might not be aware of it, but this library's collection of poetry-related material from the 1910s to the mid-Showa period is nationally recognized. Of course there are things we could do better, and limits to what we can accomplish. But rest assured we're doing our very best. I think it'd be a whole lot better if you focus on what we do *well* than what we're *unable* to do. Isn't that what you call fair?"

The tall woman looks at the short one, who looks back up at her and opens her mouth for the first time. "You've just been evading the point, mouthing empty arguments that avoid taking responsibility," she says in a really high-pitched voice. "In *reality*, to use the term for the sake of convenience, what you're doing is an easygoing attempt at self-justification. You are a totally pathetic, historical example of the phallocentric, to put it mildly."

"A *pathetic, historical example*," Oshima repeats, obviously impressed. By his tone of voice he seems to like the sound of that phrase.

"In other words you're a typical sexist, patriarchic male," the tall one pipes in, unable to conceal her irritation.

"A *patriarchic male*," Oshima again repeats.

The short one ignores this and goes on. "You're employing the status quo and the cheap phallocentric logic that supports it to reduce the entire female gender to second-class citizens, to limit and deprive women of the rights they're due. You're doing this unconsciously rather than deliberately, but that makes you even guiltier. You protect vested male interests and become inured to the pain of others, and don't even try to see what evil your blindness causes women and society. I realize that problems with restrooms and card catalogs are mere details, but if we don't begin with the small things we'll never be able to throw off the cloak of blindness that covers our society. Those are the principles by which we act."

"That's the way every sensible woman feels," the tall one adds, her face expressionless.

"*How could any woman of generous spirit behave otherwise, given the torments that I face*," Oshima says.

The two women stand there as silent as icebergs.

"*Electra*, by Sophocles. A wonderful play. And by the way, the term *gender* was originally used to indicate grammatical gender. My feeling is the word 'sex' is more accurate in terms of indicating physical sexual difference. Using 'gender' here is incorrect. To put a linguistic fine point on it."

A frozen silence follows.

"At any rate, what you've been saying is fundamentally wrong," Oshima says, calmly yet emphatically. "I am most definitely *not* a pathetic, historical example of a patriarchic male."

"Then explain, simply, what's wrong with what we've said," the shorter woman says defiantly.

"Without sidestepping the issue or trying to show off how erudite you are," the tall one adds.

"All right. I'll do just that—explain it simply and honestly, minus any sidestepping or displays of brilliance," Oshima says.

"We're waiting," the tall one says, and the short one gives a compact nod to show she agrees.

"First of all, I'm not a male," Oshima announces.

A dumbfounded silence follows on the part of everybody. I gulp and shoot Oshima a glance.

"I'm a woman," he says.

"I'd appreciate it if you wouldn't joke around," the short woman says, after a pause for breath. Not much confidence, though. It's more like she felt somebody had to say *something*.

Oshima pulls his wallet out of his chinos, takes out the driver's license, and passes it to the woman. She reads what's written there, frowns, and hands it to her tall companion, who reads it and, after a moment's hesitation, gives it back to Oshima, a sour look on her face.

"Did you want to see it too?" Oshima asks me. When I shake my head, he slips the license back in his wallet and puts the wallet in his pants pocket. He then places both hands on the counter and says, "As you can see, biologically and legally I am undeniably female. Which is why what you've been saying about me is *fundamentally* wrong. It's simply impossible for me to be, as you put it, a *typical sexist, patriarchic male*."

"Yes, but—" the tall woman says but then stops. The short one, lips tight, is playing with her collar.

"My body is physically female, but my mind's completely male," Oshima goes on. "Emotionally I live as a man. So I suppose your notion of being a *historical example* may be correct. And maybe I am sexist—who knows. But I'm not a lesbian, even though I dress this way. My sexual preference is for men. In other words, I'm a female but I'm gay. I do anal sex, and have never used my vagina for sex. My clitoris is sensitive but my breasts aren't. I don't have a period. So, what am I discriminating against? Could somebody tell me?"

The three of us listening are flabbergasted and don't say a word. One of the women clears her throat, and the jarring sound reverberates through the room. The clock on the wall loudly ticks away the seconds.

"I'm very sorry," Oshima says, "but I'm in the middle of lunch. I'm having a tuna-spinach wrap and had eaten half of it when you asked me over. If I leave it much longer the neighborhood cats will make a grab for it. People throw away kittens they don't want in the woods near the sea, so this neighborhood is full of cats. If you don't mind I'd like to get back to my lunch. So excuse me, but please take your time and enjoy the library. Our library is open to everyone. As long as you follow the rules and don't bother the other patrons, feel free to do whatever you'd like. You can look at whatever you want. Go ahead and write whatever you like in your report. We won't mind. We don't receive any funding from anywhere and pretty much do things our own way. And that's the way we like it."

After Oshima leaves the two women share a look, then they both stare at me. Maybe they figure me for Oshima's lover or something. I don't say a word and start arranging catalog cards. The two of them whisper to each other in the stacks, and before long they gather their belongings and start to pull up stakes. Frozen looks on their faces, they don't say a word of thanks when I hand back their daypacks.

After a while Oshima finishes his lunch and comes back inside. He hands me two spinach wraps made of tuna and vegetables wrapped in a kind of green tortilla with a white cream sauce on top. I have these for lunch. I boil up some water and have a cup of Earl Grey to wash it down.

"Everything I said a while ago is true," Oshima tells me when I come back from lunch.

"So that's what you meant when you told me you were a special person?"

"I wasn't trying to brag or anything," he says, "but you understand that I wasn't exaggerating, right?"

I nod silently.

Oshima smiles. "In terms of sex I'm most definitely female, though my breasts haven't developed much and I've never had a period. But I don't have a penis or testicles or facial hair. In short, I have *nothing*. A nice no-extra-baggage kind of feeling, if you want to put a positive spin on it. Though I doubt you can understand how that feels."

"I guess not," I say.

"Sometimes I don't understand it myself. Like, what the heck am I, anyway? Really, what *am* I?"

I shake my head. "Well, I don't know what *I* am, either."

"A classic identity crisis."

I nod.

"But at least you know where to begin. Unlike me."

"I don't care what you are. Whatever you are, I like you," I tell him. I've never said this to anybody in my whole life, and the words make me blush.

"I appreciate it," Oshima says, and lays a gentle hand on my shoulder. "I know I'm a *little* different from everyone else, but I'm still a

180

human being. That's what I'd like you to realize. I'm just a regular person, not some monster. I feel the same things everyone else does, act the same way. Sometimes, though, that small difference feels like an abyss. But I guess there's not much I can do about it." He picks up a long, sharpened pencil from the counter and gazes at it like it's an extension of himself. "I wanted to tell you all this as soon as I could, directly, rather than have you hear it from someone else. So I guess today was a good opportunity. It wasn't such a pleasant experience, though, was it?"

I nod.

"I've experienced all kinds of discrimination," Oshima says. "Only people who've been discriminated against can really know how much it hurts. Each person feels the pain in his own way, each has his own scars. So I think I'm as concerned about fairness and justice as anybody. But what disgusts me even more are people who have no imagination. The kind T. S. Eliot calls *hollow men*. People who fill up that lack of imagination with heartless bits of straw, not even aware of what they're doing. Callous people who throw a lot of empty words at you, trying to force you to do what you don't want to. Like that lovely pair we just met." He sighs and twirls the long slender pencil in his hand. "Gays, lesbians, straights, feminists, fascist pigs, communists, Hare Krishnas—none of them bother me. I don't care what banner they raise. But what I *can't* stand are *hollow* people. When I'm with them I just can't bear it, and wind up saying things I shouldn't. With those women—I should've just let it slide, or else called Miss Saeki and let her handle it. She would have given them a smile and smoothed things over. But I just can't do that. I say things I shouldn't, do things I shouldn't do. I can't control myself. That's one of my weak points. Do you know why that's a weak point of mine?"

" 'Cause if you take every single person who lacks much imagination seriously, there's no end to it," I say.

"That's it," Oshima says. He taps his temple lightly with the eraser end of the pencil. "But there's one thing I want you to remember, Kafka. Those are exactly the kind of people who murdered Miss Saeki's childhood sweetheart. Narrow minds devoid of imagination. Intolerance, theories cut off from reality, empty terminology, usurped ideals, inflexible systems. *Those* are the things that really frighten me. What I absolutely fear and loathe. Of course it's important to know what's right and what's wrong. Individual errors in judgment can usually be corrected. As long as you have the courage to admit mistakes, things can be turned around. But intolerant, narrow minds with no imagination are like parasites that transform the host, change form, and continue to thrive. They're a lost cause, and I don't want anyone like that coming in *here*."

Oshima points at the stacks with the tip of his pencil. What he means, of course, is the entire library.

"I wish I could just laugh off people like that, but I can't."

Chapter 20

It was already past eight p.m. when the eighteen-wheeler refrigerated truck pulled off the Tomei Highway and let Nakata out in the parking lot of the Fujigawa rest area. Canvas bag and umbrella in hand, he clambered down from the passenger seat to the asphalt.

"Good luck in finding another ride," the driver said, his head sticking out the window. "If you ask around, I'm sure you'll find something."

"Much obliged. Nakata appreciates all your help."

"Take it easy," the driver said, then waved and pulled back onto the highway.

Fu-ji-ga-wa, the driver had said. Nakata had no idea where Fu-ji-ga-wa was, though he did understand he'd left Tokyo and was heading west. No need for a compass or a map to tell him that, he knew it instinctively. Now if only a truck going west would give him a ride.

Nakata was hungry and decided to have a bowl of ramen in the rest area restaurant. The rice balls and chocolate in his bag he wanted to save for an emergency. Not being able to read, it took him a while to figure out how to purchase a meal. Before going into the dining hall you had to buy meal tickets from a vending machine, but he had to have somebody help him read the buttons. "My eyes are bad, so I can't see too well," he told a middle-aged woman, and she inserted the money for him, pushed the right button, and handed him his change. Experience had taught him it was better not to let on that he didn't know how to read. Because when he did, people stared at him like he was some kind of monster.

After his meal, Nakata, umbrella in hand, bag slung over his shoulder, made the rounds of the trucks in the parking lot, asking for a ride. I'm heading west, he explained, and I wonder if you'd be kind enough to give me a ride? But the drivers all took one look at him and shook their heads. An elderly hitchhiker was pretty unusual, and they were naturally wary of anything out of the ordinary. Our company doesn't allow us to pick up hitchhikers, they all said. Sorry.

It had taken a long time to make it from Nakano Ward to the entrance to the Tomei Highway. He'd never been out of Nakano before, and had no idea where the highway was. He had a special pass for the city bus line he could use, but he'd never ridden by himself on the subway or train, where you needed to buy a ticket.

It was just before ten a.m. when he packed a change of clothes, a toilet kit, and some snacks in his bag, carefully put the cash he'd hidden under the tatami in a money belt for safekeeping, and then, the large umbrella in hand, left his apartment. When he asked the city bus driver how he could get to the highway, the man laughed.

"This bus only goes to Shinjuku Station. City buses don't go on the highway. You'll have to take a highway bus."

"Where can I get a highway bus that goes on the *To-mei* Highway?"

"Tokyo Station," the driver replied. "Take this bus to Shinjuku Station, then take a train to Tokyo Station, where you can buy a reserved-seat ticket. The buses there will take you to the Tomei Highway."

Nakata wasn't at all sure what he meant, but went ahead and took the bus as far as Shinjuku. But when he got there he was overwhelmed. The massive station was jammed with people, and he had trouble moving through the crowds. There were so many train lines, too, that he couldn't figure out which one went to Tokyo Station. Since he couldn't read the signs, he asked a few passersby, but their explanations were too fast, too complicated, and full of place-names he didn't recognize. I might as well be talking to Kawamura, Nakata thought to himself. There was always a police box to ask directions at, but he was afraid they'd mistake him for a senile old person and take him into custody, something he'd experienced once before. As he wandered around near the station the exhaust and noise got to him and he started to feel sick. Avoiding the crowded sidewalks, he found a small park set between two high-rise buildings and sat down on a bench.

Nakata was at a complete loss. He sat there, muttering occasionally, rubbing the top of his close-cropped head. There wasn't a cat to be seen in the park. There were plenty of crows, though, squawking down and rummaging through the trash baskets. Nakata looked up at the sky a few times, and from the sun's position could guess the approximate time. Because of all the exhaust, perhaps, the sky was covered in a strange color.

At noon, office workers from the nearby buildings flooded out to eat lunch in the park. Nakata ate the bean-jam buns he'd brought with him, washing them down with hot tea from his thermos. Two young women sat down together on the bench besides his, and he decided to talk to them. How can I get to the To-mei Highway? he asked. They told him the same thing the city bus driver had said. Take the Chuo Line to Tokyo Station, then a Tomei Highway bus.

"Nakata tried that but it didn't work," Nakata admitted. "I've never been out of Nakano Ward before. So I don't know how to take the train. I just know how to ride the city bus. I can't read, so I can't buy a ticket. I took the city bus here, but don't know how to go any farther."

You can't read?! they asked, astonished. He seemed like a harmless enough old man. A nice smile, dressed neatly. Carrying an umbrella on such a fine day like this was a bit odd, but he didn't appear to be homeless. A pleasant face, especially those bright-looking eyes.

"You really mean to say you've never been outside Nakano Ward?" the girl with black hair asked.

"Yes. I've tried not to ever go out of it. If Nakata got lost, there's nobody who'd come looking for me."

"And you can't read," said the other girl, the one with dyed brownish hair.

"That's right. I can't read at all. I can understand simple numbers, but can't add."

"Hmm. I imagine it would be hard for you to take a train."

"Yes, it's very hard. I can't buy a ticket."

"If we had time we could take you to the station and make sure you get on the right train, but we have to get back to work soon. I'm really sorry."

"No, no need to apologize. I'll figure it out somehow."

"I've got it!" the girl with black hair exclaimed. "Didn't Togeguchi over in sales say he had to go to Yokohama today?"

"Yes, now that you mention it. He'd help out if we asked him. He's a little on the gloomy side, but not a bad guy, really," the brown-haired girl said.

"Since you can't read, maybe it'd be better to hitchhike," the black-haired girl said.

"Hitchhike?"

"Ask for a ride from somebody. Mostly it ends up being rides with long-haul truckers. Regular cars don't pick up hitchhikers much."

"Nakata's not sure what *long-haul truckers* are."

"As long as you go there it'll work out. I hitchhiked once when I was in college. Truck drivers are all nice guys."

"How far are you going on the Tomei Highway?" the brown-haired girl asked.

"Nakata doesn't know," Nakata replied.

"You don't know?"

"I'll know when I get there. So I'll start out going west on the *Tomei* Highway. After that I'll think about where I'll go. Anyhow, I have to go west."

The two girls looked at each other, but Nakata's words were strangely persuasive and they found themselves feeling kindly toward the old man. They finished their lunches, tossed their empty cans in the trash, and stood up.

"Why don't you come with us?" the black-haired girl said. "We'll figure something out."

Nakata followed them into a nearby building. He'd never been in such a large building before. The two girls had him sit at a bench next to the reception desk, then spoke with the receptionist and told Nakata to wait there for a while. They disappeared into one of the elevator banks in the lobby. As Nakata sat there, umbrella and canvas bag in hand, office workers streamed back inside after their lunch hour. Another scene he'd never laid eyes on before in his life. As if by mutual consent, all the people were well dressed—ties, shiny briefcases, and high heels, everyone rushing off in the same direction. For the life of him Nakata couldn't understand what so many people like this could possibly be up to.

After a time the two girls were back, acccompanied by a gangly young man wearing a white shirt and striped tie.

"This is Mr. Togeguchi," the brown-haired girl said. "He's about to drive to Yokohama. And he said he'll take you with him. He'll drop you at the Kohoku parking lot on the Tomei Highway, and hopefully you'll be able to find another ride there. Just go around telling people you want to go west, and when someone gives you a ride be sure to buy them a meal when you stop somewhere. Do you follow?"

"But do you have enough money for that?" the black-haired one asked.

"Yes, I have enough."

"Mr. Nakata's a friend of ours, so be nice to him," the brown-haired girl said to Togeguchi.

"If you'll be nice to me," the young man replied timidly.

"One of these days . . . ," the black-haired one said.

As they were saying good-bye, the girls said, "Here's a little going-away present. For when you get hungry." They handed him some rice balls and a bar of chocolate they'd bought at a convenience store.

"I don't know how to thank you enough for all you've done," Nakata said. "I'll be praying that good things happen to you both."

"I hope your prayers come true," the brown-haired one said as her companion giggled.

The young man, Togeguchi, had Nakata sit in the passenger seat of the Hi-Ace van, then drove down the Metropolitan Highway and onto the Tomei. The roads were backed up, so the two of them talked about all kinds of things as they inched along. Togeguchi was bashful, and didn't say much at first, but after he got used to having Nakata with him he started talking, to the point where it wound up less a conversation than a running monologue. There were a lot of things he wanted to talk about, and he found it easy to open up to a stranger like Nakata, whom he'd never see again. He explained that he'd broken up with his fiancée a few months ago. She'd had another boyfriend she'd been secretly seeing all the while. He said he didn't get along well with his bosses at work and was thinking of quitting. His parents had gotten divorced when he was in junior high, and his mother soon got remarried to some sleazeball. He'd lent money from his savings to a friend who didn't give any indication he'd be repaying him anytime soon. And the college student who lived in the apartment next door blasted his music so loud he couldn't get much sleep.

Nakata listened diligently, chiming in at appropriate points, tossing in an occasional opinion of his own. By the time their car pulled into the Kohoku parking area Nakata knew just about everything there was to know about the young man. There was a lot he didn't understand, but he did see the big picture of Togeguchi's life, namely that here was a poor young guy who, while trying to live an upright life, had his share of problems.

"Nakata's much obliged to you," he said. "Thank you so very much for the ride."

"I enjoyed it. Thanks to you, Mr. Nakata, I feel completely relaxed now. I've never talked to anyone like this before, and I'm happy I could tell you everything. I hope I haven't bored you with all my problems."

"No, not at all. Nakata's very happy, too, to be able to talk with you. I'm sure good things are going to happen to you, Mr. Togeguchi."

The young man took a telephone card from his wallet and handed it to Nakata. "Please take this card. My company makes them. Consider it a going-away present. I wish I could give you something better."

"Thank you very much," Nakata said, and carefully tucked it into his wallet. He had no one to phone, and didn't know how to use the card anyway, but he thought it was more polite to accept it. By now it was three p.m.

It took another hour to find someone willing to take him as far as Fujigawa. The trucker was a beefy man in his mid-forties, with arms like logs and a jutting belly, who was hauling fresh fish in a refrigerated truck.

"I hope you don't mind the fish smell," the driver said.

"Fish are one of Nakata's favorites," Nakata replied.

The driver laughed. "You're a strange one, aren't you."

"People tell me that sometimes."

"I happen to like the strange ones," the driver said. "People who look normal and live a normal life—they're the ones you have to watch out for."

"Is that so?"

"Believe me, that's how it goes. In my opinion, anyway."

"Nakata doesn't have many opinions. Though I do like eel."

"Well, that's an opinion. That you like eel."

"Eel is an opinion?"

"Sure, saying you like eel's an opinion."

Thus the two of them drove to Fujigawa. The driver said his name was Hagita.

"So, Mr. Nakata, what do you think about the way the world's going?" he asked.

"I'm very sorry, I'm not bright, so I have no idea at all about that," Nakata said.

"Having your own opinion and not being very bright are two different things."

"But Mr. Hagita, not being very bright means you can't think about things."

"But you did say you like eel."

"Yes, eel is one of Nakata's favorites."

"That's a connection, see?"

"Um."

"Do you like chicken and egg over rice?"

"Yes, that's one of Nakata's favorites too."

"Well, there's a connection there, too," Hagita said. "You build up relationships like that one after another and before you know it you have meaning. The more connections, the deeper the meaning. Doesn't matter if it's eel, or rice bowls, or grilled fish, whatever. Get it?"

"No, I still don't understand. Does food make connections between things?"

"Not just food. Streetcars, the emperor, whatever."

"But I don't ride streetcars."

"That's fine. Look—what I'm getting at is no matter who or what you're dealing with, people build up meaning between themselves and the things around them. The important thing is whether this comes about naturally or not. Being bright has nothing to do with it. What matters is that you see things with your own eyes."

"You're very bright, Mr. Hagita."

Hagita let out a loud laugh. "It isn't a question of intelligence. I'm not all that bright, I just have my own way of thinking. That's why people get disgusted with me. They accuse me of always bringing up things that are better left alone. If you try to use your head to think about things, people don't want to have anything to do with you."

"Nakata still doesn't understand, but are you saying that there's a link between liking eel and liking chicken and egg over rice?"

"You could put it that way, I suppose. There's always going to be a connection between you, Mr. Nakata, and the things you deal with. Just like there's a connection between eel and rice bowls. And as the web of these connections spreads out, a relationship between you, Mr. Nakata, and capitalists and the proletariat naturally develops."

"*Pro-le*-what?"

"The *proletariat*," Mr. Hagita said, taking his hands off the steering wheel and making a wide gesture. To Nakata they looked as massive as baseball gloves. "The people who work hard, who earn their bread through the sweat of their brow, those are the proletariat. On the other hand you've got your guys who sit on their duffs, not lifting a finger, giving orders to other people and getting a hundred times my salary. Those are your capitalists."

"I don't know about people who are capitalists. I'm poor, and I don't know anybody great like that. The greatest person I know is the Governor of Tokyo. Is the Governor a capitalist?"

"Yeah, I suppose. Governors are more likely to be capitalists' lap-dogs, though."

"The Governor is a dog?" Nakata remembered the huge black dog who took him to Johnnie Walker's house, and that ominous figure and the Governor overlapped in his mind.

"The world's swarming with those kind of dogs. Pawns of the capitalists."

"*Pawns?*"

"Like *paws*, with an 'n'."

"Are there any capitalist cats?" Nakata asked.

Hagita burst out laughing. "Boy, you *are* different, Mr. Nakata! But I like your style. *Capitalist cats!* That's a good one. A very unique opinion you have there."

"Mr. Hagita?"

"Yeah?"

"I'm poor and received a *sub city* every month from the Governor. Was this the wrong thing to do?"

"How much do you get every month?"

Nakata told him the amount.

Hagita shook his head disgustedly. "Pretty damn hard to get by on so little."

"That's not true, because Nakata doesn't use much money. Besides the *sub city*, I get money by helping people find their lost cats."

"No kidding? A professional cat-finder?" Hagita said, impressed. "You're an amazing guy, I have to say."

"Actually, I'm able to talk with cats," Nakata said. "I can understand what they say. That helps me locate the missing ones."

Hagita nodded. "I wouldn't put it past you."

"But not long ago I found out I couldn't talk with cats anymore. I wonder why."

"Things change every day, Mr. Nakata. With each new dawn it's not the same world as the day before. And you're not the same person you were, either. You get what I'm saying?"

"Yes."

"Connections change too. Who's the capitalist, who's the proletarian. Who's on the right, who's on the left. The information revolution, stock options, floating assets, occupational restructuring, multinational corporations—what's good, what's bad. Boundaries between things are disappearing all the time. Maybe that's why you can't speak to cats anymore."

"The difference between right and left Nakata understands. This is right, and this is left. Correct?"

"You got it," Hagita agreed. "That's all you need to know."

The last thing they did together was have a meal in a rest area restaurant. Hagita ordered two orders of eel, and when Nakata insisted on paying, to thank him for the ride, the driver shook his head emphatically.

"No way," he said. "I'd never let you use the pittance they give you for a subsidy to feed me."

"Much obliged, then. Thank you for such a treat," Nakata said, happy to accept his kindness.

Nakata spent an hour at the Fujigawa rest area asking drivers for a ride, but couldn't find anyone willing to take him. He didn't start to panic, though, or get depressed. In his mind, time passed very slowly. Or barely at all.

He went outside for some air and wandered around. The sky was cloudless, the surface of the moon clearly visible. Nakata strolled around the parking lot, which was filled with countless huge trucks, like giant beasts lined up shoulder to shoulder, resting. Some of the trucks had at least twenty giant tires, each one as tall as a man. So many trucks, all racing down the highway so late at night—what could they possibly be carrying inside? Nakata couldn't imagine. If he could read the writing on the sides of the trucks, he wondered, would he be able to figure it out?

After about an hour he spotted ten or so motorcycles parked in a corner of the lot where there weren't many cars. A clump of young men stood nearby in a circle, looking at something and yelling. Intrigued, Nakata approached them. Maybe they'd discovered something unusual?

When he got closer he saw that they had surrounded someone lying on the ground and were punching, kicking, and generally trying their best to hurt him. Most of the men were unarmed, though one of them had a chain in his hand. Another held a black stick that looked like a policeman's baton. They wore unbuttoned short-sleeved shirts, some in T-shirts, others in running shirts, most of them with hair dyed blond or brown, some with tattoos on their arms. The young man they were beating and kicking was dressed much the same.

As Nakata approached, tapping the asphalt surface with the tip of his umbrella, a couple of the men turned around and glared at him. They relaxed when they saw it was just some harmless old man. "Why don't you beat it, Pops," one of them growled.

Unperturbed, Nakata walked over even closer. The man on the ground seemed to be bleeding from his mouth. "Blood's coming out," Nakata said. "He might die."

Caught off guard, the men didn't react right away.

"Maybe we should kill you too, while we're at it," the one with the chain said. "Killing one or two—no skin off my nose."

"You can't kill someone for no reason," Nakata insisted.

"*You can't kill someone for no reason,*" one of them mimicked, and his friends laughed.

"We got our reasons, pal," another man said. "And it ain't got nothin' to do with you whether we kill him or not. So take your worthless umbrella and hit the road, before it starts raining."

The man on the ground started crawling forward, and a young man with a shaved head came over and kicked him hard in the ribs with his work boots.

Nakata closed his eyes. He could feel something welling up inside him, beyond his control. He felt slightly nauseous. The memory of stabbing Johnnie Walker suddenly came back to him. His hand still remembered what it felt like to plunge a knife into a man's chest. *Connections.* Could this be one of those connections that Mr. Hagita was talking about? *Eel = knife = Johnnie Walker?* The men's voices sounded distorted, and he couldn't tell them apart anymore. Their voices blended together with the ceaseless drone of tires from the high-way to make a strange tone. His heart surged blood to his extremities as night enveloped him.

Nakata looked up at the sky, then slowly opened his umbrella and held it over him. Very carefully he took a few steps backward, opening a space between himself and the gang. He looked around, then took a few more steps back.

The young men laughed when they saw this. "Hey, look at the cool old guy!" one of them said. "He's actually using his umbrella!"

But they didn't laugh for long. Suddenly, unfamiliar greasy objects began to rain down from the sky, striking the ground at their feet with a weird slap. The young men stopped kicking their prey and looked up at the sky. There weren't any clouds, but things were definitely falling one after another from a spot in the sky. At first in dribs and drabs, then gradually more and more fell, until before they knew it they were caught in a downpour. The objects pelting down from the sky were little black lumps about an inch and a half long. In the lights of the parking lot it looked like slick black snow falling on the men's shoulders, arms, and necks and sticking there. They desperately tried to yank the objects off, but couldn't.

"*Leeches!*" someone yelled.

As if given a signal, the men all shouted and raced across the parking lot to the restrooms. One of them, a young blond man, was knocked to the ground by a car he'd run in front of. He jumped up, slammed his fist on the hood of the car, and loudly cursed the driver. That was all, though, and he soon limped away toward the restrooms.

The leeches rained down hard for a time, then tapered off and stopped. Nakata folded up his umbrella, brushed off the leeches, and went over to see how the injured man was doing. A mound of the slimy creatures squirmed all around, so he couldn't get very close, and the man on the ground was buried in them. Looking closely, Nakata could see that he was bleeding from cut eyelids, and some of his teeth looked broken. Nakata knew this was too much for him to handle by himself, so he hurried back to the restaurant and told one of the employees that a man was lying in the parking lot, hurt. "You'd better call the police, or else he might die," he said.

Not long after this Nakata found a truck driver willing to give him a ride as far as Kobe. A sleepy-looking man in his mid-twenties, not very tall, with a ponytail, a pierced ear, and a Chunichi Dragons baseball team cap, he sat there in the restaurant, smoking and flipping through a comic book. A gaudy aloha shirt and oversize Nikes completed his wardrobe. He tapped his cigarette ashes into the leftover broth in his bowl of ramen, stared hard at Nakata, then gave a reluctant nod. "Yeah, okay. You can ride with me. You kind of remind me of my grandpa. The way you look, or maybe how you talk, kind of off the point. . . . At the end my grandpa got senile and died. A few years ago."

He went on to explain that they should get to Kobe by morning. He was delivering furniture to a department store warehouse there. As he pulled his truck out of the parking lot, they passed a car accident. A couple of patrol cars were already at the scene, red lights flashing, and a policeman with a signal light was directing traffic. It didn't appear to be much of an accident. A few cars had collided, the side of a minivan was dented, a car's taillight broken.

The truck driver stuck his head out the window and exchanged a few words with a patrolman, then rolled up his window. "He said a pile of leeches fell from the sky," he said, unmoved. "They got crushed by cars, the road got all slippery, and some drivers lost control. So go slow and take it easy, he told me. On top of that some local gang of bikers beat up somebody. Leeches and bikers—what a weird combination. Keeps the cops busy, at least."

He drove carefully toward the exit. Even going slow the truck slipped a couple of times, and the driver straightened it out with a subtle twist of the wheel. "Man, it really looks like a whole bunch fell down, and it's damn slippery. But, boy—leeches, that's pretty gross. Ever had a leech stick to you?"

"No, as far as Nakata can remember, I don't think so," Nakata responded.

"I was brought up in the mountains of Gifu, and it happened to me lots of times. I'd be walking in the woods and they'd fall down from the trees. Go wading in the streams and they'd stick to your legs. I know a thing or two about leeches, believe me. Once they get stuck on you they're hard to pull off. If you pull off a big sucker your skin comes off and you'll have a scar. So the best thing is to burn 'em off. Awful things, the way they suck your blood. And once they're filled up they get all soft and mushy. Pretty gross, huh?"

"Yes, it certainly is," Nakata agreed.

"But leeches aren't supposed to fall down from the sky into some rest area parking lot. I never heard of anything so stupid! The guys around here don't know the first thing about leeches. Leeches don't fall from the sky, now do they?"

Nakata was silent and didn't respond.

"A few years back a huge number of millipedes appeared all at once in Yamanashi Prefecture, and cars were slipping everywhere. Just like this, the road got all slippery and there were a lot of accidents. They got all over the tracks and the trains couldn't run either. But even millipedes aren't going to rain down from the sky. They crawl out from somewhere. Anybody can see that."

"A long time ago I lived in Yamanashi. During the war."

"No kidding," the driver said. "Which war was that?"

Chapter 21

SCULPTOR KOICHI TAMURA STABBED TO DEATH
Found in Study, Floor a Sea of Blood

The world-renowned sculptor Koichi Tamura was found dead on the afternoon of the 30th in the study in his home in Nogata, Nakano Ward. The body was discovered by a female housekeeper. Mr. Tamura was found facedown, nude, covered in blood. There were signs of a struggle and the death is being treated as a homicide. The weapon used was a knife from the kitchen discovered beside the body.

The police estimate the time of death as the evening of the 28th, and since Mr. Tamura lived alone the body was only discovered two days later. Mr. Tamura suffered several deep stab wounds to the chest from the sharp steak knife, and it is believed he died almost instantly from massive loss of blood from injuries to the heart and lungs. Several ribs were also broken from what appears to be massive blunt force. The police have not announced having found any fingerprints or anything left behind at the scene. It also appears that there were no witnesses to the crime.

Since the house was undisturbed, and valuables and a wallet near the scene were not taken, police view the crime as a personal vendetta. Mr. Tamura's home is in a quiet residential neighborhood, but no one heard anything at the time of the murder, and neighbors were shocked at the news. Mr. Tamura had little to do with his neighbors and lived quietly, and no one noticed anything out of the ordinary around the time of the incident.

Mr. Tamura lived with his son (15), but according to the

housekeeper the son hasn't been seen in some ten days. The son has also been absent from his junior high and police are tracing his whereabouts.

In addition to his residence, Mr. Tamura had an office and studio in Musashino City, and according to his secretary, until the day before the murder he was working on a new piece of sculpture as usual. On the day of the incident, there was a matter she had to contact him about, but every time she phoned his residence she got his message machine.

Mr. Tamura was born in Kokubunji, Tokyo. He entered the Dept. of Sculpture at Tokyo Arts Institute, and while still a student completed many innovative pieces that became the talk of the art world. His chief theme was the human subconscious, and his sculptures, which were in a unique style that challenged the conventional, were internationally acclaimed. His best-known work was his major "Labyrinth" series, which explored, through an uninhibited expression of the imagination, the beauty and inspiration found in the meandering contours of labyrinths. He was at present a visiting professor at an art institute, and two years ago, at the exhibition of his work at the Museum of Modern Art in New York. . . .

I stop reading at this point. There's a photo of our front gate, and one of my father in younger days, and they give the newspaper an ominous feeling. I fold it twice and put it on top of the table. Still sitting on the bed, I don't say anything, just press my fingertips against my eyes. A dull sound, at a constant frequency, pounds in my ears. I try shaking my head to get rid of it, but it won't go away.

I'm in my room in the library. It's seven p.m. Oshima and I have just shut the place up for the night, and a while ago Miss Saeki drove off in her Volkswagen Golf. It's just me and Oshima in the library now. And that irritating pounding in my ears.

"This paper's from two days ago. The article came out while you were up in the mountains. When I saw it I thought maybe this Koichi Tamura might be your father. A lot of the details fit. I should've shown it to you yesterday, but I wanted to wait until you got settled in."

I nod, still pressing my eyes. Oshima doesn't say anything more.

"I didn't kill him, you know."

"I know that," Oshima says. "On the day of the murder you were here at the library, reading until evening. You wouldn't have had enough time to go back to Tokyo, murder your father, and then get back to Takamatsu. It's impossible."

But I wasn't so sure. I did the math and figured out he was murdered the same night I woke up with my shirt covered in blood.

"But the paper does say the police are trying to locate you. As an important witness."

I nod.

"If you go to the police and prove to them you have a firm alibi, it'd make things a lot easier than trying to run around avoiding them. Of course I'll back you up."

"But if I do that, they'll take me back to Tokyo."

"I would think so. I mean, you still have to finish junior high — that's the law. You can't just go anywhere you want to at your age. The law says you still need a guardian."

I shake my head. "I don't want to explain anything to anybody. And I don't want to go back home to Tokyo, or back to school."

Quiet for a time, Oshima looks at me intently. "That's something you'll have to decide for yourself," he finally says in a calm tone. "I think you have a right to live however you want. Whether you're fifteen or fifty-one, what does it matter? But unfortunately society doesn't agree. So let's say you don't explain anything to anybody. You'll be constantly on the run from the police and society. Your life will be pretty harsh. You're only fifteen, with your whole life ahead of you. You're okay with that?"

I don't say anything.

Oshima picks up the paper and scans the article again. "According to this you're your father's only relative."

"I have a mother and an older sister," I explain, "but they left a long time ago, and I don't know where they are. Even if I did, I seriously doubt they'd come to the funeral."

"Well, if you're not there, I wonder who's going to take care of everything. The funeral, his business affairs."

"Like it said in the paper, he has a secretary at his office who's in charge of everything. She knows about his business, so I'm sure she can handle it. I don't want anything of his handed down to me. The house, his estate, whatever—they can get rid of it however they want." The only thing he's handed down to me, I think, are my genes.

"Correct me if I'm wrong," Oshima says, "but you don't seem too sad your father was murdered."

"No, I do feel sad. He's my father, after all. But what I really regret is that he didn't die sooner. I know that's a terrible thing to say. . . ."

Oshima shakes his head. "No problem. Now more than ever you have the right to be honest."

"Well, I think . . ." My voice seems weak, lacking in authority. Unsure of where they're headed, my words are sucked into the void. Oshima comes over and sits down next to me.

"All kinds of things are happening to me," I begin. "Some I chose, some I didn't. I don't know how to tell one from the other anymore. What I mean is, it feels like everything's been decided in advance— that I'm following a path somebody else has already mapped out for me. It doesn't matter how much I think things over, how much effort I put into it. In fact, the harder I try, the more I lose my sense of who I am. It's like my identity's an orbit that I've strayed far away from, and that really hurts. But more than that, it scares me. Just thinking about it makes me flinch."

Oshima reaches out to touch my shoulder. I can feel the warmth of his hand. "For the sake of argument, let's say all your choices and all your effort are destined to be a waste. You're still very much yourself and nobody else. And you're forging ahead, as *yourself*. So relax."

I raise my head and look at him. He sounds so convincing. "Why do you think that?"

"Because there's irony involved."

"Irony?"

Oshima gazes deep into my eyes. "Listen, Kafka. What you're experiencing now is the motif of many Greek tragedies. Man doesn't choose fate. Fate chooses man. That's the basic worldview of Greek drama. And the sense of tragedy—according to Aristotle—comes, ironically enough, not from the protagonist's weak points but from his good qualities. Do you know what I'm getting at? People are drawn deeper into tragedy not by their defects but by their *virtues*. Sophocles' *Oedipus Rex* being a great example. Oedipus is drawn into tragedy not because of laziness or stupidity, but because of his courage and honesty. So an inevitable irony results."

"But it's a hopeless situation."

"That depends," Oshima says. "Sometimes it is. But irony deepens a person, helps them mature. It's the entrance to salvation on a higher plane, to a place where you can find a more universal kind of hope. That's why people enjoy reading Greek tragedies even now, why they're considered prototypical classics. I'm repeating myself, but everything in life is metaphor. People don't usually kill their father and sleep with their mother, right? In other words, we accept irony through a device called metaphor. And through that we grow and become deeper human beings."

I don't say anything. I'm too involved in thinking about my own situation.

"How many people know you're in Takamatsu?" Oshima asks.

I shake my head. "Coming here was my own idea, so I don't think anybody else knows."

"Then you'd better lay low in the library for a while. Don't go out to work at the reception area. I don't think the police will be able to track you down, but if things get sticky you can always hide out at the cabin."

I look at Oshima. "If I hadn't met you, I don't think I would've made it. There's nobody else who can help me."

Oshima smiles. He takes his hand away from my shoulder and stares at his hand. "That's not true. If you hadn't met me, I'm sure you would've found another path to take. I don't know why, but I'm certain of it. I just get that feeling about you." He stands up and brings over another newspaper from the desk. "By the way, this article was in the paper the day before the other one. I remember it because it was so unusual. Maybe it's just coincidence, but it took place near your house."

FISH RAIN FROM THE SKY!
2,000 Sardines and Mackerel in Nakano Ward
Shopping District

At around 6 p.m. on the evening of the 29th, residents of the *-chome district of Nakano Ward were startled when some 2,000 sardines and mackerel rained down from the sky. Two housewives shopping in the neighborhood market received slight facial injuries when struck by the falling fish, but no other injuries were reported. At the time of the incident it was

sunny, with no clouds or wind. Many of the fish were still
alive and jumped about on the pavement. . . .

I finish reading the article and pass the paper back to Oshima. The re-
porter speculated about several possible causes of the incident, though
none of them are very convincing. The police are investigating the
possibility it involved theft and someone playing a kind of practical
joke. The Weather Service reported that there weren't any atmo-
spheric conditions present that might have led to fish raining from
the sky. And from the Ministry of Agriculture, Forestry, and Fisheries
spokesman, still no comment.

"Do you have any idea why this happened?" Oshima asks me.

I shake my head. I don't have a clue.

"The day after your father was murdered, close to where it happened, two thousand sardines and mackerel fall from the sky. Just
coincidence?"

"I suppose so."

"The newspaper also says that at the Fujigawa rest area on the
Tomei Highway, late at night on the very same day, a mess of leeches
fell from the sky in one small spot. Several fender benders resulted,
they say. Apparently the leeches were quite large. No one can explain
why leeches would rain from the sky. It was a clear night, not a cloud
in the sky. No idea why this happened, either?"

Again I shake my head.

Oshima folds up the newspaper and says, "Which leaves us with
the fact that strange, inexplicable events are happening one after the
other. Maybe it's just a series of coincidences, but it still bothers me.
There's something about it I can't shake."

"Maybe it's a metaphor?" I venture.

"Maybe . . . But sardines and mackerel and leeches raining down
from the sky? What kind of metaphor is *that*?"

In the silence I try putting into words something I haven't been
able to say for a long time. "You know something? A few years back my
father had a prophecy about me."

"A prophecy?"

"I've never told anybody this before. I figured nobody'd believe me."

Oshima doesn't say a word. His silence, though, encourages me.

"More like a curse than a prophecy, I guess. My father told me this over and over. Like he was chiseling each word into my brain." I take a deep breath and check once more what it is I have to say. Not that I really need to check it—it's always there, banging about in my head, whether I examine it or not. But I have to weigh the words one more time. And this is what I say: "*Someday you will murder your father and be with your mother,* he said."

Once I've spoken this, put this thought into concrete words, a hollow feeling grabs hold of me. And inside that hollow, my heart pounds out a vacant, metallic rhythm.

Expression unchanged, Oshima gazes at me for a long time.

"So he said that someday you would kill your father with your own hands, that you would sleep with your mother."

I nod a few more times.

"The same prophecy made about Oedipus. Though of course you knew that."

I nod. "But that's not all. There's an extra ingredient he threw into the mix. I have a sister six years older than me, and my father said I would sleep with *her*, too."

"Your father actually said this to you?"

"Yeah. I was still in elementary school then, and didn't know what he meant by 'be with.' It was only a few years later that I caught on."

Oshima doesn't say anything.

"My father told me there was nothing I could do to escape this fate. That prophecy is like a timing device buried inside my genes, and nothing can ever change it. *I will kill my father and be with my mother and sister.*"

Oshima stays silent for quite some time, like he's inspecting each word I'd spoken, one by one, examining them for clues to what this is all about. "Why in the world would your father tell you such an awful thing?" he finally asks.

"I have no idea. He didn't explain it beyond that," I say, shaking my head. "Maybe he wanted revenge on his wife and daughter who left him. Wanted to punish them, perhaps. Through me."

"Even if it meant hurting you?"

I nod. "To my father I'm probably nothing more than one of his sculptures. Something he could make or break as he sees fit."

"That's a pretty twisted way of thinking," Oshima says.

"In our home *everything* was twisted. And when everything's twisted, what's normal ends up looking weird too. I've known this for a long time, but I was a child. Where else could I go?"

"I've seen your father's works a number of times," Oshima replies. "He's a wonderful sculptor. His pieces are original, provocative, powerful. Uncompromising, is how I'd put it. Most definitely the real thing."

"Maybe so. But the dregs left over from creating these he spread everywhere, like a poison you can't escape. My father polluted everything he touched, damaged everyone around him. I don't know if he did it because he wanted to. Maybe he *had* to. Maybe it's just part of his makeup. Anyhow, I get the feeling he was connected to something very unusual. Do you have any idea what I mean?"

"Yeah, I think so," Oshima says. "Something beyond good and evil. The source of power, you might call it."

"And half my genes are made up of that. Maybe that's why my mother abandoned me. Maybe she wanted to cut herself off from me because I was born from this terrible source. Since I was polluted."

Oshima lightly presses his fingertips against his temples as he mulls this over. He narrows his eyes and stares at me. "Is there any chance he's not your biological father?"

I shake my head. "A few years ago we got tested at a hospital. The two of us had a DNA check done on our blood. No doubt about it—biologically we're father and son a hundred percent. They showed me the results of the tests."

"Very cautious of him."

"I guess he wanted me to know I was one of the works he'd created. Something he'd finished and signed."

Oshima's fingers stay pressed to his temples. "But your father's prophecy didn't come true, did it? You didn't murder him. You were here in Takamatsu when it happened. Somebody else killed him in Tokyo."

Silently I spread my hands out in front of me and stare at them. Those hands that, in the darkness of night, had been covered with blood. "I'm not so sure of that," I tell him.

And I proceed to tell him everything. About how that night, on my way back to the hotel, I'd lost consciousness for a few hours. About waking up in the woods behind the shrine, my shirt sticky with somebody's blood. About washing the blood off in the restroom. About how several hours had been erased from my memory. To save time I don't go into how I stayed overnight at Sakura's. Oshima asks the occasional question, and files away the details in his head. But he doesn't voice any opinions.

"I have no idea how that blood got all over me, or whose blood it could be. It's a complete blank," I tell him. "But maybe I did kill my father with my own hands, not metaphorically. I really get the feeling that I *did*. Like you said, I was in Takamatsu that day—I definitely didn't go to Tokyo. But *In dreams begin responsibilities*, right?"

Oshima nods. "Yeats."

"So maybe I murdered him through a dream," I say. "Maybe I went through some special dream circuit or something and killed him."

"To you that might feel like the truth, but nobody's going to grill you about your poetic responsibilities. Certainly not the police. Nobody can be in two places at once. It's a scientific fact—Einstein and all that—and the law accepts that principle."

"But I'm not talking about science or law here."

"What you're talking about, Kafka," Oshima says, "is just a theory. A bold, surrealistic theory, to be sure, but one that belongs in a science fiction novel."

"Of course it's just a theory. I know that. I don't think anybody else is going to believe such a stupid thing. But my father always used to say that without counterevidence to refute a theory, science would never progress. *A theory is a battlefield in your head*—that was his pet phrase. And right now I can't think of any evidence to counter my hypothesis."

Oshima is silent. And I can't think of anything else to say.

"Anyway," Oshima finally says, "that's why you ran away to Shikoku. To escape your father's curse."

I nod, and point to the folded-up newspaper. "But it looks like there's no escape."

Distance won't solve anything, the boy named Crow says.

"Well, you definitely need a hiding place," Oshima says. "Beyond that there's not much I can say."

I suddenly realize how exhausted I am. I lean against Oshima, and he wraps his arms around me.

I push my face up against his flat chest. "Oshima, I don't want to do those things. I don't want to kill my father. Or be with my mother and sister."

"Of course you don't," he replies, running his fingers through my short hair. "How could you?"

"Not even in dreams."

"Or in a metaphor," Oshima adds. "Or in an allegory, or an analogy." He pauses and then says, "If you don't mind, I'll stay with you here tonight. I can sleep on the chair."

But I turn him down. I think I'm better off alone for a while, I tell him.

Oshima brushes the strands of hair off his forehead. After hesitating a bit he says, "I know I'm a hopeless, damaged, homosexual woman, and if that's what's bothering you . . ."

"No," I say, "that's not it at all. I just need some time alone to think. Too many things have happened all at once. That's all."

Oshima writes down a phone number on a memo pad. "In the middle of the night, if you feel like talking to anybody, call this number. Don't hesitate, okay? I'm a light sleeper anyway." I thank him.

That's the night I see a ghost.

Chapter 22

The truck Nakata was riding in arrived in Kobe just after five in the morning. It was light out, but the warehouse was still closed and their freight couldn't be unloaded. They parked the truck in a broad street near the harbor and took a nap. The young driver stretched out on the backseat—his usual spot for napping—and was soon snoring away contentedly. His snores sometimes woke Nakata up, but each time he quickly dropped back into a comfortable sleep. Insomnia was one phenomenon Nakata had never experienced.

A little before eight the young driver sat up and gave a big yawn. "Hey, Gramps, ya hungry?" he asked. He was busy shaving with an electric razor, using the rearview mirror.

"Now that you mention it, yes, Nakata does feel a little hungry."

"Well, let's go grab some breakfast."

From the time they left Fujigawa to their arrival in Kobe, Nakata had spent most of the time sleeping. The young driver barely said a word the whole time, just drove on, listening to a late-night radio show. Occasionally he'd sing along to a song, none of which Nakata had ever heard before. He wondered if they were even in Japanese, since he could barely understand any of the lyrics, just the occasional word. From his bag he took out the chocolate and rice balls he'd gotten from the two young office girls in Shinjuku, and shared them.

The driver had chain-smoked, saying it helped keep him awake, so Nakata's clothes were reeking of smoke by the time they arrived in Kobe.

Bag and umbrella in hand, Nakata clambered down from the truck.

"You better leave that stuff in the truck," the driver said. "We're not going far, and we'll come right back after we eat."

"Yes, you're quite right, but Nakata feels better having them."

The young man frowned. "Whatever. It's not like *I'm* lugging them around. It's up to you."

"Much obliged."

"My name's Hoshino, by the way. Spelled the same as the former manager of the Chunichi Dragons. We're not related, though."

"Mr. Hoshino, is it? Very glad to meet you. My name is Nakata."

"Come on—I knew that already," Hoshino said.

He knew the neighborhood and strode off down the street, Nakata almost having to trot to keep up. They wound up in a small diner down a back street, seated among other truck drivers and stevedores from the docks. Not a single necktie in sight. All of them were intently shoveling in their breakfasts like they were filling up a gas tank. The place was filled with the clatter of dishes, the waitress yelling out orders, the morning NHK news on the TV buzzing in the corner.

Hoshino pointed to the menu taped to the wall. "Just order whatever you want, Gramps. The food's cheap here, and pretty good."

"All right," Nakata said, and did as he was told, staring at the menu until he remembered he couldn't read. "I'm sorry, Mr. Hoshino, but I'm not very bright and can't read."

"Is that right?" Hoshino said, amazed. "Can't read? That's pretty rare these days. But that's okay. I'm having the grilled fish and omelette— why don't you get the same?"

"That sounds good. Grilled fish and omelettes are some of Nakata's favorites."

"Glad to hear it."

"I enjoy eel a lot, too."

"Yeah? I like eel myself. But eel's not something you have in the morning, is it."

"That's right. And Nakata had eel last night, when Mr. Hagita bought some for me."

"Glad to hear it," Hoshino said again. "Two orders of the grilled fish set plus omelettes!" he yelled out to the waitress. "And supersize one of the rices, okay?"

"Two grilled fish sets, plus omelettes! One rice supersize!" the waitress called loudly to the cooks.

"Isn't it kind of a pain, not being able to read?" Hoshino asked.

"Yes, sometimes I have trouble because I can't read. As long as I stay in Nakano Ward in Tokyo it's not so bad, but if I go somewhere else, like now, it's very hard for me."

"I guess so. Kobe's pretty far from Nakano."

"Nakata doesn't know north and south. All I know is left and right. So I get lost, and can't buy tickets, either."

"Incredible you were able to get this far."

"Many people were kind enough to help me. You're one of them, Mr. Hoshino. I don't know how to thank you."

"That must be tough, though, not being able to read. My grandad was pretty senile, but he could still read well enough."

"I'm especially dumb."

"Is everybody in your family like that?"

"No, they aren't. My older brother is a *depart mint* head at a place called *Itoh-chew*, and my younger brother works at an office called *Em-i-tee-i*."

"Wow," Hoshino said. "Pretty elite bunch. So you're the only one who's a bit off, huh?"

"Yes, Nakata's the only one who had an accident and isn't bright. That's why I'm always being told not to go out too much and cause any trouble for my brothers, nieces, and nephews."

"Yeah, I guess most people would find it kind of awkward to have someone like you show up."

"I don't understand difficult things, but I know that as long as I stay in Nakano Ward I don't get lost. The Governor helped me out, and I got along well with cats. Once a month I got my hair cut and every once in a while I'd eat eel. But after Johnnie Walker, Nakata couldn't stay in Nakano anymore."

"Johnnie Walker?"

"That's right. He has boots and a tall black hat, and a vest and walking stick. He collects cats to get their souls."

"You don't say . . . ," Hoshino said. "I don't have much patience with long stories. So anyway, something happened and you left Nakano, right?"

"That's right. I left Nakano."

"So where are you headed?"

"Nakata doesn't know yet. But after we got here I knew I had to go across a bridge. A big bridge near here."

"Ah, so you're going to Shikoku."

"I'm very sorry, Mr. Hoshino, but I don't know geography very well. If you go over the bridge are you in Shikoku?"

"Yeah. If you're talking about a big bridge around here, that's the one to Shikoku. There're three of them, actually. One goes from Kobe to Awaji Island, then on to Tokushima. Another goes from below Kurashiki over to Sakaide. And one connects Onomichi and Imabari. One bridge would've been plenty, but politicians stuck their noses into it and they wound up with three. Typical pork-barrel projects." Hoshino poured out some water onto the resin tabletop and drew an abbreviated map of Japan with his finger, indicating the three bridges connecting Honshu and Shikoku.

"Are these bridges really big?" Nakata asked.

"They're huge."

"Is that right? Anyway, Nakata's going to cross over one of them. Probably whichever one is closest. I'll figure out what to do after that later on."

"So what you're saying is you don't have any friends or anybody where you're headed?"

"No, Nakata doesn't know anybody there."

"You're just going to cross the bridge to Shikoku and then go somewhere else."

"That's right."

"And you don't know *where* that *some*where is."

"I have no idea. But I think I'll know it when I get there."

"Jeez," Hoshino said. He brushed back his hair, gave his ponytail a tug, and put on his Chunichi Dragons cap.

Their food was served, and they started eating.

"Pretty good omelette, huh?" Hoshino asked.

"Yes, it's very good. It tastes different from the omelettes I always eat in Nakano."

"That's 'cause it's Kansai style. Not at all like those tasteless flat things that pass as omelettes in Tokyo."

The two of them then silently enjoyed their meal, the omelettes, salt-grilled mackerel, miso soup with shellfish, pickled turnips, seasoned spinach, seaweed. They didn't leave a grain of rice. Nakata made sure to chew each bite thirty-two times, so it took quite a while for him to finish.

"Get enough, Mr. Nakata?"

"Yes, plenty. How about you, Mr. Hoshino?"

"Even me, I'm stuffed. Perks up the old spirits, doesn't it, to have such a great breakfast?"

"Yes, it certainly does."

"How 'bout it? Gotta take a dump?"

"Now that you mention it, I do feel like it."

"Go right ahead. Toilet's over there."

"What about you, Mr. Hoshino?"

"I'll go later on. Take my time about it."

"Thank you. Nakata will go take a dump, then."

"Hey, not so loud. People are still eating here."

"I'm sorry. Nakata's not very bright."

"Never mind. Just go."

"Do you mind if I brush my teeth, too?"

"No, go ahead. We got time. Do whatever you want. Tell you what, I don't think you'll be needing that umbrella. You're just going to the toilet, right?"

"All right. I'll leave the umbrella."

When Nakata came back from the toilet Hoshino had already paid their bill.

"Mr. Hoshino, I have money with me, so please let me at least pay for breakfast."

Hoshino shook his head. "It's okay. I owe my grandpa big-time. Back then I was kind of wild."

"I see. But I'm not your grandfather."

"That's my problem, so don't worry about it. No arguments, okay? Just let me treat you."

After a moment's thought Nakata decided to accept the young man's generosity. "Thank you so much then. It was a wonderful meal."

"Hey, it's just some mackerel and omelettes at a nothing little diner. No need to bow like that."

"But you know, Mr. Hoshino, ever since Nakata left Nakano Ward everyone's been so nice to me I haven't had to use hardly any money at all."

"Sweet," Hoshino said, impressed.

Nakata had a waitress fill his little thermos with hot tea, then he carefully replaced it in his bag. Walking back to where the truck was parked, Hoshino said, "So, about this going to Shikoku thing . . ."

"Yes?" Nakata replied.

"Why do you want to go there?"

"I don't know."

"You don't know why you're going, or even where you're going. But you've still got to go to Shikoku?"

"That's right. Nakata's going to cross a big bridge."

"Things'll be clearer once you're on the other side?"

"I think so. I won't know anything until I cross the bridge."

"Hmm," Hoshino said. "So crossing that bridge is very important."

"Yes, that's more important than anything."

"Man alive," Hoshino said, scratching his head.

The young man had to drive his truck over to the warehouse to deliver his load of furniture, so he told Nakata to wait for him at a small park near the harbor.

"Don't move from here, okay?" Hoshino cautioned him. "There's a restroom over there, and a water fountain. You got everything you need. If you wander off somewhere, you might not find your way back."

"I understand. I'm not in Nakano Ward anymore."

"Exactly. This isn't Nakano. So sit tight, and I'll be back real soon."

"All right. I'll stay right here."

"Good. I'll be back as soon as I finish my delivery."

Nakata did as he was told, not moving from the bench, not even to use the restroom. He didn't find staying put in one place for a long time very hard. Sitting still, in fact, was his specialty.

He could see the sea from where he sat. This he hadn't seen for a long, long time. When he was little, he and his family had gone to the seaside any number of times. He'd put on trunks, splash around on the shore, gather seashells at low tide. But these memories weren't clear. It was like this had taken place in another world. Since then, he couldn't recall seeing the sea even once.

After the strange incident in the hills of Yamanashi, Nakata went back to school in Tokyo. He'd regained consciousness and physically was fine, but his memory had been wiped clean, and he never regained the ability to read and write. He couldn't read his school textbooks, and couldn't take any tests. All the knowledge he'd gained up till then had vanished, as had the ability, to a great extent, to think in abstract terms. Still, they let him graduate. He couldn't follow what was being taught, and instead sat quietly in a corner of the classroom. When the teacher told him to do something, he followed her instructions to the letter. He didn't bother anyone, so teachers tended to forget he was even there. He was more like a guest sitting in than a burden.

People soon forgot that until the accident he'd always gotten straight As. But now the school activities and events took place without him. He didn't make any friends. None of this bothered him, though. Being left alone meant he could be lost in his own little world. What absorbed him the most at school was taking care of the rabbits and goats they raised there, tending the flower beds outside and cleaning the classrooms. A constant smile on his face, he never tired of these chores.

He was essentially forgotten about at home, too. Once they learned that their eldest son couldn't read anymore or follow along with his lessons, Nakata's parents—totally focused on their children's education—ignored him and turned their attention to his younger brothers. It was impossible for Nakata to go on to public junior high, so once he graduated from elementary school he was sent to live with relatives in Nagano Prefecture, in his mother's hometown. There he attended agriculture school. Since he still couldn't read he had a hard time with his schoolwork, but he loved working in the fields. He might even have become a farmer, if his classmates hadn't tormented him so much. They enjoyed beating up this outsider, this city kid, so much. His injuries became so severe (one cauliflower ear included) that his grandparents pulled him out of school and kept him at home to help out around the house. Nakata was a quiet, obedient child, and his grandparents loved him very much.

It was about this time that he discovered he could speak with cats. His grandparents had a few cats around the house, and Nakata became good friends with them. At first he was able to speak only a few words, but he knuckled down like he was trying to master a foreign language and before long was able to carry on extended conversations. Whenever he was free he liked to sit on the porch and talk with the cats. For their part, the cats taught him a lot about nature and the world around him. Actually almost all the basic knowledge he had about the world and how it worked he learned from his feline friends.

At fifteen he was sent to a nearby furniture company to learn woodworking. It was less a factory than a small woodworking shop making folkcraft-type furniture. Chairs, tables, and chests made there were shipped to Tokyo. Nakata grew to love woodworking. His boss took a great liking to him, for he was skilled with his hands, never skipped any small details, didn't talk much, and never, ever complained. Reading a blueprint and adding figures weren't his forte, but aside from these tasks he did well at everything he set his hand to. Once he got the manufacturing steps in his mind he could repeat them endlessly, tirelessly. After a two-year apprenticeship he was given full-time employment.

Nakata worked there until he was past fifty, never once having an accident or calling in sick. He didn't drink or smoke, didn't stay up late or overeat. He never watched TV, and listened to the radio only for the morning exercise program. Day after day he just made furniture. His grandparents eventually passed away, as did his parents. Everybody liked him, though he didn't make any close friends. Perhaps that was only to be expected. When most people tried talking to Nakata, ten minutes was all it took for them to run out of things to say.

Still, he never felt lonely or unhappy. He never felt sexual desire, or even wanted to be with anyone. He understood he was different from other people. Though no one else noticed this, he thought his shadow on the ground was paler, lighter, than that of other people. The only ones who really understood him were the cats. On days off he'd sit on a park bench and spend the whole day chatting with them. Strangely enough, with cats he never ran out of things to talk about.

The owner of the furniture company passed away when Nakata was fifty-two, and the woodworking shop was closed soon afterward. That kind of gloomy, dark, traditional furniture didn't sell as well as it used to. The craftsmen were all getting on in years, and no young people were interested in learning the trade. The shop itself, originally in the middle of a field, was now surrounded by newly built homes, and complaints started to come in about both the noise and the smoke when they burned wood shavings. The owner's son, who worked in town for an accounting firm, had no interest in taking over the business, so as soon as his father passed away he sold the property to a real estate developer. For his part, the developer tore down the shop, had the land graded, and sold it to an apartment complex developer, who constructed a six-story condominium on the property. Every single apartment in the condo sold out on the first day they were put on sale.

That's how Nakata lost his job. The company had some outstanding loans to pay off, so he received only a pittance as retirement pay. Afterward he couldn't find another job. Who was going to hire an illiterate man in his fifties whose only skill was crafting antique furniture nobody wanted anymore?

Nakata had worked steadily for thirty-seven years at the plant without taking a single day of leave, so he did have a fair amount of money in his savings account at the local post office. He generally spent very little on himself, so even without finding another job he should have been able to have a comfortable old age on his savings. Since he couldn't read or write, a cousin of his who worked at city hall managed his account for him. Though kind enough, this cousin wasn't so quick on the uptake and was tricked into investing in a condominium at a ski resort by an unscrupulous real estate broker and ended up deeply in debt. Around the same time that Nakata lost his job, this cousin disappeared with his entire family to escape his creditors. Some yakuza-type loan sharks were after him, apparently. Nobody knew where this family was, or even if they were still alive.

When Nakata had an acquaintance go with him to the post office to check on the balance in his account, he found out that only a few hundred dollars were left. His retirement pay, which had been deposited directly into the account, had also vanished. One could only say that Nakata was extremely unlucky—losing his job and finding himself penniless. His relatives were sympathetic, but they'd been asked to put up collateral and likewise lost everything they'd invested with the cousin. So none of them had the resources to help Nakata in his time of need.

In the end the older of Nakata's two younger brothers in Tokyo decided to look after him for the time being. He owned a small apartment building in Nakano that catered to single men—this was part of his inheritance from his parents—and he offered one of the units to his older brother. He also looked after the money his parents had willed to Nakata—not a great amount—and arranged for him to receive a subsidy for the mentally challenged from the Tokyo Metropolitan Government. That was the extent of the brother's "care." Despite his illiteracy, Nakata was able to take care of his daily needs by himself, and as long as his rent was covered he was able to manage.

His two brothers had very little contact with him. They saw him a few times when he first moved back to Tokyo, but that was it. They had lived apart for over thirty years, and their lifestyles were too different.

Neither brother had any particular feelings toward him, and in any case they were too busy with their own careers to take care of a retarded sibling.

But this cold treatment by his relatives didn't faze Nakata. He was used to being alone and actually tensed up if people went out of their way to be nice to him. He wasn't angry, either, that his cousin had squandered his life savings. Naturally he understood it was too bad it happened, but he wasn't disappointed by the whole affair. Nakata had no idea what a resort condo was, or what "investing" meant, nor did he understand what taking out a "loan" involved. He lived in a world circumscribed by a very limited vocabulary.

Only amounts up to fifty dollars or so had any meaning to him. Anything above that—a thousand dollars, ten thousand, a hundred thousand—was all the same to him. A *lot of money*, that's all it meant. He might have savings, but he'd never seen it. They just told him, "This is how much you have in your account," and told him an amount, which to him was an abstract concept. So when it all vanished he never had the sense that he'd actually lost something real.

So Nakata lived a contented life in the small apartment his brother provided, receiving his monthly subsidy, using his special bus pass, going to the local park to chat with the cats. This little corner of Nakano became his new world. Just like dogs and cats, he marked off his territory, a boundary line beyond which, except in unusual circumstances, he never ventured. As long as he stayed there he felt safe and content. No dissatisfactions, no anger at anything. No feelings of loneliness, anxieties about the future, or worries that his life was difficult or inconvenient. Day after day, for more than ten years, this was his life, leisurely enjoying whatever came along.

Until the day that Johnnie Walker showed up.

Nakata hadn't seen the sea in years, for there was no sea in Nagano Prefecture, or in Nakano Ward. Now for the first time, he realized that he'd lost the sea for so long. He hadn't even thought about it all those many years. He nodded several times to himself, confirming this fact. He took off his hat, rubbed his closely cropped head with his palm, put his hat back on, and gazed out at the sea. This is the extent of his knowledge of the sea: it was very big, it was salty, and fish lived there.

He sat there on the bench, breathing in the scent of the sea, watching seagulls circle overhead, gazing at ships anchored far off-shore. He didn't tire of the view. An occasional white seagull would alight on the fresh summer grass in the park. The white against the green was beautiful. Nakata tried calling out to the seagull as it walked over the grass, but it didn't reply and just stared at him coolly. There were no cats around. The only animals in the park were seagulls and sparrows. As he sipped hot tea from his thermos, rain began pelting down, and Nakata opened up his precious umbrella.

By the time Hoshino came back to the park, just before twelve, it had stopped raining. Nakata was seated on the bench just as he'd left him, umbrella folded, staring out at the sea. Hoshino had parked his truck somewhere and arrived in a taxi.

"Hey, I'm sorry it took so long," he apologized. A vinyl Boston bag hung from his shoulder. "I thought I'd be finished sooner but all kinds of things came up. It's like every department store has one guy who's got to be a pain in the butt."

"Nakata didn't mind at all. I was just sitting here, looking at the sea."

"Hmm," Hoshino murmured. He looked out in the same direction, but all he saw was a shabby old pier and oil floating on the surface of the water.

"I haven't seen the sea in a long time."

"That right?"

"The last time I saw it was in elementary school. I went to the seaside at Enoshima."

"I bet that was a long time ago."

"Japan was occupied by the Americans back then. The seashore at Enoshima was filled with American soldiers."

"You gotta be kidding."

"No, I'm not kidding."

"Come on," Hoshino said. "Japan was never occupied by America."

"Nakata doesn't know the details, but America had planes called B-29s. They dropped a lot of bombs on Tokyo, so I went to Yamanashi Prefecture. That's where I got sick."

"Yeah? Whatever . . . I told you I don't like long stories. Anyway, let's head on out. It took longer than I thought, and it's gonna be dark soon if we don't get a move on."

"Where are we going?"

"Shikoku, of course. We'll cross the bridge. You said you're going to Shikoku, didn't you?"

"I did. But what about your job?"

"Don't worry about it. It'll still be there when I get back. I've been putting in some long hours and was thinking I should take a few days off. To tell the truth, I've never been to Shikoku either. Might as well check it out. Plus you can't read, right? So it'll be a whole lot easier if I'm with you to help buy the tickets. Unless you don't want me along."

"No, Nakata would be happy to have you along."

"Then let's do it. I already checked out the bus schedule. Shikoku—here we come!"

Chapter 23

I don't know if *ghost* is the right word, but it definitely isn't something of this world—that much I can tell at a glance.

I sense something and suddenly wake up and there she is. It's the middle of the night but the room is strangely light, moonlight streaming through the window. I know I closed the curtains before going to bed, but now they're wide open. The girl's silhouette is clearly outlined, bathed by the bone white light of the moon.

She's about my age, fifteen or sixteen. I'm guessing fifteen. There's a big difference between fifteen and sixteen. She's small and slim, holds herself erect, and doesn't seem delicate at all. Her hair hangs down to her shoulders, with bangs on her forehead. She's wearing a blue dress with a billowing hem that's just the right length. She doesn't have any shoes or socks on. The buttons on the cuffs of her dress are neatly done up. Her dress has a rounded, open collar, showing off her well-formed neck.

She's sitting at the desk, chin resting in her hands, staring at the wall and thinking about something. Nothing too complex, I'd say. It looks more like she's lost in some pleasant, warm memory of not so long ago. Every once in a while a hint of a smile gathers at the corners of her mouth. But the shadows cast by the moonlight keep me from making out any details of her expression. I don't want to interrupt whatever it is she's doing, so I pretend to be asleep, holding my breath and trying not to be noticed.

She's got to be a ghost. First of all, she's just too beautiful. Her features are gorgeous, but it's not only that. She's so perfect I know she can't be real. She's like a person who stepped right out of a dream. The purity of her beauty gives me a feeling close to sadness—a very natural feeling, though one that only something extraordinary could produce.

I'm wrapped in my covers, holding my breath. She continues to sit there at the desk, chin propped in her hands, barely stirring. Occasionally her chin shifts a fraction, changing the angle of her head ever so slightly. As far as anything moving in the room, that's it. I can see the large flowering dogwood just outside the window, glistening silently in the moonlight. There's no wind, and I can't hear a sound. The whole thing feels like I might've died, unknowingly. I'm dead, and this girl and I have sunk to the bottom of a deep crater lake.

All of a sudden she pulls her hands away from her chin and places them on her lap. Two small pale knees show at her hemline. She stops gazing at the wall and turns in my direction. She reaches up and touches the hair at her forehead—her slim, girlish fingers rest for a time on her forehead, as if she's trying to draw out some forgotten thought. *She's looking at me.* My heart beats dully in my chest, but strangely enough I don't feel like I'm being looked at. Maybe she's not looking at me but beyond me.

In the depths of our crater lake, everything is silent. The volcano's been extinct for ages. Layer upon layer of solitude, like folds of soft mud. The little bit of light that manages to penetrate to the depths lights up the surroundings like the remains of some faint, distant memory. At these depths there's no sign of life. I don't know how long she looks at me—not at me, maybe, but at the spot where I am. Time's rules don't apply here. Time expands, then contracts, all in tune with the stirrings of the heart.

And then, without warning, the girl stands up and heads toward the door on her slender legs. The door is shut, yet soundlessly she disappears.

I stay where I am, in bed. My eyes open just a slit, and I don't move a muscle. For all I know she might come back, I think. I *want* her to, I realize. But no matter how long I wait she doesn't return. I raise my head and glance at the fluorescent numbers on the alarm clock next to my bed. 3:25. I get out of bed, walk over to the chair she was sitting on, and touch it. It's not warm at all. I check out the desktop, in hopes of finding something—a single hair, perhaps?—she left behind. But there's nothing. I sit down on the chair, massaging my cheeks with the palms of my hands, and breathe a deep sigh.

I close the curtains and crawl back under the covers, but there's no way I can go back to sleep now. My head's too full of that enigmatic girl. A strange, terrific force unlike anything I've ever experienced is sprouting in my heart, taking root there, growing. Shut up behind my rib cage, my warm heart expands and contracts independent of my will—over and over.

I switch on the light and wait for the dawn, sitting up in bed. I can't read, can't listen to music. I can't do anything but just sit there, waiting for morning to come. As the sky begins to lighten I finally sleep a bit. When I wake up, my pillow's cold and damp with tears. But tears for *what*? I have no idea.

Around nine Oshima roars up in his Miata, and we get the library ready to open. After we get everything done I make him some coffee. He taught me how to do it just right. You grind the beans by hand, boil up some water in a narrow spouted pot, let it sit for a while, then slowly—and I mean *slowly*—pour the water through a paper filter. When the coffee's ready Oshima puts in the smallest dab of sugar, just for show, basically, but no cream—the best way, he insists. I make myself some Earl Grey tea.

Oshima has on a shiny brown short-sleeved shirt and white linen trousers. Wiping his glasses with a brand-new handkerchief he pulls from his pocket, he turns to me. "You don't look like you got much sleep."

"There's something I'd like you to do for me," I say.

"Name it."

"I want to listen to 'Kafka on the Shore.' Can you get hold of the record?"

"Not the CD?"

"If possible I'd like to listen to the record, to hear how it originally sounded. Of course we'd have to find a record player, too."

Oshima rests his fingers on his temple and thinks. "There might be an old stereo in the storeroom. Can't guarantee it still works, though."

We go into a small room facing the parking lot. There are no windows, only a skylight high up. A mess of objects from various periods are strewn around—furniture, dishes, magazines, clothes, and paintings. Some of them are obviously valuable, but some, most, in fact, don't look like they're worth much.

"Someday we've got to get rid of all this junk," Oshima remarks, "but nobody's been brave enough to take the plunge."

In the middle of the room, where time seems to have drifted to a halt, we find an old Sansui stereo. Covered in a thin layer of white dust, the stereo itself looks in good shape, though it must be over twenty-five years since this was up-to-date audio equipment. The whole set consists of a receiver, amp, turntable, and bookshelf speakers. We also find a collection of old LPs, mostly sixties pop music — Beatles, Stones, Beach Boys, Simon and Garfunkel, Stevie Wonder. About thirty albums, all told. I take some out of their jackets. Whoever listened to these took good care of them, because there's no trace of mold and not a scratch anywhere.

There's a guitar in the storeroom as well, still with strings. Plus a pile of old magazines I've never heard of, and an old-fashioned tennis racket. All like the ruins of some not-so-distant past.

"I imagine all this stuff belonged to Miss Saeki's boyfriend," Oshima says. "Like I mentioned, he used to live in this building, and they must've thrown his things down here. The stereo, though, looks more recent than that."

We lug the stereo and records to my room. We dust it off, plug it in, connect up the player and amp, and hit the switch. The little green light on the amp comes on and the turntable begins to revolve. I check the cartridge and find it still has a decent needle, then take out the red vinyl record of "Sgt. Pepper's Lonely Hearts Club Band" and put it on the turntable. The familiar guitar intro starts to play. The sound's much cleaner than I expected.

"Japan has its share of problems," Oshima says, smiling, "but we sure know how to make a sound system. This thing hasn't been used in ages, but it still sounds great."

We listen to the Beatles album for a while. Compared to the CD version, it sounds like different music altogether.

"Well, we've got something to listen to it on," Oshima concludes, "but getting hold of a single of 'Kafka on the Shore' might be a problem. That's a pretty rare item nowadays. I tell you what—I'll ask my mother. She's probably got a copy tucked away somewhere. Or at least she'll know somebody who does."

I nod.

Oshima raises a finger, like a teacher warning a pupil. "One thing, though. Make sure you never play it when Miss Saeki's here. No matter what. Understood?"

I nod again.

"Like in *Casablanca*," he says, and hums the opening bars of "As Time Goes By." "Just don't play that one song, okay?"

"Oshima, there's something I want to ask. Does any fifteen-year-old girl come here?"

"By *here* you mean the library?"

I nod.

Oshima tilts his head and gives it some thought. "Not as far as I know," he says, staring at me like he's looking into the room from a window. "That's a strange thing to ask."

"I think I saw her recently," I say.

"When was this?"

"Last night."

"You saw a fifteen-year-old girl here last night?"

"Yeah."

"What kind of girl?"

I blush a bit. "Just a girl. Hair down to her shoulders. Wearing a blue dress."

"Was she pretty?"

I nod.

"Could be a sexual fantasy," Oshima says, and grins. "The world's full of weird things. But for a healthy, heterosexual kid your age, having fantasies like that's not so strange."

I remember how Oshima saw me buck naked up at the cabin, and blush even more.

During our lunch break Oshima quietly hands me a single of "Kafka on the Shore" in a square little jacket. "Turns out my mom did have one. Five copies, if you can believe it. She really takes good care of things. A bit of a pack rat, but I guess we shouldn't complain."

"Thanks," I say.

I go back to my room and take the record out of the jacket. The record looks like it's never been played. In the record jacket's photo, Miss Saeki—she was nineteen, according to Oshima—is sitting at a piano in a recording studio. Looking straight at the camera, she's resting her chin in her hands on the music stand, her head tilted slightly to one side, a shy, unaffected smile on her face, closed lips spread pleasantly wide, with charming lines at the corners. It doesn't look like she's wearing any makeup. Her hair's held back by a plastic clip so it won't fall into her face, and part of her right ear's visible through the strands. Her light blue dress is short and loose-fitting, and she has a silver bracelet on her left wrist, her only accessory. A pair of slender sandals lie next to her piano stool, and her bare feet are lovely.

She looks like a symbol of something. A certain time, a certain place. A certain state of mind. She's like a spirit that's sprung up from a happy chance encounter. An eternal, naive innocence, never to be marred, floats around her like spores in spring. Time had come to a standstill in this photograph. 1969—a scene from long before I was even born.

I knew from the first that the young girl who visited my room last night was Miss Saeki. I never doubted it for a second, but just had to make sure.

Compared to when she was fifteen, Miss Saeki at nineteen looks more grown-up, more mature. If I had to compare the two, I'd say the outline of her face looks sharper, more defined, in the photo. A certain anxiousness is missing from the older of the two. But otherwise this nineteen-year-old and the fifteen-year-old I saw are nearly identical. The smile in the photo's the same one I saw last night. How she held her chin in her hands, and tilted her head—also the same. And in Miss Saeki now, the *real-time* Miss Saeki, I can see the same expressions and gestures. I'm delighted that those features, and her sense of the other-worldly, haven't changed a bit. Even her build is almost the same.

Still, there's something in this photo of the nineteen-year-old that the middle-aged woman I know has lost forever. You might call it an outpouring of energy. Nothing showy, it's colorless, transparent, like fresh water secretly seeping out between rocks—a kind of natural, un-spoiled appeal that shoots straight to your heart. That brilliant energy seeps out of her entire being as she sits there at the piano. Just by look-ing at that happy smile, you can trace the beautiful path that a con-tented heart must follow. Like a firefly's glow that persists long after it's disappeared into the darkness.

I sit on my bed for a long time, record jacket in hand, not thinking about anything, just letting time pass by. I open my eyes, go to the win-dow, and take a deep breath of fresh air, catching a whiff of the sea on the breeze that's come up through a pine forest. What I saw here in this room the night before was definitely Miss Saeki at age fifteen. The *real* Miss Saeki, of course, is still alive. A fifty-something woman, living a real life in the real world. Even now she's in her room upstairs at her desk, working away. To see her, all I need to do is go out of this room and up the stairs, and there she'll be. I can meet her, talk with her—

but none of that changes the fact that what I saw here was her *ghost*. Oshima told me people can't be in two places at once, but I think it's possible. In fact, I'm *sure* of it. While they're still alive, people can become ghosts.

And there's another important fact: I'm drawn to that ghost, attracted to her. Not to the Miss Saeki who's here right now, but to the fifteen-year-old who *isn't*. *Very* attracted, a feeling so strong I can't explain it. And no matter what anybody says, this is real. Maybe she doesn't really exist, but just thinking about her makes my heart—my flesh and blood, my *real* heart—thump like mad. These feelings are as real as the blood all over my chest that awful night.

As it gets near closing time Miss Saeki comes downstairs, her heels clicking as she walks. When I see her, I tense up and can hear my heart pounding. I see the fifteen-year-old girl inside her. Like some small animal in hibernation, she's curled up in a hollow inside Miss Saeki, asleep.

Miss Saeki's asking me something but I can't reply. I don't even know what she said. I can hear her, of course—her words vibrate my eardrums and transmit a message to my brain that's converted into language—but there's a disconnect between words and meaning. Flustered, I blush and stammer out something stupid. Oshima intervenes and answers her question. I nod at what he's saying. Miss Saeki smiles, says good-bye to us, and leaves for home. I listen to the sound of her Golf as it exits the parking lot, fades into the distance, and disappears.

Oshima stays behind and helps me close up for the night.

"By any chance have you fallen in love with somebody?" he asks. "You seem kind of out of it."

I don't have any idea how I should respond. "Oshima," I finally say, "this is a pretty weird thing to ask, but do you think it's possible for someone to become a ghost while they're still alive?"

He stops straightening up the counter and looks at me. "A very interesting question, actually. Are you asking about the human spirit in a literary sense—metaphorically, in other words? Or do you mean in actual fact?"

"More in actual fact, I guess," I say.

"The assumption that ghosts really exist?"

"Right."

Oshima removes his glasses, wipes them with his handkerchief, and puts them back on. "That's what's called a 'living spirit.' I don't know about in foreign countries, but that kind of thing appears a lot in Japanese literature. *The Tale of Genji*, for instance, is filled with living spirits. In the Heian period—or at least in its psychological realm—on occasion people could become living spirits and travel through space to carry out whatever desires they had. Have you read *Genji?*"

I shake my head.

"Our library has a couple of modern translations, so it might be a good idea to read one. Anyway, an example is when Lady Rokujo— she's one of Prince Genji's lovers—becomes so consumed with jealousy over Genji's main wife, Lady Aoi, that she turns into an evil spirit that possesses her. Night after night she attacks Lady Aoi in her bed until she finally kills her. Lady Aoi was pregnant with Genji's child, and that news is what activated Lady Rokujo's hatred. Genji called in priests to exorcise the evil spirit, but to no avail. The evil spirit was impossible to resist.

"But the most interesting part of the story is that Lady Rokujo had no inkling that she'd become a living spirit. She'd have nightmares and wake up, only to discover that her long black hair smelled like smoke. Not having any idea what was going on, she was totally confused. In fact, this smoke came from the incense the priests lit as they prayed for Lady Aoi. Completely unaware of it, she'd been flying through space and passing down the tunnel of her subconscious into Aoi's bedroom. This is one of the most uncanny and thrilling episodes in *Genji*. Later, when Lady Rokujo learns what she's been doing, she regrets the sins she's committed and shaves off her hair and renounces the world.

"The world of the grotesque is the darkness within us. Well before Freud and Jung shined a light on the workings of the subconscious, this correlation between darkness and our subconscious, these two forms of darkness, was obvious to people. It wasn't a metaphor, even. If you trace it back further, it wasn't even a correlation. Until Edison invented the electric light, most of the world was totally covered in darkness. The physical darkness outside and the inner darkness of the soul were mixed together, with no boundary separating the two. They were directly linked. Like this." Oshima brings his two hands together tightly.

"In Murasaki Shikibu's time living spirits were both a grotesque phenomenon and a natural condition of the human heart that was right there with them. People of that period probably couldn't conceive of these two types of darkness as separate from each other. But today things are different. The darkness in the outside world has vanished, but the darkness in our hearts remains, virtually unchanged. Just like an iceberg, what we label the ego or consciousness is, for the most part, sunk in darkness. And that estrangement sometimes creates a deep contradiction or confusion within us."

"Around your mountain cabin—that's real darkness."

"Absolutely," Oshima says. "Real darkness still exists there. Sometimes I go there just to experience it."

"What triggers people to become living spirits? Is it always something negative?"

"I'm no expert, but as far as I know, yes, those living spirits all spring up out of negative emotions. Most of the extreme feelings people have tend to be at once very individual and very negative. And these living spirits arise through a kind of spontaneous generation. Sad to say, there aren't any cases of a living spirit emerging to fulfill some logical premise or bring about world peace."

"What about because of love?"

Oshima sits down and thinks it over. "That's a tough one. All I can tell you is I've never run across an example. Of course, there is that tale, 'The Chrysanthemum Pledge,' in *Tales of Moonlight and Rain*. Have you read it?"

"No," I reply.

"*Tales of Moonlight and Rain* was written in the late Edo period by a man named Ueda Akinari. It was set, however, in the earlier Warring States period, which makes Ueda's approach a bit nostalgic or retro. Anyway, in this particular story two samurai become fast friends and pledge themselves as blood brothers. For samurai this was very serious. Being blood brothers meant they pledged their lives to each other. They lived far away from each other, each serving a different lord. One wrote to the other saying no matter what, he would visit when the chrysanthemums were in bloom. The other said he'd wait for his arrival. But before the first one could set out on the journey, he got mixed up in some trouble in his domain, was put under confinement, and wasn't allowed to go out or send a letter. Finally summer is over and fall is upon them, the season when the chrysanthemums blossom. At this rate he won't be able to fulfill his promise to his friend. To a samurai, nothing's more important than a promise. Honor's more important than your life. So this samurai commits hara-kiri, becomes a spirit, and races across the miles to visit his friend. They sit near the chrysanthemums and talk to their heart's content, and then the spirit vanishes from the face of the earth. It's a beautiful tale."

"But he had to die in order to become a spirit."

"Yes, that's right," Oshima says. "It would appear that people can't become living spirits out of honor or love or friendship. To do that they have to die. People throw away their lives for honor, love, or friendship, and only then do they turn into spirits. But when you talk about *living* spirits—well, that's a different story. They always seem to be motivated by evil."

I mull this over.

"But like you said, there might be examples," Oshima continues, "of people becoming living spirits out of positive feelings of love. I just haven't done much research into the matter, I'm afraid. Maybe it happens. Love can rebuild the world, they say, so everything's possible when it comes to love."

"Have you ever been in love?" I ask.

He stares at me, taken aback. "What do you think? I'm not a starfish or a pepper tree. I'm a living, breathing human being. Of course I've been in love."

"That isn't what I mean," I say, blushing.

"I know," he says, and smiles at me gently.

Once Oshima leaves I go back to my room, switch the stereo to 45 rpm, lower the needle, and listen to "Kafka on the Shore," following the lyrics on the jacket.

> *You sit at the edge of the world,*
> *I am in a crater that's no more.*
> *Words without letters*
> *Standing in the shadow of the door.*

> *The moon shines down on a sleeping lizard,*
> *Little fish rain down from the sky.*
> *Outside the window there are soldiers,*
> *steeling themselves to die.*

> *(Refrain)*

Kafka sits in a chair by the shore,
Thinking of the pendulum that moves the world, it seems.
When your heart is closed,
The shadow of the unmoving Sphinx,
Becomes a knife that pierces your dreams.

The drowning girl's fingers
Search for the entrance stone, and more.
Lifting the hem of her azure dress,
She gazes—
at Kafka on the shore.

I listen to the record three times. First of all, I'm wondering how a record with lyrics like this could sell over a million copies. I'm not saying they're totally obscure, just kind of abstract and surreal. Not exactly catchy lyrics. But if you listen to them a few times they begin to sound familiar. One by one the words find a home in my heart. It's a weird feeling. Images beyond any meaning arise like cutout figures and stand alone, just like when I'm in the middle of a deep dream.

The melody is beautiful, simple but different, too. And Miss Saeki's voice melts into it naturally. Her voice needs more power—she isn't what you'd call a professional singer—but it gently cleanses your mind, like a spring rain washing over stepping-stones in a garden. She played the piano and sang, then they added a small string section and an oboe. The recording budget must have kept the arrangement simple, but actually it's this simplicity that gives the song its appeal.

Two unusual chords appear in the refrain. The other chords in the song are nothing special, but these two are different, not the kind you can figure out by listening just a couple of times. At first I felt confused. To exaggerate a little, I felt betrayed, even. The total unexpectedness of the sounds shook me, unsettled me, like when a cold wind suddenly blows in through a crack. But once the refrain is over, that beautiful melody returns, taking you back to that original world of harmony and intimacy. No more chilly wind here. The piano plays its final note while the strings quietly hold the last chord, the lingering sound of the oboe bringing the song to a close.

Listening to it over and over, I start to get some idea why "Kafka on the Shore" moved so many people. The song's direct and gentle at the same time, the product of a capable yet unselfish heart. There's a kind of miraculous feel to it, this overlap of opposites. A shy nineteen-year-old girl from a provincial town writes lyrics about her boyfriend far away, sits down at the piano and sets it to music, then unhesitantly sings her creation. She didn't write the song for others to hear, but for herself, to warm her own heart, if even a little. And her self-absorption strikes a subtle but powerful chord in her listeners' hearts.

I throw together a simple dinner from things in the fridge, then put "Kafka on the Shore" on the turntable again. Eyes closed, I sit in the chair and try to picture the nineteen-year-old Miss Saeki in the studio, playing the piano and singing. I think about the love she felt as she sang. And how mindless violence severed that love forever.

The record is over, the needle lifts up and returns to its cradle.

Miss Saeki may have written the lyrics to "Kafka on the Shore" in this very room. The more I listen to the record, the more I'm sure that this Kafka on the shore is the young boy in the painting on the wall. I sit at the desk and, like she did last night, hold my chin in my hands and gaze at the same angle at the painting right in front of me. I'm positive now, this *had* to be where she wrote it. I see her gazing at the painting, remembering the young boy, writing the poem she then set to music. It had to have been at night, when it was pitch-dark outside.

I stand up, go over to the wall, and examine the painting up close. The young man is looking off in the distance, his eyes full of a mysterious depth. In one corner of the sky there are some sharply outlined clouds, and the largest sort of looks like a crouching Sphinx.

I search my memory. The Sphinx was the enemy Oedipus defeated by solving the riddle, and once the monster knew it had lost, it leaped off a cliff and killed itself. Thanks to this exploit, Oedipus got to be king of Thebes and ended up marrying his own mother. And the name Kafka. I suspect Miss Saeki used it since in her mind the mysterious solitude of the boy in the picture overlapped with Kafka's fictional world. That would explain the title: a solitary soul straying by an absurd shore.

Other lines overlap with things that happened to me. The part about "little fish rain from the sky"—isn't that exactly what happened in that shopping area back home, when hundreds of sardines and mackerel rained down? The part about how the shadow "becomes a knife that pierces your dreams"—that could be my father's stabbing. I copy down all the lines of the song in my notebook and study them, underlining parts that particularly interest me. But in the end it's all too suggestive, and I don't know what to make of it.

> *Words without letters*
> *Standing in the shadow of the door . . .*
> *The drowning girl's fingers*
> *Search for the entrance stone . . .*
> *Outside the window there are soldiers,*
> *steeling themselves to die. . . .*

What could it mean? Were all these just coincidences? I walk to the window and look out at the garden. Darkness is just settling in on the world. I go over to the reading room, sit on the sofa, and open up Tanizaki's translation of *The Tale of Genji*. At ten I go to bed, turn off the bedside light, and close my eyes, waiting for the fifteen-year-old Miss Saeki to return to this room.

Chapter 24

It was already eight p.m. when their bus from Kobe arrived in front of Tokushima Station.

"Well, Mr. Nakata, here we are. Shikoku."

"What a wonderful bridge. Nakata's never seen such a huge one before."

The two of them alighted from the bus and sat down on a bench at the station to survey their surroundings.

"So—did you have a message from God or something?" Hoshino asked. "Telling you where you're supposed to go now? What you're supposed to do?"

"No. Nakata still has no idea."

"Great . . ."

Nakata rubbed his head deliberately with his palm for a while, as if pondering weighty matters. "Mr. Hoshino?" he finally said.

"What's up?"

"I'm sorry, but Nakata really needs to go to sleep. I'm so sleepy I feel like I could fall asleep right here."

"Wait a sec—you can't fall asleep here," Hoshino said, flustered. "Tell you what, I'll find a place where you can sack out, okay? Just hang in there for a while."

"All right. Nakata will hang in there and try not to go to sleep."

"Good. Are you hungry?"

"No, just sleepy."

Hoshino quickly located the tourist information counter, found an inexpensive inn that included complimentary breakfast, and called to book a room. It was some distance from the station, so they hailed a cab. As soon as they arrived, Hoshino asked the maid to lay out their futons for them.

Nakata skipped taking a bath and undressed, lay down in bed, and in an instant was peacefully snoring away. "I'll probably sleep for a long time, so don't be alarmed," he said just before he fell asleep.

"Hey, I'm not going to bother you—sleep as much as you want," Hoshino said, but Nakata was already lost to the world.

Hoshino enjoyed a leisurely bath, went out, and strolled around to get the lay of the land, then ducked inside a sushi shop for dinner and a beer. He wasn't much of a drinker, and a medium-size bottle of beer was enough to turn his face bright red and put him in a good mood. After dinner he played pachinko and lost twenty-five dollars in a hour. His Chunichi Dragons baseball cap drew a few stares from passersby, and he decided he must be the only one in Tokushima wearing one.

Back at the inn he found Nakata just as he'd left him, sound asleep. The light was on in the room, but that obviously didn't seem to bother him. What an easygoing old guy, Hoshino concluded. He took off his cap, his aloha shirt, and his jeans, then crawled into bed and turned out the light. But he felt worked up, and the combination of this and his new surroundings kept him from falling asleep. Jeez, he thought, maybe I should've found a hooker and got laid. But as he listened to Nakata's tranquil, regular breathing, he was suddenly embarrassed by the thought, though he wasn't sure why.

Staring at the ceiling in the dark, lying in bed in a cheap inn in a town he'd never been to before next to a strange old guy he knew nothing about, he began to have doubts about himself. By this time of night he should've been driving back to Tokyo, now somewhere around Nagoya. He didn't dislike his job, and there was a girl in Tokyo who always made time for him if he wanted to see her. Still, on an impulse, as soon as he'd unloaded his cargo of furniture in Kobe, he'd called another driver he knew in town and asked him to take his place and drive his rig back to Tokyo. He phoned his company and managed to wrangle three days off, and then it was off to Shikoku with Nakata. All he had along was a small bag with a shaving kit and a change of clothes.

Hoshino originally was intrigued by the resemblance between the old man and his late grandfather, but that impression had faded, and now he was more curious about Nakata himself. The things the old guy talked about, and even *how* he talked, were definitely strange, but in an interesting way. He had to find out where the old man was going, and what he'd end up doing when he got there.

Hoshino was born into a farming family, the third of five sons. Up until junior high he was well behaved, but after entering a trade school he fell in with a bad crowd and started getting in trouble. The police hauled him in a few times. He was able to graduate but couldn't find a decent job—and trouble with a girl only compounded his difficulties—so he decided to join the Self-Defense Force. Though he was hoping to be a tank driver, he didn't make the cut and spent most of his time driving large transport trucks. After three years in the SDF he got out and found a job with a trucking company, and for the last six years he'd been driving for a living.

This suited him. He'd always loved machines, and when he was perched high up in the cab with his hands on the wheel, it was like he was in his own private little kingdom. The job's long hard hours were tiring, but he knew he couldn't stand a regular company job, commuting to a dingy office every morning only to have a boss watch his every move like a hawk.

He'd always been the feisty type who got into fights. He was skinny and on the short side, not very tough looking, but in his case looks were deceiving. He was deceptively strong, and once he reached the breaking point a crazed look would come over him that sent most opponents scurrying for cover. He'd gotten into a lot of fights, both as a soldier and as a truck driver, but only recently had started to understand that this, win or lose, never accomplished very much. At least, he thought proudly, he'd never had any serious injuries.

During his wild high school days, his grandfather was always the one who'd show up at the local precinct, bowing apologetically to the police, and they'd release Hoshino into his custody. They always stopped at a restaurant on the way home, his grandfather treating him to a delicious meal. He never lectured Hoshino, even then. Not once did his parents come to get him. They were just barely scraping by and didn't have the time or energy to worry about their no-good third son. Hoshino sometimes wondered what would've happened to him if his grandfather hadn't been there to bail him out. The old man, at least, knew he was alive and worried about him.

Despite all this, he'd never once thanked his grandfather for all he'd done. He didn't know what to say, and was also too preoccupied trying to get by. His grandfather died of cancer soon after Hoshino joined the Self-Defense Force. At the end he got senile and didn't even recognize him. Hoshino hadn't been back home once since the old man passed away.

When Hoshino woke up at eight the next morning, Nakata was still fast asleep and looked like he hadn't budged an inch all night. The volume and pace of his breathing, too, was unchanged. Hoshino went downstairs and ate breakfast with the other guests. A pretty bare-bones meal, though there were unlimited seconds on miso soup and rice.

"Will your companion be eating breakfast?" the maid called out.

"He's still out cold. Looks like he won't be needing breakfast. If you don't mind, could you not put away the futon for a while?"

At noon, with Nakata still fast asleep, Hoshino arranged for them to stay one more night. He went out to a soba place and had chicken and egg over rice. Afterward he strolled around for a while and wound up in a coffee shop, where he had a cup and a smoke and flipped through a few of the comic books.

When he got back to the inn, just before two, he found Nakata still hadn't woken up. Concerned, he felt the old man's forehead, but he didn't seem to have a fever. His breathing was calm and regular, and his cheeks had a healthy glow to them. He seemed perfectly fine. All he was doing was sleeping soundly, without ever even turning over in bed.

"Is he all right, sleeping this much?" the maid said when she looked in on them. "Maybe he's ill?"

"He's exhausted," Hoshino explained. "Let's just let him sleep as much as he wants."

"Okay, but I've never seen anybody sleep so much before. . . ."

Dinnertime came and the sleep marathon continued. Hoshino went out to a curry restaurant and had an extra-large order of beef curry and a salad. After this he went to the same pachinko place as the night before and again played for an hour. This time, though, his luck changed, and for under ten dollars he won two cartons of Marlboros. It was nine-thirty by the time he got back to the inn with his winnings, and he couldn't believe his eyes—Nakata was still asleep.

Hoshino added up the hours. The old man had been sleeping for over twenty-four hours. Sure, he said he'd sleep a long time, so not to worry, but this was ridiculous! Hoshino felt uncharacteristically help-less. Suppose the old guy never woke up? What the hell was he supposed to do then?

"Cripes," he said, and shook his head.

But the next morning, when Hoshino woke up at seven, Nakata was already awake, gazing out the window.

"Hey, Gramps, so you finally made it up, huh?" Hoshino said, relieved.

"Yes, Nakata just woke up. I don't know how long I slept, but it must have been a long time. I feel like a new man."

"No kidding it was a long time! You went to sleep at nine p.m. the day before yesterday, so you've been asleep something like thirty-four hours. You're a regular Snow White."

"Nakata's kind of hungry."

"I bet you are. You haven't had a bite in two days."

The two of them went downstairs to the dining room and had breakfast. Nakata amazed the maid at how much rice he packed away.

"You're as big an eater as you are a sleeper!" she exclaimed. "It's like two days' worth of meals in one sitting!"

"Yes, I have to eat a lot now."

"You're a really healthy person, aren't you?"

"Yes, Nakata is. I can't read, but I've never had a single cavity and don't need glasses. I never have to go to the doctor, either. My shoulders never get stiff, and I take a good dump every morning."

"Isn't that something," the maid said, impressed. "By the way, what's on your schedule for today?"

"We're headed west," Nakata declared.

"West," she mused. "That must mean you're going toward Takamatsu."

"I'm not so bright and don't know geography."

"Anyway, Gramps, why don't we go over to Takamatsu?" Hoshino chimed in. "We can figure out what's next after we get there."

"All right. Let's go to Takamatsu, then. We'll figure out what's next after we get there."

"Sort of a unique style of traveling, I must say," the maid commented.

"You got that right," Hoshino said.

Back in their room, Nakata went to the toilet, while Hoshino, still in his yukata robe, lay back on the tatami and watched the news on TV. Not much was happening. Police still didn't have any leads in the murder of a famous sculptor in Nakano—no clues, no witnesses. The police were searching for the man's fifteen-year-old son, who'd disappeared shortly before the murder.

Man alive, Hoshino thought, a fifteen-year-old kid. Why is it that these days it's always fifteen-year-olds who're involved in all these violent incidents? Of course when he was fifteen himself, he stole a motorcycle from a parking lot and went for a joyride—without, mind you, a license—so he had no right to complain. Not that you could compare borrowing a motorcycle and slicing your dad into sashimi. It was only luck, maybe, that had kept him from stabbing his own father, because he'd certainly taken his share of beatings.

The news was just winding up when Nakata emerged from the bathroom. "Mr. Hoshino, may I ask you something?"

"What's up?"

"Does your back hurt at all?"

"Yeah, it's an occupational hazard, I guess. Every trucker I know has back problems, just like pitchers all have sore shoulders. Why do you ask?"

"When I saw your back I thought maybe you had that problem."

"Huh . . ."

"Do you mind if Nakata touches your back?"

"Be my guest."

Hoshino lay facedown and Nakata straddled him. He put his hands just above the backbone and held them there. All the while Hoshino was watching some afternoon talk show featuring all the latest celebrity gossip. A famous actress had just gotten engaged to a not-so-famous young novelist. Hoshino didn't care, but there wasn't anything else on. Apparently the actress's income was ten times that of the novelist, who wasn't even particularly handsome or very intelligent looking.

Hoshino found the whole thing suspect. "That marriage won't work out, I can tell you that. There's gotta be some kind of misunderstanding going on here."

"Mr. Hoshino, your bones are out of line a bit."

"Not surprising, what with the out-of-line kind of life I've led," Hoshino replied, and yawned.

"It's going to cause all sorts of problems if you don't do something about it."

"You think?"

"You'll get headaches, you won't be able to take a good dump. And then your back will go out on you."

"That can't be good."

"This will hurt a little. Do you mind?"

"No, go right ahead."

"Honestly speaking, it's going to hurt a *lot*."

"Look, Gramps, I've been punched out my whole life—at home, at school, in the SDF—but I survived. Not to brag or anything, but the days I haven't been hit I could count on both hands. So I'm not worried that something might hurt a little. Hot or tickly, sweet or spicy—bring it on."

Nakata squinted, concentrating, carefully making sure he had his thumbs just where he wanted them. Once they were positioned just right, he ever so slowly increased the pressure, gauging Hoshino's reaction. He breathed in deeply, then let out a clipped cry like some winter bird's squawk, and pressed down with all his might on the area between muscle and backbone. The pain Hoshino felt at that instant was awful, unreasonably so. A huge flash of light went off in his brain and everything went white. He stopped breathing. It felt like he'd been thrown from the top of a tall tower into the depths of hell. He couldn't even manage a scream, so hideous was the pain. All thoughts had burned up and shot away. It was like his body had been shattered into pieces. Even death couldn't be this awful, he felt. He tried to open his eyes but couldn't. He just lay there, helpless, facedown on the tatami, drooling, tears streaming down his face. He must have endured this for some thirty seconds or so.

Finally he was able to breathe again, and he staggered as he sat up. The tatami wavered before him like the sea in a storm.

"I'm sure it was painful."

Hoshino shook his head a few times, as if checking to see that he was still alive. "Pain doesn't begin to describe it. Imagine getting skinned alive, skewered, ground down, then run over by an angry herd of bulls. What the hell did you *do* to me?"

"I put your bones back in the right position. You should be fine for the time being. Your back won't ache. And I guarantee you'll take good dumps."

As predicted, when the pain receded, like the tide going out, his back did feel better. The usual heavy, sluggish feeling had vanished. The area around his temples felt much better, and he could breathe more easily. And sure enough, he felt like going to the john.

"Yeah, I guess certain parts do feel better."

"The problem was all in the spine," Nakata said.

"But damn did that hurt," Hoshino said, and sighed.

The two of them took the JR express train from Tokushima Station bound for Takamatsu. Hoshino paid for everything, the inn and the train fare. Nakata insisted on paying his share, but Hoshino wouldn't hear of it.

"I'll pay now, and we can settle up later. I don't like it when men go all to pieces over money, okay?"

"All right. Nakata doesn't understand money very well, so I'll do as you say," Nakata said.

"I gotta tell you, though, I feel great, thanks to that shiatsu you did on me. So at least let me pay you back for it, okay? I haven't felt this good in I don't know how long. I feel like a new man."

"That's wonderful. Nakata doesn't know what shiatsu means, but I do know how important the bones are."

"I'm not sure what you call it either—shiatsu, bone-setting, chiropractic—but whatever it is, you've really got a talent for it. You could make a lot of money doing this. You could make a bundle just doing all my trucker buddies."

"As soon as I saw your back I could tell the bones were out of line. When I see something out of line I like to set it right. I made furniture for a long time and whenever I saw something crooked I just had to straighten it out. That's just how Nakata is. But this was the first time I straightened out bones."

"I guess you're a natural," Hoshino said, impressed.

"Nakata used to be able to speak with cats."

"No kidding?"

"But not so long ago I couldn't talk with them anymore. It must be Johnnie Walker's fault."

"I see."

"I'm stupid, so I don't understand difficult things. And there have been so many difficult things happening lately. Fish and leeches falling from the sky, for instance."

"Really?"

"But I'm glad I could make your back better. If you feel good, then Nakata feels good."

"I'm really happy, too," Hoshino said.

"That's good."

"Now that you mention those leeches . . ."

"Yes, Nakata remembers that very well."

"Did you have something to do with that?"

Nakata thought about it for a while, a rare occurrence. "I don't really know myself. All I know is when I opened my umbrella it started to rain leeches."

"What'ya know. . . ."

"The worst thing of all is killing other people," Nakata said, and gave a decisive nod.

"Absolutely. Killing is bad, for sure."

"That's right," Nakata said again, nodding forcefully.

The two of them got out at Takamatsu Station, then slipped inside a noodle place near the station and had udon for lunch. Outside the restaurant window there were several large cranes on the docks, covered with seagulls.

Nakata methodically enjoyed each and every noodle. "This udon is delicious," he said.

"Glad you like it," Hoshino said. "So, what do you think? Is this spot okay?"

"Yes, Nakata thinks it will do."

"So we got the right spot picked out. Now what are you going to do?"

"I've got to find the entrance stone."

"*Entrance* stone?"

"That's right."

"Hmm," Hoshino said. "I bet there's a long story behind that."

Nakata tilted his bowl and drained the last drop of soup. "Yes, it is a long story. But it's so long I don't understand it myself. Once we get there, though, Nakata thinks we'll understand."

"As usual, you gotta be there to get it?"

"Yes, that's right."

"Until we go there I won't understand it."

"Yes. Until we go there *I* won't understand it either."

"Enough already. I don't like long stories. Anyway, I guess we need to find this *entrance stone* thing."

"That is correct," Nakata said.

"So where is it?"

"Nakata has no idea."

"Like I had to ask," Hoshino said, shaking his head.

Chapter 25

I fall asleep for a short time, wake up, fall asleep again, wake up, over and over. I don't want to miss the moment she appears. But I do miss it—I look up and she's already seated at the desk, just like last night. The clock next to my bed shows a little past three. I'm positive I closed the curtains before going to bed, but again they're wide open. But there's no moon tonight—that's the only difference. There's a heavy cloud cover, and it might be drizzling outside. The room's much darker than last night, with only distant lamps in the garden casting a faint light between the trees. It takes a while for my eyes to adjust.

The girl is seated at the desk, head in her hands, gazing at the painting. She's wearing the same clothes as last night. Even if I squint and look hard, this time it's too dark to make out her face. Strangely enough, though, her body and silhouette stand out, floating there clearly in the darkness. The girl is Miss Saeki when she was young—I have absolutely no doubt about it.

She looks deep in thought. Or in the midst of a long, deep dream. Check that—maybe she herself *is* Miss Saeki's long, deep dream. At any rate, I try to breathe very quietly so as not to disturb the balance of this scene before me. I don't move an inch, just glance occasionally at the clock to check the time. Time passes slowly, regularly.

Out of the blue my heart starts beating hard, a dry sound like somebody's knocking at the door. The sound echoes through the silent, dead-of-night room, and startles me so much that I nearly leap right out of bed.

The girl's black silhouette moves ever so slightly. She looks up and listens in the dark. She's heard it—the sound of my heart. She tilts her head just a fraction, for all the world like an animal in the woods focusing on an unexpected, unknown sound. Then she turns to face me in bed. But I don't register in her eyes, I can tell. I'm not in her dream. She and I are in two separate worlds, divided by an invisible boundary.

Just as quickly as it came on, my pounding heart settles back down to normal. And so does my breathing. I'm back to being invisible, and she's no longer listening. Her gaze falls back on *Kafka on the Shore*. Head in hands like before, her heart is drawn once more toward the boy in that summer scene.

She's there for about twenty minutes, then vanishes. Just like last night, she stands up, barefoot, noiselessly glides toward the door, and, without opening it, disappears outside. I sit still for a while, then finally get up. Keeping the light off, I go over in the darkness and sit down on the seat she just occupied. I rest both hands on the desk and absorb the afterglow of her presence. I close my eyes, scooping up her shivering heart, letting it seep inside mine. I keep my eyes closed.

There's one thing, I discover, the girl and I have in common. We're both in love with someone who's no longer of this world.

A short time later I fall into a restless sleep. My body needs rest, but my mind won't allow it. I swing like a pendulum, back and forth between the two. Later, though—I'm not even sure if it's light out or not—birds begin making a racket in the garden, and their voices pull me completely awake.

I tug on jeans and pull a long-sleeved shirt over my T-shirt and go outside. It's after five o'clock and nobody else is up. I walk out of the old-looking town, through the pine forest set up as a windbreak, past the seawall and out onto the beach. There's barely a breeze against my skin. The sky's covered with a layer of gray clouds, but it doesn't look like it's going to rain anytime soon. It's a quiet, still morning. Like a layer of soundproofing, the clouds absorb every sound the earth sends up.

I walk for a while on a path that parallels the sea, picturing the boy in the painting walking the same path, canvas chair in hand, sitting on the shore. I'm not sure, though, what scene along this shore the painting depicts. The painting only shows the beach, the horizon, sky, and clouds. And an island. But there are a number of islands along the shore, and I can't exactly recall what the one in the painting looked like. I sit down on the sand, face the sea, and make a kind of picture frame with my hands. I imagine the boy sitting there. A single white seagull flits aimlessly across the windless sky. Small waves break against the shore at regular intervals, leaving behind a gentle curve and tiny bubbles on the sand.

All of a sudden I realize—I'm jealous of the boy in the painting.

"You're jealous of the boy in the painting," the boy called Crow whispers in my ear.

You're jealous of that pitiful, twenty-year-old boy mistaken for someone else and pointlessly murdered—what is it, thirty years ago? So insanely jealous it hurts. This is the first time you've ever been jealous in your life. Now you finally understand what it feels like. It's like a brush fire torching your heart.

You've never ever in your life envied anybody else, or ever wanted to be someone else—but right now you do. You want more than anything to be that boy. Even knowing that at age twenty he was going to be smashed over the head with an iron pipe and beaten to death, you'd still trade places with him. You'd do it, to be able to love Miss Saeki for those five years. And to have her love you with all her heart. To hold her as much as you want, to make love to her over and over. To let your fingers run over every single part of her body, and let her do the same to you. And after you die, your love will become a story etched forever in her heart. Every single night she'll love you in her memory.

Yup, you're in a strange position, all right. You're in love with a girl who is no more, jealous of a boy who's gone forever. Even so, this emotion you're feeling is more real, and more intensely painful, than anything you've ever felt before. And there's no way out. No possibility of finding an exit. You've wandered into a labyrinth of time, and the biggest problem of all is that you have no desire at all to get out. Am I right?

Oshima comes in a little later than yesterday. Before he does I vacuum the first and second floors, wipe down all the desks and chairs, open the windows and clean them, wash out the restroom, throw out the garbage, pour fresh water in the vases. Then I turn on all the lights and switch on the catalog computers. All that's left is to open the front gate.

Oshima checks my work and gives a satisfied nod. "You learn pretty quick, and don't fool around, do you?"

I boil some water and make him some coffee. Like yesterday, I have a cup of Earl Grey. It's started raining outside, pretty heavily. You can hear thunder off in the distance. It's not yet noon, but it's like evening it's so dark.

"Oshima, I have something I'd like you to do for me."

"What's that?"

"Can you get hold of the sheet music for 'Kafka on the Shore' somewhere?"

Oshima thinks it over. "As long as it's on a music publisher's website, I imagine you could download it for a fee. I'll check it out and let you know."

"Thanks."

He sits down on a corner of the counter, puts the tiniest lump of sugar into his coffee cup, then carefully stirs it with a spoon. "So you like the song?"

"Yeah, a lot."

"I'm fond of it myself. It's a lovely tune, quite unique. Simple yet deep. It tells you a lot about the person who composed it."

"The lyrics, though, are pretty symbolic," I venture.

"From time immemorial, symbolism and poetry have been inseparable. Like a pirate and his rum."

"Do you think Miss Saeki knew what all the lyrics mean?"

Oshima looks up, listening to the thunder as if calculating how far away it is. He turns to me and shakes his head. "Not necessarily. Symbolism and meaning are two separate things. I think she found the right words by bypassing procedures like meaning and logic. She captured words in a dream, like delicately catching hold of a butterfly's wings as it flutters around. Artists are those who can evade the verbose."

"So you're saying Miss Saeki maybe found those words in some other space—like in dreams?"

"Most great poetry is like that. If the words can't create a prophetic tunnel connecting them to the reader, then the whole thing no longer functions as a poem."

"But plenty of poems only pretend to do that."

"Right. It's a kind of trick, and as long as you know that it isn't hard. As long as you use some symbolic-sounding words, the whole thing looks like a poem of sorts."

"In 'Kafka on the Shore' I feel something urgent and serious."

"Me too," Oshima says. "The words aren't just something on the surface. But the words and melody are so inseparable in my mind, I can't look at the lyrics as pure poetry and decide how persuasive they are by themselves." He shakes his head slightly. "At any rate, she was definitely blessed with a natural talent, and had a real sense for music. She was also practical enough to grab an opportunity when it came along. If that terrible incident hadn't taken her out of circulation, I'm sure she would've developed her talent even further. In any number of ways it's a real shame. . . ."

"So where did all that talent go?"

Oshima looks at me. "You're asking where Miss Saeki's talent went after her boyfriend died?"

I nod. "If talent's a kind of natural energy, doesn't it have to find an outlet?"

"I don't know," he replies. "Nobody can predict where talent's headed. Sometimes it simply vanishes. Other times it sinks down under the earth like an underground stream and flows off who knows where."

"Maybe Miss Saeki focused her talents somewhere else, other than music," I venture.

"Somewhere else?" Oshima, obviously interested, narrows his brow. "What do you mean?"

I'm at a loss for words. "I don't know. . . . I just feel maybe that's what happened. Maybe into something intangible."

"Intangible?"

"Something other people can't see, something you pursue for yourself. An inner process."

Oshima brushes his hair off his forehead, locks of it spilling between his slender fingers. "That's an interesting idea. For all we know, after Miss Saeki came back to town maybe she used her talents somewhere out of sight—as you said, for something *intangible*. But you have to remember she disappeared for about twenty-five years, so unless you ask her yourself there's no way of knowing for sure."

I hesitate, then decide to just go ahead. "Can I ask you something really stupid?"

"Really stupid?"

I blush. "Totally off the wall."

"No problem. I don't necessarily mind stupid, off-the-wall things."

"I can't believe I'm actually saying this to somebody."

Oshima tilts his head ever so slightly, waiting for me to go on.

"Is it possible that Miss Saeki . . . is my mother?"

Oshima leans back against the counter, taking time to search for the right words. The clock on the wall ticks away as I wait.

Finally he speaks up. "So what you're saying is that when she was twenty, Miss Saeki left Takamatsu in despair and was living alone someplace when she happened to meet your father, Koichi Tamura, and they got married. They were blessed with you and then, four years later, something happened and she ran away, leaving you behind. After this there's a mysterious blank, but then she shows up back in Shikoku. Do I have that right?"

"Yeah."

"It's not impossible. What I mean is, at this point I don't have any evidence to refute your hypothesis. So much of her life is a total mystery. Rumor has it she lived in Tokyo. Plus she's about the same age as your father. When she came back to Takamatsu, though, she was alone. How old did you say your sister is?"

"Twenty-one."

"The same age as me," Oshima says. "*I'm* not your sister—that much I know for certain. I've got parents, and my brother—all related by blood. A family way too good for me." He folds his arms and looks at me for a while. "I've got a question for *you*. Have you ever looked at your family register? That would give your mother's name and age."

"Of course I have."

"So what did it say?"

"There wasn't any name," I say.

He looks surprised. "No *name*? How can that be?"

"There wasn't any. No kidding. I have no idea why. As far as the family register's concerned, I don't have a mother. Or an older sister. There's just my father's name and mine on the register. Legally, I'm a bastard. An illegitimate child."

"But you actually had a mother and a sister at one time."

I nod. "I did, until I was four. The four of us lived together. It's not just my imagination. I remember it very clearly. The two of them left soon after I turned four." I pull out my wallet and show Oshima the photo of me and my sister playing at the shore. He gazes at it for a moment, smiles, and hands it back.

" 'Kafka on the Shore,' " he says.

I nod and put the photograph back in my wallet. The wind swirls outside, pounding rain against the window. The ceiling light casts a shadow of me and Oshima on the floor, where we look like we're having an ominous talk in some alternate world.

"You don't remember your mother's face?" Oshima asks. "You lived together till you were four, so you should have some memory of what she looked like."

I shake my head. "I just can't recall, not at all. I don't know why, but the part of my memory where her face should be is dark, painted over, blank."

Oshima ponders this for a while. "Tell me more about why you think Miss Saeki might be your mother."

"That's enough," I say. "Let's just forget it. I'm making too much of it."

"It's all right—go ahead and say what's on your mind," he says. "Then the two of us can decide if you're making too much of it or not."

Oshima's shadow on the floor moves in time with his movements, though it's slightly more exaggerated.

"There are an amazing amount of coincidences between me and Miss Saeki," I say. "They're like pieces of a puzzle that fit together. I understood this when I listened to 'Kafka on the Shore.' First off is the fact that I was drawn to this library, like fate reeling me in. A straight line from Nakano to Takamatsu. Very strange, when you think about it."

"Like the plot of a Greek tragedy," Oshima comments.

"Plus," I add, "I'm in love with her."

"With Miss Saeki?"

"Yeah, probably."

"*Probably?*" Oshima repeats, frowning. "Do you mean it's *probably* Miss Saeki you're in love with? Or that you're *probably* in love with her?"

I turn red. "I can't really explain it," I reply. "It's complicated and there's a lot of stuff I still don't get."

"But you're probably in love, probably with Miss Saeki?"

"Right," I say. "Very much."

"*Probably*, but also very much."

I nod.

"At the same time it's possible she's your mother?"

Another of my patented nods.

"For a fifteen-year-old who doesn't even shave yet, you're sure carrying a lot of baggage around." Oshima takes a sip of his coffee and carefully places the cup back on its saucer. "I'm not saying that's wrong. Just that everything has a critical point."

I don't say anything.

Oshima touches his temples and is lost in thought for a time. He crosses his slim fingers together in front of his chest. "I'll try to find that sheet music as soon as I can. I can finish up here, so why don't you go back to your room."

At lunchtime I take over from Oshima at the front counter. There are fewer visitors than usual, probably due to the steady rain. When he comes back from his break, he hands me a large envelope with a computer printout of the sheet music for "Kafka on the Shore."

"Convenient world we live in," he says.

"Thanks," I tell him.

"If you don't mind, why don't you take a cup of coffee upstairs. No cream or sugar. You make really good coffee."

I make a fresh cup and take it on a tray to the second floor. As always, the door to Miss Saeki's room is open and she's at her desk, writing. When I put the cup of coffee on her desk, she looks up at me and smiles, then puts the cap back on her fountain pen and rests it on top of the paper.

"So, are you getting used to things around here?"

"Bit by bit," I answer.

"Are you free now?"

"Yes, I am," I tell her.

"Why don't you sit down, then." Miss Saeki points to the wooden chair beside her desk. "Let's talk for a while."

It's starting to thunder again. Still far away, but gradually getting closer. I do what she says and take a seat.

"How old are you again? Sixteen?"

"Fifteen. I just turned fifteen," I respond.

"You ran away from home, didn't you?"

"Yes, I did."

"Was there some reason you had to do that?"

I shake my head. What should I say?

Miss Saeki picks up the cup and takes a sip while she waits for my answer.

"I felt like if I stayed there I'd be damaged beyond repair," I say.

"Damaged?" Miss Saeki says, narrowing her eyes.

"Yes," I say.

After a pause she says, "It sounds strange for a boy your age to use a word like *damaged*, though I must say I'm intrigued. What exactly do you mean by damaged?"

I search for the right words. First I look for the boy named Crow, but he's nowhere to be found. I'm left to choose them on my own, and that takes time. But Miss Saeki waits there patiently. Lightning flashes outside, and after a time thunder booms far away.

"I mean I'd change into something I shouldn't."

Miss Saeki looks at me with great interest. "As long as there's such a thing as time, everybody's damaged in the end, changed into something else. It always happens, sooner or later."

"But even if that happens, you've got to have a place you can retrace your steps to."

"A place you can retrace your steps to?"

"A place that's worth coming back to."

Miss Saeki stares straight at me.

I blush, then summon my courage and look up at her. She has on a navy blue dress with short sleeves. She must have a whole closet of dresses in different shades of blue. Her only accessories are a thin silver necklace and a smallish wristwatch with a black leather band. I look for the fifteen-year-old girl in her and find her right away. She's hidden, asleep, like a 3-D painting in the forest of her heart. But if you look carefully you can spot her. My chest starts pounding again, like somebody's hammering a long nail into the walls surrounding it.

"For a fifteen-year-old, you make a lot of sense."

I have no idea how to respond to that. So I don't say anything.

"When I was fifteen," Miss Saeki says with a smile, "all I wanted was to go off to some other world, a place beyond anybody's reach. A place beyond the flow of time."

"But there's no place like that in this world."

"Exactly. Which is why I'm living here, in this world where things are continually damaged, where the heart is fickle, where time flows past without a break." As if hinting at the flow of time, she's silent for a while. "But you know," she goes on, "when I was fifteen, I thought there had to be a place like that in the world. I was sure that somewhere I'd run across the entrance that would take me to that other world."

"Were you lonely when you were fifteen?"

"In a sense, I guess. I wasn't alone, but I was terribly lonely. Because I knew that I would never be happier than I was then. That much I knew for sure. That's why I wanted to go—just as I was—to some place where there *was* no time."

"What I want is to grow up faster."

Miss Saeki pulls back to study my expression. "You must be much stronger and more independent than I am. At your age I was filled with illusions of escaping reality, but you're standing right up to the real world and confronting it head-on. That's a big difference."

Strong and independent? I'm neither one. I'm just being pushed along by reality, whether I like it or not. But I don't say anything.

"You know, you remind me of a fifteen-year-old boy I used to know a long time ago."

"Did he look like me?" I ask.

"You're taller and more muscular than he was, but there is a resemblance. He didn't enjoy talking with other kids his age—they were on a different wavelength—so he spent most of his time holed up in his room, reading or listening to music. He'd get the same frown lines, too, whenever the topic got difficult. And you love to read as well."

I nod.

Miss Saeki glances at her watch. "Thank you for the coffee."

Taking that as my signal to leave, I stand up and head for the door. Miss Saeki picks up her black fountain pen, slowly twists off the cap, and goes back to her writing. There's another flash of lightning outside, bathing the room for an instant in a weird color. The clap of thunder hits a moment later. This time it's closer than before.

"Kafka," Miss Saeki says.

I stop at the doorway and turn around.

"I just remembered that I wrote a book on lightning once."

I don't say anything. A book on lightning?

"I went all over Japan interviewing people who'd survived lightning strikes. It took me a few years. Most of the interviews were pretty interesting. A small publisher put it out, but it barely sold. The book didn't come to any conclusion, and nobody wants to read a book that doesn't have one. For me, though, having no conclusion seemed perfectly fine."

A tiny hammer in my head is pounding on a drawer somewhere, persistently. I'm trying to remember something, something very important—but I don't know what it is. By this time Miss Saeki's gone back to her writing and I go back to my room.

The rainstorm continues to batter us for another hour. The thunder is so incredibly loud that I'm afraid the windows in the library will shatter. Every time a bolt of lightning streaks across the sky, the stained-glass window on the landing flashes an image like some ancient ghost on the white wall across from it. By two o'clock, the storm lets up, and yellowish light begins to spill out between the clouds like a reconciliation has finally been reached. Water continues to drip down in the gentle sunlight.

When evening rolls around, I start closing up the place for the night. Miss Saeki says good-bye to me and Oshima and heads home. I hear the engine of her Golf and picture her seated at the wheel, turning the key. I tell Oshima I'll finish locking up. Whistling some aria, he goes off to wash up in the restroom, then leaves. I listen as the Mazda Miata roars off, the sound fading off in the distance. Now the library's all mine. It's much quieter than ever before.

I go to my room and study the sheet music for "Kafka on the Shore." Like I suspected, most of the chords are simple. The refrain, though, has a couple tricky ones. I go over to the reading room and try playing it on the upright piano. The fingering's really tough, so I practice it over and over, trying to get my hands around it, and somehow wind up getting it to sound right. At first the chords sound all wrong. I'm sure it's a misprint, or that the piano's out of tune. But the longer I listen to how those two chords sound one after the other, the more I'm convinced the whole song hangs on them. These two chords are what keep "Kafka on the Shore" from degrading into some silly pop song, give it a special depth and substance. But how in the world did Miss Saeki come up with them?

I go back to my room, boil water in the electric kettle, and make some tea. I take out the old records we found in the storage room and put them on the turntable one after another. Bob Dylan's *Blonde on Blonde*, the Beatles' "White Album," Otis Redding's *Dock of the Bay*, Stan Getz's *Getz/Gilberto*—all hit albums from the late sixties. That young boy—with Miss Saeki right beside him—must've done what I was doing, putting the records on the turntable, lowering the needle, listening to the music coming out of these speakers. The music felt like it was taking me and the whole room off to some different time, a world before I was even born. As I enjoy the music, I review the conversation we'd had that afternoon, trying to capture our exact words.

"When I was fifteen, I thought there had to be a place like that in the world. I was sure that somewhere I'd run across the entrance that would take me to that other world."

I can hear her voice right beside me. Inside my head something knocks at a door, a heavy, persistent knock.

An entrance?

I lift the needle off the Stan Getz album, pull out the single of "Kafka on the Shore," place it on the turntable, and lower the needle. And listen to her sing.

> *The drowning girl's fingers*
> *Search for the entrance stone, and more.*
> *Lifting the hem of her azure dress,*
> *She gazes—*
> *at Kafka on the shore.*

The girl who comes to this room most likely located that entrance stone. She's in another world, just as she was at fifteen, and at night she comes to visit this room. In her light blue dress, she comes to gaze at Kafka on the shore.

Suddenly, completely out of nowhere, I remember my father talking about how he'd once been struck by lightning. He didn't tell me himself—I'd read about it in an interview in a magazine. When he was a student in art college, he had a part-time job as a caddy at a golf course. One day he was following his golfer around the course when the sky suddenly changed color and a huge thunderstorm crashed down on them. They took refuge under a tree when it was hit by a bolt of lightning. This huge tree was split right in two. The golfer he was caddying for was killed, but my father, sensing something, leaped away from the tree in time. He got some light burns, his hair was singed, and the shock of the lightning threw him against a rock. He struck his head and lost consciousness, but survived the ordeal with only a small scar on his forehead. That's what I was trying to remember this afternoon, standing there in Miss Saeki's doorway listening to the roar of the thunder. It was after he recovered from his injuries that my father got serious about his career as a sculptor.

As Miss Saeki went around interviewing people for her book, maybe she met my father. It's entirely possible. There can't be that many people around who've been struck by lightning and lived, can there?

I breathe very quietly, waiting for the dawn. A cloud parts, and moonlight shines down on the trees in the garden. There are just too many coincidences. Everything seems to be speeding up, rushing toward one destination.

Chapter 26

It was already pretty late in the afternoon, and they had to find a place to stay for the night. Hoshino went to the tourist information booth at Takamatsu Station and had them make a reservation at an inn. It was within walking distance of the station, which was nice, but otherwise was typical and somewhat dumpy. Neither Hoshino nor Nakata minded much, though. As long as there were futons to sleep on, they were fine. As before, breakfast was provided but they were on their own for dinner. This particularly suited Nakata, who was likely to drop off to sleep any time.

Once they were in their room, Nakata had Hoshino lie facedown on the futon, got on top of him again, and pressed down with both thumbs up and down his lower back, carefully checking out the condition of his joints and muscles. This time he was much more gentle, just tracing the spine and checking out how tense the muscles were.

"Something wrong?" Hoshino asked anxiously.

"No, everything's fine. Nakata doesn't find anything wrong with you now. Your spine's in good shape."

"That's a relief," Hoshino said. "I wasn't looking forward to another torture session."

"I know. Nakata's really sorry. But you did tell me you didn't mind pain, so I went ahead and did it as hard as I could."

"Yeah, I know that's what I said. But listen, Gramps, there *are* limits. Sometimes you've gotta use common sense. But I guess I shouldn't be complaining—you did fix my back. But man alive, I never felt anything like that in my life. The pain was unimaginable! It felt like you were ripping me apart. Like I died and came back to life or something."

"Nakata was dead for three weeks once."

"No kidding," Hoshino said. Still facedown, he took a gulp of tea and munched on some crunchy snacks he'd picked up at a convenience store. "So you really were dead?"

"I was."

"Where were you all that time?"

"Nakata doesn't remember. It felt like I was somewhere far away, doing something else. But my head was floating and I can't remember anything. Then I came back to this world and found out I was dumb. I couldn't read or write anymore."

"You must've left your ability to read and write over on the other side."

"Maybe so."

The two of them were silent for a time. Hoshino decided it was best to believe whatever the old man told him, no matter how eccentric it sounded. At the same time he felt uneasy, as if pursuing this dead-for-three-weeks idea any further would lead him into some chaotic, out-of-control situation. Better to turn the conversation back to more practical matters. "So, now that we're in Takamatsu, Mr. Nakata, where are you planning to go?"

"I have no idea," Nakata replied. "I don't know what I'm supposed to do."

"What about that entrance stone?"

"That's right! Nakata completely forgot about it. We have to find the stone. But I don't have a clue where to look. My mind's floating and won't clear up. I wasn't too bright to begin with, and this kind of thing only makes it worse."

"We're in a bit of a fix, then, aren't we?"

"Yes, I'd say we are."

"Not that sitting here staring at each other's all that much fun. This won't get us anywhere."

"You're right."

"I think we should go around asking people, you know, if that stone's somewhere around here."

"If you say so, then that's what Nakata wants to do. I'm pretty dumb, so I'm used to asking people questions."

"My grandpa always said asking a question is embarrassing for a moment, but not asking is embarrassing for a lifetime."

"I agree. When you die, everything you know disappears."

"Well, that's not what he meant, exactly," Hoshino said, scratching his head. "Anyway, do you have a mental image of the stone? What *kind* of stone it is, how big it is, its shape or color? What it's used for? If we don't have some details, it's hard to ask. Nobody's going to know what the heck we're talking about if we just say, *Is there an entrance stone anywhere around here?* They'll think we're nuts. You see what I mean?"

"Yes, I do. I might be dumb, but I'm not nuts."

"Okay."

"The stone Nakata's looking for is very special. It's not so big. It's white, and doesn't have any smell. I don't know what it's used for. It's round, sort of like a rice cake." He held up his hands to indicate something the size of an LP record.

"Hmm. So if you spotted it, do you think you'd recognize it? You know, like—*Hey, here it is.*"

"Nakata would know it right away."

"There must be some kind of story or legend behind it. Maybe it's famous and on display at a shrine or someplace."

"It could be, I suppose."

"Or maybe it's just in some house, and people use it as a weight when they make pickles."

"No, that's not possible."

"Why not?"

"Because nobody can move the stone."

"Nobody except *you*, you mean."

"Yes, I think Nakata probably can."

"After you move it, then what?"

Nakata did an uncharacteristic thing—he pondered this for a good long time. At least he looked like he was, briskly rubbing his short, salt-and-pepper hair. "I don't really know about that," he finally said. "All I know is it's about time somebody moved it."

Hoshino did some pondering himself. "And that somebody's *you*, right? At least for now."

"Yes," Nakata replied, "that's correct."

"Is the stone found only in Takamatsu?"

"No, it isn't. It doesn't really matter where it is. It just happens to be here right now. It would be much easier if it was in Nakano Ward."

"But moving that kind of stone must be risky."

"That's right. Maybe Nakata shouldn't bring this up, but it is very dangerous."

"Damn," Hoshino said, slowly shaking his head. He put on his

Chunichi Dragons cap and pulled his ponytail out the hole in the back. "This is starting to feel like an Indiana Jones movie or something."

The next morning they went to the tourist information booth in the station to ask if there were any famous stones in Takamatsu or the vicinity.

"Stones?" the girl behind the counter said, frowning slightly. She'd been trained to introduce all the usual tourist places, but nothing beyond that, and the question clearly had her flustered. "What sort of stones are you looking for?"

"A round stone about so big," Hoshino said, forming his hands in a circle the size of an LP, just as Nakata had done. "It's called the entrance stone."

" 'Entrance stone'?"

"Yep. That's the name. It's pretty famous, I imagine."

"Entrance to *what*, though?"

"If I knew that I wouldn't have to go to all this trouble."

The girl thought about it for a while. Hoshino gazed at her face the whole time. Kind of pretty, he judged, though her eyes are a bit too far apart, giving her the look of a cautious bovine. She made a few calls, but it didn't look like she was getting anywhere.

"I'm sorry," she finally said. "Nobody's heard of a stone by that name."

"Nobody?"

She shook her head. "Excuse me for asking, but are you here just to find this stone?"

"Yeah, I don't know if it's *just* to see it. Anyway, I'm from Nagoya. The old guy's from Nakano Ward in Tokyo."

"Yes, Nakata's from Nakano Ward," Nakata chimed in. "I rode in a lot of trucks, and even got treated to eel once. I came this far and haven't spent a cent of my own money."

"I see . . . ," the girl said.

"Not to worry. If nobody's heard about the stone, what're ya gonna do, huh? It's not your fault. But maybe they call it something else. Are there any other famous stones around here? You know, something with a legend behind it, maybe? Or some stone people pray to? Anything like that?"

The girl looked timidly at Hoshino with her too-far-apart eyes, taking in his Chunichi Dragons cap, his hair and ponytail, his green-tinted sunglasses, pierced ear, and rayon aloha shirt. "I'd be happy to tell you how to get to the city public library. You could research the stone there. I don't know much about stones myself, I'm afraid."

The library, however, yielded nothing. There wasn't a single book in the place devoted to stones in or around Takamatsu. The reference librarian, saying they might run across a reference somewhere, plunked down a stack of books in front of them: *Legends of Kagawa Prefecture*, *Legends of Kobo Daishi in Shikoku*, *A History of Takamatsu*, and the like. Sighing deeply, Hoshino started leafing through them. For his part, Nakata carefully turned one page after another in a photo collection entitled *Famous Stones of Japan*.

"I can't read," he said, "so this is the first library I've ever been in."

"I'm not proud of it," Hoshino said, "but this is a first for me, too. Even though I *can*."

"It's kind of interesting now that we're here."

"Glad to hear it."

"There's a library in Nakano Ward. I think I'll stop by there every now and then. The best thing is they don't charge anything. Nakata had no idea they'd let you in if you can't read."

"I've got a cousin who was born blind, but he goes to see movies," Hoshino said. "What fun could that be?"

"I can see, but I've never been to a movie theater."

"You're kidding! I'll have to take you sometime."

The librarian came over and warned them to keep their voices down, so they stopped talking and went back to their books. When he finished with *Famous Stones of Japan*, Nakata put it back on the shelf and began flipping through *Cats of the World*.

Grumbling all the while, Hoshino managed to look through all the books piled up next to him. Unfortunately, he couldn't find any matches in any of them. There were several references to the stone walls of Takamatsu Castle, but the stones in those walls were so massive that for Nakata to pick one up was out of the question. There was also a promising legend about Kobo Daishi, a famous scholarly monk of the Heian period. It was claimed that when he lifted up a stone in a wilderness, a spring gushed out and the place became a fertile rice field, but that was the end of the story. Hoshino also read about one shrine that had a stone called the Treasure of Children Stone, but it was more than a yard tall and shaped like a phallus. No way that could be the one Nakata was looking for.

The two of them gave up, left the library, and went to a nearby diner for dinner. They both had noodles topped with tempura, Hoshino ordering an extra bowl of noodles and broth.

"I enjoyed the library," Nakata said. "I had no idea there were so many kinds of cats in the world."

"The stone thing didn't pan out, but that's all right," Hoshino told him. "We just got started. Let's get a good night's sleep and see what tomorrow brings."

The next morning they went back to the library. Like the day before, Hoshino read through a huge stack of books, one after the other. He'd never read so many books in his life. By now he was fairly conversant with the history of Shikoku, and he'd learned that people had worshipped different kinds of stones for centuries. But what he really wanted—a description of this entrance stone—was nowhere to be found. By afternoon his head was starting to ache, so they left the library, laid down on the grass in a park for a long while, and gazed at the clouds drifting by. Hoshino smoked, Nakata sipped at hot tea from his thermos.

"It's going to thunder again tomorrow," Nakata said.

"Meaning *you're* going to make it thunder?"

"No, Nakata can't do that. The thunder comes by itself."

"Thank God for that," Hoshino said.

They went back to their inn, took a bath, and then Nakata went to bed and was soon fast asleep. Hoshino watched a baseball game on TV with the sound down low, but since the Giants were soundly beating Hiroshima he got disgusted with the whole thing and turned it off. He wasn't sleepy yet and felt thirsty, so he went out and found a beer hall, and ordered a draft and a plate of onion rings. He was thinking of striking up a conversation with a young girl sitting nearby, but figured it wasn't the time or place to make a pass. Tomorrow morning, after all, it was back to searching for the elusive stone.

He finished his beer, pulled on his Chunichi Dragons cap, left, and just wandered around. Not the most appealing-looking city, he decided, but it felt pretty good to be walking around wherever he wanted in a place he'd never been before. He always enjoyed walking, anyway. A Marlboro between his lips, hands stuck in his pockets, he wandered from one main street to another and down various alleys. When he wasn't smoking he whistled. Some parts were lively and crowded, others deserted and deathly quiet. No matter where he found himself, he kept up the same pace. He was young, healthy, carefree, with nothing to fear.

He was walking down a narrow alley full of karaoke bars and clubs that looked like they'd be operating under different names in six months, and had just come to a dark, deserted spot when somebody called out behind him, "Hoshino! Hoshino!" in a loud voice.

At first he couldn't believe it. Nobody knew him in Takamatsu—it had to be some other Hoshino. It wasn't that common a name, but not that uncommon, either. He didn't turn around and kept walking. But whoever it was followed him, calling out his name.

Hoshino finally stopped and turned around. Standing there was a short old man in a white suit. White hair, a serious pair of glasses, a white mustache and goatee, white shirt, and string tie. His face looked Japanese, but the whole outfit made him look more like some country gentleman from the American South. He wasn't much over five feet tall but looked less like a short person than a miniature, scaled-down version of a man. He held both hands out in front of him like he was carrying a tray.

"Mr. Hoshino," the old man said, his voice clear and piercing, with a bit of an accent.

Hoshino stared at the man in blank amazement.

"Right you are! I'm Colonel Sanders."

"You look just like him," Hoshino said, impressed.

"I don't just look like Colonel Sanders. It's who I *am*."

"The fried-chicken guy?"

The old man nodded heavily. "One and the same."

"Okay, but how do you know my name?"

"Chunichi Dragons fans I always call Hoshino. Nagashima's your basic Giants name—likewise, for the Dragons it's got to be Hoshino, right?"

"Yeah, but Hoshino happens to be my real name."

"Pure coincidence," the old man boomed out. "Don't blame me."

"So what do you want?"

"Have I got a girl for you!"

"Oh, I get it," Hoshino said. "You're a pimp. That's why you're dolled up like that."

"Mr. Hoshino, I don't know how many times I have to say this, but I'm not dressed up as anybody. I *am* Colonel Sanders. Don't get mixed up here, all right?"

"Okay. . . . But if you're the real Colonel Sanders, what the heck are you doing working as a pimp in a back alley in Takamatsu? You're famous, and must be raking in the dough from license fees alone. You should be kicking back at a poolside somewhere in the States, enjoying your retirement. So what's the story?"

"There's a kind of a warp at work in the world."

"A warp?"

"You probably don't know this, but that's how we have three dimensions. Because of the warp. If you want everything to be nice and straight all the time, then go live in a world made with a triangular ruler."

"You're pretty weird, you know that?" Hoshino said. "But hanging out with weird old guys seems to be my fate these days. Any more of this and I won't know up from down."

"That may be, Mr. Hoshino, but how about it? How about a nice girl?"

"You mean like one of those massage parlor places?"

"Massage parlor? What's that?"

"You know, those places where they won't let you do the dirty deed but can manage a BJ or a hand job. Let you come that way, but no in-and-out."

"No, no," Colonel Sanders said, shaking his head in irritation. "That's not it at all. My girls do it all—hand job, BJ, whatever you want, including the old in-and-out."

"Ah hah—so you're talking a soapland."

"*What* land?"

"Quit kidding around, okay? I've got somebody with me, and we've got an early start in the morning. So I don't have time for any fooling around tonight."

"So you don't want a girl?"

"No girl. No fried chicken. I'm going back to get some sleep."

"But maybe you won't get to sleep that easily?" Colonel Sanders said knowingly. "When a person's looking for something and can't find it, they usually can't sleep very well."

Hoshino stood there, mouth agape, staring at him. "Looking for something? How'd you know I'm looking for something?"

"It's written all over your face. By nature you're an honest person. Everything you're thinking is written all over your face. It's like one side of a split-open dried mackerel—everything inside your head's laid out for all to see."

Instinctively, Hoshino reached up and rubbed his cheek. He spread his hand open and stared at it, but there was nothing there. *Written all over my face?*

"So," Colonel Sanders said, one finger held up for emphasis. "Is what you're looking for by any chance round and hard?"

Hoshino frowned and said, "Come on, old man, *who* are you? How could you know that?"

"I told you—it's written all over your face. You don't get it, do you?" Colonel Sanders said, shaking his finger. "I haven't been in this business all these years for my health, you know. So you really don't want a girl?"

"I'm looking for a kind of stone. It's called an entrance stone."

"I know all about it."

"You do?"

"I don't lie. Or tell jokes. I'm a straight-ahead, no-nonsense type of guy."

"Do you know where the stone is?"

"I know exactly where it is."

"So, could you—tell me where?"

Colonel Sanders touched his black-framed glasses and cleared his throat. "Are you *sure* you don't want a girl?"

"If you'll tell me where the stone is, I'll think about it," Hoshino said dubiously.

"Great. Come with me." Without waiting for a reply, he walked briskly away down the alley.

Hoshino scrambled to keep up. "Hey, old man. Colonel. I've only got about two hundred bucks on me."

Colonel Sanders clicked his tongue as he trotted down the road. "That's plenty. That'll get you a fresh-faced, nineteen-year-old beauty. She'll give you the full menu—BJ, hand job, in-and-out, you name it. And afterward I'll throw this in for free—I'll tell you all about the stone."

"Jeez Louise," Hoshino gasped.

Chapter 27

It's 2:47 when I notice the girl's here—a little earlier than last night. I glance at the clock by my bed to remember the time. This time I stay up, waiting for her to appear. Other than the occasional blink I don't close my eyes once. I thought I was paying attention, but somehow I miss the actual moment she appears.

She has on her usual light blue dress and is sitting there the same as before, head in hands, silently gazing at the painting of *Kafka on the Shore*. And I'm gazing at her with bated breath. Painting, girl, and me—we form a still triangle in the room. She never tires of looking at the picture, and likewise I never tire of gazing at her. The triangle is fixed, unwavering. And then something totally unexpected happens.

"Miss Saeki," I hear myself say. I hadn't planned on speaking her name, but the thought welled up in me and spilled out. In a very small voice, but she hears it. And one side of the triangle collapses. Maybe I was secretly hoping it would—I don't know.

She looks in my direction, though not like she's straining to see. Her head's still in her hands as she quietly turns her face. Like something— she's not sure what—has made the air tremble ever so slightly.

I don't know if she can see me, but I want her to. I pray she notices me and knows I exist. "Miss Saeki," I repeat. I can't keep myself from saying her name. Maybe she'll be frightened by my voice and leave the room, never to return. I'd feel terrible if that happened. No—not terrible, that's not what I mean. *Devastated* is more like it. If she never came back everything would be lost to me forever. All meaning, all direction. *Everything*. I know this, but I go ahead and risk it anyway, and call her name. Of their own accord, almost automatically, my tongue and lips form her name, over and over.

She's not looking at the painting anymore, she's looking at me. Or at least I'm in her field of vision. From where I sit I can't see her expression. Clouds move outside and the moonlight flickers. It must be windy, but I can't hear it.

"Miss Saeki," I say again, carried away by some urgent, compelling, overwhelming force.

She takes her head out of her hands, holds up her right hand in front of her as if to tell me not to say anything more. But is that what she really wants to say? If only I could go up to her and gaze into her eyes, to see what she's thinking right now, what emotions are running through her. What is she trying to tell me? What is she hinting at? Damn, I wish I knew. But this heavy, just-before-three-a.m. darkness has snatched away all meaning. It's hard to breathe, and I close my eyes. There's a hard lump of air in my chest, like I've swallowed a rain-cloud whole. When I open my eyes a few seconds later, she's vanished. All that's left is an empty chair. A shadow of a cloud slides across the wall above the desk.

I get out of bed, go over to the window, and look at the night sky. And think about time that can never be regained. I think of rivers, of tides. Forests and water gushing out. Rain and lightning. Rocks and shadows. All of these are in me.

The next day, in the afternoon, a detective stops by the library. I'm lying low in my room and don't know he's there. The detective questions Oshima for about twenty minutes and then leaves. Oshima comes to my room later to fill me in.

"A detective from a local precinct was asking about you," Oshima says, then takes a bottle of Perrier from the fridge, uncaps it, pours the water into a glass, and takes a drink.

"How did he know I was here?"

"You used a cell phone. Your dad's phone."

I check my memory and nod. That night I ended up all bloody in the woods behind that shrine, I called Sakura on the cell phone. "I did, but just once."

"The police checked the calling record and traced you to Takamatsu. Usually police don't get into details, but while we were chatting I got him to explain how they traced the call. When I want to I can turn on the charm. He also let out that they couldn't trace the person you called, so it must've been a prepaid phone. Anyhow, they know you were in Takamatsu, and the local police have been checking all the hotels. They found out that a boy named Kafka Tamura matching your description stayed in a business hotel in town, through a special arrangement with the YMCA, until May 28th. The same day somebody murdered your father."

At least the police didn't find out about Sakura. I'm thankful for that, having bothered her enough already.

"The hotel manager remembered that you'd asked about our library. Remember how he called to see if you were really coming here?"

I nod.

"That's why the police stopped by." Oshima takes a sip of Perrier. "Naturally I lied. I told the detective I hadn't seen you since the 28th. That you'd been coming every day, but not once since."

"You might get into trouble," I say.

"If I didn't lie, you'd be in a whole lot more trouble."

"But I don't want to get you involved."

Oshima narrows his eyes and smiles. "You don't get it, do you? You already *have* gotten me involved."

"Yeah, I guess so—"

"Let's not argue, okay? What's done is done. Talking about it now won't get us anywhere."

I nod, not saying a word.

"Anyway, the detective left his card and told me to call him right away if you ever showed up again."

"Am I a suspect?"

Oshima slowly shakes his head. "I doubt it. But they do think you might be able to help them out. I've been following all this in the newspaper. The investigation isn't getting anywhere, and the police are getting impatient. No fingerprints, no clues, no witnesses. You're the only lead they have. Which explains why they're trying so hard to track you down. Your dad's famous, too, so the murder's been covered in detail on TV and in magazines. The police aren't about to sit around and twiddle their thumbs."

"But if they find out you lied to them, they won't accept you as a witness anymore—and there goes my alibi. They might think I did it."

Oshima shook his head again. "Japanese police aren't that stupid, Kafka. Lacking in imagination, yes, but they're not incompetent. I'm sure they've already checked all the passenger lists for planes from Tokyo to Shikoku. I don't know if you're aware of this, but they have video cameras set up at all the gates at airports, to photograph all the boarding passengers. By now they know you didn't fly back to Tokyo around the time of the incident. Information in Japan is micromanaged, believe me. So the police don't consider you a suspect. If they did, they wouldn't send some local cop, but detectives from the National Police Agency. If that happened they would've grilled me pretty hard and there's no way I could've outsmarted them. They just want to hear from you whatever information you can provide about the incident."

It makes perfect sense, what he says.

"Anyhow, you'd better keep a low profile for a while," he says. "The police might be staking out the area, keeping an eye out for you. They had photos of you with them. Copies of your official junior high class picture. Can't say it looked much like you, though. You looked really mad in the photo."

That was the only photograph I left behind. I always tried to avoid having my picture taken, but not having this one taken wasn't an option.

"The police said you were a troublemaker at school. There were some violent incidents involving you and your classmates. And you were suspended three times."

"Twice, not three times. And I wasn't suspended, just officially grounded," I explain. I breathe in deeply, then slowly breathe out. "I have times like that, yeah."

"You can't control yourself," Oshima says.

I nod.

"And you hurt other people?"

"I don't mean to. But it's like there's somebody else living inside me. And when I come to, I find out I've hurt somebody."

"Hurt them how much?" Oshima asks.

I sigh. "Nothing major. No broken bones or missing teeth or anything."

Oshima sits down on the bed, crosses his legs, and brushes his hair off his forehead. He's wearing navy blue chinos, a black polo shirt, and white Adidas. "Seems to me you have a lot of issues you've got to deal with."

A lot of issues. I look up. "Don't you have any?"

Oshima holds his hands in the air. "Not all that many. But there is one thing. For me, inside this physical body—this defective container—the most important job is surviving from one day to the next. It could be simple, or very hard. It all depends on how you look at it.

Either way, even if things go well, that's not some great achievement. Nobody's going to give me a standing ovation or anything."

I bite my lip for a while, then ask, "Don't you ever think about getting out of that container?"

"You mean leaving my physical body?"

I nod.

"Symbolically? Or for real?"

"Either one."

Oshima flips his hair back with a hand. I can picture the gears going full speed just below the surface of his pale forehead. "Are you thinking you'd like to do that?"

I take a breath. "Oshima, to tell you the unvarnished truth, I don't like the container I'm stuck in. Never have. I *hate* it, in fact. My face, my hands, my blood, my genes . . . I hate everything I inherited from my parents. I'd like nothing better than to escape it all, like running away from home."

He gazes into my face and smiles. "You have a nice, muscular body. No matter who you inherited it from, you're quite handsome. Well, maybe a little too unique to be called handsome, exactly. But you're not bad looking. At least I like the way you look. You're smart, you're quick. You've got a nice cock, too. I envy you that. You're going to have tons of girls fall for you, guaranteed. So I can't see what you're dissatisfied with about *your* container."

I blush.

"Okay, I guess that's all beside the point," Oshima continues. "I'm not crazy about the container I'm in, that's for sure. How could I be—this crummy piece of work? It's pretty inconvenient, I can tell you. Still, inside here, this is what I think: If we reverse the outer shell and the essence—in other words, consider the outer shell the essence and the essence only the shell—our lives might be a whole lot easier to understand."

I stare at my hands, thinking about all that blood on them, how sticky they felt. I think about my own essence, my own shell. The essence of me, surrounded by the shell that's me. But these thoughts are driven away by one indelible image: all that blood.

"How about Miss Saeki?" I ask.

"What do you mean?"

"You think she has issues to overcome?"

"You'd better ask her yourself," Oshima says.

At two I take a cup of coffee on a tray up to Miss Saeki's room, where she's sitting at her desk. Like always there's writing paper and a fountain pen on the desk, but the pen is still capped. Both hands resting on the desk, she's staring off into space. Not like she's looking at anything, just gazing at a place that isn't there. She seems tired. The window behind her is open, the early summer breeze rustling the white lace curtain. The scene looks like some beautiful allegorical painting.

"Thank you," she says when I put the coffee cup on her desk.

"You look a little tired."

She nods. "I imagine I look a lot older when I get tired."

"Not at all. You look wonderful, like always."

She smiles. "For someone so young, you certainly know how to flatter a woman."

My face reddens.

Miss Saeki points to a chair. The same chair as yesterday, in exactly the same position. I take a seat.

"I'm used to being tired, but I don't imagine you are."

"I guess not."

"When I was fifteen I wasn't either, of course." She picks up the coffee cup and takes a sip. "Kafka, what can you see outside?"

I look out the window behind her. "I see trees, the sky, and some clouds. Some birds on tree branches."

"Nothing out of the ordinary. Right?"

"That's right."

"But if you knew you might not be able to see it again tomorrow, everything would suddenly become special and precious, wouldn't it?"

"I suppose so."

"Have you ever thought about that?"

"I have."

A surprised look comes over her. "When?"

"When I'm in love," I tell her.

She smiles faintly, and it continues to hover around her lips. This puts me in mind of how refreshing water looks after someone's sprinkled it in a tiny hollow outside on a summer day.

"Are you in love?" she asks.

"Yes."

"And her face and whole being are special and precious to you, each time you see her?"

"That's right. And I might lose those."

Miss Saeki looks at me for a while, and the smile fades away. "Picture a bird perched on a thin branch," she says. "The branch sways in the wind, and each time this happens the bird's field of vision shifts. You know what I mean?"

I nod.

"When that happens, how do you think the bird adjusts?"

I shake my head. "I don't know."

"It bobs its head up and down, making up for the sway of the branch. Take a good look at birds the next time it's windy. I spend a lot of time looking out that window. Don't you think that kind of life would be tiring? Always shifting your head every time the branch you're on sways?"

"I do."

"Birds are used to it. It comes naturally to them. They don't have to think about it, they just do it. So it's not as tiring as we imagine. But I'm a human being, not a bird, so sometimes it does get tiring."

"You're on a branch somewhere?"

"In a manner of speaking," she says. "And sometimes the wind blows pretty hard." She places the cup back on the saucer and takes the cap off her fountain pen.

This is my signal, so I stand up. "Miss Saeki, there's something I've got to ask you."

"Something personal?"

"Yes. And maybe out of line, too."

"But it's important?"

"For me it is."

She puts the pen back on the desk, and her eyes fill with a kind of neutral glow. "All right. Go ahead."

"Do you have any children?"

She takes in a breath and pauses. The expression on her face slowly retreats somewhere far away, then comes back. Kind of like a parade that disappears down a street, then marches back up the same street toward you again.

"Why do you want to know that?"

"It's personal. It's not just some spur-of-the-moment question."

She lifts up her Mont Blanc like she's testing the thickness and heft of it, then sets it on the desk and looks up. "I'm sorry, but I can't give you a yes or no answer. At least right now. I'm tired, and there's a strong wind blowing."

I nod. "Sorry. I shouldn't have asked."

"It's all right. I'm not blaming you," she says gently. "Thank you for the coffee. You make excellent coffee."

I leave and go back down the stairs to my room. I sit on my bed and try to read, but nothing seems to filter into my head. I feel like I'm gazing at some table of random numbers, just following the words with my eyes. I put my book down, go over to the window, and look at the garden. There are birds on some of the branches, but no wind to speak of. Am I in love with Miss Saeki when she was fifteen? Or with the real, fifty-something Miss Saeki upstairs? I don't know anymore. The boundary line separating the two has started to waver, to fade, and I can't focus. And that confuses me. I close my eyes and try to find some center inside to hold on to.

But you know, she's right. Every single day, each time I see her face, see *her*, it's utterly precious.

Chapter 28

For a man his age Colonel Sanders was light on his feet, and so fast that he resembled a veteran speed walker. And he seemed to know every nook and cranny of the city. He took short cuts up dark, narrow staircases, turning sideways to squeeze through the narrow passages between houses. He leaped over a ditch, hushing a barking dog behind a hedge with a short command. Like some restless spirit searching for its home, his small white-suited figure raced through the back alleys of the town. It was all Hoshino could do to keep up. He was soon out of breath, his armpits soaked. Colonel Sanders never once looked back to see if he was following.

"Hey, are we almost there?" Hoshino finally called out impatiently.

"What are you talking about, young fellow? I wouldn't even call this a walk," Colonel Sanders replied, still not turning around.

"Yeah, but I'm a customer, remember? What's going to happen to my sex drive if I'm all pooped out?"

"What a disgrace! And you call yourself a man? If a little walk's going to kill your desire, you might as well not have any from the beginning."

"Jeez," Hoshino muttered.

Colonel Sanders cut across another side street, crossed a main road, oblivious to the traffic light, and continued walking. He strode over a bridge and ducked into a shrine. A fairly big shrine, by the looks of it, but it was late and no one else was around. Colonel Sanders pointed to a bench in front of the shrine office, indicating that Hoshino should take a seat. A mercury lamp was next to the bench, and everything was as bright as day. Hoshino did as he was told, and Colonel Sanders sat down next to him.

"You're not going to make me do it *here*, are you?" Hoshino asked worriedly.

"Don't be an idiot. We're not like those deer that hang around the famous shrines and go at it. I'm not about to have you do it in a shrine. Who do you think I *am*, anyway?" Then he extracted a silver cell phone from his pocket and punched in a three-digit number. "Yeah, it's me," he said when the other person answered. "The usual place. The shrine. I've got a young man named Hoshino here with me. That's right . . . the same as usual. Yes, I got it. Just get here as soon as you can." He switched off the phone and slipped it back into the pocket of his white suit.

"Do you always call up the girls from this shrine?" Hoshino asked.

"Anything wrong with that?"

"No, not really. I was just thinking there's got to be a better place. Someplace more . . . normal? A coffee shop, or maybe have me wait in a hotel room?"

"A shrine's quiet. And the air's crisp and clean."

"True, but waiting for a girl on a bench in front of a shrine office — it's hard to relax. I feel like I'm going to fall under the spell of one of those fox spirits or something."

"What are you talking about? You're not making fun of Shikoku now, are you? Takamatsu's a proper city—the prefectural capital, in fact. Not some hick town. We don't have any foxes here."

"Okay, okay, just kidding. . . . But you're in the service industry, so I was just thinking you'd better worry more about creating an *atmosphere*, you know what I'm saying? Something luxurious, to get you in the mood. I don't know, maybe it's none of my business."

"You're right. It isn't," Colonel Sanders intoned. "Now about that stone . . ."

"Right! The stone . . . Tell me about it."

"*After* you do the deed. Then we talk."

"Doing the deed's important, huh?"

Colonel Sanders nodded gravely a couple of times, and tugged at his goatee. "That's right. It's a formality you have to go through. Then we'll talk about the stone. I know you're going to like this girl. She's our top girl. Luscious breasts, skin like silk. A nice, curvy waist, hot and wet right where you like it, a regular sex machine. To use a car metaphor, she's four-wheel drive in bed, turbocharged desire, step on the gas, the surging gearshift in her hands, you round the corner, she shifts gears ecstatically, you race out in the passing lane, and bang! You're there — Hoshino's dead and gone to heaven."

"You're quite a character, you know that?" Hoshino said admiringly.

"Like I said, I'm not in this business for my health."

Fifteen minutes later the girl arrived, and Colonel Sanders was right—she *was* a knockout. Tight miniskirt, black high heels, a small black-enamel shoulder bag. She could easily have been a model. Generous breasts, too, spilling out of her low-cut top.

"Will she do?" Colonel Sanders asked.

Hoshino was too stunned to reply, and just nodded.

"A veritable sex machine, Hoshino. Have yourself a ball," Colonel Sanders said, smiling for the first time. He gave Hoshino a pinch on the rump.

The girl took Hoshino to a nearby love hotel, where she filled up the bathtub, quickly slipped out of her clothes, and then undressed him. She washed him carefully all over, then commenced to lick him, sliding into a totally artistic act of fellatio, doing things to him he'd never seen or heard of in his life. He couldn't think of anything else but coming, and come he did.

"Man alive, that was fantastic. I've never felt like that," Hoshino said, languidly sinking back in the hot tub.

"That's just the beginning," the girl said. "Wait till you see what's next."

"Yeah, but man that was good."

"How good?"

"Like there's no past or future anymore."

"*The pure present is an ungraspable advance of the past devouring the future. In truth, all sensation is already memory.*"

Hoshino looked up, mouth half open, and gazed at her face. "What's that?"

"Henri Bergson," she replied, licking the semen from the tip of his penis. "*Mame mo memelay.*"

"I'm sorry?"

"*Matter and Memory.* You ever read it?"

"I don't think so," Hoshino replied after a moment's thought. Except for the special SDF driver's manual he was forced to study—and the books on Shikoku history he'd just gone through at the library—he couldn't remember reading anything except manga.

"Have you read it?"

The girl nodded. "I had to. I'm majoring in philosophy in college, and we have exams coming up."

"You don't say," Hoshino said. "So this is a part-time job?"

"To help pay tuition."

She took him over to the bed, stroked him all over with her finger-tips and tongue, getting another erection out of him. A firm hard-on, a Tower of Pisa at carnival time.

"See, you're ready to go again," the girl remarked, slowly segueing into her next set of motions. "Any special requests? Something you'd like me to do? Mr. Sanders asked me to make sure you got everything you want."

"I can't think of anything special, but could you quote some more of that philosophy stuff? I don't know why, but it might keep me from coming so quick. Otherwise I'll lose it pretty fast."

"Let's see. . . . This is pretty old, but how about some Hegel?"

"Whatever."

"I recommend Hegel. He's sort of out of date, but definitely an oldie but goodie."

"Sounds good to me."

"At the same time that 'I' am the content of a relation, 'I' am also that which does the relating."

"Hmm . . ."

"Hegel believed that a person is not merely conscious of self and object as separate entities, but through the projection of the self via the mediation of the object is volitionally able to gain a deeper under-standing of the self. All of which constitutes self-consciousness."

"I don't know what the heck you're talking about."

"Well, think of what I'm doing to you right now. For me I'm the self, and you're the object. For you, of course, it's the exact opposite—you're the self to you and I'm the object. And by exchanging self and object, we can project ourselves onto the other and gain self-consciousness. Volitionally."

"I still don't get it, but it sure feels good."

"That's the whole idea," the girl said.

Afterward he said good-bye to the girl and returned to the shrine, where Colonel Sanders was sitting on the bench just as he'd left him.

"You been waiting here the whole time?" Hoshino asked.

Colonel Sanders shook his head irritably. "Don't be a moron. Do I really look like I have that much time on my hands? While you were sailing off to heaven, I was working the back alleys again. She called me when you finished, and I rushed over. So, how was our little sex machine? Pretty good, I'll bet."

"She was great. No complaints by me. I got off three times. *Volitionally* speaking. I must've lost five pounds."

"Glad to hear it. Now, about the stone . . ."

"Right, that's what I came here for."

"Actually, the stone's in the woods right here in this shrine."

"We're talking about the entrance stone?"

"That's right. The entrance stone."

"Are you sure you're not just making this up?"

Colonel Sanders's head shot up. "What are you talking about, you dingbat? Have I ever lied to you? Do I just make up things? I told you I'd get you a supple young sex machine, and I kept my end of the bargain. At a bargain-basement price, too—only \$120, and you were brazen enough to shoot off three times, no less. All that and you still doubt me?"

"Don't blow a fuse! Of course I believe you. It's just that when things are going along a little too smoothly, I get a bit suspicious, that's all. I mean, think about it—I'm walking along and a guy in a funny getup calls out to me, tells me he knows where to find the stone, then I go with him and get off with this drop-dead-gorgeous babe."

"*Three* times, you mean."

"Whatever. So I get off three times, and then you tell me the stone I'm looking for is right over there? That would confuse anybody."

"You still don't get it, do you? We're talking about a *revelation* here," Colonel Sanders said, clicking his tongue. "A revelation leaps over the borders of the everyday. A life without revelation is no life at all. What you need to do is move from reason that *observes* to reason that *acts*. That's what's critical. Do you have any idea what I'm talking about, you gold-plated whale of a dunce?"

"The projection and exchange between self and object . . . ?" Hoshino timidly began.

"Good. I'm glad you know that much at least. That's the point. Follow me, and you can pay your respects to your precious stone. A special package deal, just for you."

Chapter 29

I call up Sakura from the public phone in the library. I realize I haven't been in touch once since that night at her place—just a short note and that was it. I'm kind of embarrassed about the way I said good-bye. After I left her apartment I went right to the library, Oshima drove me up to the cabin for a few days, well out of range of any phone. Then I came to live and work at the library, encountering Miss Saeki's living spirit—or something like it—every night. And I've fallen head over heels for that fifteen-year-old girl. A ton of things happened, one after another—enough to keep anybody busy. Not that that's any excuse.

It's around nine p.m. when I call, and she answers after six rings.

"Where in the world have you been?" Sakura asks in a hard voice.

"I'm still in Takamatsu."

She doesn't say anything for a while. In the background I hear a music program on TV.

"Somehow I've survived," I add.

Silence, then a kind of resigned sigh.

"What did you mean by disappearing like that? I was worried about you, so I came home a little early that day. Even did some shopping for us."

"I know it was wrong. I *do*. But I had to leave. My mind was all messed up and I had to get away to think things out, try to get back on my feet. Being with you was—I don't know—I can't put it into words."

"Overstimulating?"

"Yeah. I've never been near a girl like that before."

"No kidding?"

"You know, the scent of a girl. All kinds of things . . ."

"Pretty rough being young, huh?"

"I guess," I say. "So how's your job going?"

"It's been a madhouse. But I wanted to work and save up some money, so I shouldn't complain."

I pause, then tell her about the police looking for me.

She's silent for a while, then cautiously says, "All that business with the blood?"

I decide to hold back on telling the truth. "No, that's not it. Nothing about the blood. They're after me because I'm a runaway. They want to catch me and ship me back to Tokyo, that's all. So the cops might get in touch with you. The other day, the night I stayed over, I called your cell phone using mine, and they traced the phone records and found I was here in Takamatsu."

"Don't worry," she says. "It's a prepaid phone, so there's no way they can trace the owner."

"That's a relief," I say. "I didn't want to cause you any more trouble than I already have."

"You're so sweet you're going to make me cry, you know that?"

"No, that's how I really feel."

"I know," she says like she'd rather not admit it. "So where's our little runaway staying these days?"

"Somebody I know is letting me stay over."

"Since when do you know anybody here?"

How could I possibly summarize everything that's happened to me in the past few days? "It's a long story," I say.

"With you it's always long stories."

"I don't know why, but it always turns out that way."

"Sort of a tendency of yours?"

"I guess so," I reply. "I'll tell you all about it someday when I have the time. It's not like I'm hiding anything. I just can't explain it well over the phone."

"That's okay. I just hope you're not into anything you shouldn't be."

"No, nothing like that. I'm okay, don't worry."

She sighs again. "I can understand wanting to be out on your own, but just don't get mixed up with anything illegal, okay? It isn't worth it. I don't want to see you die some miserable teenage death like Billy the Kid."

"Billy the Kid didn't die in his teens," I correct her. "He killed twenty-one people and died when he was twenty-one."

"If you say so. . . . Anyway, was there something you wanted?"

"I just wanted to thank you. I feel bad about leaving like that after you were so nice."

"Thanks, but why don't we just forget that, okay?"

"I wanted to hear your voice, too," I say.

"I'm happy to hear that, but how does that help anything?"

"I don't know how to put it exactly. . . . This might sound strange, but you're living in the real world, breathing real air, speaking real words. Talking with you makes me feel, for the time being, connected to reality. And that's really important to me now."

"The people you're with now *aren't*?"

"I'm not sure," I tell her.

"So what you're saying is you're in some unreal place, with people cut off from reality?"

I think about that for a while. "You might say that."

"Kafka," Sakura says. "I know it's your life and I shouldn't butt in, but I think you'd better get out of there. I don't know what kind of place you're in, but I get the feeling that's the smart move. Call it a hunch. Why don't you come over to my place? You can stay as long as you like."

"Why are you so nice to me?"

"What are you, a dunce?"

"What do you mean?"

"'Cause I *like* you—can't you figure that out? I'm a basically curious type, but I wouldn't do this for just anybody. I've done all this for you because I *like* you, okay? I don't know how to put it, but you feel like a younger brother to me."

I hold the phone without saying a word. For a second I'm completely confused, even dizzy. Nobody's ever said anything like that to me. Ever.

"You still there?" Sakura asks.

"Yeah," I manage to say.

"Well, then *say* something."

I stand up straight and take a deep breath. "Sakura, I wish I could do that. I really do. But I can't right now. Like I told you, I can't leave here. I'm in love."

"With some complicated, *unreal* person?"

"You could say that."

I hear her sigh again—a deep, profound kind of sigh. "You know, when kids your age fall in love they tend to get a little spacey, so if the person you're in love with isn't connected to reality, that's a major problem. You follow me?"

"Yeah, I get it."

"Kafka?"

"Hmm?"

"If anything happens, call me, okay? Don't hesitate, at all."

"I appreciate it."

I hang up, go back to my room, put the single of "Kafka on the Shore" on the turntable, and lower the needle. And once more, whether I like it or not, I'm swept away to that *place*. To that *time*.

I sense a presence and open my eyes. It's totally dark. The fluorescent numbers on the alarm clock next to my bed show it's after three. I must've fallen asleep. In the faint light from the lamppost out in the garden I see her sitting there. As always she's at the desk, gazing at the painting on the wall. Motionless, head in her hands. And I'm lying in bed as before, trying hard not to breathe, eyes barely open, gazing at her silhouette. Outside the window the breeze from the sea is rustling the branches of the dogwood.

After a while, though, I sense that something's different. Something in the air that disturbs the perfect harmony of our little world. I strain to see through the gloom. What *is* it? The wind momentarily picks up, and the blood coursing through my veins begins to feel strangely thick and heavy. The dogwood branches draw a nervous maze on the windowpane. Finally it comes to me. The silhouette isn't that of the young girl. It looks a lot like her, almost an exact match. But it isn't *exactly* the same. Like a copy of a drawing laid over the real thing, some of the details are off. Her hairstyle is different, for one thing. And she has on different clothes. Her whole *presence* is different. Unconsciously I shake my head. It isn't the girl sitting there — it's *someone else*. Something's happening, something very important. I'm clutching my hands tightly beneath the covers, and my heart, unable to stand it anymore, starts pounding hard, beating out an unexpected, erratic rhythm.

As if that sound is the signal, the silhouette in the chair starts to move, slowly changing its angle like some massive ship changing course. She takes her head out of her hands and turns in my direction. With a start I realize it's Miss Saeki. I gulp and can't let my breath out. It's the Miss Saeki of the *present*. The *real* Miss Saeki. She looks at me for a while, quietly concentrating like when she's looking at the painting, and a thought hits me—*the axis of time*. Somewhere I don't know about, something weird is happening to time. Reality and dreams are all mixed up, like seawater and river water flowing together. I struggle to find the meaning behind it all, but nothing makes any sense.

Finally she gets to her feet and slowly comes toward me, holding herself as erect as always. She's barefoot, and the floorboards faintly creak as she walks. Silently she sits down on the edge of the bed, and remains still for a time. Her body has a definite density and weight. She has on a white silk blouse and a navy blue skirt that reaches to her knees. She reaches out and touches my head, her fingers groping through my short hair. Her hand is real, with real fingers touching me. She stands up again, and in the faint light shining in from outside— like it's the most natural thing to do—begins to undress. She's in no hurry, but she doesn't hesitate, either. In smooth, natural motions she unbuttons her blouse, slips out of her skirt, and steps out of her panties. Piece by piece her clothing falls to the floor, the soft fabric hardly making a sound. She's asleep, I realize. Her eyes are open but it's like she's sleepwalking.

Once she's naked she crawls into the narrow bed and wraps her pale arms around me. Her warm breath grazes my neck, her pubic hair pushing up against my thigh. She must think I'm her dead boyfriend from long ago, and that she's doing what they used to do here in this very room. Fast asleep, dreaming, she goes through the motions from long ago.

I figure I'd better wake her up. She's making a big mistake, and I have to let her know. This isn't a dream—it's *real life*. But everything's happening so fast, and I don't have the strength to resist. Thrown totally off balance, I feel like I'm being sucked into a time warp.

And you're sucked into a time warp.

Before you know it, her dream has wrapped itself around your mind. Gently, warmly, like amniotic fluid. Miss Saeki will take off your T-shirt, pull off your boxers. She'll kiss your neck over and over, then reach out and hold your penis, which is already porcelain-hard. Gently she wraps her hand around your balls, and wordlessly guides your fingers to her pubic hair. Her vagina is warm and wet.

She kisses your chest, sucking your nipples. Your fingers are slowly sucked inside her.

Where does your responsibility begin here? Wiping away the nebula from your sight, you struggle to find where you really are. You're trying to find the direction of the flow, struggling to hold on to the axis of time. But you can't locate the borderline separating dream and reality. Or even the boundary between what's real and what's possible. All you're sure of is that you're in a delicate position. Delicate—and dangerous. You're pulled along, a part of it, unable to pin down the principles of prophecy, or of logic. Like when a river overflows, washing over a town, all road signs have sunk beneath the waves. And all you can see are the anonymous roofs of the sunken houses.

You're faceup, and Miss Saeki gets on top of you. She guides your rock-hard cock inside her. You're helpless—she's the one who's in charge. She bends and twists her waist as if tracing a picture with her body. Her straight hair falls on your shoulders and trembles noiselessly, like the branches of a willow. Little by little you're sucked down into the warm mud. The whole world turns warm, wet, indistinct, and all that exists is your rigid, glistening cock. You close your eyes and your own dream begins. It's hard to tell how much time is passing. The tide comes in, the moon rises. And soon you come. There's nothing you can do to stop it. You come over and over inside her. The warm walls inside her contract, gathering in your semen. All this while she's still asleep with her eyes wide open. She's in a different world, and that's where your seed goes—swallowed down into a place apart.

A long time passes. I can't move. Every part of me is paralyzed. Paralyzed, or else maybe I just don't feel like trying to move. She gets off and lies down beside me. After a while she gets up, tugs on her panties, pulls on her skirt, and buttons up her blouse. She gently reaches out again and tousles my hair. All this takes place without a word passing between us. She hasn't said a thing since she entered the room. The only sounds are the creak of the floorboards, the wind blowing ceaselessly outside. The room breathing out, the windowpane shivering. That's the chorus behind me.

Still asleep, she crosses the room and leaves. The door's open just a crack but she slips right out like a delicate, dreamy fish. Silently the door closes. I watch from the bed as she makes her exit, still unable to move. I can't even raise a finger. My lips are tightly sealed. Words are asleep in a corner of time.

Unable to move a muscle, I lie there straining to hear. I imagine I'll catch the roar of her Golf in the parking lot. But I never hear it, no matter how long I listen. The wind blows clouds over, then scatters them away. The branches of the dogwood quiver, and countless knives flash in the darkness. The window is my heart's window, the door my soul's door. I lie there awake until dawn, gazing at the empty chair.

Chapter 30

The two of them scrambled over the low hedge into the woods. Colonel Sanders took a small flashlight out of his pocket and illuminated the narrow path. The woods weren't very deep, but the trees were hugely ancient, the tangle of their branches looming darkly above. A strong grassy odor came from the ground below.

Colonel Sanders took the lead, for once maintaining a leisurely pace. Shining the flashlight to make sure of his footing, he cautiously took one step at a time.

Hoshino followed right behind. "Hey, Unc, is this some kind of dare or something?" he said to the Colonel's white back. "Whoa—a ghost!"

"Why don't you zip it for a change," Colonel Sanders said without turning around.

"Okay, okay." Hoshino suddenly wondered how Nakata was doing. Probably still sound asleep. It's like the term *sound asleep* was invented just to describe him—once he falls asleep, that's all she wrote. What kind of dreams does he have, though, during those record-breaking sleeps? Hoshino couldn't imagine. "Are we there yet?"

"Almost," Colonel Sanders replied.

"Tell me something," Hoshino began.

"What?"

"Are you *really* Colonel Sanders?"

Colonel Sanders cleared his throat. "Not really. I'm just taking on his appearance for a time."

"That's what I figured," Hoshino said. "So what are you *really*?"

"I don't have a name."

"How do you get along without one?"

"No problem. Originally I don't have a name or a shape."

"So you're kind of like a fart."

"You could say that. Since I don't have a shape I can become any-thing I want."

"Huh . . ."

"This time I decided to take on a familiar shape, that of a famous capitalist icon. I was toying with the idea of Mickey Mouse, but Disney's particular about the rights to their characters."

"I don't think I'd want Mickey Mouse pimping for me anyway."

"I see your point."

"Dressing up like Colonel Sanders fits your character, too."

"But I don't have a character. Or any feelings. *Shape I may take, converse I may, but neither god nor Buddha am I, rather an insensate being whose heart thus differs from that of man.*"

"What the—?"

"A line from Ueda Akinari's *Tales of Moonlight and Rain*. I doubt you've read it."

"You got me there."

"I'm appearing here in human form, but I'm neither god nor Buddha. My heart works differently from humans' hearts because I don't have any feelings. That's what it means."

"Hmm," Hoshino said. "I'm not sure I follow, but what you're say-ing is you're not a person and not a god or Buddha either, right?"

"*Neither god nor Buddha, just the insensate. As such, of the good and bad of man I neither inquire nor follow.*"

"Meaning?"

"Since I'm neither god nor Buddha, I don't need to judge whether people are good or evil. Likewise I don't have to act according to stan-dards of good and evil."

"In other words you exist beyond good and evil."

"You're too kind. I'm not beyond good and evil, exactly—they just don't matter to me. I have no idea what's good or what's evil. I'm a very pragmatic being. A neutral object, as it were, and all I care about is consummating the function I've been given to perform."

"*Consummate* your function? What's that?"

"Didn't you go to school?"

"Yeah, I went to high school, but it was a trade school. I spent all my time screwing around on motorcyles."

"I'm kind of an overseer, supervising something to make sure it ful-fills its original role. Checking the correlation between different worlds, making sure things are in the right order. So results follow causes and meanings don't get all mixed up. So the past comes before the present, the future after it. Things can get a *little* out of order, that's okay. Nothing's perfect. If the account book's basically in balance, though, that's fine by me. To tell you the truth, I'm not much of a detail person. The technical term for it is 'Abbreviating Sensory Processing of Continuous Information,' but I don't want to get into all that. It'd take too long to explain, and I know it's beyond you. So let's cut to the chase. What I'm getting at is I'm not going to complain about each and every little thing. Of course if the accounts don't eventually balance, that is a problem. I do have my responsibility to consider."

"I got a question for you. If you're such an important person, how come you're a pimp in a back alley in Takamatsu?"

"I am not a *person*, okay? How many times do I have to tell you?"

"Whatever . . ."

"Pimping's just a means of getting you here. There's something I need you to lend me a hand with, so as a reward I thought I'd let you have a good time first. A kind of formality we have to go through."

"Lend you a hand?"

"As I've explained, I don't have any form. I'm a metaphysical, conceptual object. I can take on any form, but I lack substance. And to perform a real act, I need someone with substance to help out."

"And at this particular point that substance happens to be me."

"Exactly," Colonel Sanders replied.

They cautiously continued down the path, and came to a smaller shrine beneath a thick oak tree. The shrine was old and dilapidated, with no offerings or decorations of any kind.

Colonel Sanders shined his flashlight on it. "The stone's inside there. Open the door."

"No way!" Hoshino replied. "You're not supposed to open up shrines whenever you feel like it. You'll be cursed. Your nose will fall off. Or your ears or something."

"Not to worry. I said it's all right, so go ahead and open it. You won't be cursed. Your nose and ears won't fall off. God, you can be really old-fashioned."

"Then why don't *you* open it? I don't want to get mixed up in that."

"How many times do I have to explain this?! I told you already I don't have substance. I'm an abstract concept. I can't do anything on my own. That's why I went to the trouble of dragging you out here. And letting you do it three times at a discount rate."

"Yeah, man, she was fantastic . . . but robbing a shrine? No way! My grandfather always told me not to mess with shrines. He was really strict about it."

"Forget about your grandfather. Don't lay all your Gifu Prefecture, country-bumpkin morality on me, okay? We don't have time for that."

Grumbling all the while, Hoshino hesitantly opened the door of the shrine, and Colonel Sanders shined his flashlight inside. Sure enough, there was an old round stone inside. Just like Nakata said, it was about the size of a big rice cake, a smooth white stone.

"This is it?" Hoshino asked.

"That's right," Colonel Sanders said. "Take it out."

"Hold on a minute. That's stealing."

"No matter. Nobody's going to notice if a stone like this is missing. And nobody'll care."

"Yeah, but the stone is owned by God, right? He's gonna be pissed if we take it out."

Colonel Sanders folded his arms and stared straight at Hoshino. "What is God?"

The question threw Hoshino for a moment.

Colonel Sanders pressed him further. "What does God look like, and what does He do?"

"Don't ask *me*. God's *God*. He's everywhere, watching what we do, judging whether it's good or bad."

"Sounds like a soccer referee."

"Sort of, I guess."

"So God wears shorts, has a whistle sticking out of His mouth, and keeps an eye on the clock?"

"You know that's not what I mean," Hoshino said.

"Are the Japanese God and the foreign God relatives, or maybe enemies?"

"How should *I* know?"

"Listen—God only exists in people's minds. Especially in Japan, God's always been kind of a flexible concept. Look at what happened after the war. Douglas MacArthur ordered the divine emperor to quit being God, and he did, making a speech saying he was just an ordinary person. So after 1946 he wasn't God anymore. That's what Japanese gods are like—they can be tweaked and adjusted. Some American chomping on a cheap pipe gives the order and *presto change-o*—God's no longer God. A very postmodern kind of thing. If you think God's there, He is. If you don't, He isn't. And if that's what God's like, I wouldn't worry about it."

"Okay . . ."

"Anyway, just get the stone out, would you? I'll take full responsibility. I might not be a god or a Buddha, but I do have a few connections. I'll make sure you aren't cursed."

"You sure?"

"I won't go back on my word."

Hoshino reached out and carefully, like he was inching out a land mine, picked up the stone. "It's pretty heavy."

"This isn't tofu we're dealing with. Stones tend to be heavy."

"But even for a stone it's heavy," Hoshino said. "So what do you want me to do with it?"

"Take it home and put it next to your bed. After that things will take their course."

"You want me to take it back to the inn?"

"You can take a cab if it's too heavy," Colonel Sanders replied.

"Yeah, but is it okay to take it so far away?"

"Listen, every object's in flux. The Earth, time, concepts, love, life, faith, justice, evil—they're all fluid and in transition. They don't stay in one form or in one place forever. The whole universe is like some big FedEx box."

"Hm."

"This stone's temporarily there in the form of a stone. Moving it isn't going to change anything."

"All right, but what's so special about this stone? It doesn't look like much of anything."

"The stone itself is meaningless. The situation calls for something, and at this point in time it just happens to be this stone. Anton Chekhov put it best when he said, 'If a pistol appears in a story, eventually it's got to be fired.' Do you know what he means?"

"Nope."

Colonel Sanders sighed. "I didn't think so, but I had to ask. It's the polite thing to do."

"Much obliged."

"What Chekhov was getting at is this: necessity is an independent concept. It has a different structure from logic, morals, or meaning. Its function lies entirely in the role it plays. What doesn't play a role shouldn't exist. What necessity requires *does* need to exist. That's what you call dramaturgy. Logic, morals, or meaning don't have anything to do with it. It's all a question of relationality. Chekhov understood dramaturgy very well."

"Whoa—you're way over *my* head."

"The stone you're carrying there is Chekhov's pistol. It will have to be fired. So in that sense it's important. But there's nothing sacred or holy about it. So don't worry yourself about any curse."

Hoshino frowned. "This stone's a pistol?"

"Only in the metaphorical sense. Don't worry—bullets aren't about to shoot out." Colonel Sanders took a huge furoshiki cloth from a pocket and handed it to Hoshino. "Wrap it up in this. Better for people not to see it."

"I told you it was stealing!"

"Are you deaf? It's not stealing. We need it for something important, so we're just borrowing it for a while."

"Okay, okay. I get it. Following the rules of dramaturgy, we're of necessity moving matter."

"Precisely," Colonel said, nodding. "See, you *do* understand what I'm talking about."

Carrying the stone wrapped in the navy blue cloth, Hoshino followed the path back out of the woods, Colonel Sanders lighting the way for him with his flashlight. The stone was much heavier than it looked and Hoshino had to stop a few times to catch his breath. They quickly cut across the well-lit shrine grounds so no one would see them, then came out on a main street. Colonel Sanders hailed a cab and waited for Hoshino to climb in with the stone.

"So I should put it next to my pillow, huh?" Hoshino asked.

"Right," Colonel Sanders said. "That's all you have to do. Don't try anything else. Just having it there's the main thing."

"I should thank you. For showing me where the stone was."

Colonel Sanders grinned. "No need—just doing my job. Just consummating my function. But hey—how 'bout that girl, Hoshino?"

"She was amazing."

"I'm glad to hear it."

"She was real, right? Not a fox spirit or some abstraction or something messed up like that?"

"No spirit, no abstraction. Just one real, live sex machine. Genuine four-wheel-drive lust. It wasn't easy to find her. So rest assured."

"Whew!" Hoshino sighed.

By the time Hoshino laid the cloth-wrapped stone next to Nakata's pillow it was already past one a.m. He figured putting it next to Nakata's pillow instead of his own lessened the chance of any curse. As he'd imagined, Nakata was still out like the proverbial log. Hoshino untied the cloth so the stone was visible. He changed into his pajamas, crawled into the other futon, and instantly fell asleep. He had one short dream—of a god in short pants, hairy shins sticking out, racing around a field playing a flute.

At five that morning, Nakata woke up and found the stone beside his pillow.

Chapter 31

Just after one o'clock I take coffee up to the second-floor study. The door, as always, is open. Miss Saeki's standing by the window gazing outside, one hand resting on the windowsill. Lost in thought, unaware that her other hand's fingering the buttons on her blouse. This time there's no pen or writing paper on the desk. I place the coffee cup on the desk. A thin layer of clouds covers the sky, and the birds outside are quiet for a change.

She finally notices me and, pulled back from her thoughts, comes away from the window, sits down at the desk, and takes a sip of coffee. She motions for me to sit in the same chair as yesterday. I sit down and look at her across the desk, sipping her coffee. Does she remember anything at all about what happened last night? I can't tell. She looks like she knows everything, and at the same time like she doesn't know a thing. Images of her naked body come to mind, memories of how different parts felt. I'm not even sure that was the body of the woman who's here in front of me. At the same time, though, I'm a hundred percent sure.

She has on a light green, silky-looking blouse and a tight beige skirt. There's a thin silver necklace at her throat, very chic. Like some neatly crafted object, her slim fingers on the desk are beautifully intertwined. "So, do you like this area now?" she asks me.

"Do you mean Takamatsu?"

"Yes."

"I don't know. I haven't seen much of it, just a few things along the way. This library, of course, a gym, the station, the hotel . . . those kinds of places."

"Don't you find it boring?"

I shake my head. "I don't know yet. I haven't had time to get bored, and cities look the same anyway. Why do you ask? Do you think it's a boring town?"

She gave a slight shrug. "When I was young I did. I was dying to get out. To leave here and go someplace else, where something special was waiting, where I could find more interesting people."

"Interesting people?"

Miss Saeki shakes her head slightly. "I was young," she says. "Most young people have that feeling, I suppose. Haven't you?"

"No, I never felt that if I go somewhere else there'll be special things waiting for me. I just wanted to *be* somewhere else, that's all. Anywhere but *there*."

"*There?*"

"Nogata, Nakano Ward. Where I was born and grew up."

At the sound of this name something flashed across her eyes. At least it looked like it.

"As long as you left there, you didn't particularly care where you went?" she asks.

"That's right," I say. "Where I went wasn't the issue. I had to get out of there or else I knew I'd get totally messed up. So I left."

She looks down at her hands resting on the desk, a very detached look in her eyes. Then, very quietly, she says, "When I left here when I was twenty, I felt the same way. I had to leave or else I wouldn't survive. And I was convinced I'd never see this place again as long as I lived. I never considered coming back, but things happened and here I am. Like I'm starting all over again." She turns around and looks out the window.

The clouds covering the sky are the same tone as before, and there isn't any wind to speak of. The whole thing looks as still as the painted background scenery in a movie.

"Incredible things happen in life," she says.

"You mean I might go back to where I started?"

"I don't know. That's up to you, sometime well in the future. But I think where a person is born and dies is very important. You can't choose where you're born, but where you die you can—to some degree." She says all this in a quiet voice, staring out the window like she's talking to some imaginary person outside. Remembering I'm here, she turns toward me. "I wonder why I'm confessing all these things to you."

"Because I'm not from around here, and our ages are so different."

"I suppose so," she says.

For twenty, maybe thirty seconds, we're lost in our own thoughts. She picks up her cup and takes another sip of coffee.

I decide to come right out and say it. "Miss Saeki, I have something I need to confess, too."

She looks at me and smiles. "We're exchanging secrets, I see."

"Mine isn't a secret. Just a theory."

"A theory?" she repeats. "You're confessing a *theory*?"

"Yes."

"Sounds interesting."

"It's a sequel to what we're talking about," I say. "What I mean is, did you come back to this town to die?"

Like a silvery moon at dawn, a smile rises to her lips. "Perhaps I did. But it doesn't seem to matter. Whether you come to a place to live or to die, the things you do every day are about the same."

"Are you hoping to die?"

"I wonder . . . ," she says. "I don't know myself."

"My father was hoping to die."

"Your father died?"

"Not long ago," I tell her. "Very recently, in fact."

"Why was your father trying to die?"

I take a deep breath. "For a long time I couldn't figure it out. But now I think I have. After coming here I finally understand."

"Why?"

"My father was in love with you, but couldn't get you back. Or maybe from the very beginning he couldn't really make you *his*. He knew that, and that's why he wanted to die. And that's also why he wanted his son—*your* son, too—to murder him. *Me*, in other words. He wanted me to sleep with you and my older sister, too. That was his prophecy, his curse. He programmed all this inside me."

Miss Saeki returns her coffee cup to the saucer with a hard, neutral sound. She looks straight at me, but she's not really seeing me. She's gazing at some void, some blank space somewhere else. "Do I know your father?"

I shake my head. "As I told you, it's just a theory."

She rests her hands on the desk, one on top of the other. Faint traces of a smile remain. "In your theory, then, I'm your mother."

"That's right," I say. "You lived with my father, had me, and then went away, leaving me behind. In the summer when I'd just turned four."

"So that's your theory."

I nod.

"Which explains why you asked me yesterday whether I have any children?"

Again I nod.

"I told you I couldn't answer that. Couldn't give you a yes or a no."

"I know."

"So your theory remains speculative."

I nod again. "That's right."

"So tell me, how did your father die?"

"He was murdered."

"You didn't murder him, did you?"

"No, I didn't. I have an alibi."

"But you're not entirely sure?"

I shake my head. "I'm not sure at all."

She lifts the coffee cup again and takes a tiny sip, as if it has no taste. "Why did your father put you under that curse?"

"He must've wanted me to take over his will," I say.

"To desire me, you mean."

"That's right," I say.

Miss Saeki stares into the cup in her hand, then looks up again.

"So do you—desire me?"

I give one clear nod.

She closes her eyes. I gaze at her closed eyelids for a long time, and through them I can see the darkness that she's seeing. Odd shapes loom up in it, floating up only to disappear.

Finally she opens her eyes. "You mean in theory you desire me."

"No, apart from the theory. I want you, and that goes way beyond any theory."

"You want to have sex with me?"

I nod.

She narrows her eyes like something's shining in them. "Have you ever had sex with a girl before?"

I nod again. *Last night*—with *you*, I think. But I can't say it out loud. She doesn't remember a thing.

Something close to a sigh escapes her lips. "Kafka, I know you realize this, but you're fifteen and I'm over fifty."

"It's not that simple. We're not talking about that sort of time here. I know you when you were fifteen. And I'm in love with you at that age. *Very* much in love. And through *her*, I'm in love with *you*. That young girl's still inside you, asleep inside you. Once *you* go to sleep, though, she comes to life. I've seen it."

She closes her eyes once more, her eyelids trembling slightly.

"I'm in love with you, and that's what's important. I think you understand that."

Like someone rising to the surface of the sea from deep below, she takes a deep breath. She searches for the words to say, but they lie beyond her grasp. "I'm sorry, Kafka, but would you mind leaving? I'd like to be alone for a while," she says. "And close the door on your way out."

I nod, stand up, and start to go, but something pulls me back. I stop at the door, turn around, and walk across the room to where she is. I reach out and touch her hair. Through the strands my hand brushes her small ear. I just can't help it.

Miss Saeki looks up, surprised, and after a moment's hesitation lays her hand on mine. "At any rate, you—and your theory—are throwing a stone at a target that's very far away. Do you understand that?"

I nod. "I know. But metaphors can reduce the distance."

"We're not metaphors."

"I know," I say. "But metaphors help eliminate what separates you and me."

A faint smile comes to her as she looks up at me. "That's the oddest pickup line I've ever heard."

"There're a lot of odd things going on—but I feel like I'm slowly getting closer to the truth."

"Actually getting closer to a metaphorical truth? Or metaphorically getting closer to an actual truth? Or maybe they supplement each other?"

"Either way, I don't think I can stand the sadness I feel right now," I tell her.

"I feel the same way."

"So you did come back to this town to die."

She shakes her head. "To be honest about it, I'm not trying to die. I'm just waiting for death to come. Like sitting on a bench at the station, waiting for the train."

"And do you know when the train's going to arrive?"

She takes her hand away from mine and touches her eyelids with the tips of her fingers. "Kafka, I've worn away so much of my own life, worn myself away. At a certain point I should have stopped living, but didn't. I knew life was pointless, but I couldn't give up on it. So I ended up just marking time, wasting my life in pointless pursuits. I wound up hurting myself, and that made me hurt others around me. That's why I'm being punished now, why I'm under a kind of curse. I had something too complete, too perfect, once, and afterward all I could do was despise myself. That's the curse I can never escape. So I'm not afraid of death. And to answer your question—yes, I have a pretty good idea of when the time is coming."

Once more I take her hand in mine. The scales are shaking, and just a tiny weight would send them tipping to one side or the other. I have to think. I have to decide. I have to take a step forward. "Miss Saeki, would you sleep with me?" I ask.

"You mean even if I were your mother in that theory of yours?"

"It's like everything around me's in flux—like it all has a doubled meaning."

She ponders this. "That might not be true for me, though. For me, things might not be so nuanced. It might be more like all or nothing."

"And you know which it is."

She nods.

"Do you mind if I ask you a question?"

"About what?"

"Where did you come up with those two chords?"

"*Chords?*"

"The ones in the bridge in 'Kafka on the Shore.'"

She looks at me. "You like them?"

I nod.

"I found those chords in an old room, very far away. The door to the room was open then," she says quietly. "A room that was far, far away." She closes her eyes and sinks back into memories. "Kafka, close the door when you leave," she says.

And that's exactly what I do.

After we close up the library for the night, Oshima drives me to a seafood restaurant a little way away. Through a large window in the restaurant we can see the night sea, and I think about all the creatures living under the water.

"Sometimes you've got to get out and eat some decent food," he tells me. "Relax. I don't think the cops have staked the place out. We both needed a change of scenery."

We eat a huge salad, and split an order of paella.

"I'd love to go to Spain someday," Oshima says.

"Why Spain?"

"To fight in the Spanish Civil War."

"But that ended a long time ago."

"I know that. Lorca died, and Hemingway survived," Oshima says. "But I still have the right to go to Spain and be a part of the Spanish Civil War."

"Metaphorically."

"Exactly," he says, giving me a wry look. "A hemophiliac of undetermined sex who's hardly ever set foot outside Shikoku isn't about to actually go off to fight in Spain, I would think."

We attack the mound of paella, washing it down with Perrier.

"Have there been any developments in my father's case?" I ask.

"Nothing to report, really. Except for a typical smug memorial piece in the arts section, there hasn't been much in the papers. The investigation must be stuck. The sad fact is the arrest rate's been going down steadily these days—just like the stock market. I mean, the police can't even track down the son who's disappeared."

"The fifteen-year-old youth."

"Fifteen, with a history of violent behavior," Oshima adds. "The obsessed young runaway."

"How about that incident with things falling from the sky?"

Oshima shakes his head. "They're taking a break on that one. Nothing else weird has fallen from the sky—unless you count that award-winning lightning we had two days ago."

"So things have settled down?"

"It seems like it. Or maybe we're just in the eye of the storm."

I nod, pick up a clam, yank out the meat with a fork, then put the shell on a plate full of empty shells.

"Are you still in love?" Oshima asks me.

I nod. "How about you?"

"Am I in love, do you mean?"

I nod again.

"In other words, you're daring to get personal and ask about the antisocial romance that colors my warped, homosexual, Gender-Identity-Disordered life?"

I nod, and he follows suit.

"I have a partner, yes," he admits. He makes a serious face and eats a clam. "It's not the kind of passionate, stormy love you find in a Puccini opera or anything. We keep a careful distance from each other. We don't get together that often, but we do understand each other at a deep, basic level."

"Understand each other?"

"Whenever Haydn composed, he always made sure to dress formally, even to wearing a powdered wig."

I look at him in surprise. "What's Haydn got to do with anything?"

"He couldn't compose well unless he did that."

"How come?"

"I have no idea. That's between Haydn and his wig. Nobody else would understand. Inexplicable, I imagine."

I nod. "Tell me, when you're alone do you sometimes think about your partner and feel sad?"

"Of course," he says. "It happens sometimes. When the moon turns blue, when birds fly south, when—"

"Why *of course*?" I ask.

"Anyone who falls in love is searching for the missing pieces of themselves. So anyone who's in love gets sad when they think of their lover. It's like stepping back inside a room you have fond memories of, one you haven't seen in a long time. It's just a natural feeling. You're not the person who discovered that feeling, so don't go trying to patent it, okay?"

I lay my fork down and look up.

"A fond, old, faraway room?"

"Exactly," Oshima says. He holds his fork straight up for emphasis. "Just a metaphor, of course."

Miss Saeki comes to my room after nine that night. I'm sitting at the desk reading a book when I hear her Golf pull into the parking lot. The door slams shut. Rubber-soled shoes slowly crunch across the parking lot. And finally there's a knock at my door. I open the door, and there she is. This time she's wide awake. She has on a pinstriped silk blouse, thin blue jeans, white deck shoes. I've never seen her in pants before.

"I haven't seen this room in a long time," she says. She stands by the wall and looks at the painting. "Or this picture, either."

"Is the place in the painting around here?" I ask.

"Do you like it?"

I nod. "Who painted it?"

"A young artist who boarded that summer with the Komuras," she says. "He wasn't very famous, at least at the time. I've forgotten his name. He was a very friendly person, though, and I think he did a good job with the painting. There's something, I don't know—*powerful* about it. I sat beside him the whole time and watched him work. I made all kinds of half-joking suggestions as he painted. We got along well. It was a summer a long time ago. I was twelve then. The boy in the painting was twelve, too."

"It looks like the sea around here."

"Let's go for a walk," she says. "I'll take you there."

I walk with her to the shore. We cut through a pine forest and walk down the sandy beach. The clouds are breaking up and a half moon shines down on the waves. Small waves that barely reach the shore, barely break. She sits down at a spot on the sand, and I sit down next to her. The sand's still faintly warm.

Like she's checking the angle, she points to a spot on the shoreline. "It was right over there," she says. "He painted that spot from here. He put the deck chair over there, had the boy pose in it, and set up his easel right around here. I remember it well. Do you notice how the position of the island is the same as in the painting?"

I follow where she's pointing, and sure enough it's the same. No matter how long I gaze at it, though, it doesn't look like the place in the painting. I tell her that.

"It's changed completely," Miss Saeki replies. "That was forty years ago, after all. Things change. A lot of things affect the shoreline— waves, wind, typhoons. Sand gets washed away, they truck more in. But this is definitely the spot. I remember what occurred there very well. That was the summer I had my first period, too."

We sit there looking at the scenery. The clouds shift and the moon-light dapples the sea. Wind blows through the pine forest, sounding like a crowd of people sweeping the ground at the same time. I scoop up some sand and let it slowly spill out between my fingers. It falls to the beach and, like lost time, becomes part of what's already there. I do this over and over.

"What are you thinking about?" Miss Saeki asks me.

"About going to Spain," I reply.

"What are you going to do there?"

"Eat some delicious paella."

"That's all?"

"And fight in the Spanish Civil War."

"That ended over sixty years ago."

"I know," I tell her. "Lorca died, and Hemingway survived."

"But you want to be a part of it."

I nod. "Yup. Blow up bridges and stuff."

"And fall in love with Ingrid Bergman."

"But in reality I'm here in Takamatsu. And I'm in love with you."

"Tough luck."

I put my arm around her.

You put your arm around her.

She leans against you. And a long spell of time passes.

"Did you know that I did this exact same thing a long time ago? Right in this same spot?"

"I know," you tell her.

"How do you know that?" Miss Saeki asks, and looks you in the eyes.

"I was there then."

"Blowing up bridges?"

"Yes, I was there, blowing up bridges."

"Metaphorically."

"Of course."

You hold her in your arms, draw her close, kiss her. You can feel the strength deserting her body.

"We're all dreaming, aren't we?" she says.

All of us are dreaming.

"Why did you have to die?"

"I couldn't help it," you reply.

Together you walk along the beach back to the library. You turn off the light in your room, draw the curtains, and without another word climb into bed and make love. Pretty much the same sort of lovemaking as the night before. But with two differences. After sex, she starts to cry. That's one. She buries her face in the pillow and silently weeps. You don't know what to do. You gently lay a hand on her bare shoulder. You know you should say something, but don't have any idea what. Words have all died in the hollow of time, piling up soundlessly at the dark bottom of a volcanic lake. And this time as she leaves you can hear the engine of her car. That's number two. She starts the engine, turns it off for a time, like she's thinking about something, then turns the key again and drives out of the parking lot. That blank, silent interval between leaves you sad, so terribly sad. Like fog from the sea, that blankness wends its way into your heart and remains there for a long, long time. Finally it's a part of you.

She leaves behind a damp pillow, wet with her tears. You touch the warmth with your hand and watch the sky outside gradually lighten. Far away a crow caws. The Earth slowly keeps on turning. But beyond any of those details of the real, there are dreams. And everyone's living in them.

Chapter 32

When Nakata woke up at five a.m. he saw the big stone right next to his pillow. Hoshino was still sound asleep on the futon next to his, mouth half open, hair sticking every which way, Chunichi Dragons cap tossed beside him. His sleeping face had a determined *no-matter-what-don't-dare-wake-me-up* look to it.

Nakata wasn't particularly surprised to find the stone there. His mind adapted immediately to the new reality, accepted it, didn't question why it happened to be there. Figuring out cause and effect was never his strong suit.

He sat down formally beside his bed, legs tucked neatly under him, and spent some quality time with the stone, gazing intently at it. Finally he reached out and, like he was stroking a large, sleeping cat, touched it. At first gingerly, with only his fingertips, and when that seemed safe he ran his entire hand carefully over the whole surface. All the while he rubbed it, he was thinking—or at least had the pensive look of someone thinking. As if reading a map, he ran his hand over every part of the stone, memorizing every bump and cranny, getting a solid sense of it. Then he suddenly reached up and rubbed his short hair, searching, perhaps, for the correlation between the stone and his own head.

Finally he gave what might have been a sigh, stood up, opened the window, and stuck his face out. All that was visible was the rear of the building next door. A shabby, miserable sort of building. The kind where shabby people spend one shabby day after another doing their shabby work. The kind of fallen-from-grace sort of building you find in any city, the kind Charles Dickens could spend ten pages describing. The clouds floating above the building were like hard clumps of dirt from a vacuum cleaner no one ever cleaned. Or maybe more like all the contradictions of the Third Industrial Revolution condensed and set afloat in the sky. Regardless, it was going to rain soon. Nakata looked down and spied a skinny black cat, tail alert, patrolling the top of a narrow wall between the two buildings. "There's going to be lightning today," he called out. But the cat didn't appear to hear him, didn't even turn around, just continued its languid walk and disappeared in the shadows of the building.

Nakata set off down the hall, plastic bag with toilet kit inside in hand, to the communal sinks. He washed his face, brushed his teeth, and shaved with a safety razor. Each operation took time. He carefully washed his face, taking his time, carefully brushed his teeth, taking his time, carefully shaved, taking his time. He trimmed his nose hairs with a pair of scissors, straightened up his eyebrows, cleaned out his ears. He was the type who took his time no matter what he did, but this morning he took everything at an even slower pace than usual. No one else was up washing his face at this early hour, and it was still a while before breakfast was ready. Hoshino didn't look like he'd be getting up anytime soon. With the whole place to himself, Nakata looked in the mirror, leisurely preparing for the day, and pictured the faces of all the cats he'd seen in the book in the library two days before. Unable to read, he didn't know the names of the cats, but a clear picture of each and every cat's face was etched in his memory.

"There really are a lot of cats in the world, that's for sure," he said as he cleaned out his ears with a Q-tip. His first-ever visit to a library had made him painfully aware of how little he knew. The amount of things he didn't know about the world was infinite. The infinite, by definition, has no limits, and thinking about it gave him a mild migraine. He gave up and turned his thoughts back to *Cats of the World*. How nice it would be, he thought, to be able to talk with each and every cat in there. There must be all kinds of cats in the world, all with different ways of thinking and talking. Would foreign cats speak in foreign languages? he wondered. But this was another difficult subject, and again his head began to throb.

After washing up, he went to the toilet and took care of business as usual. This didn't take as long as his other ablutions. Finished, he took his plastic bag with the toilet kit inside back to the room. Hoshino was sound asleep, exactly as he'd left him. Nakata picked up the discarded aloha shirt and jeans, folding them up neatly. He set them down on top of each other next to Hoshino's futon, adding the Chunichi Dragons baseball cap on top like a summary title given to a motley collection of ideas. He took off his yukata robe and put on his usual trousers and shirt, then rubbed his hands together and took a deep breath.

He sat down again in front of the stone, gazing at it for a while before hesitantly reaching out to touch it. "There's going to be thunder today," he pronounced to no one in particular. He may have been addressing the stone. He punctuated this with a couple of nods.

Nakata was over next to the window, running through an exercise routine, when Hoshino finally woke up. Humming the radio exercise music quietly to himself, Nakata moved in time to the tune.

Hoshino squinted at his watch. It was just after eight. He craned his neck to make sure the stone was where he'd put it. In the light the stone looked much bigger and rougher than he'd remembered. "So I wasn't dreaming after all," he said.

"I'm sorry—what did you say?" Nakata asked.

"The stone," Hoshino said. "The stone's right there. It wasn't a dream."

"We have the stone," Nakata said simply, still in the midst of his exercises, making it sound like some central proposition of nineteenth-century German philosophy.

"It's a long story, though, Gramps, about how the stone *got to be there*."

"Yes, Nakata thought that might be the case."

"Anyway," Hoshino said, sitting up in bed and sighing deeply. "It doesn't matter. The important thing is it's here. To make a long story short."

"We have the stone," Nakata repeated. "That's what matters."

Hoshino was about to respond but suddenly noticed how famished he was. "Hey, what d'ya say we grab some breakfast?"

"Nakata's quite hungry."

After breakfast, as he was drinking tea, Hoshino said, "So what are you going to do with the stone?"

"What should Nakata do with it?"

"Gimme a break," Hoshino said, shaking his head. "You said you had to find that stone, so that's why I managed to come up with it last night. Don't hit me now with this *Gee whiz, what should I do with it* stuff. Okay?"

"Yes, you are right. But to tell the truth, I don't know yet what I'm supposed to do with it."

"That's a problem."

"A problem indeed," Nakata replied, though you'd never know it from his expression.

"So if you spend some time thinking about it, you'll figure out what to do?"

"I think so. It takes Nakata much longer to do things than other people."

"Okay, but listen here, Mr. Nakata."

"Yes, Mr. Hoshino?"

"I don't know who gave it that name, but since it's called the entrance stone I'm guessing it's gotta be the entrance to something a long time ago, don't you think? There must be some legend or explanation about it."

"Yes, that must be the case."

"But you have no idea what kind of entrance we're talking about here?"

"No, not yet. I used to talk with cats all the time, but I've never spoken to a stone."

"Doesn't sound like it'd be too easy."

"It's very different from talking with a cat."

"But still, ripping that stone off from a shrine—you sure we won't be cursed or something? That's really bothering me. Taking it's one thing, but dealing with it now that we have it could be a total pain in the butt. Colonel Sanders told me there wouldn't be any curse, but I can't totally trust the guy, you know what I mean?"

"Colonel Sanders?"

"There's an old guy by that name. The guy on the Kentucky Fried Chicken ads. With the white suit, beard, stupid glasses. You don't know who I mean?"

"I'm very sorry, but I don't believe I know that person."

"You don't know Kentucky Fried Chicken? That's kind of unusual. Well, whatever. The old guy's an abstract concept anyway. He's not human, not a god or a Buddha. He doesn't have any shape, but has to take on some sort of appearance, so he just happened to choose the Colonel."

Nakata looked perplexed and rubbed his salt-and-pepper hair. "I don't understand."

"Well, to tell you the truth, I don't get it either, though I'm the one spouting off," Hoshino said. "Anyhow, this weird old guy suddenly pops up out of nowhere and rattles off all those things to me. Long story short, the old guy helped me out so I could locate the stone, and I lugged it back here. I'm not trying to win your sympathy or anything, but it was a long, hard night, I can tell you. What I'd really like to do right now is hand the whole thing to you and let you take over."

"I will."

"That was quick."

"Mr. Hoshino?" Nakata said.

"What?"

"There's going to be a lot of thunder soon. Let's wait for that."

"You're telling me the thunder's going to do something to help with the stone?"

"I don't know for sure, but I'm starting to get that feeling."

"Thunder, huh? Sounds kind of cool. Okay, we'll wait and see what happens."

When they got back to their room Hoshino flopped facedown on the futon and switched on the TV. Nothing was on except a bunch of variety shows targeted at housewives, but since there was no other way of killing time, he kept watching, giving a running critique of everything on the screen.

Nakata, meanwhile, sat in front of the stone, gazing at it, rubbing it, occasionally mumbling. Hoshino couldn't catch what he was saying. For all he knew the old man might actually be talking to the stone.

After a couple of hours, Hoshino ran out to a nearby convenience store and came back with a sack full of milk and sweet rolls the two of them had for lunch. While they were eating, the maid showed up to clean the room, but Hoshino told her not to bother, they were fine.

"You're not going out anywhere?" she asked.

"Nope," he answered. "We've got something to do here."

"Because there's going to be thunder," Nakata added.

"Thunder. I see . . . ," the maid said dubiously before she left, looking like she'd rather not have anything more to do with this weird pair.

Around noon thunder rumbled dully off in the distance, and, as if waiting for a signal, it started sprinkling. Unimpressive thunder, a lazy dwarf trampling on a drum. Before long, though, the raindrops grew larger, and it was soon a regular downpour, wrapping the world in a wet, stuffy smell.

Once the thunder started, the two sat down across from each other, the stone between them, like Indians passing a peace pipe. Nakata was still mumbling to himself, rubbing the stone or his head. Hoshino puffed on a Marlboro and watched.

"Mr. Hoshino?" Nakata said.

"What's up?"

"Would you stay with me for a while?"

"Sure. I'm not going anywhere in this rain."

"There's a chance something strange might happen."

"Are you kidding me?" Hoshino began. "Everything's been strange enough already."

"Mr. Hoshino?"

"Yeah."

"All of a sudden I was wondering—what am I, anyway? What is Nakata?"

Hoshino pondered this. "That's a tough one. A little out of left field. I mean, I don't even know what *I* am, so I'm not the guy to ask. Thinking isn't exactly my thing, you know? But I know you're an okay, honest guy. You're out of kilter big-time, but you're somebody I trust. That's why I came with you all the way to Shikoku. I may not be so bright, either, but I do have an eye for people."

"Mr. Hoshino?"

"Yeah?"

"It's not just that I'm dumb. Nakata's *empty* inside. I finally understand that. Nakata's like a library without a single book. It wasn't always like that. I used to have books inside me. For a long time I couldn't remember, but now I can. I used to be normal, just like everybody else. But something happened and I ended up like a container with nothing inside."

"Yeah, but if you look at it like that we're all pretty much empty, don't you think? You eat, take a dump, do your crummy job for your lousy pay, and get laid occasionally, if you're lucky. What else is there? Still, you know, interesting things do happen in life—like with us now. I'm not sure why. My grandpa used to say that things never work out like you think they will, but that's what makes life interesting, and that makes sense. If the Chunichi Dragons won every single game, who'd ever watch baseball?"

"You liked your grandfather a lot, didn't you?"

"Yeah, I did. If it hadn't been for him I don't know what would've happened to me. He made me feel like I should try and make something of myself. He made me feel—I don't know—*connected*. That's why I quit the motorcycle gang and joined the Self-Defense Force. Before I knew it, I wasn't getting in trouble anymore."

"But you know, Mr. Hoshino, Nakata doesn't *have* anybody. Nothing. I'm not connected at all. I can't read. And my shadow's only half of what it should be."

"Everybody has their shortcomings."

"Mr. Hoshino?"

"Yeah?"

"If I'd been my normal self, I think I would've lived a very different kind of life. Like my two younger brothers. I would have gone to college, worked in a company, gotten married and had a family, driven a big car, played golf on my days off. But I wasn't normal, so that's why I'm the Nakata I am today. It's too late to do it over. I understand that. But still, even for a short time, I'd like to be a *normal* Nakata. Up until now there was never anything in particular I wanted to do. I always did what people told me as best I could. Maybe that just became a habit. But now I want to go back to being *normal*. I want to be a Nakata with his own ideas, his own meaning."

Hoshino sighed. "If that's what you want, then go for it. Not that I have a clue what a normal Nakata's like."

"Nakata doesn't either."

"I just hope it works out. I'll be praying for you—that you can be normal again."

"Before I get back to being normal, though, there are some things I have to take care of."

"Like what?"

"Like Johnnie Walker."

"Johnnie Walker?" Hoshino said. "Yeah, you mentioned that before. You mean the whisky guy?"

"Yes. I went to the police right away, and told them about him. I knew I had to report to the Governor, but they wouldn't listen. So I have to find a solution on my own. I have to take care of that before I can be a normal Nakata again. If that's possible."

"I don't really get it, but I guess you're saying you need this stone to do whatever it is you need to do."

"That's right. I have to get the other half of my shadow back."

By this time the thunder was deafening. Lightning zigzagged across the sky, followed, a moment later, by the roar of thunder. The air shook, and the loose windowpanes rattled nervously. Dark clouds capped the whole sky, and it got so dark inside they could barely make out each other's faces. They left the light off, however. They were still seated as before, with the stone between them. The rain was lashing down so hard it felt suffocating just to look at it. Each flash of lightning lit up the room for an instant. They didn't say anything for a while.

"Okay, but why do you have to have anything to do with this stone, Mr. Nakata?" Hoshino asked when the thunder had died down a bit. "Why does it have to be *you*?"

"Because I'm the one who's gone in and come out again."

"I don't follow you."

"I left here once, and came back again. It happened when Japan was in a big war. The lid came open, and I left here. By chance I came back. That's why I'm not normal, and my shadow's only half of what it was. But then I could talk with cats, though I can't do it well anymore. I can also make things fall from the sky."

"Like those leeches?"

"Yes."

"A pretty unique talent, that's for sure."

"That's right, not everybody can do it."

"And that's because you went out and came back again? I guess you really *are* pretty extraordinary."

"After I came back I wasn't normal anymore. I couldn't read. And I've never touched a woman."

"That's hard to believe."

"Mr. Hoshino?"

"Yeah?"

"I'm scared. As I told you, I'm completely empty. Do you know what it means to be completely empty?"

Hoshino shook his head. "I guess not."

"Being empty is like a vacant house. An unlocked, vacant house. Anybody can come in, anytime they want. That's what scares me the most. I can make things rain from the sky, but most of the time I don't have any idea what I'm going to make rain next. If it were ten thousand knives, or a huge bomb, or poison gas—I don't know what I'd do. . . . I could say I'm sorry to everybody, but that wouldn't be enough."

"You got that right," Hoshino said. "Just apologizing wouldn't cut it. Leeches are bad enough, but those things are even worse."

"Johnnie Walker went inside Nakata. He made me do things I didn't want to. Johnnie Walker used me, but I didn't have the strength to fight it. Because I don't have anything inside me."

"Which explains why you want to go back to being a normal Nakata. One with substance?"

"That's exactly right. I'm not very bright, but I could build furniture, and I did it day after day. I liked making things—desks, chairs, chests. It's nice to make things with nice shapes. Those years I made furniture, I never thought about wanting to be normal again. And there wasn't anyone I knew who tried to get inside me. Nakata never felt afraid of anything. But after meeting Johnnie Walker I got very afraid."

"So what did this Johnnie Walker make you do after he got inside you?"

A loud rumble ripped through the sky, and the lightning was close by, by the sound of it. Hoshino's eardrums were stinging from the roar.

Nakata inclined his head slightly to one side, listening carefully, slowly rubbing the surface of the stone all the while. "He made me shed blood."

"Blood?"

"Yes, but it didn't stick to Nakata's hands."

Hoshino pondered this for a while, puzzled. "Anyway, once you open the entrance stone, all sorts of things will naturally settle back where they're meant to be, right? Like water flowing from high places to low places?"

Nakata considered this. "It might not be that easy. Nakata's job is to find the entrance stone, and open it. What happens after that, I'm afraid I don't know."

"Okay, but why's the stone in Shikoku?"

"The stone is everywhere. Not just in Shikoku. And it doesn't have to be a stone."

"I don't get it. . . . If it's everywhere, then you could've done all this back home in Nakano. That would've saved a lot of time and effort."

Nakata rubbed a palm over his close-cropped hair. "That's a hard question. I've been listening to the stone for a while now but can't understand it all that well yet. But I do think both of us had to come here. We had to cross a big bridge. It wouldn't have worked in Nakano Ward."

"Can I ask you something else?"

"Yes."

"If you do open the entrance stone here, is something amazing going to happen? Like is what's-his-name, that genie, going to pop out like in *Aladdin*? Or a prince that's been turned into a frog will French-kiss me? Or else we'll be eaten alive by Martians?"

"Something might happen, but then again maybe nothing. I haven't opened it yet, so I don't know. You can't know until you open it."

"But it might be dangerous, huh?"

"Yes, exactly."

"Jeez." Hoshino pulled a Marlboro out of his pocket and lit it. "My grandpa used to always tell me that my bad point was running off with people I didn't know without thinking what I was doing. I guess I must have always done that. The child's the father of the man, like they say. Anyhow, there's nothing I can do about it now. I've come all this way, and gone to all the trouble of locating the stone, so I can't just head on home without seeing it through. We know it might be dangerous, but what the hell. Why don't we open it up and see what happens? At least it'll make a great story for the grandkids."

"Nakata has a favor to ask you, Mr. Hoshino."

"What's that?"

"Could you pick up the stone?"

"No problem."

"It's a lot heavier than when you brought it."

"I know I'm no Schwarzenegger, but I'm stronger than I look. In the SDF I got second place in our unit's arm-wrestling contest. Plus you've cured my back problems, so I can give it everything I've got."

Hoshino stood up, grabbed the stone in both hands, and tried to lift it. The stone didn't budge an inch. "You're right, it is a lot heavier," he said, gasping. "A while ago, lifting it up was no problem. Now it feels like it's nailed to the floor."

"It's the valuable entrance stone, so it can't be moved easily. If it could, *that* would be a problem."

"I suppose so."

Right then a few irregular flashes of light ripped through the sky, and a series of thunderclaps shook the earth to its core. It's like somebody just opened the lid to hell, Hoshino thought. One final clap of thunder boomed nearby and suddenly there was a thick, suffocating silence. The air was damp and stagnant, with a hint of something suspicious, as if countless ears were floating in the air, waiting to pick up a trace of some conspiracy. The two men were frozen, wrapped in the midday darkness. Suddenly the wind picked up again, lashing rain against the window. Thunder rumbled, but not as violently as before. The center of the storm had passed the city.

Hoshino looked up and swept the room with his eyes. Everything seemed strangely cold and distant, the four walls even more blank than before. The Marlboro butt in the ashtray had turned to ash. He swallowed and brushed the silence from his ears. "Hey, Mr. Nakata?"

"What is it, Mr. Hoshino?"

"I feel like I'm having a bad dream."

"Well, at least we're having the same dream."

"You're right," Hoshino said, and scratched his earlobe in resignation. "Right you are, right as rain, rain rain go away, come again some other day. . . . Anyway, that makes me feel better." He then stood up once more, to try to move the stone. He took a deep breath, grabbed it, and focused all his strength in his hands. With a low grunt he managed to lift the stone an inch or two.

"You moved it a little," Nakata said.

"So we know it's not nailed down. But I've got to move it more than that, I guess."

"You need to flip it completely over."

"Like a pancake."

Nakata nodded "That's right. Pancakes are one of Nakata's favorites."

"Glad to hear it. So they have pancakes in hell, huh? Anyway, let me give it one more try. I think I can flip this thing over."

Hoshino closed his eyes and summoned up every ounce of strength, concentrating it on this one action. *This is it!* he told himself. *Now or never!*

He got a good grip, carefully tightened it, then took a huge breath, let out a gut-wrenching yell, and all at once lifted the stone, holding it in the air at a forty-five-degree angle. That was the limit of his strength. Somehow, he was able to hold it in that position. He gasped, his whole body aching, his bones and muscles and nerves screaming in pain, but he wasn't about to give up. He took in one last deep breath and gave out a battle cry, but couldn't hear his own voice. He had no idea what he was saying. Eyes shut tight, he managed to drag out a strength he never knew he had, strength that should have been beyond him. Lack of oxygen made everything go white. One after another his nerves snapped like popping fuses. He couldn't see or hear a thing, or even think. There wasn't enough air. Still, he inched the stone upward and, with a final yell, tipped it over. He lost his grip, and the weight of the stone itself flipped it over. A massive thud rattled the room as if the whole building was shaking.

The recoil sent Hoshino tumbling backward. He lay there, sprawled faceup on the tatami, gasping for air, his head filled with soft mud whirling round and round. I don't think, he thought, I'll ever lift something this heavy again as long as I live. (Later on, though, it turned out that this prediction was overly optimistic.)

"Mr. Hoshino?"

"Wh—what?"

"The entrance opened up, thanks to you."

"You know something, Gramps? I mean, Mr. Nakata?"

"What is it?"

Faceup, eyes still shut, Hoshino took another long, deep breath and exhaled. "It *better* have opened up. Otherwise I killed myself for nothing."

Chapter 33

I get the library all ready to open up before Oshima arrives. Vacuum all the floors, wipe the windows, clean the restroom, wipe off all the chairs and desks. Spray the banister, polish it up nicely. Carefully dust the stained glass on the landing. Sweep the garden, switch on the AC in the reading room and the storeroom's dehumidifier. Make coffee, sharpen pencils. A deserted library in the morning— there's something about it that really gets to me. All possible words and ideas are there, resting quietly. I want to do what I can to preserve this place, keep it neat and tidy. Sometimes I come to a halt and gaze at all the silent books on the stacks, reach out and touch the spines of a few. At ten-thirty, as always, the Mazda Miata roars into the parking lot and Oshima appears, looking a little sleepy. We chat for a while till it's time to open up.

"If it's okay, I'd like to go out for a while," I tell him right after we open up.

"Where to?"

"I need to go to the gym and work out. I haven't gotten any exercise for a while."

That isn't the only reason. Miss Saeki comes in to work late in the morning, and I don't want to run into her. I need some time to get my head together before I see her again.

Oshima looks at me and, after a pause, nods. "Watch out, though. I don't want to henpeck you, but you can't be too careful, okay?"

"Don't worry, I'll be careful," I assure him.

Backpack slung from one shoulder, I board the train. At Takamatsu Station I take a bus to the fitness club. I change into my gym clothes in the locker room, then do some circuit training, plugged into my Walkman, Prince blasting away. It's been a while and my muscles complain, but I manage. It's the body's normal reaction—muscles screaming out, resisting the extra burden put on them. Listening to "Little Red Corvette," I try to soothe that reaction, suppress it. I take a deep breath, hold it, exhale. Inhale, hold, exhale. Even breathing, over and over. One by one I push my muscles to the limit. I'm sweating like crazy, my shirt's soaked and heavy. I have to go over to the cooler a few times to gulp down water.

I go through the machines in the usual order, my mind filled with Miss Saeki. About the sex we had. I try to clear my head, blank everything out, but it's not easy. I focus on my muscles, absorb myself in the routine. The same machines as always, same weights, same number of reps. Prince is singing "Sexy Motherfucker" now. The end of my penis is still a bit sore and stings a little when I take a leak. The tip's red. My fresh-from-the-foreskin cock is still plenty young and tender. Condensed sexual fantasies, Prince's slippery voice, quotes from all kinds of books—the whole confused mess swirls around in my brain, and my head feels like it's about to burst.

I take a shower, change into fresh underwear, and take the bus back to the station. Hungry, I duck inside a diner and have a quick meal. As I'm eating I realize this is where I ate on my first day in Takamatsu. Which gets me wondering how many days I've been here. It's been a week or so since I started staying at the library, so I must have gotten to Shikoku about three weeks ago.

I have some tea after I'm finished eating and watch the people hustling back and forth in front of the station. They're all headed somewhere. If I wanted to, I could join them. Take a train to some other place. Throw away everything here, head off somewhere I've never been, start from scratch. Like turning a new page in a notebook. I could go to Hiroshima, Fukuoka, wherever. Nothing's keeping me here. I'm one hundred percent free. Everything I need to get by for a while is in my backpack. Clothes, toilet kit, sleeping bag. I've hardly touched the cash I took from my father's study.

But I know I can't go anywhere.

"But you can't go anywhere, you know that very well," the boy named Crow says.

You held Miss Saeki, came inside her so many times. And she took it all. Your penis is still stinging, still remembering how it felt to be inside her. One of the places that's just for you. You think of

the library. The tranquil, silent books lining the stacks. You think of Oshima. Your room. *Kafka on the Shore* hanging on the wall, the fifteen-year-old girl gazing at the painting. You shake your head. There's no way you can leave here. You aren't free. But is that what you really want? To be free?

Inside the station I pass by patrolmen making their rounds, but they don't pay me any mind. Seems like every other guy I pass is some tanned kid my age shouldering a backpack. And I'm just one of them, melting into the scenery. No need to get all jumpy. Just act natural, and nobody'll notice me.

I jump on the little two-car train and return to the library.

"Hey, you're back," Oshima says. He looks at my backpack, dumbfounded. "My word, do you always lug around so much luggage with you? You're a regular Linus."

I boil some water and have a cup of tea. Oshima's twirling his usual long, freshly sharpened pencil. Where his pencils wind up when they get too short I have no idea.

"That backpack's like your symbol of freedom," he comments.

"Guess so," I say.

"Having an object that symbolizes freedom might make a person happier than actually getting the freedom it represents."

"Sometimes," I say.

"Sometimes," he repeats. "You know, if they had a contest for the world's shortest replies, you'd win hands down."

"Perhaps."

"Perhaps," Oshima says, as if fed up. "Perhaps most people in the world *aren't* trying to be free, Kafka. They just *think* they are. It's all an illusion. If they really were set free, most people would be in a real bind. You'd better remember that. People actually prefer *not* being free."

"Including you?"

"Yeah. I prefer being unfree, too. Up to a point. Jean-Jacques Rousseau defined civilization as when people build fences. A very perceptive observation. And it's true—all civilization is the product of a fenced-in lack of freedom. The Australian Aborigines are the exception, though. They managed to maintain a fenceless civilization until the seventeenth century. They're dyed-in-the-wool free. They go where they want, when they want, doing what they want. Their lives are a literal journey. Walkabout is a perfect metaphor for their lives. When the English came and built fences to pen in their cattle, the

Aborigines couldn't fathom it. And, ignorant to the end of the principle at work, they were classified as dangerous and antisocial and were driven away, to the outback. So I want you to be careful. The people who build high, strong fences are the ones who survive the best. You deny that reality only at the risk of being driven into the wilderness yourself."

I go back to my room and lay down my backpack. Next I head to the kitchen, brew up some coffee, and take it to Miss Saeki's room. Metal tray in both hands, I carefully walk up each step, the old floorboards creaking. On the landing, I step through a rainbow of brilliant colors from the stained glass.

Miss Saeki's sitting at her desk, writing. I put down the coffee cup, and she looks up and asks me to sit down in my usual chair. Today she has on a café-au-lait-colored shirt over a black T-shirt. Her hair's pinned back, and she's wearing a pair of small pearl earrings.

She doesn't say anything for a while. She's looking over what she's just written. Nothing in her expression looks out of the ordinary. She screws on the cap of her fountain pen and lays it on top of her writing paper. She spreads her fingers, checking for ink stains. Sunday-afternoon sunlight is shining through the window. Somebody's outside in the garden, talking.

"Mr. Oshima told me you went to the gym," she says, studying my face.

"That's right," I say.

"What kind of exercise do you do there?"

"I use the machines and the free weights," I reply.

"Anything else?"

I shake my head.

"Kind of a lonely type of sport, isn't it?"

I nod.

"I imagine you want to become stronger."

"You have to be strong to survive. Especially in my case."

"Because you're all alone."

"Nobody's going to help me. At least no one has up till now. So I have to make it on my own. I have to get stronger—like a stray crow. That's why I gave myself the name Kafka. That's what Kafka means in Czech, you know—*crow*."

"Hmm," she says, mildly impressed. "So you're Crow."

"That's right," I say.

That's right, the boy named Crow says.

"There must be a limit to that kind of lifestyle, though," she says. "You can't use that strength as a protective wall around you. There's always going to be something stronger that can overcome your fortress. At least in principle."

"Strength itself becomes your morality."

Miss Saeki smiles. "You catch on quickly."

"The strength I'm looking for isn't the kind where you win or lose. I'm not after a wall that'll repel power coming from outside. What I want is the kind of strength to be able to *absorb* that outside power, to stand up to it. The strength to quietly endure things—unfairness, misfortune, sadness, mistakes, misunderstandings."

"That's got to be the most difficult strength of all to make your own."

"I know. . . ."

Her smile deepens one degree. "You seem to know everything."

I shake my head. "That's not true. I'm only fifteen, and there're plenty of things I don't know. I should know them, but I don't. I don't know anything about *you*, for one thing."

She picks up the coffee cup and takes a sip. "There's nothing that you have to know, nothing inside me you need to know."

"Do you remember my theory?"

"Of course," she says. "But that's *your* theory, not mine. So I have no responsibility for it, right?"

"Exactly. The person who comes up with the theory is the one who has to prove it," I say. "Which leads me to a question."

"About?"

"You told me you'd published a book about people who'd been struck by lightning."

"That's right."

"Is it still available?"

She shakes her head. "They didn't print that many copies to begin with. It went out of print a long time ago, and I imagine any leftover copies were destroyed. I don't even have a copy. Like I said before, nobody was interested."

"Why were you interested in that topic?"

"I'm not sure. I guess there was something symbolic about it. Or maybe I just wanted to keep myself busy, so I set a goal that kept me running around and my mind occupied. I can't recall now what the original motivation was. I came up with the idea and just started researching it. I was a writer then, with no money worries and plenty of free time, so I could mostly do whatever sparked my interest. Once I got into it, though, the topic itself was fascinating. Meeting all kinds of people, hearing all kinds of stories. If it weren't for that project, I probably would've withdrawn even further from reality and ended up completely isolated."

"When my father was young he worked as a caddy at a golf course and was hit by lightning. He was lucky to survive. The guy with him didn't make it."

"A lot of people are killed by lightning on golf courses—big, wide-open spaces, with almost nowhere to take shelter. And lightning loves golf clubs. Is your father also named Tamura?"

"Yes, and I think he was about your age."

She shakes her head. "I don't remember anybody named Tamura. I didn't interview anybody by that name."

I don't say anything.

"That's part of your theory, isn't it? That your father and I met while I was researching the book, and as a result you were born."

"Yes."

"Well, that puts an end to it, doesn't it? That never happened. Your theory doesn't stand up."

"Not necessarily," I say.

"What do you mean?"

"Because I don't believe everything you're telling me."

"Why not?"

"Well, you immediately said you'd never interviewed anybody called Tamura without even giving it any thought. Twenty years is a long time, and you must've interviewed quite a number of people. I don't think you'd be able to recall so quickly whether one of them was or wasn't named Tamura."

She shakes her head and takes another sip of coffee. A faint smile springs to her lips. "Kafka, I—" She stops, looking for the right words.

I wait for her to find them.

"I feel like things are starting to change around me," she says.

"How so?"

"I can't really say, but something's happening. The air pressure, the way sounds reverberate, the reflection of light, how bodies move and time passes—it's all transforming, bit by bit. It's like each small change is a drop that's steadily building up into a stream." She picks up her black Mont Blanc pen, looks at it, puts it back where it was, then looks straight at me. "What happened between us in your room last night is probably part of that flow. I don't know if what we did last night was right or not. But at the time I decided not to force myself to judge anything. If the flow is there, I figured I'd just let it carry me along where it wanted."

"Can I tell you what I think?"

"Go right ahead."

"I think you're trying to make up for lost time."

She thinks about it for a while. "You may be right," she says. "But how do you know that?"

"Because I'm doing the same thing."

"Making up for lost time?"

"Yes," I say. "A lot of things were stolen from my childhood. Lots of important things. And now I have to get them back."

"In order to keep on living."

I nod. "I have to. People need a place they can go back to. There's still time to make it, I think. For me, *and* for you."

She closes her eyes, and tents her fingers on top of her desk. Like she's resigned to it, she opens her eyes again. "Who *are* you?" she asks. "And why do you know so much about everything?"

You tell her she must know who you are. I'm Kafka on the Shore, you say. Your lover—and your son. The boy named Crow. And the two of us can't be free. We're caught up in a whirlpool, pulled beyond time. Somewhere, we were struck by lightning. But not the kind of lightning you can see or hear.

That night you make love again. You listen as the blank within her is filled. It's a faint sound, like fine sand on a shore crumbling in the moonlight. You hold your breath, listening. You're inside your theory now. Then you're outside. And inside again, then outside. You inhale, hold it, exhale. Inhale, hold it, exhale. Prince sings on, like some mollusk in your head. The moon rises, the tide comes in. Seawater flows into a river. A branch of the dogwood just outside the window trembles nervously. You hold her close, she buries her face in your chest. You feel her breath against your bare skin. She traces your muscles, one by one. Finally, she gently licks your swollen penis, as if healing it. You come again, in her mouth. She swallows it down, as if every drop is precious. You kiss her vagina, touching every soft, warm spot with your tongue. You become someone else there, *something* else. You are somewhere else.

"There's nothing inside me you need to know," she says. Until Monday morning dawns you hold each other, listening to time passing by.

Chapter 34

The massive bank of thunderclouds crossed the city at a lethargic pace, letting loose a flurry of lightning bolts as if probing every nook and cranny for a long-lost morality, finally dwindling to a faint, angry echo from the eastern sky. And right then the violent rain came to a sudden halt, followed by an unearthly silence. Hoshino stood up and opened the window to let in some air. The storm clouds had vanished, the sky covered once more by a thin membrane of pale clouds. All the buildings were wet, the moist cracks in their walls dark, like old people's veins. Water dripped off power lines and formed puddles on the ground. Birds flew out from where they'd sought shelter, chirping loudly as they vied for the bugs that were out themselves now that the storm had abated.

Hoshino rotated his neck from side to side a couple of times, checking out his spine. He gave one big stretch, sat down beside the window, and gazed outside, then pulled out his pack of Marlboros and lit up.

"You know, though, Mr. Nakata, after all that effort to turn that stone over and open the entrance, nothing out of the ordinary happened. No frog appeared, no demons, nothing strange at all. Which is fine by me, of course. . . . The stage was set with all that noisy thunder, but I gotta tell you I'm kind of disappointed."

He didn't get a reply, so he turned around. Nakata was leaning forward with both hands on the floor and his eyes closed. The old man looked like a feeble bug.

"What's the matter? Are you all right?" Hoshino asked.

"I'm sorry, I just seem to be a little tired. Nakata doesn't feel so well. I'd like to lie down and sleep for a while."

Nakata's face did look awfully pale. His eyes were sunken, his fingers trembling. Just a few hours was all it took, it seemed, for him to have aged terribly.

"Okay, I'll lay out the futon for you. Feel free to sleep as much as you want," Hoshino said. "But are you sure you're okay? Does your stomach hurt? Do you feel like you're gonna hurl? Any ringing in your ears? Or maybe you have to take a dump. Should I get a doctor? Do you have insurance?"

"Yes, the Governor gave me an insurance card, and I keep it safe in my bag."

"That's good," Hoshino said, dragging the futon out of the closet and spreading it out. "I know this isn't the time to go into details, but it isn't the Governor of Tokyo who gave you the card. It's a National Health card, so it's the Japanese government that issued it to you. I don't know all that much about it, but I'm sure that's the case. The Governor himself isn't looking after every little detail of your life, okay? So forget about him for a while."

"Nakata understands. The Governor didn't give me the insurance card. I'll try to forget about him for a while. Anyway, I don't think I need a doctor. If I can just get some sleep I should be all right."

"Wait a sec. You're not going to pull one of those thirty-six-hour marathons, are you?"

"I don't know. I don't decide how long I'm going to sleep and then stick to that."

"Well, I guess that makes sense," Hoshino admitted. "Nobody does that. Okay—just sleep as long as you like. It's been a rough day. All that thunder, plus talking with the stone, right? And that entrance thing opening up. Not something you see every day, that's for sure. You had to use your head a lot, so you must be tired. Don't worry about anything, just relax and catch some shut-eye. Let old Hoshino handle the rest."

"Much obliged. I'm always putting you out, aren't I? Nakata can never thank you enough for all you've done. If you hadn't been with me, I wouldn't have known what to do. And you have your own important work to do."

"Yeah, I guess so," Hoshino said in a gloomy voice. So many things had happened, he'd completely forgotten about his job. "Now that you mention it, I really should be getting back to work soon. The boss's blowing a gasket as we speak, I'll bet. I phoned him and said I had to take a few days off to take care of something, but haven't checked in since. Once I get back he'll really let me have it."

He lit up a fresh Marlboro, leisurely exhaling the smoke. He stared at a crow perched on top of a telephone pole and made silly faces at it.

"But who cares? He can say what he likes—blow steam out of his ears for all I care. Look, I've been pulling more than my weight for years, working my tail off. *Hey, Hoshino, we're shorthanded, so how 'bout making a night run to Hiroshima? Okay, boss, I'm on it.* . . . Always did what they told me to do, never a complaint. Thanks to which my back got shot to hell. If you didn't fix it for me things would've gone from bad to worse. I'm only in my mid-twenties, so why should I ruin my health over some crummy job, right? What's wrong with a few days off now and then? But you know, Mr. Nakata, I—"

Hoshino suddenly realized the old man was sound asleep. Eyes shut tight, face pointed toward the ceiling, lips firmly pressed together, Nakata was breathing peacefully. The flipped-over stone lay near his pillow.

Man, I've never seen anyone fall asleep as fast as him, Hoshino thought admiringly.

With time on his hands, he stretched out and watched some television, but he couldn't stand any of the insipid afternoon programs so he decided to go out. He'd run out of clean underwear and needed to buy some. He detested washing clothes. Better to buy some cheap underpants, he always figured, than bother with washing the old scuzzy ones. He went to the front desk of the inn to pay for the next day and told them his companion was asleep and they weren't to wake him up. "Not that you could if you tried," he added.

He wandered down the streets, sniffing the post-rain scent in the air, dressed in his usual Dragons cap, green-tinted Ray-Bans, and aloha shirt. He picked up a newspaper at a kiosk at the station and checked how the Dragons were doing—they lost to Hiroshima in an away game—then scanned the movie schedule and decided to see the latest Jackie Chan film. The timing was perfect. He asked directions at the police box and found out it was close by, so he walked. He bought his ticket, went inside, and watched the movie, munching on peanuts.

When he got out of the movie it was already evening. He wasn't all that hungry, but since he couldn't think of anything else to do he decided to have dinner. He popped into a place nearby and ordered sushi and a beer. He was more tired than he realized, and only finished half the beer.

That makes sense, though, he thought. Lifting that heavy stone, of course I'm beat. I feel like I'm the oldest of the Three Little Pigs. All the mean old wolf's gotta do is huff and puff and I'll be blasted all the way to Okayama.

He left the sushi bar and happened to run across a pachinko place. Before he knew it, he was down twenty dollars. He figured it just wasn't his day, so he gave up on pachinko and wandered around. He remembered he still hadn't bought any underwear. *Damn*—that was the whole point of going out, he told himself. He went into a discount store in the shopping district and bought underpants, white T-shirts, and socks. Now he could finally toss his dirty underwear. He decided it was about time for a new aloha shirt and scoured a few shops looking for one, only to conclude that the pickings in Takamatsu were pretty slim. Summer and winter alike he always wore aloha shirts, but that didn't mean just any aloha shirt would do.

He stopped at a nearby bakery and bought some bread, in case Nakata woke up hungry in the middle of the night, as well as a small carton of orange juice. Next he went to a bank and used the ATM to withdraw five hundred dollars. Checking his balance, he found there was still quite a lot left. These past few years had been so busy that he'd hardly had time to spend any money.

By this time it was completely dark, and he had a sudden yearning for a cup of coffee. He looked around, spotting a sign for a café just off the main drag. It turned out to be the kind of old-fashioned coffee shop you don't find much anymore. He went inside, eased back onto a soft, comfortable chair, and ordered a cup. Chamber music filtered out of the solid, British-made walnut speakers. Hoshino was the only customer. He sank back in his chair and, for the first time in quite a while, felt completely at ease. Everything in the shop was calming, natural, easy to feel comfortable with. The coffee, served in a fancy cup, was rich and delicious. Hoshino closed his eyes, breathing in quietly, and listened to the intertwining of strings and piano. He'd hardly ever listened to classical music before, but it was soothing and put him in an introspective mood.

Sunk back in his soft chair, eyes closed, lost in the music, a number of thoughts crossed his mind—mostly having to do with himself. But the more he thought about himself, the less reality his existence seemed to have. He began to feel like some meaningless appendage sitting there.

I've always been a great fan of the Chunichi Dragons, he thought, but what are the Dragons to me, anyway? Say they beat the Giants— how's that going to make me a better person? How *could* it? So why the heck have I spent all this time getting worked up like the team was some extension of myself?

Mr. Nakata said he's empty. Maybe he is, for all I know. But what does that make *me*? He said an accident when he was little made him that way—empty. But *I* never had an accident. If Mr. Nakata's empty, that makes me *worse* than empty! At least he has something about him—whatever it was that made me drop everything and follow him to Shikoku. Don't ask me what that something is, though. . . .

Hoshino ordered another cup of coffee.

"You like our coffee, then?" the gray-haired owner came over and asked. (Hoshino didn't know this, of course, but the man used to be an official in the Ministry of Education. After retirement, he came back to his hometown of Takamatsu and opened up this coffee shop, where he made fine coffee and played classical music.)

"It's great. Such a nice aroma."

"I roast the beans myself. Select each bean individually."

"No wonder it's so good."

"The music doesn't bother you?"

"The music?" Hoshino replied. "No, it's great. I don't mind it at all. Not one bit. Who's playing?"

"The Rubinstein, Heifetz, and Feuermann trio. The Million-Dollar Trio, they were dubbed. Consummate artists. This is an old 1941 recording, but the brilliance hasn't faded."

"It really hasn't. Good things never grow old, do they?"

"Some people prefer a more structured, classic, straightforward version of the *Archduke* Trio. Like the Oistrach Trio's version."

"No, I think this one's nice," Hoshino said. "It has a, I don't know, gentle feel to it."

"Thank you very much," the owner said, thanking him on behalf of the Million-Dollar Trio, and went back behind the counter.

As Hoshino enjoyed his second cup he went back to his reflections. But I *am* helping Mr. Nakata out. I read things for him, and I was the one who found the stone, after all. I've hardly ever noticed this before, but it feels kind of nice to be helpful to someone. . . . I don't regret any of it—skipping out on work, coming over to Shikoku. All those crazy things happening one after another.

I feel like I'm exactly where I belong. When I'm with Mr. Nakata I can't be bothered with all this *Who am I?* stuff. Maybe this is going overboard, but I bet Buddha's followers and Jesus' apostles felt the same way. *When I'm with the Buddha, I always feel I'm where I belong—* something like that. Forget about culture, truth, all that junk. That kind of inspiration's what it's all about.

When I was little, Grandpa told me stories about Buddha's disciples. One of them was named Myoga. The guy was a complete moron and couldn't memorize even the simplest sutra. The other disciples always teased him. One day the Buddha said to him, "Myoga, you're not very bright, so you don't have to learn any sutras. Instead, I'd like you to sit at the entrance and polish everybody's shoes." Myoga was an obedient guy, so he didn't tell his master to go screw himself. So for ten years, twenty years, he diligently polished everybody's shoes. Then one day he achieved enlightenment and became one of the greatest of all the Buddha's followers. That's a story Hoshino always remembered, because he'd thought that had to be the crappiest kind of life, polishing shoes for decades. You gotta be kidding, he thought. But when he considered it now, the story started to take on a different undertone. Life's crappy, no matter how you cut it. He just hadn't understood that when he was little.

These thoughts occupied him till the music, which was helping him meditate, stopped playing.

"Hey," he called out to the owner. "What was that music called again? I forget."

"Beethoven's *Archduke* Trio."

"March Duke?"

"*Arch. Arch*duke. Beethoven dedicated it to the Austrian archduke Rudolph. It's not the official name, more like the piece's nickname. Rudolph was the son of Emperor Leopold the Second. He was a very skilled musician, who studied piano and music theory with Beethoven starting when he was sixteen. He looked up to Beethoven. Archduke Rudolph didn't make a name for himself as either a pianist or a composer, but sort of stood in the shadows lending a helping hand to Beethoven, who didn't know much about getting ahead in the world. If it hadn't been for him, Beethoven would have had a much tougher time."

"Those kind of people are necessary in life, huh?"

"Absolutely."

"The world would be a real mess if everybody was a genius. Somebody's got to keep watch, take care of business."

"Exactly. A world full of geniuses would have significant problems."

"I really like that piece."

"It's beautiful. You never get tired of listening to it. I'd say it's the most refined of all Beethoven's piano trios. He wrote it when he was forty, and never wrote another. He must have decided he'd reached the pinnacle in the genre."

"I think I know what you mean. Reaching the pinnacle's important in everything," Hoshino said.

"Please come again."

"Yeah, I'll do that."

When he got back to the room Nakata was, as expected, out cold. He'd gone through this before, so this time it didn't strike him as odd. Just let him sleep as much as he wants, he decided. The stone was still there, right next to his pillow, and Hoshino put his sack of bread down beside it. He took a bath and changed into his new underwear, then balled up his old set inside a paper bag and tossed it in the trash. He crawled into his futon and was soon sound asleep.

He woke up the next morning just before nine. Nakata was still asleep, his breathing quiet and regular.

Hoshino went to eat breakfast alone, asking the maid not to wake up his companion. "You can just leave the futon like it is," he said.

"Is he all right, sleeping that long?" the maid asked.

"Don't worry, he's not about to die on us. He needs to sleep to regain his strength. I know exactly what's best for him."

He bought a paper at the station and sat on a bench and looked through the movie listings. A theater near the station was having a François Truffaut retrospective. Hoshino had no idea who Truffaut was, or even if it was a man or a woman, but a double feature was a good way of killing time till evening, so he decided to go. The featured films were *The 400 Blows* and *Shoot the Piano Player*. There were only a handful of customers in the theater. Hoshino wasn't by any means a movie buff. Occasionally he'd go see one, a kung fu or action film. So these early works of Truffaut were over his head in spots, the pace, as you'd expect of older films, a bit sluggish. Still, he enjoyed the unique mood, the overall look of the films, how suggestively the characters' inner worlds were portrayed. At the very least he wasn't bored. I wouldn't mind seeing some more films by that guy, he told himself afterward.

He exited the theater, walked to the shopping district, and went inside the same coffee shop as the night before. The owner remembered him. Hoshino sat in the same chair and ordered coffee. As before, he was the sole customer. Something with stringed instruments was playing on the stereo.

"Haydn's first cello concerto. Pierre Fournier's playing the solo," the owner explained as he brought over Hoshino's coffee.

"It's a real natural sound," Hoshino commented.

"It is, isn't it?" the owner said. "Pierre Fournier's one of my absolute favorite musicians. Like an elegant wine, his playing has an aroma and substance that warms the blood and gently encourages you. I always refer to him as Maestro Fournier out of respect. I don't know him personally, of course, but I've always felt like he's my mentor."

Listening to Fournier's flowing, dignified cello, Hoshino was drawn back to his childhood. He used to go to the river every day to catch fish. Nothing to worry about back then, he reminisced. Just live each day as it came. As long as I was alive, I was *something*. That was just how it was. But somewhere along the line it all changed. Living turned me into *nothing*. Weird . . . People are born in order to live, right? But the longer I've lived, the more I've lost what's inside me—and ended up empty. And I bet the longer I live, the emptier, the more worthless, I'll become. Something's wrong with this picture. Life isn't supposed to turn out like this! Isn't it possible to shift direction, to change where I'm headed?

"Excuse me . . . ," Hoshino called out to the owner at the register.

"Can I help you?"

"I was wondering, if you had time, could you come over and talk with me? I'd like to know more about this Haydn guy."

The owner was happy to give a mini lecture on Haydn, the man and his music. He was basically a reserved sort of person, but when it came to classical music he was eloquent. He explained how Haydn became a hired musician, serving different patrons over his long life, composing who knows how many compositions to order. Haydn was practical, affable, humble, and generous, he said, yet also a complex person with a silent darkness all his own inside.

"Haydn was an enigmatic figure. Nobody really knows the amount of intense pathos he held inside him. In the feudal time he was born in, though, he was compelled to skillfully cloak his ego in submissiveness and display a smart, happy exterior. Otherwise he would have been crushed. A lot of people compare him unfavorably to Bach and Mozart—both his music and the way he lived. Over his long life he was innovative, to be sure, but never exactly on the cutting edge. But if you really pay attention as you listen, you can catch a hidden longing for the modern ego. Like a far-off echo full of contradictions, it's all there in Haydn's music, silently pulsating. Listen to that chord—hear it? It's very quiet—right?—but it has a persistent, inward-moving spirit that's filled with a pliant, youthful sort of curiosity."

"Like François Truffaut's films."

"Exactly!" the owner exclaimed happily, patting Hoshino's arm reflexively. "You've hit it right on the head. You find the same spirit animating Truffaut. A persistent, inward-moving spirit that's filled with a pliant, youthful sort of curiosity," he repeated.

When the Haydn concerto was over Hoshino asked him to play the Rubinstein-Heifetz-Feuermann version of the *Archduke* Trio again. While listening to this, he again was lost in thought. Damn it, I don't care what happens, he finally decided. I'm going to follow Mr. Nakata as long as I live. To hell with the job!

Chapter 35

When the phone rings at seven a.m. I'm still sound asleep. In my dream I was deep inside a cave, bent over in the dark, flashlight in hand, searching for something. I hear a voice far away at the cave's entrance calling out a name faintly. I yell out a reply, but whoever it is doesn't seem to hear me. The person calls out my name, over and over. Reluctantly I stand up and start heading for the entrance. A little longer and I would've found it, I think. But inside I'm also relieved I didn't find it. That's when I wake up. I look around, collecting the scattered bits of my consciousness. I realize the phone's ringing, the phone at the library's reception desk. Bright sunlight's shining in through the curtains, and Miss Saeki's no longer next to me. I'm alone in bed.

I get out of bed in my T-shirt and boxers and go out to the phone. It takes me a while to get there but the phone keeps on ringing.

"Hello?"

"Were you asleep?" Oshima asks.

"Yeah."

"Sorry to get you up so early on a day off, but we've got a problem."

"A problem?"

"I'll tell you about it later, but you'd better not hang around there for a while. We're going to head off soon, so get your things together. When I get there, just come out to the parking lot and get right in the car without saying anything. Okay?"

"Okay," I reply.

I go back to my room and pack up. There's no need to rush since it only takes five minutes to get ready. I take down the laundry I had hanging in the bathroom, stuff my toilet kit, books, and diary in my backpack, then get dressed and straighten up the bed. Pull the sheets tight, plump up the pillows, straighten out the covers. Covering up all traces of what went on here. I sit down in the chair and think about Miss Saeki, who'd been with me until a few hours before.

I have time for a quick bowl of cornflakes. Wash up the bowl and spoon and put them away. Brush my teeth, wash my face. I'm checking out my face in the mirror when I hear the Miata pull into the parking lot.

Even though the weather's perfect, Oshima has the tan top up. I shoulder my pack, walk over to the car, and climb into the passenger seat. As before, Oshima does a good job of tying my pack down on top of the trunk. He's wearing a pair of Armani-type sunglasses, and a striped linen shirt over a white V-neck T-shirt, white jeans, and navy blue, low-cut Converse All-Stars. Casual day-off clothes.

He hands me a navy blue cap with a North Face logo on it. "Didn't you say you lost your hat somewhere? Use this one. It'll help hide your face a little."

"Thanks," I say, and tug on the cap.

Oshima checks me out in the cap and nods his approval. "You have sunglasses, right?"

I nod, take my sky blue Revos from my pocket, and put them on.

"Very cool," he says. "Try putting the cap on backward."

I do as he says, turning the cap around.

Oshima nods again. "Great. You look like a rap singer from a nice family." He shifts to first, slowly steps on the gas, and lets out the clutch.

"Where are we going?" I ask.

"The same place as before."

"The mountains in Kochi?"

Oshima nods. "Right. Another long drive." He flips on the stereo. It's a cheerful Mozart orchestral piece I've heard before. The "Posthorn Serenade," maybe?

"Are you tired of the mountains?"

"No, I like it there. It's quiet, and I can get a lot of reading done."

"Good," Oshima says.

"So what was the problem you mentioned?"

Oshima shoots a sullen look at the rearview mirror, glances over at me, then faces forward again. "First of all, the police got back in touch with me. Phoned my place last night. Sounds like they're getting serious about tracking you down. They seemed pretty intense about the whole thing."

"But I have an alibi, don't I?"

"Yes, you do. A solid alibi. The day the murder took place you were in Shikoku. They don't doubt that. What they're thinking is you might've conspired with somebody else."

"Conspired?"

"You might have had an accomplice."

Accomplice? I shake my head. "Where'd they get that idea?"

"They're pretty tight-lipped about it. They're pushy about asking questions, but get all low key when you try turning the tables on them. So I spent the whole night online, downloading information about the case. Did you know there're a couple of websites up already about it? You're pretty famous. The wandering prince who holds the key to the puzzle."

I give a small shrug. *The wandering prince?*

"With online information it's hard to separate fact from wishful thinking, but you could summarize it like this: The police are now after a guy in his late sixties. The night of the murder he showed up at a police box near the Nogata shopping district and confessed to just having murdered somebody in the neighborhood. Said he stabbed him. But he spouted out all kinds of nonsense, so the young cop on the beat tagged him as crazy and sent him on his way without getting the whole story. Of course when the murder came to light, the policeman knew he'd blown it. He hadn't taken down the old man's name or address, and if his superiors heard about it there'd be hell to pay, so he kept quiet about it. But something happened—I have no idea what—and the whole thing came to light. The cop was disciplined, of course. Poor guy'll probably never live it down."

Oshima downshifts to pass a white Toyota Tercel, then nimbly slips back into the lane. "The police went all out and were able to identify the old man. They don't know his background, but he appears to be mentally impaired. Not retarded, just a teeny bit off. He lives by himself on welfare and some support from relatives. But he's disappeared from his apartment. The police traced his movements and think he was hitchhiking, heading for Shikoku. An intercity bus driver thinks he might've ridden his bus out of Kobe. He remembered him because he had an unusual way of talking and said some weird things. Apparently he was with some young guy in his mid-twenties. The two of them got out at Tokushima Station. They've located the inn where they stayed, and according to a housekeeper, they took a train to Takamatsu. The old man's movements and yours overlap exactly. Both of you left Nogata in Nakano Ward and headed straight for Takamatsu. A little too much of a coincidence, so naturally the police are reading something into it—thinking that the two of you planned the whole thing together. The National Police Agency's even getting in the act, and now they're scouring the city. We might not be able to hide you at the library anymore, so I decided you'd better lie low in the mountains."

"A mentally impaired old man from Nakano?"

"Ring any bells?"

I shake my head. "None."

"His address isn't far from your house. A fifteen-minute walk, apparently."

"But tons of people live in Nakano. I don't even know who lives next door."

"There's more," Oshima says, and glances at me. "He's the one who made all those mackerel and sardines rain down from the sky in the Nogata shopping district. At least he predicted to the police that lots of fish would fall from the sky the day before it happened."

"That's amazing," I say.

"Isn't it?" Oshima says. "And the same day, in the evening, a huge amount of leeches rained down on the Fujigawa rest stop on the Tomei Highway. Remember?"

"Yeah, I do."

"None of this slipped past the police, of course. They're guessing there's got to be some connection between these events and this mystery man they're after. His movements parallel everything so closely."

The Mozart piece ends, and another begins.

Hands on the steering wheel, Oshima shakes his head a couple of times. "A really strange turn of events. It started out weird and is getting even weirder as it goes along. Impossible to predict what'll happen next. One thing's for sure, though. Everything seems to be converging right here. The old man's path and yours are bound to cross."

I close my eyes and listen to the roar of the engine. "Maybe I should go to some other town," I tell him. "Apart from anything else, I don't want to cause you or Miss Saeki any more trouble."

"But where would you go?"

"I don't know. But I can figure it out if you take me to the station. It doesn't really matter."

Oshima sighs. "I don't think that's such a smart idea. The station has to be crawling with cops, all on the lookout for a cool, tall, fifteen-year-old boy lugging a backpack and a bunch of obsessions."

"So why not take me to a station far away that they're not staking out?"

"It's all the same. In the end they'll find you."

I don't say anything.

"Look, they haven't issued a warrant for your arrest. You're not on the most-wanted list or anything, okay?"

I nod.

"Which means you're still free. So I don't need anybody's permission to take you anywhere I want. I'm not breaking the law. I mean, I don't even know your real first name, Kafka. So don't worry about me. I'm a very cautious person. Nobody's going to nab me so easily."

"Oshima?" I say.

"Yes?"

"I didn't plan anything with anybody. If I had to kill my father, I wouldn't ask anybody to do it."

"I know."

He stops at a red light and checks the rearview mirror, then pops a lemon drop into his mouth and offers me one.

I slip it in my mouth. "What comes after that?"

"What do you mean?" Oshima asks.

"You said *first of all*. About why I have to go hide in the hills. If there's a first reason, there's got to be a second."

Oshima stares at the red light, but it doesn't change. "Compared to the first, the second isn't very important."

"I still want to hear it."

"It's about Miss Saeki," he says. The light finally turns green and he steps on the gas. "You're sleeping with her, right?"

I don't know how to answer that.

"Don't worry, I'm not blaming you or anything. I just have a sense for these things, that's all. She's a wonderful person, a very attractive lady. She's—special, in all sorts of ways. She's a lot older than you, sure, but so what? I understand your attraction to her. You want to have sex with her, so why not? She wants to have sex with you? More power to her. It doesn't bother me. If you guys are okay with that, it's fine by me." Oshima rolls the lemon drop around in his mouth. "But I think it's best if you two keep your distance for a while. And I don't mean because of that bloody mess in Nakano."

"Why, then?"

"She's in a very delicate place right now."

"How so?"

334

"Miss Saeki . . . ," he begins, searching for the rest. "What I mean is, she's dying. I've felt it for a long time."

I raise my sunglasses and look at him closely. He's looking straight ahead as he drives. We've turned onto the highway to Kochi. This time, surprisingly, he keeps to the speed limit. A Toyota Supra whooshes past us.

"When you say she's dying . . . ," I begin. "You mean she's got an incurable disease? Cancer or leukemia or something?"

Oshima shakes his head. "That could be. But I don't know anything about her health. For all I know she might be saddled with a disease like that. I think it's more of a psychological issue. The will to live—something to do with that."

"You're saying she's lost the will to live?"

"I think so. Lost the will to go on living."

"Do you think she's going to kill herself?"

"No, I don't," Oshima replies. "It's just that very quietly, very steadily, she's heading toward death. Or else death is heading toward her."

"Like a train heading toward the station?"

"Something like that," Oshima said, and stopped, his lips taut. "But then *you* showed up, Kafka. Cool as a cucumber, mysterious as the real Kafka. The two of you were drawn together and, to use the classic expression, you have a relationship."

"And then?"

For a brief moment Oshima lifts both hands off the wheel. "That's it." I slowly shake my head. "I bet you're thinking *I'm the train*."

Oshima doesn't say anything for a long time. "Exactly," he finally says. "That's it, exactly."

"That I'm bringing about her death?"

"I'm not blaming you for this, mind you," he says. "It's actually for the best."

"Why?"

He doesn't answer this. You're *supposed to find the answer to that*, his silence tells me. Or maybe he's saying, *It's too obvious to even think about.*

I lean back in my seat, shut my eyes, and let my body go limp. "Oshima?"

"What is it?"

"I don't know what to do anymore. I don't even know what direction

335

I'm facing in. What's right, what's wrong—whether I should keep on going ahead or turn around. I'm totally lost."

Oshima keeps silent, no answer forthcoming.

"You've got to help me. What am I supposed to do?" I ask him.

"You don't have to do anything," he says simply.

"Nothing?"

He nods. "Which is why I'm taking you to the mountains."

"But what should I do once I get there?"

"Just listen to the wind," he says. "That's what I always do."

I mull this over.

He gently lays a hand over mine. "There are a lot of things that aren't your fault. Or mine, either. Not the fault of prophecies, or curses, or DNA, or absurdity. Not the fault of Structuralism or the Third Industrial Revolution. We all die and disappear, but that's because the mechanism of the world itself is built on destruction and loss. Our lives are just shadows of that guiding principle. Say the wind blows. It can be a strong, violent wind or a gentle breeze. But eventually every kind of wind dies out and disappears. Wind doesn't have form. It's just a movement of air. You should listen carefully, and then you'll understand the metaphor."

I squeeze his hand back. It's soft and warm. His smooth, sexless, delicately graceful hand. "So you think it's better for me to be away from Miss Saeki for the time being?"

"I do, Kafka. It's the best thing right now. We should let her be by herself. She's bright, and tough. She's managed to put up with a terrible kind of loneliness for a long time, a lot of painful memories. She can make whatever decisions she needs to make alone."

"So I'm just a kid who's getting in the way."

"That's not what I mean," Oshima says softly. "That's not it at all. You did what you had to do. What made sense to you, and to her. Leave the rest up to her. This might sound cold, but there's nothing you can do for her now. You need to get into the mountains and do your own thing. For you, the time is right."

"*Do my own thing?*"

"Just keep your ears open, Kafka," Oshima replied. "Just listen. Imagine you're a clam."

Chapter 36

When he got back to the inn, Hoshino found Nakata—no surprise—still fast asleep. The sack he'd put next to him with bread and orange juice was untouched. The old man hadn't shifted an inch, probably hadn't woken up once the whole time. Hoshino counted up the hours. Nakata had gone to sleep at two the previous afternoon, which meant he'd been asleep for thirty solid hours. What day is it, anyway? Hoshino wondered. He was completely losing track of time. He took his memo book out of his bag and checked. Let's see, he told himself, we arrived in Tokushima on a Saturday on the bus from Kobe, then Nakata slept till Monday. On Monday we left Tokushima for Takamatsu, Thursday was all that ruckus with the stone and thunder, and that afternoon he went to sleep. So skip ahead one night and that would make today . . . Friday. It's like the old guy came to Shikoku to attend some Sleep Festival or something.

Like the night before, Hoshino took a bath, watched TV for a while, then climbed into his futon. Nakata was still breathing peacefully, sound asleep. Whatever, Hoshino thought. Just go with the flow. Let him sleep as much as he wants. No need to worry about that. And he himself fell asleep, at ten-thirty.

At five the next morning the cell phone in his bag went off, jolting him awake. Nakata was still out like a light.

Hoshino reached for the phone. "Hello."

"Mr. Hoshino!" A man's voice.

"Colonel Sanders?" Hoshino said, recognizing the voice.

"The very one. How's it hanging, sport?"

"Fine, I guess. . . . But how'd you get this number? I didn't give it to you, and the phone's been turned off all this time so those clowns from work won't bother me. So how could you call me? You're kind of freaking me out here."

"It's like I told you, I'm neither a god nor a Buddha, not a human being. I'm something else again—a *concept*. So making your phone ring is a cinch. Piece of cake. Whether it's turned on or not makes not one jot of difference, my friend. Don't let every little thing get to you, okay? I could've run over and been right there beside you when you woke up, but I figured that'd be a bit of a shock."

"You bet it would."

"Which explains the phone call. I'm a well-mannered person, after all."

"I appreciate it," Hoshino said. "So anyway, what're we supposed to do with the stone? Nakata and I managed to flip it over so that entrance thing opened up. Lightning was flashing like crazy outside, and the stone weighed a ton. Oh, that's right—I haven't told you about Nakata yet. He's the guy I'm traveling with."

"I know all about Mr. Nakata," Colonel Sanders said. "No need to explain."

"You know about him?" Hoshino said. "Okay. . . . Anyhow, Nakata went into hibernation after that, and the stone's still here. Don't you think we should get it back to the shrine? We might be cursed for taking it without permission."

"You never give up, do you? How many times did I tell you there's no curse?" Colonel Sanders said disgustedly. "Keep the stone there for the time being. You opened it up, and eventually you'll have to close it again. Then you can take it back. But it's not time for that yet. Get it? We okay here?"

"Yeah, I get it," Hoshino said. "Things that are open have to be shut. Things you have, you gotta return the way they were. All *right* already! Anyhow, I've decided not to think about things so much. I'll go along with whatever you want, no matter how crazy it sounds. I had a kind of revelation last night. Taking crazy things seriously is—a serious waste of time."

"A very wise conclusion. There's that saying, 'Pointless thinking is worse than no thinking at all.'"

"I like that."

"Very suggestive, don't you think?"

"Have you heard the saying 'Sheepish butlers' surgical bottle battles'?"

"What on earth is that supposed to mean?"

"It's a tongue-twister. I made it up."

"Your point being?"

"No point, really. I just felt like saying it."

"Can the stupid comments, all right? I don't have much patience with inanity. You'll drive me nuts if you keep it up."

"Sorry," Hoshino said. "But why'd you call me, anyway? You must have had a reason to call so early."

"That's right. It completely slipped my mind," Colonel Sanders said. "Here's the thing—I want you to leave that inn right this minute. No time to eat breakfast. Just wake up Mr. Nakata, grab the stone, and get out. Get a cab, but don't have the inn call one for you. Go out to the main street and flag one down. Then give the driver this address. Do you have something to write with?"

"Yep, just a sec," Hoshino replied, grabbing a pen and his note-book from his bag. "Broom and dustpan, check."

"Enough with the stupid jokes already!" Colonel Sanders yelled into the phone. "I'm serious here. Not a minute to lose."

"Okay, okay. Go ahead."

Colonel Sanders recited the address and Hoshino wrote it down, repeating it to make sure he got it right: "Apartment 308, Takamatsu Park Heights 16-15, 3-chome. Is that it?"

"That's fine," Colonel Sanders replied. "You'll find the key under a black umbrella stand at the front door. Unlock the door and go inside. You can stay there as long as you like. There's a stock of food and things, so you won't have to go out for the time being."

"That's your place?"

"It is indeed. I don't own it, though. It's rented. So make yourself at home. I got the place for you two."

"Colonel?"

"Yeah?"

"You told me you're not a god, or a Buddha, or a human being, correct?"

"Correct."

"So I'm assuming you're not of this world."

"You got it."

"Then how could you rent an apartment? You're not human, so you don't have all the papers and stuff you need, right? A family reg-ister, local registration, proof of income, official stamp and seal and all that. If you don't have those, nobody's gonna rent you a place. Did you cheat or something? Like change a leaf by magic into an official

339

stamp? Enough underhanded stuff's gone on already, I don't want to get mixed up in any more."

"You just don't get it, do you?" Colonel Sanders said, clicking his tongue. "You are one major dimwit. Is your brain made out of Jell-O, you spineless twit? A *leaf*? What do you think I am, one of those magical raccoons? I'm a *concept*, get it? *Con-cept!* Concepts and raccoons aren't exactly the same, now are they? What a dumb thing to say. . . . Do you really think I went over to the real estate agent's, filled out all the forms, bargained with them to lower the rent? Ridiculous! I have a secretary take care of *temporal* things. My secretary gets all the necessary documents and things together. What do you expect?"

"Ah—so you have a *secretary*!"

"Damn right I do! Who do you think I am, anyway? You're way out of line. I'm a busy man, so why shouldn't I have a secretary?"

"All right, all right—don't blow a gasket. I was just pulling your leg. Anyway, why do we have to leave so fast? Can't we at least have a bite before we go? I'm starved, and Mr. Nakata's out like a light. I couldn't wake him up no matter how hard I try."

"Listen up. This is no joke. The police are scouring the town for you. First thing this morning, they've been making the rounds of hotels and inns, questioning everyone. They've already got a description of both of you. So once they start nosing around it's only a matter of time. The two of you stand out, let's face it. There's not a moment to lose."

"The cops?" Hoshino shouted. "Gimme a break! We haven't done anything wrong. Sure, I ripped off a few motorcycles back in high school. Just joyriding—it wasn't like I was gonna sell them or anything. I always took them back. Never done anything illegal since. Taking that stone from the shrine is about the worst thing I've done. And you *told* me to."

"This has nothing to do with the stone," Colonel Sanders said flatly. "You're a real dunce sometimes. Forget the stone. The police don't know anything about it, and wouldn't give a damn if they did. They're not going to be up at the crack of dawn beating down doors over some stone. We're talking about something much more serious."

"What do you mean?"

"The police are after Mr. Nakata because of it."

"I don't get it. He's the last person you'd ever imagine committing a crime. What kind of crime? And how could he be involved?"

"No time to go into that now. You have to get him out of there. Everything depends on you. Are we clear here?"

"I don't get it," Hoshino repeated, shaking his head. "It just doesn't make any sense. So they're gonna tag me as an accomplice?"

"No, but I'm sure they'll question you. Time's a-wasting. Don't bother your head over it now, just do as I say."

"Listen, you gotta understand one thing about me. I *hate* cops. They're worse than the yakuza—worse than the SDF. They're awful, the things they do. They strut around and love nothing better than tormenting the weak. I had plenty of run-ins with cops when I was in high school, even after I started driving trucks, so the last thing I need is to get into a fight with them. There's no way you can win, plus you can't shake 'em off afterward. You know what I mean? God, how'd I get mixed up in all this? You see, what I—"

The phone went dead.

"*Jeez*," Hoshino said. He sighed deeply and tossed the cell phone into his bag, then tried to wake Nakata up.

"Hey, Mr. Nakata. Gramps. Fire! Flood! Earthquake! Revolution! Godzilla's on the loose! Get *up*, already!"

It was some time before Nakata woke up. "I finished the beveling," he said. "The rest I used as kindling. No, cats don't take baths. I'm the one who took the bath." Obviously in his own little world.

Hoshino shook the old man's shoulder, pinched his nose, tugged at his ears, and finally roused him to the land of the living.

"Is that you, Mr. Hoshino?" he asked.

"Yeah, it's me," Hoshino replied. "Sorry to wake you up."

"No problem. Nakata was going to get up soon anyway. Don't worry about it. I finished with the kindling."

"Good. But something's come up—something not so good—and we have to get out of here right now."

"Is it about Johnnie Walker?"

"That I don't know. I've got my sources, and they told me we better make ourselves scarce. The cops are after us."

"Is that right?"

"That's what he said. But what happened with you and this Johnnie Walker guy?"

"Didn't Nakata already tell you?"

"No, you didn't."

"I feel like I did, though."

341

"No, you never told me the most important part."

"Well, what happened was—Nakata killed him."

"You gotta be kidding!"

"No, I'm not."

"Jeez Louise," Hoshino muttered.

Hoshino threw his belongings into his bag and wrapped the stone back up in its cloth. It was the same weight as it had been originally. Not light, but at least he could carry it. Nakata put his things in his canvas bag. Hoshino went to the front desk and told them something had come up suddenly and they had to check out. Since he'd paid in advance, it didn't take long. Nakata was still a bit unsteady on his feet but could walk. "How long did I sleep?" he asked.

"Let me see," Hoshino said, doing the math. "About forty hours, give or take."

"I feel like I slept well."

"No wonder. If you don't feel refreshed after that kind of record-breaking sleep, then sleep's kind of pointless, isn't it. Hey, you hungry?"

"Yes, I am. Very hungry."

"Can you hold off a while? First we have to get out of here, as soon as we can. Then we'll eat."

"That's all right. I can wait."

Hoshino helped him out onto the main street and flagged down a cab. He told the driver the address, and the driver nodded and sped off. The cab left the city, drove down a main thoroughfare, and entered a suburb. The neighborhood was upscale and quiet, quite a contrast from the noisy area near the station where they'd been staying. The ride took about twenty-five minutes.

They stopped in front of a typical five-story neat-as-a-pin apartment building. Takamatsu Park Heights, the sign said, though it was on a level expanse with no park in sight. They rode the elevator up to the third floor, where Hoshino found the key, sure enough, under the umbrella stand. The apartment was a standard two-bedroom place, with a dinette kitchen, a living room, and a bathroom. The place was brand new, by the looks of it, the furniture barely used. The living room contained a wide-screen TV, a small stereo, a sofa and a love seat, and each bedroom had a bed already made up. The kitchen had the usual utensils, the shelves stocked with a passable set of plates, cups, and bowls. There were smart-looking framed prints on the walls, and the whole place looked like some model apartment a developer might come up with to show new clients.

"Not bad at all," Hoshino remarked. "Not much character, but at least it's clean."

"It's very pretty," Nakata added.

The large, off-white fridge was packed with food. Muttering to himself, Nakata checked out everything, finally taking out some eggs, a green pepper, and butter. He rinsed off the pepper, sliced it into thin strips, and sautéed it. Next he broke the eggs into a bowl and whipped them up with chopsticks. He pulled out a frying pan and proceeded to make two green-pepper omelettes with a practiced touch. He topped this off with toast and took the whole meal over to the dining table, along with hot tea.

"You're quite the cook," Hoshino said. "I'm impressed."

"I've always lived alone, so I'm used to it."

"I live alone too, but don't ask me to cook anything, 'cause I stink at it."

"Nakata has a lot of free time and nothing else to do."

The two of them ate their toast and omelettes. They were still hungry, so Nakata went back to the kitchen and sautéed some bacon and spinach, which they had with two more slices of toast each. Starting to feel human again, they sank back on the sofa and had a second cup of tea.

"So," Hoshino said, "you killed somebody, huh?"

"Yes, I did," Nakata answered, and gave a detailed account of how he stabbed Johnnie Walker to death.

"Man alive," Hoshino said when he'd finished. "What a freaky story. The police would never believe that, no matter how honest you are about it. I mean, *I* believe you, but if you'd told me that a week ago I would have sent you packing."

"I don't understand it myself."

"At any rate, somebody's been murdered, and murder's not something you just shrug off. The police aren't fooling around on this one, not if they've trailed you out here to Shikoku."

"Nakata's sorry you had to get involved."

"Aren't you gonna give yourself up?"

"No, I'm not," Nakata said with uncharacteristic firmness. "I already tried to, but right now I don't feel like doing that. There are some other things Nakata has to do. Otherwise it's pointless for me to have come all this way."

"You have to close that entrance again."

"That's right. Things that are open have to be shut. Then I will be normal again. But there are some things Nakata has to take care of first."

"Colonel Sanders, the guy who told me where the stone is," Hoshino said, "is helping us lie low. But why's he doing this? Is there some connection between him and Johnnie Walker?"

The more Hoshino tried to unravel it, though, the more confused he got. Better not to try to make sense, he decided, of what basically doesn't make any. "Pointless thinking is worse than no thinking at all," he concluded out loud, his arms crossed.

"Mr. Hoshino?" Nakata said.

"What's up?"

"I smell the sea."

Hoshino went to the window, opened it, went out on the narrow veranda, and breathed in deeply. No sea smells that he could detect. Off in the distance, white summer clouds floated above a pine forest. "I don't smell anything," he said.

Nakata came over beside him and started sniffing, his nose twitching like a squirrel. "I can. The sea's right over there." He pointed to the forest.

"You have quite a nose there," Hoshino said. "I have a touch of a sinus problem myself, so I'm always a bit stuffed up."

"Mr. Hoshino, why don't we walk over to the ocean?"

Hoshino thought about it. How could a little walk on the beach hurt anything? "Okay, let's go."

"Nakata has to take a dump first, if it's all right."

"Take your time, we're in no rush."

While Nakata was in the toilet Hoshino walked around the apartment, checking it out. Like the Colonel said, there was pretty much everything they needed. Shaving cream in the bathroom, a couple of new toothbrushes, Q-tips, Band-Aids, nail clippers. All the basics. Even an iron and ironing board. Very considerate of him, Hoshino thought, though I imagine his secretary did all the work. They haven't forgotten a thing.

He opened the closet and found fresh underwear and clothes. No aloha shirts, unfortunately, just some ordinary striped shirts and polo shirts, brand-new Tommy Hilfigers. "And here I was thinking Colonel

Sanders was pretty quick on the uptake," Hoshino complained to no one in particular. "He should've figured out I only wear aloha shirts. If he went to all this trouble, he at least could've bought me one." He noticed the shirt he had on was getting a bit rank, so he took it off and pulled on a polo shirt. It was a perfect fit.

They walked through the pines, up over a breakwater, and down to the beach. The Inland Sea was calm. They sat down side by side on the sand, not speaking for a long time, watching the waves rise up like sheets being fluffed into the air and then, with a faint sound, break apart. Several small islands were visible offshore. Neither of them had been to the sea very often in their lives, and they feasted their eyes on the scene.

"Mr. Hoshino?" Nakata said, breaking the silence.

"What is it?"

"The sea is a really nice thing, isn't it?"

"Yeah, it is. Makes you feel calm."

"Why is that?"

"Probably 'cause it's so big, with nothing on it," Hoshino said, pointing. "You wouldn't feel so calm if there was a 7-Eleven over there, or a Seiyu department store, would you? Or a pachinko place over there, or a Yoshikawa pawnshop? But as far as the eye can see there's *nothing*—which is pretty darn nice."

"I suppose you're right," Nakata said, giving it some thought. "Mr. Hoshino?"

"What's up?"

"I have a question about something else."

"Shoot."

"What's at the bottom of the sea?"

"There's like another world down there, all kinds of fish, shellfish, seaweed, and stuff. You've never been to an aquarium?"

"No, I've never been. The place where Nakata lived for a long time, Matsumoto, didn't have one of those."

"No, I don't imagine it would," Hoshino said. "A town like that off in the hills—I guess a mushroom museum or something would be about all you could expect. Anyhow, there's all kinds of stuff at the bottom of the sea. The animals are different than us—they take oxygen from the water and don't need air to breathe. There're some beautiful things down there, some delicious things, plus some dangerous things. And things that'd totally creep you out. If you've never seen it, it's hard

345

to explain, but it's completely different than what we're used to. Way down at the bottom it's totally dark and there are some of the grossest creatures you've ever seen. What do you say when all this blows over we check out an aquarium? They're kind of fun, and I haven't been to one in a long time. I'm sure there's one around here."

"Yes, I'd love to go to a place like that."

"There's something I wanted to ask *you*."

"Yes?"

"The other day we lifted up that stone and opened the entrance, right?"

"Yes, you and I opened up the entrance. After that Nakata fell sound asleep."

"What I want to know is—did something take place because the entrance opened up?"

Nakata gave a nod. "Yes. It did."

"But you still don't know what that is."

Nakata gave a decisive shake of his head. "No, Nakata doesn't know yet."

"So maybe it's happening someplace else, right this minute?"

"Yes, I think that's true. As you said, it's happening. And I'm waiting for it to *finish* happening."

"And once whatever it is finishes taking place, everything will work itself out?"

Another definitive shake of the head. "That Nakata doesn't know. I'm doing what I'm doing because I *must*. But I have no idea what will happen because of what I do. I'm not so bright, so it's too hard for me to figure out. I don't know what's going to happen."

"At any rate, it's gonna take some time, right? For whatever this is to finish up and some conclusion or something to happen?"

"That is correct."

"And while we're waiting we have to make sure the cops don't grab us. 'Cause there's still stuff that needs doing?"

"Correct. I don't mind visiting the police. I'm ready to do whatever the Governor tells me to do. But now is just not a good time to do that."

"You know what? If the cops heard your crazy story, they'd just blow it off and make up some convenient confession, something anyone would believe. Like you were robbing the house and you heard somebody, so you grabbed a knife from the kitchen and stabbed him. They don't give a damn what the real facts are, or what's right. Framing somebody just to jack up their arrest rate. They wouldn't bat an eye. Next thing you know, you're thrown in jail or some maximum-security psycho ward. They'd lock you up and throw away the key. You don't have enough money to hire some fancy lawyer, so they'd stick you with some court-appointed bozo who couldn't care less, so it's obvious how it'd end up."

"I'm afraid I don't understand all—"

"I'm just telling you what cops are like. Believe me, I know," Hoshino said. "So I really don't want to take 'em on, okay? Cops and me just don't hit it off."

"I'm sorry to cause so many problems for you."

Hoshino sighed deeply. "As they say, though, 'Take the poison, take the plate.'"

"What does that mean?"

"If you're gonna take poison, you might as well eat the plate it came on."

"But if you eat a plate, you'll die. It's not good for your teeth, either. And it'll hurt your throat."

"I'd have to agree," Hoshino said, puzzling over it. "Yeah—why *do* you have to eat the plate?"

"I'm not so bright, so I really can't tell you. But aside from the poison, the plate's way too hard."

"Um. You got that right. I'm starting to get confused myself. I never was one for using my head, either. What I'm trying to say is, I've come this far so I'll stick with you and make sure you escape. I can't believe you did anything bad, and I'm not going to just abandon you here. I've got my honor to consider."

"Much obliged. Nakata can't thank you enough. I'll presume on you again, though, and ask one more favor."

"Go for it."

"We'll need a car."

"Would a rental car be okay?"

"Nakata doesn't really know what that is, but any kind is fine. Big or small is all right as long as it's a car."

"No problem. Now you're talking my specialty. I'll go pick one up in a while. So we're gonna be heading out somewhere?"

"I think so. We probably will be headed out somewhere."

"You know something, Mr. Nakata?"

"Yes?"

347

"I never get bored when I'm with you. All kinds of off-the-wall things happen, but that much I can say for sure—being with you's never boring."

"Thank you for saying that. I feel relieved to hear it. But Mr. Hoshino?"

"What's up?"

"I'm not really sure I understand what being *bored* means."

"You've never been bored before?"

"No, not even once."

"You know, I kind of had the feeling that might be the case."

Chapter 37

We stop at a town to have a bite to eat and stock up on food and mineral water at a supermarket, then drive up the unpaved road through the hills and arrive at the cabin. Inside, it's exactly as I left it a week ago. I open the window to air out the place, then stow away the food.

"I'm going to take a nap before I head back," Oshima says, nearly covering his face with his hands as he lets out a huge yawn. "I didn't sleep well last night."

He must really be exhausted, because as soon as he gets under the covers and turns toward the wall, he's out. I make some coffee and pour it in a thermos for his ride back, then head down to the brook with the aluminum pail to fill up on water. The forest hasn't changed a bit—the same smell of grasses, birdcalls, babbling water in the brook, the rush of wind through the trees, the same shadows of rustling leaves. The clouds above me look really close. I feel nostalgic to see them again, for they've become a part of me.

While Oshima sleeps I sit on the porch, sip tea, and read a book about Napoleon's 1812 invasion of Russia. Some 400,000 French soldiers lost their lives in that huge country in this massive, pointless campaign. The battles themselves were awful, of course, but there weren't enough doctors or medical supplies, so most of the severely wounded soldiers were left to die in agony. More froze to death or died of starvation, equally terrible ways to die. Seated there on the porch, sipping hot herb tea, birds whistling all around me, I tried to picture the battlefield in Russia and these men trudging through blizzards.

I get about a third of the way through the book and go check to see if Oshima's okay. I know he's exhausted, but he's so quiet it's like he's not even there, and I'm a little worried. But he's all right, wrapped in the covers, breathing quietly. I walk over next to him and notice his shoulders rising and falling slightly. Standing there, I suddenly remember that he's a woman. Most of the time I forget that, and think of him as a man. Which is exactly what he wants, of course. But when he's sleeping, he looks like he's *gone back* to being a woman.

I go out on the porch again and pick up where I left off in the book. Back to a road outside Smolensk lined with frozen corpses.

Oshima sleeps for a couple of hours. After he wakes up he walks out on the porch and looks at his car. The dusty, unpaved road has turned the green Miata almost white. He gives a big stretch and sits down next to me. "It's the rainy season," he says, rubbing his eyes, "but there's not much rain this year. If we don't get some soon, Takamatsu's going to run out of water."

I venture a question: "Does Miss Saeki know where I am?"

He shakes his head. "No, I didn't tell her anything. She doesn't even know I have a cabin up here. It's better to keep her in the dark, so she won't get mixed up in all this. The less she knows, the less she needs to hide."

I nod. That's exactly what I wanted to hear.

"She's gotten mixed up in enough before," Oshima says. "She doesn't need this now."

"I told her about my father dying recently," I tell him. "How somebody murdered him. I left out the part about the police looking for me."

"She's pretty smart. Even if neither of us mentioned it, I get the feeling she's figured out most of what's going on. So if I tell her tomorrow that you had something you had to do and will be gone for a while, and tell her hi from you, I doubt she'll quiz me about the details. Even if that's all I tell her, I know she'll just let it pass."

I nod.

"But you want to see her, don't you?"

I don't reply. I'm not sure how to express it, but the answer isn't hard to guess.

"I feel kind of sorry for you," Oshima says, "but like I said, I think you two shouldn't see each other for a while."

"But I might never see her again."

"Perhaps," Oshima admits, after giving it some thought. "This is pretty obvious, but until things happen, they haven't happened. And often things aren't what they seem."

"But how does Miss Saeki feel?"

Oshima narrows his eyes and looks at me. "About what?"

"I mean—if she knows she'll never see me again, does she feel the same about me as I feel about her?"

Oshima grins. "Why are you asking me this?"

"I have no idea, which is probably why I'm asking you. Loving somebody, wanting them more than anything—it's all a new experience. The same with having somebody want *me*."

"I imagine you're confused and don't know what to do."

I nod. "Exactly."

"You don't know if she shares the same strong, pure feelings you have for her," Oshima comments.

I shake my head. "It hurts to think about it."

Oshima's silent for a time as he gazes out at the forest, eyes narrowed. Birds are flitting from one branch to the next. His hands are clasped behind his head. "I know how you feel," he finally says. "But this is something you have to figure out on your own. Nobody can help you. That's what love's all about, Kafka. You're the one having those wonderful feelings, but you have to go it alone as you wander through the dark. Your mind and body have to bear it all. All by yourself."

It's after two when he gets ready to leave.

"If you divide up the food," he tells me, "it should last you a week. I'll be back by then. If something comes up and I can't make it, I'll send my brother here with supplies. He only lives about an hour away. I've told him about you being here. So no worries, okay?"

"Okay."

"And like I told you before, be extra cautious if you go into the woods. If you get lost, you'll never find your way out."

"I'll be careful."

"Just before World War II started, a large unit of Imperial troops carried out some training exercises here, staging mock battles with the Soviet army in the Siberian forests. Did I tell you this already?"

"No."

"Seems like I forgot the most important thing," Oshima says sheepishly, tapping his temple.

"But this doesn't look like Siberian forests," I say.

"You're right. The trees here are all broadleaf types, the ones in those forests would have to be evergreens, but I guess the military didn't worry about details. The point was to march into the forest in full battle gear and conduct their war games."

He pours out a cup of the coffee I made from the thermos, spoons in a dollop of sugar, and seems pleased with the results. "The military asked my great-grandfather to let them use the mountain for their training, and he said sure, be my guest. Nobody else was using it, after all. The unit marched up the road we drove here on, then went into the forest. But when the exercises were finished and they took roll call, they discovered two soldiers were missing. They'd just disappeared, full battle gear and all, during the training, both brand-new draftees. The army conducted a huge search, but the two soldiers never turned up." Oshima takes another sip of coffee. "To this day nobody knows if they simply got lost or ran away. The forest around here is incredibly deep, and there's hardly anything you could forage for food."

I nod.

"There's another world that parallels our own, and to a certain degree you're able to step into that other world and come back safely. As long as you're careful. But go past a certain point and you'll lose the path out. It's a labyrinth. Do you know where the idea of a labyrinth first came from?"

I shake my head.

"It was the ancient Mesopotamians. They pulled out animal intestines—sometimes human intestines, I expect—and used the shape to predict the future. They admired the complex shape of intestines. So the prototype for labyrinths is, in a word, guts. Which means that the principle for the labyrinth is inside you. And that correlates to the labyrinth *outside*."

"Another metaphor," I comment.

"That's right. A reciprocal metaphor. Things outside you are projections of what's inside you, and what's inside you is a projection of what's outside. So when you step into the labyrinth outside you, at the same time you're stepping into the labyrinth *inside*. Most definitely a risky business."

"Sort of like Hansel and Gretel."

"Right—just like them. The forest has set a trap, and no matter what you do, no matter how careful you are, some sharp-eyed birds are going to eat up all your bread crumbs."

"I promise I'll be careful," I tell him.

Oshima lowers the top on the Miata and climbs in. He puts on his sunglasses and rests his hand on the gearshift. The forest echoes with the sound of that familiar roar. He brushes back his hair, gives an abbreviated wave, and is gone. Dust swirls around where he was, but the wind soon carries it away.

I go back inside the cabin. I lie down on the bed he'd been using and shut my eyes. Come to think of it, I didn't get much sleep last night either. The pillow and covers still show signs of Oshima having been there. Not him, really—more like his *sleep*. I sink down in those signs. I've slept for half an hour when there's a loud thump outside the cabin, like a tree branch snapped and tumbled to the ground. The sound jolts me awake. I get up and walk out to the porch to have a look, but everything looks the same. Maybe this is some mysterious sound the forest makes from time to time. Or maybe it was part of a dream. I can't tell one from the other.

Until the sun sinks down in the west, I sit out on the porch, reading my book.

I make a simple meal and eat it in silence. After clearing away the dishes I sink back in the old sofa and think about Miss Saeki.

"Like Oshima said, Miss Saeki's a smart person. Plus she has her own way of doing things," the boy named Crow says. He's sitting next to me on the sofa, just like when we were in my father's den. "She's very different from you," he tells me.

She's very different from you. She's overcome all kinds of obstacles—and not what you'd call normal obstacles, either. She knows all kinds of things you're clueless about, she's experienced a range of emotions you've never felt. The longer people live, the more they learn to distinguish what's important from what's not. She's had to make a lot of critical decisions, and has seen the results. Again, very different from you. You're only a child who's lived in a narrow world and experienced very little. You've worked hard to become stronger, and in some areas you actually have. That's a fact. But now you find yourself in a new world, in a situation you've never been in before. It's all new to you, so no wonder you feel confused.

No wonder you feel confused. One thing you don't understand

very well is whether women have sexual desire. Theoretically, of course they do. That much even *you* know. But when it comes to how this desire comes about, what it's like—you're lost. Your own sexual desire is a simple matter. But women's desire, especially Miss Saeki's, is a total mystery. When she held you did she feel the same physical ecstasy? Or is it something altogether different?

The more you think about it, the more you hate being fifteen. You feel hopeless. If only you were twenty—no, even *eighteen* would be good, anything but fifteen—you could understand better what her words and actions mean. Then you could respond the right way. You're in the middle of something wonderful, something so tremendous you may never experience it again. But you can't really understand how wonderful it is. That makes you impatient. And that, in turn, leads to despair.

You try to picture what she's doing right now. It's Monday, and the library's closed. What does she do on her days off? You imagine her alone in her apartment. She does the laundry, cooks, cleans, goes out shopping—each scene flashes in your imagination. The more you imagine, the harder it gets to sit still here. You want to turn into a dauntless crow and fly out of this cabin, zoom out over these mountains, come to rest outside her apartment, and gaze at her forever.

Perhaps she stops by the library and goes into your room. She knocks but there's no answer. The door's unlocked. She discovers you're no longer there. The bed's made, and all your things are gone. She wonders where you disappeared to. Perhaps she waits a while for you to come back, sitting at the desk, head in hands, gazing at *Kafka on the Shore*. Thinking of the past that's enveloped in that painting. But no matter how long she waits, you don't return. She finally gives up and leaves. She walks over to her Golf in the parking lot and starts the engine. The last thing you want is to let her leave like this. You want to hold her, and know what each and every movement of her body means. But you're not there. You're all alone, in a place cut off from everyone.

You climb into bed and turn off the light, hoping that she'll show up in *this* room. It doesn't have to be the real Miss Saeki—that fifteen-year-old girl would be fine. It doesn't matter what form she takes—a living spirit, an illusion—but you have to see her, have to have her beside you. Your brain is so full of her it's ready to burst, your body about to explode into pieces. Still, no matter how much you want her to be here, no matter how long you wait, she never appears. All you hear is the faint rustle of wind outside, birds softly cooing in the night. You hold your breath, staring off into the gloom. You listen to the wind, trying to read something into it, straining to catch a hint of what it might mean. But all that surrounds you are different shades of darkness. Finally, you give up, close your eyes, and fall asleep.

Chapter 38

Hoshino looked up rental car agencies in the Yellow Pages, picked one at random, and phoned them. "I just need a car for a couple of days," he explained, "so an ordinary sedan's fine. Nothing too big, nothing that stands out."

"Maybe I shouldn't say this," the rental clerk said, "but since we only rent Mazdas, we don't have a single car that stands out. So rest assured."

"Great."

"How about a Familia? A very reliable car, and I swear nobody will notice it at all."

"Sounds good. The Familia it is." The rental agency was near the station, and Hoshino told them he'd be over in an hour to pick up the car.

He took a taxi over, showed them his credit card and license, then rented the car for two days. The white Familia parked in the lot was, as advertised, totally unobtrusive. Turn away from it for a moment and every memory of what it looked like vanished. A notable achievement in the field of anonymity.

Driving back to the apartment, Hoshino stopped at a bookstore and picked up maps of Takamatsu city and the Shikoku highway system. He popped into a CD shop nearby to see if they had a copy of Beethoven's *Archduke* Trio, but the little shop had only a small classical section and one cheap, discount-bin version of the piece. Not the Million-Dollar Trio, unfortunately, but Hoshino went ahead and paid his eight dollars.

Back in the apartment, a soothing fragrance filled the place. Nakata was bustling around the kitchen preparing some steamed daikon and deep-fried flat tofu. "I had nothing to do, so I made a few dishes," he explained.

"That's great," Hoshino said. "I've been eating out too much these days, and it'll be nice to have a home-cooked meal for a change. Oh, hey—I got the car. It's parked outside. Do you need it right away?"

"No, tomorrow would be fine. Nakata has to talk more with the stone today."

"Good idea. Talking things over is important. Whether you're talking with people, or things, or whatever, it's always better to discuss things. You know, when I'm driving trucks I often talk to the engine. You can hear all kinds of things if you listen closely."

"Nakata can't talk with engines, but it *is* important to discuss things."

"So how's it going with the stone? You able to communicate?"

"We're starting to."

"That's good. I was wondering—is the stone upset we brought it here?"

"No, not at all. As far as I can make out, the stone doesn't much care where it is."

"Whew—*that's* a relief," Hoshino sighed. "After all we've been through, if the stone turns on us we're up a creek."

Hoshino spent the afternoon listening to his new CD. The performance wasn't as spontaneous and memorable as the one he'd heard in the coffee shop. It was more restrained and steady, but overall not so bad. As he lay back on the couch and listened, the lovely melody got to him, the subtle convolutions of the fugue stirring up something deep inside.

If I'd listened to this music a week ago, he told himself, I wouldn't have understood the first thing about it—or even wanted to. But chance brought him to that little coffee shop, where he sank back in that comfortable chair, enjoyed the coffee, and listened to the music. And now look at me, he thought, I'm into *Beethoven*—can you believe it? A pretty amazing development.

He played the piece over and over, testing out his newfound appreciation for music. The CD contained a second Beethoven trio, the *Ghost*. Not such a bad piece, he thought, though the *Archduke* was definitely his favorite. More depth, he concluded. All the while, Nakata was off in a corner, facing the white stone and muttering. Occasionally he'd nod or scratch his head. Two men off in their own little worlds.

"Does the music bother you?" Hoshino asked him.

"No, it's fine. Music doesn't bother me. To me it's like the wind."

"The wind, huh?"

At six Nakata made dinner—grilled salmon and a salad, plus a number of little side dishes he'd concocted. Hoshino switched on the TV and watched the news to see if there were any developments in the murder case. But there wasn't a word about it. Just other news—a kidnapping of an infant girl, the usual Israeli and Palestinian reprisals, a massive traffic accident on a highway in western Japan, a carjacking ring headed by foreigners, some cabinet minister's stupid discriminatory remark, layoffs at companies in the communication industry. Not a single upbeat story.

The two of them sat at the table and ate their dinner.

"This is really good," Hoshino said. "You're quite a cook."

"Much obliged. But you're the first person I've ever cooked for."

"You're telling me you never eat with friends or relatives or anybody?"

"Nakata knew many cats, but what we eat is very different."

"Well, yeah," Hoshino said. "But, anyway, this is delicious. Especially the vegetables."

"I'm happy you like it. Nakata can't read, so sometimes I make some terrible mistakes in the kitchen. So I always use the same ingredients and cook things the same way. If I could read, I could make all kinds of different dishes."

"These are just fine."

"Mr. Hoshino?" Nakata said in a serious tone, sitting up straight.

"Yeah?"

"Not being able to read makes life tough."

"I imagine so," Hoshino said. "The commentary with this CD says Beethoven was deaf. He was a famous composer, the top pianist in Europe when he was young. But then one day, maybe because of illness, he started to go deaf. In the end he couldn't hear a thing. Pretty rough to be a composer who can't hear. You know what I mean?"

"I think so."

"A deaf composer's like a cook who's lost his sense of taste. A frog that's lost its webbed feet. A truck driver with his license revoked. That would throw anybody for a loop, don't you think? But Beethoven didn't let it get to him. Sure, he must have been a little depressed at first, but he didn't let misfortune get him down. It was like, *Problem? What* problem? He composed more than ever and came up with better music than anything he'd ever written. I really admire the guy. Like this *Archduke* Trio—he was nearly deaf when he wrote it, can you believe it? What I'm trying to say is, it must be tough on you not being able to read, but it's not the end of the world. You might not be able to read, but there are things only *you* can do. *That's* what you gotta focus on—your strengths. Like being able to talk with the stone."

"Yes, I am able to talk with it a little now. Nakata used to be able to talk with cats."

"No one else can do that, right? Other people can read all the books they want and they're still not gonna know how to talk to stones or cats."

"These days, though, Nakata's having a lot of dreams. In my dreams, for some reason, I'm able to read. I'm not as dumb as I am now. I'm so happy and I go to the library and read lots of books. And I'm thinking how wonderful it is to be able to read. I'm reading one book after another, but then the light in the library goes out and it's dark. Somebody turned off the light. I can't see a thing. I can't read any more books. And then I wake up. Even if it's only in a dream, it's wonderful to be able to read."

"Interesting . . . ," Hoshino said. "And here I'm able to read and hardly ever pick up a book. The world's a mixed-up place, that's for sure."

"Mr. Hoshino?" Nakata asked.

"What's up?"

"What day of the week is it today?"

"It's Saturday."

"So tomorrow would be Sunday?"

"Normally, yeah."

"Would you drive me tomorrow morning?"

"Sure, but where do you want to go?"

"Nakata doesn't know. I'll think about it after I get in the car."

"Believe it or not," Hoshino said, "I had a feeling that's what you were going to say."

Hoshino woke up the next morning just after seven. Nakata was already up cooking breakfast. Hoshino went to the bathroom, scrubbed his face with cold water, and shaved with an electric razor. They breakfasted on rice, miso soup with eggplant, dried mackerel, and pickles. Hoshino had a second helping of rice.

While Nakata washed the dishes Hoshino watched the news on TV. This time there was a short piece on the murder in Nakano. "Ten days have passed since the incident, but the police still have no leads," the NHK announcer droned. An impressive front gate of a house flashed on the screen, cordoned off, with a patrolman stationed outside.

"The search continues for the missing fifteen-year-old son of the deceased, though his whereabouts remain unknown. The search continues as well for a man in his sixties who lives in the neighborhood and stopped by a police station right after the incident to provide information regarding the murder. It remains unclear whether or not there is a connection between these two people. Because the inside of the house was undisturbed, the police believed that the crime was an act of personal revenge rather than a robbery gone bad and are investigating Mr. Tamura's friends and acquaintances. At the Tokyo National Modern Art Museum, where Mr. Tamura's artistic achievements are being honored—"

"Hey, Gramps," Hoshino called out to Nakata in the kitchen.

"Yes? What is it?"

"Do you know the son of this guy that was murdered in Nakano? This fifteen-year-old?"

"No, I don't. As I told you, all Nakata knows about is Johnnie Walker and his dog."

"Yeah?" Hoshino replied. "The police are looking for that boy, too. An only child, it sounds like, and there's no mention of his mom. I guess he ran away from home just before the murder and he's still missing."

"Is that so . . ."

"A hard nut to crack, this murder," Hoshino said. "But the police are a pretty tight-lipped bunch—they always know more than they let on. According to Colonel Sanders, they're on to you, and know you're in Takamatsu. Plus they know some handsome guy like me's with you. But they haven't leaked that to the media yet. They're afraid if they let on we're here, we'll hightail it somewhere else. That's why they're insisting they don't know where we are, publicly. A delightful bunch, cops."

At eight-thirty they went out to the rental car and climbed in. As he settled down into the passenger seat, Nakata had his usual thermos of hot tea with him, as well as his faithful shapeless hat, umbrella, and canvas bag. As they were leaving the apartment Hoshino was about to put on his Chunichi Dragons cap when he glanced in the mirror and was brought up short. The police must know the young guy they were looking for would be decked out in a Dragons ball cap, green Ray-Bans, and an aloha shirt. There couldn't be many people with Dragons caps on here in Takamatsu, and add on Ray-Bans and the shirt and he'd stick out like a sore thumb. So that's why Colonel Sanders stocked the place with inconspicuous navy blue polo shirts—he must've anticipated this. Nothing gets by him, Hoshino thought, and tossed the sunglasses and cap aside.

"So, where to?" he asked.

"Anywhere is fine," Nakata replied. "Just circle around the city."

"You sure?"

"You can go wherever you like. I'll just enjoy the scenery."

"This is a first," Hoshino said. "I've done my share of driving—both in the Self-Defense Force and with the truck company—and I'm a decent driver, if I say so myself. But every time I get behind the wheel, I know where I'm going and beeline it right there. That's just the way I am, I guess. Nobody's ever told me, *You can go wherever you like—anywhere is fine*. You're kind of baffling me here."

"Nakata is very sorry."

"It's okay—no need to apologize. I'll do my best," Hoshino said. He slipped the CD of the *Archduke* Trio into the player. "I'll just drive all over the city while you enjoy the view. Is that okay?"

"Yes, that would be fine."

"I'll stop the car when you find what you're looking for. And then the story will develop in a new direction. Do I have that right?"

"Yes, that's what might happen," Nakata said.

"Let's hope so," Hoshino said, and unfolded the city map in his lap.

The two of them drove through the city, Hoshino marking each street on a block to make sure they'd covered every one, then heading over to the next. They took an occasional break so Nakata could enjoy a cup of tea, and Hoshino a Marlboro. The *Archduke* Trio played over and over. At noon they stopped by a diner and had curry.

"But what the heck are you looking for?" Hoshino asked after they'd eaten.

"I don't know. But I think—"

"—that you'll know it when you see it. And until you see it, you won't know what it is."

"Yes, that's correct."

Hoshino shook his head listlessly. "I knew what you were gonna say, but I just had to be sure."

"Mr. Hoshino?"

"Yeah?"

"It might take some time before I find it."

"That's okay. We'll do our best. The boat's left the dock, and we're stuck on it."

"Are we going to take a boat?" Nakata asked.

"No. No boats for the time being."

At three they went into a coffee shop, where Hoshino had a cup of coffee. Nakata puzzled over his order, finally going with the iced milk. By this time Hoshino was exhausted from all the driving and didn't feel like talking. He'd had his fill of Beethoven. Driving around in a circle, getting nowhere, didn't suit him. He had to keep his speed down and pay careful attention to what he was doing, and he was getting bored. An occasional patrol car would pass by, and Hoshino did his best to avoid eye contact. He also tried to avoid passing in front of any police boxes. The Mazda Familia might be just about the most inconspicuous car on the road, but if the police spotted the same car passing by a few times they might very well pull him over. He drove cautiously, making absolutely sure he didn't rear-end anybody. An accident would put everything in jeopardy.

As Hoshino drove around the city, checking the map as he went, Nakata sat motionless, hands on the window, scanning the passing scenery, intently searching for something, for all the world like a child or a well-behaved dog. They each concentrated on their task until evening, and hardly a word passed between them.

"What are you searching for?" Out of desperation Hoshino started singing an Inoue Yosui tune. He couldn't recall the rest of the lyrics, so he made them up as he went along.

> *Haven't you found it yet?*
> *The sun is soon setting . . .*
> *And Hoshino's stomach is growling.*
> *Driving round and round sets my head spinning.*

They went back to the apartment at six.

"Let's continue tomorrow," Nakata said.

"We covered a lot of territory today. We can probably finish up the whole city tomorrow," Hoshino said. "Hey—I got a question for you."

"And what might that be?"

"If you don't find what you're looking for in Takamatsu, then what?"

Nakata gave his head a good rub. "If we can't find it in Takamatsu, then we'll have to look farther out."

"And if you still can't find it, then what're we supposed to do?"

"If that happens, then we have to search even more."

"We'll just make bigger and bigger circles and eventually we'll find it. Like the saying goes, if a dog walks on, it's bound to bump into a stick."

"Yes, I think that will happen," Nakata said. "But Nakata doesn't understand. Why does a dog have to hit a stick if it walks? If there's a stick in front of it, the dog can go around it."

Hoshino puzzled this over. "Yeah, I guess you're right. I never thought about it before. . . ."

"It's very strange."

"Let's put the dog and the stick aside for a minute, okay?" Hoshino said. "That only complicates things. What I want to know is how far are we going to search? If we don't watch out, before we know it we'll wind up in another prefecture—Ehime or Kochi or someplace. Summer will be over and it'll be fall by then."

"That may well be. But I have to find it, even if it's fall or winter. I know I can't ask you to help me forever. Nakata will just walk alone and keep on searching."

"Let's not worry about that for right now," Hoshino stammered. "But can't the stone be a pal and give us a hint or something? Even an approximate location would help."

"Nakata's very sorry, but the stone doesn't say much."

"Yeah, it doesn't strike me as the talkative type," Hoshino said. "I don't imagine it's much good at swimming, either. Whatever. . . . We don't need to think about it now. Let's get a good night's sleep and see what tomorrow brings."

The next day it was the same routine, with Hoshino this time circling the western half of the city. By now his city map was full of yellow lines. Only the increased number of yawns coming from the driver set this day apart from the previous one. Nakata kept his face plastered against the window, intently studying the passing scenery, and they hardly spoke. Whatever Nakata was looking for, he didn't find it.

"Would today be Monday?" Nakata asked.

"Yup. Yesterday was Sunday, so today's Monday," Hoshino said. Then, almost in desperation, he made up a melody to some words that popped into his head:

> If today is Monday,
> tomorrow must be Tuesday.
> Ants are hard workers, swallows like to dress up.
> The chimney's tall, the setting sun red.

"Mr. Hoshino," Nakata said after a while.

"Yeah?"

"You can look at ants working for a long time and never tire of it."

"I suppose you're right," Hoshino replied.

At noon they stopped by a restaurant specializing in eel and ordered the lunch special, a bowl of rice topped with eel. At three they went to a coffee shop, where Hoshino had coffee, Nakata kelp tea. By six p.m. the map was a mass of yellow marks, the anonymous tires of the Familia having traversed every square inch of road in the city. But still no luck.

What are you searching for? Hoshino sang again in a listless voice: *Haven't you found it yet? / We've gone everywhere in town. / My butt's aching, so can't we go home?*

After he finished, he said, "We keep this up much longer, I'll turn into a regular singer-songwriter," Hoshino said.

"What would that be?" Nakata asked.

"Never mind. Just a harmless joke."

Calling it a day, they left the city, got on the highway, and headed back to the apartment. Lost in thought, Hoshino failed to turn left when he should. He tried to get back on the highway, but the road curved off at a strange angle into a maze of one-way streets and he was soon totally lost. Before he realized it they were in a residential area they'd never seen before, an old-looking, elegant neighborhood with high walls surrounding the homes. The road was strangely quiet, with not a soul in sight.

"I don't think we're too far from our apartment, but I have no idea where we are," Hoshino admitted. He parked the car in an empty lot, cut the engine, set the parking brake, and spread out his map. He checked the name of the neighborhood and street number on a nearby lightpole and looked for it on the map. Maybe his eyes were too tired, but he couldn't find it.

"Mr. Hoshino?" Nakata asked.

"Yeah?"

"I'm sorry to bother you, but what does it say on that sign over there on that gate?"

Hoshino looked up from his map and glanced where Nakata was pointing, down a high wall with an old-fashioned gate, and next to it a large wooden sign. The black gate was shut tight. "*Komura Memorial Library,*" Hoshino read. "Huh, a library in this deserted part of town? Doesn't even look like a library. More like an old mansion."

"*Ko-mu-ra-Me-mori-al-Li-bra-ry?*"

"You got it. Must be made to commemorate somebody named Komura. Who this Komura guy is, though, I have no idea."

"Mr. Hoshino?"

"Yup?"

"That's it."

"What do you mean—*that?*"

"The place Nakata's been searching for."

Hoshino looked up from his map again and gazed into Nakata's eyes. He frowned, looked at the sign, and slowly read it again. He patted a Marlboro out of the box, put it between his lips, and lit it with his plastic lighter. He slowly inhaled, then blew smoke out the open window. "Are you sure?"

"Yes, this is it."

"*Chance* is a scary thing, isn't it?" Hoshino said.

"It certainly is," Nakata agreed.

Chapter 39

My second day on the mountain passes by leisurely, seamlessly. The only thing that distinguishes one day from the next is the weather. If the weather was the same I couldn't tell one day from another. Yesterday, today, tomorrow—they'd all blur into one. Like an anchorless ship, time floats aimlessly across the broad sea.

I do the math and come up with today as Tuesday. The day Miss Saeki gives a tour of the library, provided there are any people who want to take it. Just like the very first day I came to the place. . . . Spike heels clicking on the stairs, she walks up to the second floor, the sound reverberating through the stillness. Her glistening stockings, bright white blouse, tiny pearl earrings, her Mont Blanc pen on top of her desk. Her calm smile, tinged with the long shadow of resignation. All these details seem so far away now—and no longer real.

Sitting on the sofa in the cabin, the odor of the faded fabric all around me, memories of our lovemaking rise up in my head. Miss Saeki slowly removing her clothes, getting into bed. My cock, not surprisingly, is rock hard as these thoughts filter through my mind, but the tip's not red or sore anymore and doesn't sting.

Tiring of these sexual fantasies, I wander outside and go into my usual exercise routine. I hang on to the porch railing and go through an ab workout. Then I do some quick squats, followed by hard stretching. By this time I'm covered in sweat, so I wet my towel in the stream and wipe myself off. The cold water helps calm my nerves. I sit down on the porch and listen to Radiohead on my Walkman. Since I ran away I've been listening to the same music over and over—Radiohead's *Kid A*, Prince's *Very Best of*. Sometimes Coltrane's *My Favorite Things*.

At two p.m.—just when the library tour is starting—I head out into the forest. I follow the same path, walk for a while, and arrive at the clearing. I sit down on the grass, lean back against a tree trunk, and gaze up at the round opening of sky through the branches. The edges of white summer clouds are visible. Up to this point, I'm safe. I can find my way back to the cabin. A maze for beginners—if this were a video game I've easily cleared Level 1. If I go any farther, though, I'll enter a more elaborate, more challenging labyrinth. The path gets narrower and I'll get swallowed up by the sea of ferns.

I ignore this and forge on ahead.

I want to see how deep this forest really is. I know it's dangerous, but I want to see—and *feel*—what kind of danger lies ahead, how dangerous it really is. I *have* to. Something's shoving me forward.

I cautiously go down a kind of path. The trees tower higher and higher, the air growing denser by the minute. Up above, the mass of branches nearly blots out the sky. All signs of summer have vanished, and it's like seasons never existed. Soon I no longer know if what I'm following is a path or not. It looks like a path, is shaped like one—but then again it doesn't, and isn't. In the middle of all this stuffy, overgrown greenery all definitions start to get a bit fuzzy around the edges. What makes sense, and what doesn't, it's all mixed up. Above me, a crow gives out a piercing caw that sounds like a warning, it's so jarring. I stop and cautiously survey my surroundings. Without the proper equipment it's too dangerous to go any farther. I have to turn around.

Which isn't easy. Like Napoleon's army on the retreat, going back is more difficult than going forward, I discover. The path back is misleading, the dense vegetation forming a dark wall in front of me. My own breathing sounds loud in my ears, like a wind blowing at the edge of the world. A huge black butterfly about the size of my palm appears from the shade of the trees and flutters into my line of sight, its shape reminding me of that bloodstain on my T-shirt. It flies slowly across an open space, then disappears among the trees again, and once it vanishes everything suddenly seems even more oppressive, the air chillier. I'm seized by panic—not knowing how to get out of here. The crow squawks out shrilly again—the same bird as before, sending the same message. I stand still and look up, but can't see it. A breeze, a real one, blows up from time to time, ominously rustling the dark leaves at my feet. I sense shadows racing past behind me, but when I spin around they've hidden themselves.

Somehow I'm able to make it back to my safety zone—the little round clearing in the forest. I plop down on the grass and take a deep breath. I look up at the patch of real sky above me a couple of times, just to convince myself I've made it back to the world I came from. Signs of summer—so precious now—surround me. Sunlight envelopes me like a film, warming me up. But the fear I felt clings to me like a clump of unmelted snow in the corner of a garden. My heart beats irregularly from time to time, and my skin still has a slightly creepy feeling.

That night I lie there in the darkness, breathing quietly with my eyes wide open, hoping to catch a figure appearing in the dark. Praying for it to appear, and not knowing if prayers have any effect. Concentrating for all I'm worth, wanting badly for it to happen. Hoping that wanting it so badly will make my wish come true.

But my wish doesn't come true, my desires are shot down. Like the night before, Miss Saeki doesn't show up. Not the real Miss Saeki, not an illusion, not her as a fifteen-year-old girl. The darkness remains just that—darkness. Right before I fall asleep I have a massive erection, harder than any I've ever had, but I don't jack off. I've made up my mind to hold the memory of making love with Miss Saeki untouched, at least for now. Hands clenched tight, I fall asleep, hoping to dream of her.

Instead, I dream of Sakura.

Or is it a dream? It's all so vivid, clear, and consistent, but I don't know what else to call it, so dream seems the best label. I'm in her apartment and she's asleep in bed. I'm in my sleeping bag, just like that night I spent at her place. Time's been rewound, setting me down at a turning point.

I wake up in the middle of the night dying of thirst, get out of my sleeping bag, and drink some water. Glass after glass—five or six. My skin's covered with a sheen of sweat, and the front of my boxers is tented in another huge erection. My cock's like some animal with a mind of its own, operating on a different wavelength from the rest of me. When I drink some water my cock automatically absorbs it. I can hear the faint sound of it soaking up the water.

I put the glass next to the sink and lean back against the wall. I want to check the time but can't find the clock. In this, the deepest hour of the night, even the clock's been swallowed up in the depths. I'm standing beside Sakura's bed. Light from a streetlight filters in through the curtain. She's facing away from me, fast asleep, her small, shapely feet sticking out from under the thin covers. Behind me I hear a small, hard sound, like someone's turned on a switch. Thick branches cut off my field of vision. There is no season here. I make a decision and crawl in next to Sakura. The single bed creaks with the extra weight. I breathe in the smell of the faintly sweaty back of her neck. Gently I wrap my arms around her. She makes a small sound but continues to sleep. The crow squawks loudly. I glance up but can't spot the bird. I can't even see the sky.

I pull up Sakura's T-shirt and fondle her soft breasts. I tweak her nipples like I'm adjusting a radio dial. My rock-hard cock slaps against the back of her thigh, but she doesn't make any noise and her breathing stays the same. She must be dreaming deeply, I figure. Again the crow cries out, sending me a message, but I can't figure out what it's trying to tell me.

Sakura's body is warm, and as sweaty as mine. I decide to pull her around toward me, slowly pulling her closer so she's faceup. She exhales deeply but still doesn't show any signs of waking. I rest my ear against her paper-flat stomach, trying to catch the echoes of the dreams within that labyrinth.

My erection's not letting up, so rigid it looks like it'll last forever. I slip off her small cotton panties, taking my time to get them down her legs and off. I rest my palm against her pubic hair, gently letting my finger go in deeper. It's wet, invitingly wet. I slowly move my finger. Still she doesn't wake up. Lost in her dream, she merely exhales deeply again.

At the same time, in a hollow inside me, something struggles to break out of its shell. Before I realize what's happening, there's a pair of eyes turned in on me, and I can observe this whole scene. I don't yet know if this thing inside me is good or bad, but whichever it is, I can't hold it back or stop it. It's still a slimy, faceless being, but it will soon break free of its shell, show its face, and slough off its jelly-like coating. Then I'll know what it really is. Now, though, it's just a formless *sign*. It's reaching out its hands-that-won't-be-hands, breaking apart the shell at its softest point. And I can see each and every one of its movements.

I make up my mind.

No, actually I haven't made up my mind about anything. Making

up your mind means you have a choice, and I don't. I strip off my boxers, releasing my cock. I hold Sakura, spread her legs, and slip inside
her. It's easy—she's so soft and I'm so hard. My cock no longer hurts.
In the past few days the tip's become even harder. Sakura's still dreaming, and I bury myself inside her dream.

Suddenly she snaps awake and realizes what's going on.

"Kafka, what are you *doing*?!"

"It would seem that I'm inside you," I reply.

"But why?" she asks in a dry, raspy voice. "Didn't I tell you that's
off-limits?"

"I can't help it."

"Stop already. Get it out of me."

"I can't," I say, shaking my head emphatically.

"Listen to me. First of all, I've got a steady boyfriend, okay? And second, you've come into my dream without permission. That's not right."

"I know."

"It's still not too late. You're inside me, but you haven't started moving, you haven't come yet. It's just quietly inside me, like it's thinking
about something. Am I right?"

I nod.

"Take it out," she admonishes me. "And let's pretend this never
happened. I can forget it, and so should you. I'm your sister, and you're
my brother. Even if we're not blood related, we're most definitely
brother and sister. You understand what I'm saying? We're part of a
family. We shouldn't be doing this."

"It's too late," I tell her.

"Why?"

"Because I decided it is."

"Because you decided it is," says the boy named Crow.

**You don't want to be at the mercy of things outside you any-
more, or thrown into confusion by things you can't control. You've
already murdered your father and violated your mother—and now
here you are inside your sister. If there's a curse in all this, you mean
to grab it by the horns and fulfill the program that's been laid out
for you. Lift the burden from your shoulders and *live*—not caught
up in someone else's schemes, but as *you*. That's what you want.**

**She covers her face with her hands and cries a little. You feel
sorry for her, but there's no way you're going to leave her body. Your
cock swells up inside her, gets even harder, like it's set down roots.**

"I understand," she says. "I won't say any more. But I want you to remember something: You're raping me. I like you, but this isn't how I want it to be. We might never see each other again, no matter how much we want to meet later on. Are you okay with that?"

You don't respond. Your mind's switched off. You draw her close to you and start to move your hips. Carefully, cautiously, in the end violently. You try to remember the shapes of the trees to help you get back, but they all look the same and are soon swallowed up in the anonymous sea. Sakura closes her eyes and gives herself up to the motion. She doesn't say a word or resist. Her face is expressionless, turned away from you. But you feel the pleasure rising up in her like an extension of yourself. Now you understand it. The entwined trees stand like a dark wall blocking your view. The bird no longer sends its message. And you come.

I come.

And I wake up. I'm in bed, alone. It's the middle of the night. The darkness is as deep as it can be, all clocks lost within. I get out of bed, strip off my underpants, go over to the kitchen, and rinse the semen off them. Gooey, white, and heavy, like some illegitimate child born of the darkness. I gulp down glass after glass of water, but nothing slakes my thirst. I feel so alone I can't stand it. In the darkness, in the middle of the night, surrounded by a deep forest, I couldn't be more alone. There are no seasons here, no light. I walk back to the bed, sit down, and breathe a huge sigh. The darkness wraps itself around me.

The thing inside you has revealed itself. The shell is gone, completely shattered, nowhere to be seen, and it's there, a dark shadow, resting. Your hands are sticky with something—human blood, by the look of it. You hold them out in front of you, but there's not enough light to see. It's far too dark. Both inside, and out.

Chapter 40

Next to the sign that read KOMURA MEMORIAL LIBRARY was an information placard informing them that the library's hours were eleven to five, except for Monday, when it was closed, that admission was free, and that tours were conducted every Tuesday at two p.m. Hoshino read all this aloud for Nakata.

"Today's Monday, so it's closed," Hoshino said. He glanced at his watch. "Not that it matters much, since it's way past their closing time anyway. Same difference."

"Mr. Hoshino?"

"Yeah?"

"This place doesn't look at all like the library we went to before," Nakata said.

"That was a large public library and this one's private. So the scale's different."

"When you say a private library, what does that mean?"

"It means some man of property who likes books puts up a building and makes all the books he's collected available to the public. This guy must have really been something. You can tell from the gate he had to be pretty impressive."

"What is a man of property?"

"A rich person."

"What's the difference between the two?"

Hoshino tilted his head in thought. "I don't know. Seems to me a man of property's more cultured than just a regular rich guy."

"Cultured?"

"Anybody who has money is rich. You or me, as long as we had money, we'd be rich. But becoming a man of property isn't so easy. It takes time."

"It's difficult to become one?"

"Yeah, it is. Not that we need to worry about it. I don't see either of us becoming rich, let alone cultured."

"Mr. Hoshino?"

"Yeah?"

"Since they're closed on Monday, if we come here tomorrow morning at eleven they should be open, right?" Nakata asked.

"I suppose so. Tomorrow's Tuesday."

"Will Nakata be able to go inside the library?"

"The sign says it's open to everybody. Of course you can."

"Even if I can't read?"

"No problem," Hoshino said. "They don't quiz people at the entrance about whether they can read or not."

"I want to go inside, then."

"We'll come back tomorrow, first thing, and go in together," Hoshino said. "I got a question for you first, though. This *is* the place you were looking for, right? And the thing you're looking for's inside?"

Nakata removed his cap and rubbed his close-cropped hair vigorously. "Yes. I think it's here."

"So we can give up our search?"

"That's right. The search is over."

"Thank God," Hoshino said. "I was starting to wonder if we'd really be driving around till fall."

The two of them drove back to Colonel Sanders's apartment, slept soundly, and set off at eleven the next morning for the library. It was only a twenty-minute walk from the apartment, so they decided to stroll over. Hoshino had already returned the rental car.

The gate of the library was open wide when they arrived. It looked like it was going to be a hot, humid day, and someone had splashed water on the pavement to keep the dust down. Past the gate was a neat, well-kept garden.

"Mr. Nakata?" Hoshino said in front of the gate.

"Yes, how can I help you?"

"What do we do after we go inside the library? I'm always afraid you're all of a sudden gonna come up with some off-the-wall idea, so I'd like to know about it ahead of time. I have to prepare myself."

Nakata gave it some thought. "Nakata has no idea what to do once we get in. This is a library, though, so I thought we might start by reading books. I'll find a photo collection or book of paintings, and you can pick whatever you'd like to read."

"Gotcha. Starting off by reading — that makes sense."

"Then after a while we can think about what to do next."

"Okay," Hoshino said. "We'll think about what comes later — *later*. Sounds like a plan."

They walked through the beautiful garden and into the antique-looking entrance. There was a reception area right inside, with a handsome, slim young man seated behind the counter. He had on a white button-down shirt and small glasses. Long, fine hair hung over his forehead. Someone you might expect to see in a black-and-white Truffaut film, Hoshino thought.

The young man looked up at them and beamed.

"Good morning," Hoshino said cheerfully.

"Good morning," the young man replied. "Welcome to the library."

"We'd, uh — like to read some books."

"Of course," Oshima nodded. "Feel free to read whatever you like. We're open to the public. The stacks are completely open, so take any books you'd like to read. You can look books up in our card catalog or online. And if you have any questions, don't hesitate to ask. I'd be more than happy to help."

"That's very kind of you."

"Is there a particular field or book you're looking for?"

Hoshino shook his head. "Not really. Actually we're more interested in the library itself than books. We happened to pass by and thought the place looked interesting. It's a beautiful building."

Oshima gave a graceful smile and picked up a neatly sharpened pencil. "A lot of people just stop by like that."

"Glad to hear it," Hoshino said.

"If you have the time, you might consider the short tour of the place that takes place at two. We have one every Tuesday, as long as there are people who'd like to join in. The head of the library explains the background of the library. And today just happens to be Tuesday."

"That sounds like fun. Hey, what d'ya say, Mr. Nakata?"

All the time Hoshino and Oshima had been talking at the counter, Nakata stood off to one side, cap in hand, gazing vacantly at his surroundings. At the sound of his name, he came out of his daze. "Yes, how can I help you?"

"They have a tour of the library at two. You want to go on it?"

"Yes, Mr. Hoshino, thank you. Nakata would like to."

Oshima watched this exchange with great interest. Messrs. Hoshino and Nakata—what sort of relationship did they have to each other? They didn't seem like relatives. A strange combo, these two—with a vast difference in age and appearance. What could they possibly have in common? And this Mr. Nakata, the older one, had an odd way of speaking. There was something about him Oshima couldn't quite pin down. Not anything *bad*, though. "Have you traveled far to get here?" he asked.

"We came from Nagoya," Hoshino said hurriedly before Nakata could open his mouth. If he started in about being from Nakano, things could get a little sticky. The TV news had already put out the word that an old man like Nakata was connected with the murder there. Fortunately, though, as far as Hoshino knew, Nakata's photograph hadn't been made public.

"That's quite a journey," Oshima commented.

"Yes, we crossed a bridge to get here," Nakata said. "A long, wonderful bridge."

"It *is* pretty long, isn't it?" Oshima said. "Though I've never been over it myself."

"Nakata had never seen such a long bridge in all his life."

"It took a lot of time and a tremendous amount of money to build it," Oshima went on. "According to the newspaper, each year the public corporation that operates the bridge and the highway over it is a billion dollars in the red. Our taxes make up the shortfall."

"Nakata has no idea how much a billion is."

"I don't either, to tell you the truth," Oshima said. "After a certain point amounts like that aren't real anymore. Anyway, it's a huge amount of money."

"Thanks so much," Hoshino butted in. There was no telling what Nakata might say next, and he had to nip that possibility in the bud. "We should be here at two for the tour, right?"

"Yes, two would be fine," Oshima said. "The head librarian will be happy to show you around then."

"We'll be reading until then," Hoshino said.

Twirling his pencil in his hand, Oshima watched the retreating figures and then went back to work.

They picked some books from the stacks, Hoshino going for *Beethoven and His Generation*. Nakata picked out some photo collections and placed them on the table. Next, much like a dog might, he circled the room, carefully checking out everything, touching things, sniffing their odor, stopping at select spots to stare fixedly. They had the reading room to themselves until past twelve, so no one else noticed the old man's eccentric behavior.

"Hey, Gramps?" Hoshino whispered.

"Yes, how may I help you?"

"This is kind of sudden, but I'd appreciate it if you wouldn't mention to anyone that you're from Nakano."

"Why is that?"

"It's a long story, just take my word for it. If people find out that's where you're from, it might cause them some trouble."

"I understand," Nakata said, nodding deeply. "It's not good to trouble others. Nakata won't say a word about being from Nakano."

"That'd be great," Hoshino said. "Oh—did you find whatever it is you're looking for?"

"No, nothing so far."

"But this is definitely the place?"

Nakata nodded. "It is. Last night I had a good talk with the stone before I went to bed. I'm sure this is the place."

"Thank God."

Hoshino nodded and returned to his biography. Beethoven, he learned, was a proud man who believed absolutely in his own abilities and never bothered to flatter the nobility. Believing that art itself, and the proper expression of emotions, was the most sublime thing in the world, he thought political power and wealth served only one purpose: to make art possible. When Haydn boarded with a noble family, as he did most of his professional life, he had to eat with the servants. Musicians of Haydn's generation were considered employees. (The unaffected and good-natured Haydn, though, much preferred this arrangement to the stiff and formal meals put on by the nobility.)

Beethoven, in contrast, was enraged by any such contemptuous treatment, on occasion smashing things against the wall in anger. He insisted that as far as meals went he be treated with no less respect than the nobility he ostensibly served. He often flew off the handle, and once angry was hard to calm down. On top of this were radical political ideas that he made no attempt to hide. As his hearing deteriorated, these tendencies became even more pronounced. As he aged his music also became both more expansive and more densely inward looking. Only Beethoven could have balanced these two contrasting tendencies. But the extraordinary effort this required had a progressively deleterious effect on his life, for all humans have physical and emotional limits, and by this time the composer had more than reached his.

Geniuses like that don't have it easy, Hoshino thought, impressed, and laid down his book. He remembered the bronze bust of a scowling Beethoven in the music room of his school, but until now he'd had no idea of the hardships the man had endured. No wonder the guy looked so sour. *I'm* never gonna be a genius, that's for sure, Hoshino thought.

He looked over at Nakata, who was deep into a photo collection of traditional folk furniture, and working an imaginary chisel and plane. These photos must've made him unconsciously feel like he was back at his old job. And Nakata—who knows? *He* might become a great person someday, Hoshino thought. Most people can't do the kinds of things he does. The old codger's definitely in a class all his own.

After twelve, two other readers, middle-aged women, came into the reading room, so Hoshino and Nakata used the opportunity to take a breather outside. Hoshino had brought some bread along for their lunch, while Nakata was lugging around his usual thermos of hot tea. Hoshino first asked Oshima at the counter whether it was all right to eat on the library grounds.

"Of course," Oshima replied. "It's nice to sit on the veranda overlooking the garden. Afterward, feel free to come in for a cup of coffee. I've already made some, so help yourself."

"Thanks," Hoshino said. "This is quite a homey place you have here."

Oshima smiled and brushed back his hair. "It is a little different from your normal library. Homey is a good way to describe it. What we're trying to create is sort of an intimate space where people can relax and enjoy reading."

Hoshino found Oshima an appealing young man. Intelligent, well groomed, obviously from a good family. And quite kind. He's got to be gay, right? Not that Hoshino cared. To each his own, was his thinking. Some men talk with stones, and some sleep with other men. Go figure.

After lunch, Hoshino stood up, stretched his whole body, then went back to the reception area to take Oshima up on his offer of a cup of coffee. Since Nakata didn't drink coffee, he stayed on the veranda sipping his tea and gazing at the birds flitting around the garden.

"So, did you find anything interesting to read?" Oshima asked Hoshino.

"Yeah, I've been reading a biography of Beethoven," Hoshino replied. "I like it. His life really gives you a lot to think about."

Oshima nodded. "He went through a lot—to put it mildly."

"He did have a tough time," Hoshino said, "but I think it was mainly his fault. I mean, he was so self-centered and uncooperative. All he thought about was himself and his music, and he didn't mind sacrificing whatever he had to for it. He must've been tough to get along with. *Hey, Ludwig, gimme a break!* That's what I would have said if I knew him. No wonder his nephew went off his rocker. But I have to admit his music is wonderful. It really gets to you. It's a strange thing."

"Absolutely," Oshima agreed.

"But why did he have to live such a hard, wild life? He would've been better off with a more normal type of life."

Oshima twirled the pencil around in his fingers. "I see your point, but by Beethoven's time people thought it was important to express the ego. Earlier, when there was an absolute monarchy, this would've been considered improper, socially deviant behavior and suppressed quite severely. Once the bourgeoisie came to power in the nineteenth century, however, that suppression came to an end and the individual ego was liberated to express itself. Freedom and the emancipation of the ego were synonymous. And art, music in particular, was at the forefront of all this. Those who came after Beethoven and lived under his shadow, so to speak—Berlioz, Wagner, Liszt, Schumann—all lived eccentric, stormy lives. Eccentricity was seen as almost the ideal lifestyle. The age of Romanticism, they called it. Though I'm sure living like that was pretty hard on them at times. So, you like Beethoven's music?"

"I can't really say if I do or not. I haven't heard that much," Hoshino admitted. "Hardly any at all, actually. I just kind of like that piece called the *Archduke* Trio."

"That *is* nice, yes."

"The Million-Dollar Trio's great," Hoshino added.

"I prefer the Czech group, the Suk Trio, myself," Oshima said. "They have a beautiful balance. You feel like you can smell the wind wafting over a green meadow. But I do know the Million-Dollar Trio version—Rubinstein, Heifetz, and Feuermann. It's an elegant performance."

"Um, Mr.—Oshima?" Hoshino asked, looking at the nameplate on the counter. "You know a lot about music, I can tell."

Oshima smiled. "Not a lot. I just enjoy listening to it."

"Do you think music has the power to change people? Like you listen to a piece and go through some major change inside?"

Oshima nodded. "Sure, that can happen. We have an experience—like a chemical reaction—that transforms *something* inside us. When we examine ourselves later on, we discover that all the standards we've lived by have shot up another notch and the world's opened up in unexpected ways. Yes, I've had that experience. Not often, but it has happened. It's like falling in love."

Hoshino had never fallen head over heels in love himself, but he went ahead and nodded anyway. "That's gotta be a very important thing, right?" he said. "For our lives?"

"It is," Oshima answered. "Without those peak experiences our lives would be pretty dull and flat. Berlioz put it this way: A life without once reading *Hamlet* is like a life spent in a coal mine."

"A coal mine?"

"Just typical nineteenth-century hyperbole."

"Well, thanks for the coffee," Hoshino said. "I'm happy we could talk."

Oshima gave him a big grin in reply.

Hoshino and Nakata read books until two, Nakata going through his carpenter's motions as he leafed through the collection of furniture photographs. Besides the middle-aged ladies, three other readers had joined them after lunch. But only Hoshino and Nakata asked to join the tour of the library.

"You don't mind if it's just the two of us?" Hoshino asked. "I feel bad you have to go to all this trouble just for us."

"No trouble at all," Oshima said. "The head librarian is happy to conduct the tour, even for one person."

At two on the dot a good-looking middle-aged woman came down the stairs. Back held straight, she had an impressive walk. She wore a dark blue suit with severe lines, black high heels, a thin silver necklace at her wide, open neckline, her hair gathered in the back. Nothing extraneous, altogether a highly refined, tasteful look.

"Hello. My name is Miss Saeki. I'm the head librarian here," the woman said, and smiled calmly.

"I'm Hoshino."

"I'm Nakata, and I'm from Nakano," the old man said, hiking hat in hand.

"We're glad you've come to visit us from so far away," Miss Saeki said.

A chill ran down Hoshino's spine at Nakata's words, but Miss Saeki didn't look suspicious.

Nakata was typically oblivious. "Yes, I crossed over a very big bridge," he said.

"This is a wonderful building," Hoshino interjected, trying to cut off any talk of bridges.

"The building was built in the early Meiji period as the library and guesthouse of the Komura family," Miss Saeki began. "Many literati visited and lodged here. It's been designated a historical site by the city."

"*Litter oddy?*" Nakata asked.

Miss Saeki smiled. "Artists—poets, novelists, and so forth. In the past men of property in various localities helped support artists. Art was different back then, and wasn't viewed as something one should make a living at. The Komuras were men of property in this region who sponsored culture and the arts. This library was built, and is operated, to pass down that legacy to future generations."

"*Man of property*—Nakata knows what that means," Nakata said. "It takes a long time to become one."

Smiling, Miss Saeki nodded. "You're quite right, it does. No matter how much money you accumulate, you can't buy time. Well, we'll begin our tour on the second floor."

They toured the rooms upstairs one by one. Miss Saeki gave her usual talk about the various literati who had stayed there, and showed the two men the calligraphy and paintings these artists had left behind. During the tour Nakata seemed to turn a deaf ear to what she was saying, instead curiously examining each and every item. In the study Miss Saeki used as her office, a fountain pen was sitting on the desk. It was up to Hoshino to follow along and make all the appropriate noises. All the while he was on pins and needles, worried the old man would suddenly do something bizarre. But all Nakata did was continue to scrutinize the items they passed by. Miss Saeki didn't seem to care what Nakata did. Smiling all the while, she briskly showed them around. Hoshino was impressed by how calm and collected she was.

The tour ended in twenty minutes, and the two men thanked their guide. Miss Saeki's smile never failed the entire time. The more Hoshino watched her, though, the more confused he grew. She smiles and looks at us, he told himself, but she doesn't *see* anything. She's looking at us, but she's *seeing* something else. Though all the time she was giving the tour, even if her mind was elsewhere, she was perfectly polite and kind. Whenever he asked a question, she gave a kind, easy-to-follow response. It's not like she's doing this against her will or anything. A part of her enjoys doing a meticulous job. But her heart isn't in it.

The two men returned to the reading room and settled down on the sofa with their books. But as he turned the pages, Hoshino couldn't get Miss Saeki out of his mind. There was something very unusual about that beautiful woman, but he couldn't quite put his finger on it. He gave up and went back to reading.

At three o'clock, totally without warning, Nakata stood up. His movements were uncharacteristically decisive. He held his hat firmly in his hand.

"Hey, what's up? Where are you going?" Hoshino whispered.

But there was no response. Lips set in a determined look, Nakata was already hurrying toward the main entrance, his belongings left behind on the floor.

Hoshino shut his book and stood up. Something was definitely wrong. "Hey, wait up!" he called. Realizing the old man wasn't about to, he scrambled after him. The other readers looked up and watched him leave.

Before he got to the entrance, Nakata turned left and without hesitating started up to the second floor. A NO VISITORS ALLOWED BEYOND THIS POINT sign at the foot of the stairs didn't deter him, since he couldn't read. His worn tennis shoes squeaked on the floorboards as he climbed up the stairs.

"Excuse me," Oshima said, leaning over the counter to call out to the retreating figure. "That area is closed now."

Nakata didn't seem to hear him.

Hoshino ran up the stairs after him. "Gramps. It's closed. You can't go there."

Oshima came out from behind the counter and followed them up the stairs.

Undaunted, Nakata strode down the corridor and into the study. The door was open. Miss Saeki, her back to the window, was sitting at the desk reading a book. She heard the footsteps and looked up. When he got to the desk, Nakata stood there looking down at her face. Neither one of them said a word. A moment later Hoshino arrived, soon followed by Oshima.

"There you are," Hoshino said, tapping the old man on the shoulder. "You're not supposed to be here. It's off-limits. We have to leave, okay?"

"Nakata has something to say," Nakata said to Miss Saeki.

"And what would that be?" Miss Saeki asked quietly.

"I want to talk about the stone. The entrance stone."

For a while Miss Saeki silently studied the old man's face. Her eyes shone with a noncommittal light. She blinked a few times, then silently closed her book. She rested both hands on the desk and looked up again at Nakata. She looked undecided about how to proceed, but then gave a small nod.

She looked over at Hoshino, then at Oshima. "Would you mind leaving us alone for a while?" she said to Oshima. "We're going to have a talk. Please close the door on your way out."

Oshima hesitated, then nodded. He gently took Hoshino's arm, led him out to the corridor, and shut the door.

"Are you sure it's okay?" Hoshino asked.

"Miss Saeki knows what she's doing," Oshima said as he escorted Hoshino back down the stairs. "If she says it's all right, it's all right. No need to worry about her. So, Mr. Hoshino, why don't we go have a cup of coffee while we're waiting?"

"Well, when it comes to Mr. Nakata, worrying's a total waste of time," Hoshino said, shaking his head. "That I can guarantee."

Chapter 41

When I go into the woods this time I've outfitted myself with everything I might need: compass, knife, canteen, some emergency food, work gloves, a can of yellow spray paint, and the small hatchet I'd used before. I stuff all this into a small nylon daypack that was also in the tool shed, and head off into the forest. I'm wearing a long-sleeved shirt, a towel wrapped around my neck, and the cap Oshima gave me, and I've sprayed insect repellent over all the exposed parts of my body. The sky's overcast, and it's hot and sticky like it could rain any minute, so I throw a poncho into the pack just in case. A flock of birds screech at each other as they cut across the low, leaden sky.

I make it easily to that round clearing in the forest. Checking my compass to make sure I'm generally heading north, I step deeper into the woods. This time I spray yellow markings on tree trunks to mark the route. Unlike Hansel and Gretel's bread crumbs, spray paint's safe from hungry birds.

I'm better prepared, so I'm not as afraid. I'm nervous, sure, but my heart's not pounding. Curiosity's what's leading me on. I want to know what lies down this path. Even if there's nothing there, I want to know that. I *have* to know. Memorizing the scenery as I pass by, I move steadily forward, step by careful step.

Occasionally there's some weird sound. A thud like something hitting the ground, a creak like floorboards groaning under weight, and others I can't even describe. I have no idea what these mean, since there's no knowing what they are. Sometimes they sound far away, sometimes right near by—the sense of distance expanding and contracting. Bird wings echo above me, sounding louder, more exaggerated, than they should. Every time I hear this I stop and listen intently, holding my breath, waiting for something to happen. Nothing does, and I walk on.

Besides these sudden, unexpected sounds, everything else is still. There's no wind, no rustle of leaves in the treetops, just my own footsteps as I push through the brush. When I step on a fallen branch, the snap reverberates through the air.

I grasp the hatchet, which I'd sharpened, and it feels rough in my gloveless hands. Up to this point it hasn't come in handy, but its heft is comforting, and makes me feel protected. But from what? There aren't any bears or wolves in this forest. A few poisonous snakes, perhaps. The most dangerous creature here would have to be me. So maybe I'm just scared of my own shadow.

Still, as I walk along I get the feeling something, somewhere, is watching me, listening to me, holding its breath, blending into the background, watching my every move. Somewhere far off, something's listening to all the sounds I make, trying to guess where I'm headed and why. I try not to think about *it*. The more you think about illusions, the more they'll swell up and take on form. And no longer be an illusion.

I try whistling to fill in the silence. The soprano sax from Coltrane's "My Favorite Things," though of course my dubious whistling doesn't come anywhere near the complex, lightning-quick original. I just add bits so what I hear in my head approximates the sound. Better than nothing, I figure. I glance at my watch—it's ten-thirty. Oshima must be getting the library ready to open. Today would be . . . Wednesday. I picture him sprinkling water in the garden, wiping off the desks with a cloth, boiling water and brewing up some coffee. All the tasks I normally take care of. But now I'm here, deep in the forest, heading even deeper. Nobody has any idea I'm here. The only ones who do are me, and *them*.

I continue down the path. Calling it a path, though, isn't quite right. It's more like some natural kind of channel that water's carved out over time. When there's a downpour in the forest, rushing water gouges out the dirt, sweeping the grasses before it, exposing the roots of trees. When it hits a boulder it makes a detour around it. Once the rain lets up you're left with a dry riverbed that's something like a path. This pseudo-path is covered with ferns and green grass, and if you don't pay attention you'll lose it entirely. It gets steep every once in a while, and I scramble up by grabbing hold of tree trunks.

Somewhere along the line Coltrane's soprano sax runs out of steam. Now it's McCoy Tyner's piano solo I hear, the left hand carving out a repetitious rhythm and the right layering on thick, forbidding chords. Like some mythic scene, the music portrays somebody's—a nameless, faceless *somebody*'s—dim past, all the details laid out as clearly as entrails being dragged out of the darkness. Or at least that's how it sounds to me. The patient, repeating music ever so slowly breaks apart the real, rearranging the pieces. It has a hypnotic, menacing smell, just like the forest.

I hike along, spraying marks on the trees as I go, sometimes turning to make sure these yellow marks are still visible. It's okay—the marks that lead me home are like an uneven line of buoys in the sea. Just to be doubly sure, every once in a while I hack out a notch in a tree trunk. My little hatchet isn't very sharp, so I pick out the thinner, softer-looking trunks to hack. The trees receive these blows in silence.

Huge black mosquitoes buzz me like reconnaissance patrols, aiming for the exposed skin around my eyes. When I hear their buzz I brush them away or squash them. Whenever I smush one it makes a squish, already bloated with blood it's sucked out of me. It feels itchy only later. I wipe the blood off my hands on the towel around my neck.

The army marching through these woods, if it was summer, must have had the same problems with mosquitoes. Full battle gear—how much would that have weighed? Those old-style rifles like a clump of iron, ammunition belt, bayonet, steel helmet, a couple of grenades, food and rations, of course, entrenching tools to dig foxholes, mess kit . . . All that gear must add up to well over forty pounds. Damn heavy, and a lot more than my little daypack. I have the distinct feeling I'm going to bump into those soldiers around the next bend, even though they disappeared here more than sixty years ago.

I remember Napoleon's troops marching into Russia in the summer of 1812. They must have swatted away their share of mosquitoes, too, on that long road to Moscow. Of course mosquitoes weren't the only problem. They had to struggle to survive all kinds of other things— hunger, thirst, muddy roads, infectious disease, sweltering heat, Cossack commandos attacking their thin supply lines, lack of medical supplies, not to mention huge battles with the regular Russian army. When the French forces finally straggled into a deserted Moscow, their number had been reduced from 500,000 to a mere 100,000.

I stop and take a swig of water from my canteen. My watch shows exactly eleven o'clock. The library is just opening up. Oshima's unlocking the door, taking his usual seat behind the counter, a stack of long, neatly sharpened pencils on the desk. He picks one up and twirls it, gently pushing the eraser end against his temple. I can see it all clearly. But that place is so far away.

I've never had periods, says Oshima. I do anal sex and have never used my vagina for sex. My clitoris is sensitive but my breasts aren't.

I remember Oshima asleep in the bed in the cabin, his face to the wall. And the signs he/she left behind. Cloaked in those signs, I went to sleep in the same bed.

I give up thinking about it anymore. Instead I think about war. The Napoleonic Wars, the war the Japanese soldiers had to go off and fight. I feel the heft of the hatchet in my hands. That pale, sharp blade glints and I have to turn my eyes away from it. Why do people wage war? Why do hundreds of thousands, even millions of people group together and try to annihilate each other? Do people start wars out of anger? Or fear? Or are anger and fear just two aspects of the same spirit?

I hack another notch in a tree with my hatchet. The tree cries out silently, bleeding invisible blood. I keep on trudging. Coltrane picks up his soprano sax again. Once more the repetition breaks apart the real, rearranging the pieces.

Before long my mind wanders into the realm of dreams. They come back so quietly. I'm holding Sakura. She's in my arms, and I'm inside her. I don't want to be at the mercy of things outside me anymore, thrown into confusion by things I can't control. I've already murdered my father and violated my mother—and now here I am inside my sister. If there's a curse in all this, I mean to grab it by the horns and fulfill the program that's been laid out for me. Lift the burden from my shoulders and live—not caught up in someone else's schemes, but as *me*. That's what I really want. And I come inside her.

"Even if it's in a dream, you shouldn't have done that," the boy named Crow calls out. He's right behind me, walking in the forest. "I tried my best to stop you. I wanted you to understand. You heard, but you didn't *listen*. You just forged on ahead."

I don't respond or turn around, just silently keep on trudging.

"You thought that's how you could overcome the curse, right? But was it?" Crow asks.

But was it? You killed the person who's your father, violated your mother, and now your sister. You thought that would put an end to the curse your father laid on you, so you did everything that was prophesied about you. But nothing's really over. You didn't over-

come anything. That curse is branded on your soul even deeper than before. You should realize that by now. That curse is part of your DNA. You breathe out the curse, the wind carries it to the four corners of the Earth, but the dark confusion inside you remains. Your fear, anger, unease—nothing's disappeared. They're all still inside you, still torturing you.

"Listen up—there's no war that will end all wars," Crow tells me. "War breeds war. Lapping up the blood shed by violence, feeding on wounded flesh. War is a perfect, self-contained being. You need to know that."

"Sakura—my sister," I say. I shouldn't have raped her. *Even if it was in a dream.* "What should I do?" I ask, staring at the ground in front of me.

"You have to overcome the fear and anger inside you," the boy named Crow says. "Let a bright light shine in and melt the coldness in your heart. That's what being tough is all about. Do that and you really *will* be the toughest fifteen-year-old on the planet. You following me? There's still time. You can still get your *self* back. Use your head. Think about what you've got to do. You're no dunce. You should be able to figure it out."

"Did I really murder my father?" I ask.

No reply. I swing around, but the boy named Crow is gone and the silence swallows my question.

Alone in such a deep forest, the person called *me* feels empty, horribly empty. Oshima once used the term *hollow men.* Well, that's exactly what I've become. There's a void inside me, a blank that's slowly expanding, devouring what's left of who I am. I can hear it happening. I'm totally lost, my identity dying. There's no direction where I am, no sky, no ground. I think of Miss Saeki, of Sakura, of Oshima. But I'm light-years away from them. It's like I'm looking through the wrong end of a pair of binoculars, and no matter how far I stretch out my hand, I can't touch them. I'm all alone in the middle of a dim maze. Listen to the wind, Oshima told me. I listen, but no wind's blowing. Even the boy named Crow has vanished.

Use your head. Think about what you've got to do.

But I can't think anymore. No matter how much I try, I wind up at a dead end in the maze. What is it inside me that makes up *me*? Is this what's supposed to stand up to the void?

If only I could wipe out this *me* who's here, right here and right now. I seriously consider it. In this thick wall of trees, on this path that's not a path, if I stopped breathing, my consciousness would silently be buried in the darkness, every last drop of my dark violent blood dripping out, my DNA rotting among the weeds. Then my battle would be over. Otherwise, I'll eternally be murdering my father, violating my mother, violating my sister, lashing out at the world forever. I close my eyes and try to find my center. The darkness that covers it is rough and jagged. There's a break in the dark clouds, like looking out the window to see the leaves of the dogwood gleaming like a thousand blades in the moonlight.

I feel something rearranging itself under my skin, and there's a tinkling sound in my head. I open my eyes and take a deep breath. I throw away the can of spray paint, the hatchet, the compass. From far away I hear them all clatter to the ground. I feel lighter. I slip the daypack off my shoulders and toss it aside. My sense of touch seems suddenly acute. The air around me's grown more transparent. My sense of the forest has grown more intense. Coltrane's labyrinthine solo plays on in my ears, never ending.

Thinking it over, I reach into the daypack and take out the hunting knife and stuff it in my pocket. The razor-sharp knife I stole from my father's desk. If need be, I could use it to slash my wrists and let every drop of blood inside me gush out onto the ground. That would destroy the device.

I head off into the heart of the forest, a hollow man, a void that devours all that's substantial. There is nothing left to fear. Not a thing.

And I head off into the heart of the forest.

Chapter 42

O nce the two of them were alone, Miss Saeki offered Nakata a chair. He thought about it for a moment before sitting down. They sat there for a time without speaking, eyeing each other across the desk. Nakata placed his hiking hat on his lap and gave his short hair a good rub with his hand. Miss Saeki rested both hands on the desktop, quietly watching him go through his routine.

"Unless I'm mistaken, I think I've been waiting for you to come," she said.

"I believe that's true," Nakata replied. "But it took some time for Nakata to get here. I hope I didn't make you wait too long. I did my best to get here as quickly as I could."

Miss Saeki shook her head. "No, it's perfectly all right. If you'd come any earlier, or any later, I would've been even more at a loss, I suppose. For me, right now is the perfect time."

"Mr. Hoshino was very kind to me and helped me out a lot. If I had to do it alone it would've taken even longer. Nakata can't read, after all."

"Mr. Hoshino is your friend, isn't he?"

"Yes," Nakata replied, and nodded. "I think he is. But to tell the truth, I'm not all too sure about that. Besides cats, I've never had what you would call a friend in my life."

"I haven't had any friends either, for quite some time," Miss Saeki said. "Other than in memories."

"Miss Saeki?"

"Yes?" she replied.

"Actually, I don't have any memories either. I'm dumb, you see, so could you tell me what memories are like?"

Miss Saeki stared at her hands on the desk, then looked up at Nakata again. "Memories warm you up from the inside. But they also tear you apart."

Nakata shook his head. "That's a tough one. Nakata still doesn't understand. The only thing I understand is the present."

"I'm the exact opposite," Miss Saeki said.

A deep silence settled over the room.

Nakata was the one who broke it, lightly clearing his throat. "Miss Saeki?"

"Yes?"

"You know about the entrance stone, don't you?"

"Yes, I do," she said. She brushed the Mont Blanc pen on the desk with her fingers. "I happened to come across it a long time ago. Perhaps it would've been better if I'd never known about it. But I had no choice in the matter."

"Nakata opened it again a few days ago. The afternoon when there was lightning. Lots of lightning falling all over town. Mr. Hoshino helped me. I couldn't have done it myself. Do you know the day I'm talking about?"

Miss Saeki nodded. "Yes, I remember."

"I opened it because I had to."

"I know. You did that so things would be restored to the way they should be."

It was Nakata's turn to nod. "Exactly."

"And you had the right to do it."

"Nakata doesn't know about that. In any case, it wasn't something I chose. I have to tell you this—I murdered someone in Nakano. I didn't want to kill anybody, but Johnnie Walker was in charge and I took the place of the fifteen-year-old boy who should've been there, and I murdered someone. Nakata had to do it."

Miss Saeki closed her eyes, then opened them and looked him in the face. "Did all that happen because I opened the entrance stone a long time ago? Does that still have an effect even now, distorting things?"

Nakata shook his head. "Miss Saeki?"

"Yes?" she said.

"Nakata doesn't know about that. My role is to restore what's here now to the way it *should* be. That's why I left Nakano, went across a huge bridge, and came to Shikoku. And as I'm sure you're aware, you can't stay here anymore."

Miss Saeki smiled. "I know," she said. "It's what I've been hoping for, Mr. Nakata, for a long time. Something I longed for in the past, what I'm longing for right now. No matter how I tried, though, I couldn't grasp it. I simply had to sit and wait for that time—*now*, in other words—to come. It wasn't always easy, but suffering is something I've had to accept."

"Miss Saeki," Nakata said, "I only have half a shadow. The same as you."

"I know."

"Nakata lost it during that war. I don't know why that had to happen, and why it had to be me. . . . At any rate, a long time has passed since then, and it's nearly time for *us* to leave here."

"I understand."

"Nakata's lived a long time, but as I said, I don't have any memories. So this 'suffering' you talked about I don't rightly understand. But what I think is—no matter how much suffering you went through, you never wanted to let go of those memories."

"That's true," Miss Saeki said. "It hurt more and more to hold on to them, but I never wanted to let them go, as long as I was alive. It was the only reason I had to go on living, the only thing that proved I was alive."

Nakata nodded silently.

"Living longer than I should have has only ruined many people and many things," she went on. "Just recently I had a sexual relationship with that fifteen-year-old boy you mentioned. In that room I became a fifteen-year-old girl again, and made love to *him*. I don't know if that was the right thing to do or not, but I couldn't help it. But those actions must surely have caused something else to be ruined. That's my only regret."

"Nakata doesn't know about sexual desire. Just like I don't have memories, I don't have any desire. So I don't understand the difference between right or wrong sexual desire. But if something did happen, it happened. Whether it's right or wrong, I accept everything that happens, and that's how I became the person I am now."

"Mr. Nakata?"

"Yes?"

"I have a favor to ask." Miss Saeki picked up the bag at her feet, took out a small key and unlocked a desk drawer, then pulled out some thick file folders and laid them on top of the desk.

"Ever since I came back to this town," she said, "I've been writing this. A record of my life. I was born nearby and fell deeply in love with a boy who lived in this house. I couldn't have loved him more, and he was deeply in love with me. We lived in a perfect circle, where everything inside was complete. Of course that couldn't go on forever. We grew up, and times changed. Parts of the circle fell apart, the outside world came rushing into our private paradise, and things inside tried to get out. All quite natural, I suppose, yet at the time I couldn't accept it. And that's why I opened up the entrance stone—to prevent our perfect, private world from collapsing. I can't remember now how I managed to do it, but I decided I had to open the stone no matter what—so I wouldn't lose him, so things from the outside wouldn't destroy our world. I didn't understand at the time what it would mean. And of course I received my punishment."

She stopped speaking here, picked up the fountain pen, and closed her eyes. "My life ended at age twenty. Since then it's been merely a series of endless reminiscences, a dark, winding corridor leading nowhere. Nevertheless, I had to live it, surviving each empty day, seeing each day off still empty. During those days I made a lot of mistakes. No, that's not correct—sometimes I feel that *all* I did was make mistakes. I felt like I was living at the bottom of a deep well, completely shut up inside myself, cursing my fate, hating everything outside. Occasionally I ventured outside myself, putting on a good show of being alive. Accepting whatever came along, numbly slipping through life. I slept around a lot, at one point even living in a sort of marriage, but it was all pointless. Everything passed away in an instant, with nothing left behind except the scars of things I injured and despised."

She laid her hands on top of the three files on her desk. "All the details are in here. I wrote this to put it all in order, to make sure one more time about the life I lived. I have only myself to blame, but it's a gut-wrenching process. And I've finally finished it. I've written everything I need to write. I don't need this anymore, and I don't want anybody else to read it. If someone else happened to see it, it might cause harm all over again. So I want it all burned up, every last page, so nothing's left. If you wouldn't mind, I'd like you to take care of it. You're the only person I can depend on, Mr. Nakata. I'm sorry to bother you with this, but could you do it for me?"

"Nakata understands," he said, nodding seriously. "If that's what you'd like, Miss Saeki, I'll be happy to burn it all up for you. You can rest assured."

"Thank you," Miss Saeki said.

"Writing things was important, wasn't it?" Nakata asked.

"Yes, it was. The process of writing *was* important. Even though the finished product is completely meaningless."

"I can't read or write, so I can't write things down. Nakata's just like a cat."

"Mr. Nakata?"

"How can I help you?"

"I feel like I've known you for ages," Miss Saeki said. "Weren't *you* in that painting? A figure in the sea in the background? White pants legs rolled up, dipping your feet in the water?"

Nakata silently stood up and came over to stand in front of Miss Saeki. He laid his hard, sunburned hands on top of hers on the files. And as if listening carefully to something, he felt the warmth there filter from her hand to his. "Miss Saeki?"

"Yes?"

"I think I understand a little now."

"About what?"

"What memories are. I can feel them, through your hands."

She smiled. "I'm glad."

Nakata kept his hands on top of hers for a long while. Eventually Miss Saeki closed her eyes, quietly giving herself over to memories. There was no more pain there, for someone had siphoned it off forever. The circle was once again complete. She opens the door of a faraway room and finds two beautiful chords, in the shape of lizards, asleep on the wall. She gently touches them and can feel their peaceful sleep. A gentle wind is blowing, rustling the old curtain from time to time. A significant rustling, like some parable. She's wearing a long blue dress. A dress she wore somewhere a long time ago. Its hem swishes faintly as she walks. The shore is visible outside the window. And you can hear the sound of waves, and someone's voice. There's a hint of the sea in the breeze. And it's summer. Always it's summer. Small white clouds are etched against the azure sky.

Nakata carried the three thick files downstairs. Oshima was at the counter talking with one of the patrons. When he saw Nakata, he grinned. Nakata gave a polite bow in return, and Oshima went back to his conversation. Hoshino was in the reading room all the while, deep in a book.

"Mr. Hoshino?" Nakata said.

Hoshino laid his book down and looked up. "Hey, that took a while. You all finished?"

"Yes, Nakata's all finished here. If it's all right with you, I was thinking we can leave pretty soon."

"Fine by me. I'm nearly finished with this book. Beethoven just died, and I'm at the part about the funeral. Man, what a funeral! Twenty-five thousand Viennese joined the procession, and they closed all the schools for the day."

"Mr. Hoshino?"

"Yeah, what's up?"

"I have one more favor to ask of you."

"Shoot."

"I need to burn this somewhere."

Hoshino looked at the files the old man was carrying. "Hmm, that's a lot of stuff. We can't just burn it anywhere. We'd need a dry riverbed or someplace."

"Mr. Hoshino?"

"Yeah?"

"Let's go find one then."

"Maybe this is a stupid question, but is that really so important? Can't we just toss it somewhere?"

"Yes, it's very important and we have to burn it all up. It has to turn into smoke and rise into the sky. And we have to watch it, to make sure it all burns up."

Hoshino stood up and stretched. "Okay, let's find a big riverbed. I have no idea where, but I'm sure Shikoku's gotta have at least one—if we look long enough."

The afternoon was busier than it had ever been. Lots of people came to use the library, several with detailed, specialized questions. It was all Oshima could do to respond, and to run around collecting materials that had been requested. Several items he had to locate on the computer. Normally he'd ask Miss Saeki to help out, but today it didn't look like he'd be able to. Various tasks took him away from his desk and he didn't even notice when Nakata left. When things settled down for a moment he looked around, but the strange pair was nowhere to be seen. Oshima walked upstairs to Miss Saeki's study. Strangely, the door was shut. He knocked twice and waited, but there was no response. He knocked again. "Miss Saeki?" he said from outside the door. "Are you all right?"

He softly turned the knob. The door was unlocked. Oshima opened it a crack and peeked inside. And saw Miss Saeki facedown on the desk. Her hair had tumbled forward, hiding her face. He didn't know what to do. Maybe she was just tired and had fallen asleep. But he'd never once seen her take a nap. She wasn't the type to doze off at work. He walked into the room and went over to the desk. He leaned over and whispered her name in her ear, but got no response. He touched her shoulder, then held her wrist and pressed his finger against it. There was no pulse. Her skin retained a faint warmth, but it was already fading away.

He lifted her hair and checked her face. Both eyes were slightly open. She looked like she was having a pleasant dream, but she wasn't. She was dead. A faint trace of a smile was still on her lips. Even in death she was graceful and dignified, Oshima thought. He let her hair fall back and picked up the phone on the desk.

He'd resigned himself to the fact that it was only a matter of time before this day came. But now that it had, and he was alone in this quiet room with a dead Miss Saeki, he was lost. He felt as if his heart had dried up. I needed her, he thought. I needed someone like her to fill the void inside me. But I wasn't able to fill the void inside her. Until the bitter end, the emptiness inside her was hers alone.

Somebody was calling out his name from downstairs. He felt like he'd heard that voice. He'd left the door wide open and could hear the sounds of people bustling around. A phone rang on the first floor. He ignored it all. He sat down and gazed at Miss Saeki. You want to call my name, he thought, go right ahead. You want to call on the phone— be my guest. Finally he heard an ambulance siren that seemed to be getting closer. In a few moments people will be rushing upstairs to take her away—forever. He raised his left arm and glanced at his watch. It was 4:35. 4:35 on a Tuesday afternoon. I have to remember this time, he thought. I have to remember this day, this afternoon, forever.

"Kafka Tamura," he whispered, staring at the wall, "I have to tell you what happened. If you don't already know."

Chapter 43

With all my baggage gone I can travel light now, forging on deeper into the forest. I focus totally on moving forward. No need to mark any more trees, no need to remember the path back. I don't even look at my surroundings. The scenery's always the same, so what's the point? A canopy of trees towering above thick ferns, vines trailing down, gnarled roots, lumps of decaying leaves, the dry, sloughed-off skins of various bugs. Hard, sticky spiderwebs. And endless branches—a regular tree branch universe. Menacing branches, branches fighting for space, cleverly hidden branches, twisted, crooked branches, contemplative branches, dried-up, dying branches—the same scenery repeated again and again. Though with each repetition the forest grows a bit deeper.

Mouth tightly shut, I continue down what passes for a path. It's running uphill, but not so steeply, at least for now. Not the kind of slope that's going to get me out of breath. Sometimes the path threatens to get lost in a sea of ferns or thorny bushes, but as long as I push on ahead the pseudo-path pops up again. The forest doesn't scare me anymore. It has its own rules and patterns, and once you stop being afraid you're aware of them. Once I grasp these repetitions, I make them a part of me.

I'm empty-handed now. The can of yellow spray paint, the little hatchet— they're history. The daypack's gone as well. No canteen, no food. Not even the compass. One by one I left these behind. Doing this gives a visible message to the forest: *I'm not afraid anymore. That's why I chose to be totally defenseless.* Minus my hard shell, just flesh and bones, I head for the core of the labyrinth, giving myself up to the void.

The music that had been playing in my head has vanished, leaving behind some faint white noise like a taut white sheet on a huge bed. I touch that sheet, tracing it with my fingertips. The white goes on forever. Sweat beads up under my arms. Sometimes I can catch a glimpse of the sky through the treetops. It's covered with an even, unbroken layer of gray clouds, but it doesn't look like it's going to rain. The clouds are still, the whole scene unchanging. Birds in the high branches call out clipped, meaningful greetings to each other. Insects buzz prophetically among the weeds.

I think about my deserted house back in Nogata. Most likely it's all shut up now. Fine by me. Let the bloodstains be. What do I care? I'm never going back there. Even before that bloody incident took place, that house was a place where lots of things had died. Check that— were *murdered*.

Sometimes from above me, sometimes from below, the forest tries to threaten me. Blowing a chill breath on my neck, stinging like needles with a thousand eyes. Trying anything to drive this intruder away. But I gradually get better at letting these threats pass me by. This forest is basically a part of me, isn't it? This thought takes hold at a certain point. The journey I'm taking is *inside me*. Just like blood travels down veins, what I'm seeing is my inner self, and what seems threatening is just the echo of the fear in my own heart. The spiderweb stretched taut there is the spiderweb inside me. The birds calling out overhead are birds I've fostered in my mind. These images spring up in my mind and take root.

Like I'm being shoved from behind by some huge heartbeat, I continue on and on through the forest. The path leads to a special place, a light source that spins out the dark, the place where soundless echoes come from. I need to see with my own eyes what's there. I'm carrying an important, sealed, personal letter, a secret message to myself.

A question. Why didn't she love me? Don't I deserve to have my mother love me?

For years that question's been a white-hot flame burning my heart, eating away at my soul. There had to be something fundamentally wrong with me that made my mother not love me. Was there something inherently polluted about me? Was I born just so everyone could turn their faces away from me?

My mother didn't even hold me close when she left. She turned her face away and left home with my sister without saying a word. She disappeared like quiet smoke. And now that face is gone forever.

The birds screech above me again, and I look up at the sky. Nothing there but that flat, expressionless layer of gray clouds. No wind at all. I trudge along. I'm walking by the shores of consciousness. Waves of consciousness roll in, roll out, leave some writing, and just as quickly new waves roll in and erase it. I try to quickly read what's written there, between one wave and the next, but it's hard. Before I can read it the next wave's washed it away. All that's left are puzzling fragments.

My mind wanders back to my house on the day my mother left, taking my sister with her. I'm sitting alone on the porch, staring out at the garden. It's twilight, in early summer, and the trees cast long shadows. I'm alone in the house. I don't know why, but I already knew I was abandoned. I understood even then how this would change my world forever. Nobody told me this—I just *knew* it. The house is empty, deserted, an abandoned lookout post on some far-off frontier. I'm watching the sun setting in the west, shadows slowly stealing over the world. In a world of time, nothing can go back to the way it was. The shadows' feelers steadily advance, eroding away one point after another along the ground, until my mother's face, there until a moment ago, is swallowed up in this dark, cold realm. That hardened face, turned away from me, is automatically snatched away, deleted from my memory.

Trudging along in the woods, I think of Miss Saeki. Her face, that calm, faint smile, the warmth of her hand. I try imagining her as my mother, leaving me behind when I was four. Without realizing it, I shake my head. The picture is all wrong. Why would Miss Saeki have done that? Why does she have to hurt me, to permanently screw up my life? There had to be a hidden, important reason, something deeper I'm just not getting.

I try to feel what she felt then and get closer to her viewpoint. It isn't easy. *I'm* the one who was abandoned, after all, she's the one who did the abandoning. But after a while I take leave of myself. My soul sloughs off the stiff clothes of the self and turns into a black crow that sits there on a branch high up in a pine tree in the garden, gazing down at the four-year-old boy on the porch.

I turn into a theorizing black crow.

"It's not that your mother didn't love you," the boy named Crow says from behind me. "She loved you very deeply. The first thing you have to do is believe that. That's your starting point."

"But she abandoned me. She disappeared, leaving me alone where I shouldn't be. I'm finally beginning to understand how much that hurt. How could she do that if she really loved me?"

"That's the reality of it. It did happen," the boy named Crow says. "You were hurt badly, and those scars will be with you forever. I feel

398

sorry for you, I really do. But think of it like this: It's not too late to recover. You're young, you're tough. You're adaptable. You can patch up your wounds, lift up your head, and move on. But for her that's not an option. The only thing she'll ever be is lost. It doesn't matter whether somebody judges this as good or bad—that's not the point. *You're* the one who has the advantage. You ought to consider that."

I don't respond.

"It all really happened, so you can't undo it," Crow tells me. "She shouldn't have abandoned you then, and you shouldn't have *been* abandoned. But things in the past are like a plate that's shattered to pieces. You can never put it back together like it was, right?"

I nod. *You can never put it back together like it was.* He's hit the nail on the head.

The boy named Crow continues. "Your mother felt a gut-wrenching kind of fear and anger inside her, okay? Just like you do now. Which is why she had to abandon you."

"Even though she loved me?"

"Even though she loved you, she had to abandon you. You need to understand how she felt then, and learn to accept it. Understand the overpowering fear and anger she experienced, and feel it as your own—so you won't inherit it and repeat it. The main thing is this: You have to *forgive* her. That's not going to be easy, I know, but you have to do it. That's the only way you can be saved. There's no other way!"

I think about what he's said. The more I think about it, the more confused I get. My head's spinning, and I feel like my skin's being ripped away. "Is Miss Saeki really my mother?" I ask.

"Didn't she tell you that theory is still functional?" the boy named Crow says. "So that's the answer. *It's still a functioning hypothesis.* That's all I can tell you."

"A working hypothesis until some good counterevidence comes along."

"You got it," Crow says.

"And I have to pursue that hypothesis as far as it'll take me."

"That's it," Crow replies pointedly. "A theory that still doesn't have any good counterevidence is one worth pursuing. And right now, pursuing it's the only choice you have. Even if it means sacrificing yourself, you have to pursue it to the bitter end."

"Sacrifice myself?" That certainly has a strange ring to it. I can't quite grasp it.

There's no reply. Worried, I turn around. The boy named Crow is still there. He's right behind, keeping pace.

"What sort of fear and anger did Miss Saeki have at that time?" I ask him as I turn back around and walk on. "And where did it come from?"

"What kind of fear and anger do *you* think she had?" the boy named Crow asks in return. "Think about it. You've got to figure it out yourself. That's what your head's for."

So I do just that. I have to understand it, accept it, before it's too late. But I still can't make out that delicate writing left on the shore of my consciousness. There's not enough time between one wave and the next.

"I'm in love with Miss Saeki," I say. The words slip out naturally.

"I know that," the boy named Crow says curtly.

"I've never felt that before," I go on. "And it's more important to me than anything else I've ever experienced."

"Of course it is," Crow says. "That goes without saying. That's why you've come all this way."

"But I still don't get it. You're telling me my mother loved me very much. I want to believe you, but if that's true, I just don't get it. Why does loving somebody mean you have to hurt them just as much? I mean, if that's the way it goes, what's the point of loving someone? Why the hell does it have to be like that?"

I wait for an answer. I keep my mouth shut for a long time, but there's no response, so I spin around. The boy named Crow is gone. From up above I hear the flap of wings.

You're totally confused.

Not long afterward, the two soldiers appear.

They're wearing battle fatigues of the old Imperial army. Short-sleeved summer uniforms, gaiters, and knapsacks. No helmets, just caps with bills, and some kind of black face paint. Both of them are young. One of them's tall and thin, with round, metal-framed glasses. The other one's short, broad-shouldered, and muscular. They're both sitting on a flat rock, neither one looking like he's about to leap into battle. Their Arisaka rifles are on the ground by their feet. The tall soldier seems bored and is chewing on a stem of grass. The two of them look completely natural, like they belong here. Unperturbed, they watch as I approach.

There's a small flat clearing around them, like a landing on a staircase.

"Hey," the tall soldier calls out cheerfully.

"How ya doing?" the brawny one says with the smallest of frowns.

"How are you?" I greet them back. I know I should be amazed to see them, but somehow it doesn't seem weird at all. It's entirely within the realm of possibility.

"We were waiting for you," the tall one says.

"For me?" I ask.

"Sure," he replies. "No one else is coming out here, that's for sure."

"We've been waiting a long time," the brawny one says.

"Not that time's much of a factor here," the tall one adds. "Still, you took longer than I figured."

"You're the two guys who disappeared in this forest a long, long time ago, right?" I ask. "During maneuvers?"

The brawny soldier nods. "That's us."

"They searched everywhere for you," I say.

"Yeah, I know," he says. "I know they were looking for us. I know everything that goes on in this forest. But they're not about to find us, no matter how hard they look."

"Actually, we didn't get lost," the tall one says. "We ran away."

"Not running away so much as just stumbling onto this spot and deciding to stay put," the brawny one adds. "That's different from getting lost."

"Not just anybody can find this place," the tall soldier says. "But we did, and now you have too. It was a stroke of luck—for us, at least."

"If we hadn't found this spot, they would've shipped us overseas," the brawny one explains. "Over there it was kill or be killed. That wasn't for us. I'm a farmer, originally, and my buddy here just graduated from college. Neither one of us wants to kill anybody. And being killed's even worse. Kind of obvious, I'd say."

"How 'bout you?" the tall one asks me. "Would you like to kill anybody, or be killed?"

I shake my head. No, neither one, definitely not.

"Everybody feels like that," the tall one says. "Or the vast majority, at least. But if you say, Hey, I don't want to go off to war, the country's not about to break out in smiles and give you permission to skip out. You can't run away. Japan's a small country, so where are you going to run to? They'll track you down so fast it'll make your head spin. That's why we stayed here. This is the only place we could hide." He shakes his head and goes on. "And we've stayed here ever since. Like you said, from a *long, long time ago*. Not that time's a major factor here. There's almost no difference at all between now and a long, long time ago."

"No difference at all," the brawny one says, waving something away with his hand.

"You knew I was coming?" I ask.

"Sure thing," the brawny one replies.

"We've been standing guard here for a long time, so we know if somebody's coming," the other one said. "We're like part of the forest."

"This is the entrance," the brawny one says. "And we're guarding it."

"And right now the entrance happens to be open," the tall one explains. "Before long, though, it'll close up. If you want to come in, now's the time. It doesn't open up all that often."

"We'll lead the way," the brawny one says. "The path's hard to follow, so you need someone to guide you in."

"If you don't come in, then go back where you came from," the tall one says. "It's not all that hard to find your way back, so don't worry about it. You'll do fine. Then you'll return to the world you came from, to the life you've been living. The choice is entirely up to you. Nobody's going to force you to do one or the other. But once you're in, it isn't easy to turn back."

"Take me inside," I answer without a moment's hesitation.

"Are you sure?" the brawny one asks.

"Somebody's inside I have to see," I say. "At least I think so. . . ."

Slowly, silently, the two of them get up off the rock and shoulder their rifles. They exchange a glance and walk on ahead of me.

"You must think it's strange we still lug around these heavy lumps of steel," the tall one says, turning around. "They're worthless. Never had any bullets anyway."

"But they're a kind of *sign*," the brawny one says, not looking back at me. "A sign of what we left behind."

"Symbols are important," the tall one adds. "We happen to have these rifles and soldiers' uniforms, so we play the part of sentries. That's our role. Symbols guide us to the roles we play."

"Do you have anything like that with you?" the brawny one asks. "Something that can be a sign?"

I shake my head. "No, I don't have anything. Just memories."

"Hmm . . . ," the brawny one says. "Memories, huh?"

"That's okay. Doesn't matter," the tall one says. "Memories can be a great symbol too. Course I don't have any idea how well memories will stand up, how long they'll last."

"Something that has a form or a shape is best, if you can manage it," the brawny one says. "It's easier to understand."

"Like a rifle," the tall one says. "By the way, what's your name?"

"Kafka Tamura," I answer.

"Kafka Tamura," they both repeat.

"Weird name," the tall one says.

"You got that right," the brawny one adds.

After this we walk in silence down the path.

Chapter 44

They took the three files to a riverbed along the highway and burned them. Hoshino had bought lighter fluid at a convenience store, and doused the files before setting them ablaze. Then he and Nakata stood by silently as they watched each page become engulfed in flames. There was barely a hint of wind, and the smoke rose straight up, getting lost among the low-hanging gray clouds.

"So we can't read any of these papers?" Hoshino asked.

"No, we're not supposed to," Nakata replied. "I promised Miss Saeki we wouldn't, and my job is to keep that promise."

"Yeah, keeping promises *is* important," Hoshino said, wiping away sweat from his forehead. "It would be nice if we had a shredder, though. That would sure make it a lot easier. Copy shops have big shredders you can rent pretty cheap. Don't get me wrong, I'm not complaining. It's just kind of hot to make a bonfire at this time of year. If it were winter, that'd be another story."

"I'm sorry, but I promised Miss Saeki I'd burn it all up. So that's what Nakata has to do."

"Okay, then. I'm in no rush. A little heat's not going to kill me. It was just a, what do you call it—a suggestion."

A cat sauntering along stopped to watch, a skinny, brown-striped cat whose tail was slightly bent at the tip. A personable cat, by the looks of it. Nakata badly wanted to talk with it but decided he'd better not, since Hoshino was with him. The cat wouldn't be able to relax unless they were alone. Besides, Nakata wasn't at all confident he could speak with cats like he used to. The last thing he wanted was to blurt out something weird and frighten the poor animal. Before long, the cat grew bored of watching the bonfire, stood up, and padded away.

A long while later, after the files were completely burned, Hoshino stomped the ashes into dust. The next strong wind would scatter all the remains. The sun was nearly setting by then, and crows were flying back to their nests.

"Nobody's gonna read it now," Hoshino said. "I don't know what was written in it, but it's all gone. A bit of shape and form has disappeared from the world, increasing the amount of nothingness."

"Mr. Hoshino?"

"What's up?"

"I have a question I'd like to ask."

"Fire away."

"Can nothingness increase?"

Hoshino puzzled this one over for a while. "That's a tough one," he admitted. "If something returns to nothing it becomes zero, but even if you add zero to zero, it's still zero."

"I don't understand."

"I don't get it either. Thinking about those kinds of things always gives me a headache."

"So maybe we should stop thinking about it."

"Fine with me," Hoshino said. "Anyhow, the manuscript's all burned up. All the words in it have disappeared. It's gone back to nothing—that's what I wanted to say."

"That's a load off my mind."

"So this pretty much wraps up what we need to do here, right?" Hoshino asked.

"Yes, we've almost finished what we need to do," Nakata said. "All that's left is to close up the entrance again."

"That's pretty important, huh?"

"It is. What's opened has to be shut."

"Well, let's get to it. Strike while the iron is hot and all that."

"Mr. Hoshino?"

"Yeah?"

"We can't do it now."

"Why not?"

"It's not time yet," Nakata said. "We have to wait for the right time to shut the entrance. Before that, I have to get some sleep. Nakata's so sleepy."

Hoshino looked at the old man. "Wait a sec—you're not going to sack out for days on end again, are you?"

"I can't say, but it may turn out like that."

"Can't we take care of business before you zonk out? Look—once you shift into sleep mode things kind of come to a halt."

"Mr. Hoshino?"

"What's up?"

"I wish we could shut the entrance first. That would be wonderful. But I have to get some sleep first. I can't keep my eyes open anymore."

"Like your batteries have fizzled out or something?"

"I suppose. It took longer than I thought to do what we needed to do. All my energy's gone. Would you take me back to where Nakata can get some sleep?"

"No problem. We'll grab a cab and head back to the apartment. Then you can sleep like a log if you want."

Once they'd settled into the cab Nakata started to nod out.

"You can sleep as much as you want once we're back in the apartment," Hoshino said. "But hang in there until we get home, okay?"

"Mr. Hoshino?"

"Yup?"

"I'm sorry to have put you to so much trouble," Nakata murmured vaguely.

"Yeah, I guess you have," Hoshino admitted. "But nobody asked me to come—I tagged along of my own free will. Like volunteering to shovel snow. So don't worry about it."

"If you hadn't helped me, Nakata wouldn't have known what to do. I wouldn't have finished even half of what I had to do."

"Well, if you put it that way, I guess it was worth the effort."

"I'm very grateful to you."

"But you know what?" Hoshino said.

"What?"

"I have a lot to thank *you* for too, Mr. Nakata."

"Is that right?"

"It's been about ten days since all this began," Hoshino said. "I've skipped out on work the whole time. The first couple of days I got in touch with them and asked for some time off, but right now I'm sort of AWOL. I probably won't get my old job back. Maybe, if I get down on my knees and apologize, they might forgive me. But it's no big deal. Not to brag or anything, but finding another job won't be hard—I'm a great driver and a good worker. So I'm not worried about that, and neither should you be. What I'm trying to say is that I don't have any regrets about being with you. These past ten days there's been a lot of bizarre stuff going on. Leeches falling from the sky, Colonel Sanders popping up out of thin air, hot sex with this drop-dead-gorgeous philosophy major, swiping the entrance stone from that shrine. . . . A lifetime of weird stuff packed into ten days. Like we've been doing test runs on a roller coaster or something."

Hoshino stopped here, thinking how to go on. "But you know what, Gramps?"

"Yes?"

"The most amazing thing of all has been *you*, Mr. Nakata. *You* changed my life. These past ten days, I don't know—things look *different* to me now. Stuff I never would've given a second glance before seems different. Like music, for instance—music I used to think was boring really gets to me now. I feel like I've gotta tell somebody about this or bust, somebody who'll understand what I've gone through. Nothing like this ever happened to me before. And it's all because of *you*. I've started to see the world through *your* eyes. Not *everything*, mind you. I like how you look at life, so that's why it happened. That's why I've stayed with you through thick and thin, why I couldn't leave you. It's been one of the most meaningful times I've ever had in my life. So there's no need for you to be thanking me—not that I mind it. I should be thanking *you*. All I'm trying to say is you've done me a lot of good, Mr. Nakata. Do you know what I'm saying?"

But Nakata wasn't listening anymore. His eyes were shut, his breathing regular as he slept.

"What a happy-go-lucky guy," Hoshino said, and sighed.

Hoshino carried the old man in his arms up to the apartment and put him to bed. He took off Nakata's shoes but left his clothes on, and covered him with a light comforter. Nakata squirmed a bit, then settled down as usual, on his back facing the ceiling. His breathing was quiet and he was still.

Bet we're in for another three-day sleep marathon, Hoshino thought to himself.

But that's not how things turned out. Before noon the next day, Wednesday, Mr. Nakata was dead. He died peacefully in his sleep. His face was as calm as always, and he looked like he was just sleeping—only not breathing. Hoshino shook the old man's shoulders and called out his name, but there was no mistaking it—he was dead. Hoshino checked his pulse—nothing—and even put a hand mirror near his mouth, but it didn't cloud up. He'd stopped breathing completely. In this world, at least, he was never going to wake up again.

Alone in the room with the corpse, Hoshino noticed how, very gradually, all sounds disappeared. How the real sounds around him steadily lost their reality. Meaningful sounds all ended up as silence. And the silence grew, deeper and deeper, like silt on the bottom of the sea. It accumulated at his feet, reached up to his waist, then up to his chest. He watched as the layers of silence rose up higher and higher. He sat down on the sofa and gazed at Nakata's face, trying to accept the fact that he was really gone. It took him a long time to accept it. As he sat there the air began to feel strangely heavy and he could no longer tell if his thoughts and feelings were really *his*. But there were a few things he started to understand.

Maybe death would take Nakata back to the way he used to be. When he was alive, he was always good old Nakata, a not-so-bright, cat-talking old man. Maybe death was the only road back to being the "normal Nakata" he'd always talked about.

"Hey, Gramps," Hoshino said. "Maybe I shouldn't say this, but if you gotta die, this isn't such a bad way to go."

Nakata had passed away calmly in his sleep, most likely not thinking of anything. His face was peaceful, with no signs of suffering, regret, or confusion. Very Nakata-like, Hoshino concluded. But what his life had really meant, Hoshino had no idea. Not that anybody's life had more clear-cut meaning to it. What's really important for people, what really has dignity, is *how* they die. Compared to that, he thought, how you lived doesn't amount to much. Still, how you live determines how you die. These thoughts ran through his head as he stared at the face of the dead old man.

But one critical thing remained. *Someone had to close up the entrance stone.* Nakata had finished everything he'd set out to do except that. The stone was right there, at Hoshino's feet, and he knew that when the time came he had to roll it over and shut up the entrance. But Nakata had warned him that if you mishandled it, the stone could be very dangerous. There had to be a right way of turning the stone over—but also a *wrong* way. If you just powered it over, that could screw up the entire world.

"I can't do anything about your having died, Gramps, but you've left me in a real bind here," Hoshino said, addressing the corpse, which of course didn't respond.

There was also the question of what to do with the body. The normal response would be to ring up the police or the hospital and have them take it. Ninety-nine percent of the people in the world would have done exactly that, and Hoshino wanted to. But the police were hunting for Nakata in connection with that murder case, and getting in touch with the authorities at this point would definitely put Hoshino in a precarious position. The police would haul him off and grill him for hours. Explaining everything that had happened was the last thing he wanted to do, plus there was the fact that he was no fan of law enforcement. If he could avoid having anything to do with cops, so much the better.

And how the hell do I explain this apartment? he wondered.

An old man dressed up like Colonel Sanders lent us the place. Said he'd prepared it specially for us and that we could use it as long as we liked. Would the police really buy that? *Colonel Sanders? Is he with the U.S. army? No, you know—the Kentucky Fried Chicken guy. You must've seen their billboards, right, detective? Yeah, that's the guy—glasses, white goatee. . . . He was a pimp working the back alleys of Takamatsu. He got a girl for me.* Explain stuff like that and the cops would call him an idiot and give him a swift punch to the head. Cops, Hoshino concluded, not for the first time in his life, are just gangsters who get paid by the state.

He let out a deep sigh.

What I've got to do, he thought, is get out of here right now, as far away as I can. I can make an anonymous call to the cops from a pay phone at the station. Give them the address here, say that somebody's died. Then hop a train back to Nagoya. They'll never connect me to the case. The old man died a natural death, so the cops won't launch some investigation. They'll hand over the body to his relatives and there'll be a simple funeral, end of story. Then I'll go to my company, bow and scrape in front of the president: *It'll never happen again, I swear. I'll work hard from now on.* Whatever it takes to get my old job back.

He started packing, cramming a change of clothes in his bag. He put on his Chunichi Dragons cap, pulling his ponytail through the opening in back, and his dark green sunglasses. Thirsty, he got a Diet Pepsi from the refrigerator. As he leaned back against the fridge and drank, he noticed the round stone next to the sofa. He went into the bedroom and looked at Nakata's corpse one more time. He still didn't look like he was dead. He looked like he was quietly breathing, and Hoshino half expected him to suddenly sit up and say, *Mr. Hoshino, it's all a mistake. Nakata's not really dead!* But he didn't. Nakata was most definitely deceased. There weren't going to be any miracles. The old man had already crossed the great divide.

Pepsi in hand, Hoshino stood there, shaking his head. I can't just go off and leave the stone behind, he thought. If I did, Mr. Nakata won't be able to truly rest in peace. He was such a conscientious type, always making sure things were done just right. And he would've finished this final task, if his batteries hadn't run out. Hoshino crushed the empty aluminum can and tossed it in the trash. Still thirsty, he went back into the kitchen and popped open another Pepsi.

Mr. Nakata told me how he wanted, if only one time, to be able to read, Hoshino remembered. He said he wanted to go to a library and be able to choose any book and read it. But he died before he could make that dream come true. Maybe now that he's dead he's gone on to another world, where he's become a *normal Nakata*, and *can* read. As long as he was in *this* world, though, he never could. In fact, his final act on earth was quite the opposite—burning up writing. Sending all those words on the pages off into the void. Kind of ironic, when you think about it. That being the case, though, Hoshino thought, I need to fulfill his final wish. *I've got to close the entrance.* I wasn't able to take him to the movies, or the aquarium—so it's the least I can do for him, now that he's gone.

He drained his second can of Pepsi, went over to the sofa, crouched down, and tried lifting the stone. It wasn't so heavy. Not exactly light, either, but it didn't take all that much to lift it up. About as heavy as when he and Colonel Sanders had stolen it from the shrine. About as heavy as the kind of stones used to weigh down pickles as they ferment. That means right now it's just a stone, Hoshino thought. When the stone's acting as an entrance, it's so heavy you have to kill yourself to pick it up. But when it's light like this, it's just an ordinary stone. Something extraordinary has to happen first, for the stone to become as heavy as it did and change into the entrance stone. Like lightning striking all over town or something . . .

Hoshino went to the window, opened the curtain, and gazed up at the sky from the veranda. The sky was the same as the day before, a mass of drab gray clouds. But it didn't look like it was going to rain, much less thunder. He perked up his ears and sniffed the air, but everything seemed the same as yesterday. *Steady as she goes* seemed to be today's theme for the world.

"Hey, Gramps," he said aloud to the dead man. "Guess I just have to wait here with you for something out of the ordinary to happen. What the heck that could be, I have no idea. Or even *when* it might take place. Plus it's June, and your body's gonna decay and start to stink pretty soon. I know you don't want to hear this, but that's nature for you. And the more time that passes, and the later I get in touch with the cops, the worse it'll get for me. I mean, I'll do whatever I can, but I just wanted you to know the situation, okay?"

There was no reply, of course.

Hoshino wandered around the room. *That's* it! Colonel Sanders might get in touch! *He'd* know what to do with the stone. Him you could always count on for some warmhearted, practical advice. But no matter how long he stared at the phone, it just sat there, a silent, unnecessarily introspective object. Nobody knocked on the door, not a single letter arrived. And nothing out of the ordinary happened. The weather stayed the same, and no flashes of inspiration struck him. One expressionless moment after another ticked by. Noon came and went, the afternoon quietly reeling into twilight. The hands of the electric clock on the wall skimmed smoothly over the surface of time like a whirligig beetle, and on the bed Mr. Nakata was still dead. Hoshino didn't feel hungry at all. He had a third can of Pepsi and dutifully munched on some crackers.

At six p.m. he sat down on the sofa, picked up the remote, and switched on the TV. He watched the NHK evening news, but nothing caught his attention. It had been an ordinary day, a slow news day. The announcer's voice started to grate on his nerves, and when the program was over he turned off the TV. It was getting darker outside, and finally night took over. An even greater stillness and quiet enveloped the room.

"Hey, Gramps," Hoshino said to Nakata. "Could you get up, just for a few minutes? I don't know what the hell to do. And I miss your voice."

Naturally Nakata didn't reply. He was still on the other side of the divide. Wordlessly he continued as he was, dead. The silence grew deeper, so deep that if you listened carefully you might very well catch the sound of the earth revolving on its axis.

Hoshino went out to the living room and put on the *Archduke* Trio. As he listened to the first theme, tears came to his eyes, then the floodgates opened. Jeez, he thought, when was the last time I cried? He couldn't remember.

Chapter 45

As advertised, the path from the "entrance" on is hard to follow. Actually, it's pretty much given up on trying to be a path. The farther we go, the deeper and more enormous the forest gets. The slope gets a whole lot steeper, the ground more overgrown with bushes and undergrowth. The sky has just about disappeared, and it's so dim that it seems like twilight. Thick spiderwebs loom up all over the place, and the air's thick with the smell of plants. The silence gets even deeper, like the forest is trying to reject this invasion of its territory by human beings. The soldiers, rifles slung across their backs, seem oblivious as they easily cut through openings in the thick foliage. They're amazingly fast as they slip past the low-hanging branches, clamber up rocks, leap over hollows, neatly avoiding all the thorns.

I scramble to keep up and not lose sight of them as they forge on ahead. They never check to see if I'm still there. It's like they're testing me, to see how much I can handle. I don't know why, but it almost feels like they're angry with me. They don't say a word, not just to me but to each other. They're totally focused on walking. Without a word between them, they take turns in the lead. The black barrels of the rifles on their backs swing back and forth in front of me, as regular as a metronome. The whole thing starts to get hypnotic after a while. My mind starts to wander, like it's slipping on ice, to somewhere else. But I still have to focus on keeping up with their relentless pace, so I march on, the sweat pouring off me now.

"We going too fast for you?" the brawny soldier finally turns around and asks. He's not out of breath at all.

"No, I'm fine," I tell him. "I'm hanging in there."

"You're young, and look like you're in good shape," the tall one comments without looking around.

"We know this path real well, so sometimes we speed up too

much," the brawny one explains. "So tell me if we're going too fast. Don't be shy, okay? Just say the word and we'll slow down. But understand we don't want to go any slower than we have to. You know what I'm saying?"

"I'll let you know if I can't keep up," I tell him, forcing myself not to breathe too hard, so they won't have any idea how tired this is making me. "Do we have far to go?"

"No, not really," the tall one answers.

"We're almost there," the other one adds.

I'm not sure I really believe him. Like they said, time's not much of a factor here.

So we walk on for a while without talking, at a less blistering pace than before. It seems like they've finished testing me.

"Are there any poisonous snakes in this forest?" I ask, since it's been worrying me.

"Poisonous snakes, eh?" the tall one with the glasses says without turning around. He never turns around when he talks, always facing forward like something absolutely critical's about to leap out in front of us at any moment. "I never thought about it."

"Could be," the brawny one says, turning to look at me. "I haven't seen any, but there might be some. Not that it matters even if there are."

"What we're trying to say," the tall one adds casually, "is that the forest isn't out to harm you."

"So you don't need to worry about snakes or anything," the brawny one says. "Feel better now?"

"Yes," I reply.

"No *other* here—poisonous snakes or mushrooms, venomous spiders or insects—is going to do you any harm," the tall soldier says, as always without turning around.

"*Other*?" I ask. I can't get a mental picture of what he means. I must be tired.

"An *other*, no *other* thing," he says. "No thing's going to harm you here. We're in the deepest part of the forest, after all. And no one—not even yourself—is going to hurt you."

I try to figure out what he means. But what with the exhaustion, sweat, and hypnotic effect of this repetitive journey through the woods, my brain can't form a coherent thought.

"When we were soldiers they used to force us to practice ripping open the enemy's stomach with a bayonet," the brawny one says. "You know the best way to stab someone with a bayonet?"

"No," I reply.

"Well, first you stab your bayonet deep into his belly, then you twist it sideways. That rips the guts to ribbons. Then the guy dies a horrible, slow, painful death. But if you just stab without twisting, then your enemy can jump up and rip *your* guts to shreds. That's the kind of world we were in."

Guts. Oshima told me once that intestines are a metaphor for a labyrinth. My head's full of all kinds of thoughts, all intertwined and tangled. I can't tell the difference between one thing and another.

"Do you know why people have to do such cruel things like that to other people?" the tall soldier asks.

"I have no idea," I reply.

"Neither do I," he says. "I don't care who the enemy is—Chinese soldiers, Russians, Americans. I never wanted to rip open their guts. But that's the kind of world we lived in, and that's why we ran away. Don't get me wrong, the two of us weren't cowards. We were actually pretty good soldiers. We just couldn't put up with that rush to violence. I don't imagine you're a coward, either."

"I really don't know," I answer honestly. "But I've always tried to get stronger."

"That's very important," the brawny one says, turning in my direction again. "*Very* important—to do your best to get stronger."

"I can tell you're pretty strong," the tall one says. "Most kids your age wouldn't make it this far."

"Yeah, it is pretty impressive," the brawny one pipes in.

The two of them come to a halt at this point. The tall soldier takes off his glasses, rubs the sides of his nose a couple of times, then puts his glasses on again. Neither one's out of breath or has even worked up a sweat.

"Thirsty?" the tall one asks me.

"A little," I reply. Actually, my canteen gone along with my day-pack, I'm dying of thirst. He unhooks the canteen from his waist and hands it to me. I take a few gulps of the lukewarm water. The liquid quenches every pore of my body. I wipe the mouth of the canteen off and hand it back. "Thanks," I say. The tall soldier nods silently.

"We've reached the ridge," the brawny soldier says.

"We're going to go straight to the bottom without stopping, so watch your footing," the tall one says.

I follow them carefully down the tricky, slippery slope. We get about halfway down, then turn a corner and cut through some trees, and all of a sudden a world opens up below us. The two soldiers stop, and turn around to look at me. They don't say a thing, but their eyes speak volumes. *This is the place*, they're telling me. *The place you're going to enter*. I stand there with them and gaze out at that world.

The whole place is a basin neatly carved out of the natural contours of the land. How many people might be living there I have no idea, but there can't be many—the place isn't big enough. There're a couple of roads, with buildings here and there along either side. Small roads, and equally small buildings. Nobody's out on the roads. The buildings are all expressionless, built less for beauty than to withstand the elements. The place is too small to be called a *town*. There aren't any shops as far as I can tell. No signs or bulletin boards. It's like a bunch of buildings, all the same size and shape, just happened to come together to make up a little community. None of the buildings have gardens, and not a single tree lines the roads. Like with the forest all around there's no need for any extra plants or trees.

A faint breeze is cutting through the woods, making the leaves of the trees around me tremble. That anonymous rustling forms ripples on the folds of my mind. I rest a hand against a tree trunk and close my eyes. Those ripples seem to be a sign, a signal of some sort, but it's like a foreign language I can't decipher. I give up, open my eyes, and gaze out again at this brand-new world before me. Standing there halfway down the slope, staring down at this place with two soldiers, I feel those ripples shifting inside me. These signs reconfigure themselves, the metaphors transform, and I'm drifting away, away from myself. I'm a butterfly, flitting along the edges of creation. Beyond the edge of the world there's a space where emptiness and substance neatly overlap, where past and future form a continuous, endless loop. And hovering about there are signs no one has ever read, chords no one has ever heard.

I try to calm my ragged breathing. My heart still isn't back in one piece, but at least I'm not afraid.

Without a word the soldiers start walking again, and silently I follow along. As we go farther down the slope, the town draws closer. I see a small stream running alongside a road, with a stone wall as an embankment. The beautiful clear water gurgles pleasantly. Everything here is simple, and cozy. Slim poles with wires strung between them dot the area, which means they must have electricity. Electricity? Out here?

The place is surrounded by a high, green ridge. The sky's still a mass of gray clouds. The soldiers and I walk down the road but don't pass a single person. Everything's completely still, not a sound to be heard. Maybe they're all shut up inside their homes, holding their breath, waiting for us to go.

My companions take me to one of the dwellings. Strange thing is, it's the same size and shape as Oshima's cabin. Like one was the model for the other. There's a porch out front, and a chair. The building has a flat roof with a stovepipe sticking out the top. There's a plain single bed in the bedroom, all neatly made up. The only differences are that the bedroom and living room are separate from each other, and there's a toilet inside and the place has electricity. There's even a fridge in the kitchen, a small, old-fashioned model. A light hangs down from the ceiling. And there's a TV. *A TV?*

"For the time being, you're supposed to stay here till you get settled," the brawny soldier says. "It won't be for that long. *For the time being.*"

"Like I said before, time isn't much of a factor here," the tall one says.

The other one nods in agreement. "Not a factor at all."

"Where could the electricity be coming from?"

They look at each other.

"There's a small wind-power station farther on in the forest," the tall one explains. "The wind's always blowing there. Gotta have electricity, right?"

"No electricity and you can't use the fridge," the brawny one says. "No fridge and you can't keep food for long."

"You'd manage somehow without it," the tall one says. "Though it sure is a nice thing to have."

"If you get hungry," the brawny one adds, "help yourself to whatever's in the fridge. There isn't much, I'm afraid."

"There's no meat here, no fish, coffee, or liquor," the tall one says. "It's hard at first, but you'll get used to it."

"But you do have eggs and cheese and milk," the brawny soldier says. "Gotta have your protein, right?"

"They don't make those other things here," the tall one explains, "so you have to go somewhere else to get them. And swap something for them."

"Somewhere *else?*"

The tall one nods. "That's right. We're not cut off from the world here. There *is* a somewhere else. It might take a while, but you'll understand."

"Someone will be along in the evening to make dinner for you," the brawny soldier says. "If you get bored before then, you can watch TV."

"They have shows on the TV?"

"Well, I don't know what's on," the tall one replies, a bit flustered. He tilts his head and looks at his companion.

His brawny friend tilts his head too, a doubtful look on his face. "To be honest with you, I don't know much about TV. I've never watched it."

"They put the TV there for people who've just come here," the tall one says.

"But you should be able to watch *something*," the brawny one says.

"Just rest up for a while," the tall one says. "We have to get back to our post."

"Thanks for bringing me here."

"No problem," the brawny one says. "You have much stronger legs than the others we've brought here. Lots of people can't keep up. Some we even have to carry on our backs. So you were one of the easy ones."

"If memory serves," the tall soldier says, "you said there's somebody you want to see here."

"That's right."

"I'm sure you'll meet whoever that is before long," he says, nodding a couple of times for emphasis. "It's a small world here."

"I hope you get used to it soon," the brawny soldier says.

"Once you get used to it, the rest is easy," the tall soldier adds.

"I really appreciate it."

The two of them stand at attention and salute, then shoulder their rifles and leave, walking quickly down the road back toward their post. They must guard the entrance there day and night.

I go to the kitchen and check out what's in the fridge. There are some tomatoes, a chunk of cheese, eggs, carrots, turnips even, and a large porcelain jug of milk. Butter, too. A loaf of bread's on a shelf, and I tear off a piece and taste it. A little hard, but not bad.

The kitchen has a sink and a faucet. I turn the faucet and water comes out, clear and cold. Since they have electricity, they must pump water up from a well. I fill up a cup and drink it.

I go over to the window and look outside. The sky's still covered with gray clouds, though it doesn't look like it's going to rain anytime soon. I stare out the window a long time but still don't see any sign of other people. It's like the town's dead. Or else for some reason everybody's trying to avoid me.

I walk away from the window and sit down in a hard, straight-backed wooden chair. There're three chairs altogether, and a square dining table that's been varnished a number of times. Nothing at all's hanging on the plaster walls, no paintings, no photos, not even a calendar. Just pure white walls. A single bulb dangles from the ceiling, with a simple glass shade that's discolored by heat.

The room has been nicely cleaned. I run my finger over the table-top and the window frame and there's no dust at all. The windows, too, are sparkling clean. The pots, plates, and various utensils in the kitchen aren't new, but it's clear they've been well cared for and are all clean. Next to the work space in the kitchen are two old electric hot plates. I switch one of them on, and right away the coil turns red.

There's an old color TV in a heavy wooden cabinet that I'm guessing is fifteen or twenty years old. There's no remote control. It looks like something that was thrown away and then retrieved. Which could be said of all the electric items, all of which look like they were saved from the trash. Not that they were dirty or anything, or didn't work, just that they're all faded and out-of-date.

I turn on the switch on the TV, and an old movie's playing, *The Sound of Music*. My teacher took us all to see it on a wide-screen movie theater when I was in grade school. No adults were around to take me to the theater, so it's one of the few movies I saw when I was a kid. On TV they're at the part where the difficult, uptight father, Captain von Trapp, has gone to Vienna on business, and Maria, the children's tutor, takes them on an outing in the mountains. They all sit together on the grass and she plays guitar and they sing a couple of harmless songs. It's a famous scene. I plant myself in front of the TV, glued to the movie. Just like when I first saw it, I wonder how things would've turned out if I'd had someone like Maria with me. Needless to say, nobody like that ever showed up in my life.

I flash back to reality. Why in the world do I have to watch *The Sound of Music* right now? Why *that* movie? Maybe the people here have hooked up some sort of satellite dish and can get the signal from a station. Or is it a videotape being played somewhere and shown on this set? I'd guess it's a tape, because when I change channels the other ones show only sandstorms. A vicious sandstorm's exactly what it reminds me of, the gravelly white, inorganic static.

They're singing "Edelweiss" when I turn off the set. Quiet returns to the room. I'm thirsty, so I go to the kitchen and drink some milk from the jug. The milk's thick and fresh, and tastes a hundred times better than those packs of milk you buy in convenience stores. As I down glass after glass, I suddenly remember the scene in François Truffaut's film *400 Blows* where Antoine runs away from home and, early one morning, gets hungry and steals a bottle of milk that's been delivered to somebody's front door, then drinks it as he makes his getaway. It's a large bottle, so it takes him a while to drink it all down. A sad, distressing scene—though it's hard to believe that just drinking milk could be so sad. That's another one of the few movies from my childhood. I was in fifth grade, and the title caught my attention, so I took the train to Ikebukuro alone, saw the film, then rode the train back. As soon as I got out of the theater, I bought some milk and drank it. I couldn't help it.

After drinking all that milk now I get sleepy. An overwhelming, almost nauseous sleepiness comes over me. My thoughts slow down, and finally stop, like a train pulling into a station, and I can't think straight anymore, like the core of my body's coagulating. I walk into the bedroom, make a tangle out of getting my pants and shoes off, then slump down on the bed, bury my face in the pillow, and close my eyes. The pillow smells like the sunlight, a precious smell. I quietly breathe it in, breathe it out, and fall asleep before I know it.

When I wake up it's dark all around. I open my eyes and try to figure out where I am. Two soldiers led me through the forest to a small town next to a stream, right? Slowly my memory's coming back. The scene comes into focus, and I hear a familiar melody. "Edelweiss." Out in the kitchen there's a faint, intimate clattering of pots and pans. Light spills into the bedroom through a crack in the door, forming a yellow line on the floor. Kind of an old-fashioned, powdery yellow light.

I try to get out of bed but my body's numb all over. I take a deep breath and look up at the ceiling. I hear the sound of plates, of someone scurrying busily across the floor, preparing a meal for me, I imagine. I'm finally able to stand up. Though it takes a while, I struggle into my pants, my socks and shoes. Quietly I grab the knob and open the door.

A young girl's in the kitchen cooking. Her back to me, she's leaning over a pot, tasting the food with a spoon, but when she hears the door open she looks up and turns around. It's her. The same girl who visited my room in the library and gazed at the painting on the wall. The fifteen-year-old Miss Saeki. She's wearing the same clothes, a long-sleeved, light blue dress. The only thing different is now her hair's pinned back. She gives me a small, warm smile, and a powerful emotion overwhelms me, like the whole world's been turned upside down, like everything tangible had fallen apart but has now been put back together. But this girl is no illusion, certainly no ghost. She's a living, breathing young girl, someone you can touch, standing in a real kitchen at twilight, cooking me a real meal. Her small breasts jut beneath her dress, her neck as white as porcelain fresh from the kiln. It's all real.

"Oh, you're awake?" she asks.

No voice comes out of me. I'm still trying to pull myself together.

"You seem to have slept very well," she says. She turns back to tasting the dish. "If you didn't wake up I was going to put the meal on the table and leave."

"I wasn't planning to sleep so much," I finally manage to say.

"You came all the way through the forest," she says, "so you must be hungry."

"I'm not sure. But I think I am." I want to reach out and see if I can actually touch her. But I can't. I just stand there, drinking her in. I listen to the sounds she makes as she bustles around the kitchen.

She ladles hot stew onto a plain white plate and carries it over to the table. There's a bowl of salad, too, tomatoes and greens, and a large loaf of bread. There are potatoes and carrots in the stew. The fragrance brings back fond memories. I breathe it all in deeply and realize I'm starving. I have to eat something. As I pick up a scuffed fork and spoon and begin eating, the girl sits in a chair to the side and watches me with a serious expression on her face, like watching me eat is a critical part of her job. Occasionally she brushes back her hair.

"They told me you're fifteen," she says.

"That's right," I reply, buttering a slice of bread. "I just turned fifteen."

"I'm fifteen too," she says.

I nod. *I know that*, I almost say. But it's too soon to say that. I take another bite.

"I'll be making the meals here for a while," she says. "The cleaning and washing as well. There are clothes in the dresser in the bedroom, so feel free to help yourself. You can just put your laundry in the basket and I'll take care of it."

"Somebody gave you these jobs?"

She looks fixedly at me but doesn't answer. It's like my question's taken a wrong turn and been sucked into some nameless space.

"What's your name?" I ask, trying a different tack.

She shakes her head slightly. "I don't have a name. We don't have names here."

"But if you don't have a name, how can I call you?"

"There's no need to call me," she says. "If you need me, I'll be here."

"I guess I don't need my name here, either."

She nods. "You're *you*, you see, and nobody else. You *are* you, right?"

"I guess so," I say. Though I'm not so sure. Am I really me?

All the while she's steadily gazing at me.

"Do you remember the library?" I come right out and ask her.

"The library?" She shakes her head. "No. . . . There's a library far away, but not here."

"There's a library?"

"Yes, but there aren't any books in it."

"If there aren't any books, then what *is* there?"

She tilts her head but doesn't respond. Again my question's taken a wrong turn and vanished.

"Have you ever been there?"

"A long time ago," she says.

"But it's not for reading books?"

She nods. "There aren't any books there."

I eat in silence for a time. The stew, the salad, the bread. She doesn't say anything either, just observes me with that serious look.

"How was the food?" she asks after I finish eating.

"It was really good."

"Even without any meat or fish?"

I point to the empty plate. "Well, I didn't leave anything, right?"

"I made it."

"It was really good," I repeat. It's the truth.

Being with her I feel a pain, like a frozen knife stuck in my chest. An awful pain, but the funny thing is I'm thankful for it. It's like that frozen pain and my very existence are one. The pain is an anchor, mooring me *here*. The girl stands up to boil some water and make tea. While I'm sitting at the table drinking it, she carries the dirty dishes out to the kitchen and starts washing them. I watch her do all this. I want to say something, but when I'm with her words no longer function as they're supposed to. Or maybe the meaning that ties them together has vanished? I stare at my hands and think of the dogwood outside the window, glinting in the moonlight. That's where the blade that's stabbing me in the heart is.

"Will I see you again?" I ask.

"Of course," the girl replies. "Like I said before, if you need me, I'll be here."

"You're not going to suddenly disappear?"

She doesn't say anything, just gazes at me with a strange look on her face, like *Where-do-you-think-I'd-go?*

"I've met you before," I venture. "In another land, in another library."

"If you say so," she says, touching her hair to check that it's still pinned back. Her voice is expressionless, like she's trying to let me know the topic doesn't interest her.

"I think I've come here to meet you one more time. You, and one other woman."

She looks up and nods seriously. "Going through the deep woods to get here."

"That's right. I had to see you and that other woman again."

"And you've met me."

I nod.

"It's like I told you," she says. "If you need me, I'll be here."

After she washes up, she puts the pots and plates back on the shelf and drapes a canvas bag across her shoulder. "I'll be back tomorrow morning," she tells me. "I hope you get used to being here soon."

I stand at the door and watch as she vanishes into the gloom. I'm alone again in the little cabin, inside a closed circle. Time isn't a factor here. Nobody here has a name. She'll be here as long as I need her. She's fifteen here. Eternally fifteen, I imagine. But what's going to happen to *me*? Am I going to stay fifteen here? Is age, too, not a factor here?

I stand in the doorway long after she's disappeared, gazing vacantly at the scenery outside. There's no moon or stars in the sky. Lights are on in a few other buildings, spilling out of the windows. The same antique, yellowish light that illuminates this room. But I still can't see anybody else. Just the lights. Dark shadows widen their grip on the world outside. Farther in the distance, blacker than the darkness, the ridge rises up, and the forest surrounding this town like a wall.

Chapter 46

After Nakata's death, Hoshino couldn't pull himself away from the apartment. With the entrance stone there, something might happen, and when it *did* he wanted to be close enough that he could react in time. Watching over the stone had been Nakata's job, and now it was his. He set the AC in Nakata's room to the lowest possible temperature and turned it on full blast, checking that the windows were shut tight. The air in the room had that special solidity found only in a room with a corpse in it. "Not too cold for you, I hope?" he said to Nakata, who naturally didn't have an opinion one way or the other.

Hoshino plopped down on the living-room sofa, trying to pass the time. He didn't feel like listening to music or reading. Twilight came on, the room by degrees turning dark, but he didn't even get up to switch on the light. He felt completely drained, and once ensconced on the sofa couldn't rouse himself enough to get up. Time came slowly and passed slowly, so leisurely that at times he could swear it had stealthily doubled back on itself.

When his own grandfather died, he thought, it was hard, but nothing like this. He'd suffered through a long illness, and they all knew it was just a matter of time. So when he did die, they were prepared. It makes a big difference whether or not you have a chance to steel yourself for the inevitable. But that's not the only difference, Hoshino concluded. There was something about Nakata's death that forced him to think long and hard.

Suddenly hungry, he went to the kitchen, defrosted some fried rice in the microwave, and ate half of it along with a beer. Afterward he went back to check on Nakata. Maybe he'd come back to life, he thought. But no, the old man was still dead. The room was like a walk-in freezer, so cold you could store ice cream in there.

Spending a night in the same house as a corpse was a first, and Hoshino couldn't settle down. Not that he was scared or anything, he told himself. It didn't make his flesh crawl. He just didn't know how he should act with a dead man beside him. The flow of time is so different for the dead and the living. Same with sounds. That's why I can't calm down, he decided. But what can you do? Mr. Nakata's already gone over to the world of the dead, and I'm still in the land of the living. Of course there's going be a gap. He got up from the sofa and sat down next to the stone. He started stroking it with his palms, like he was petting a cat.

"What the heck am I supposed to do?" he asked the stone. "I want to turn Mr. Nakata over to somebody who'll take care of him, but until I take care of you, I can't. You want to clue me in?"

But there was no reply. For the moment the stone was just a stone, and Hoshino understood this. He could ask till he was blue in the face but couldn't expect a response. Even so, he sat beside the stone, rubbing it. He tossed out a couple questions, made an appeal to logic, and did his best to win the sympathy vote. Though he knew it was pointless, he couldn't think of an alternative. Mr. Nakata had sat here all the time talking to the stone, so why shouldn't he?

Still, talking to a stone, trying to get it to feel your pain—that's pretty pathetic, he thought. I mean, isn't that where they get that expression? *As heartless as a stone?*

He stood up, thinking he'd watch the news on TV, but thought better of it and sat down again beside the stone. Silence is probably best for now, he decided. Got to listen carefully, wait for whatever it is that's going to happen. "But waiting around isn't exactly my thing," Hoshino said to the stone. Come to think of it, I've always been the impatient type, and man have I paid for it! Always leaping before I look, always screwing things up. You're as antsy as a cat in heat, my grandpa used to tell me. But now I've got to sit tight and wait. Gut it out!

Everything was quiet except for the groan of the AC going full blast next door. The clock showed nine, then ten, but nothing happened. Time passed, the night grew deeper, nothing else. Hoshino dragged his blankets into the living room, lay down on the sofa, and pulled them over him. He figured that it was better, even asleep, to be near the stone in case something happened. He turned off the light and shut his eyes.

"Hey, stone! I'm going to sleep now," he called out. "We'll talk again tomorrow. It's been a long day, and I need some shut-eye." Man, he thought, was that an understatement. Long did not begin to describe it. "Hey, Gramps!" he called out more loudly. "Mr. Nakata? You hear me?" No reply.

Hoshino sighed, closed his eyes, adjusted his pillow, and fell asleep. He slept the whole night without a break, without a single dream. In the next room, Nakata slept his own deep, dreamless, stone-hard sleep.

As soon as he got up, just past seven the next morning, Hoshino went right in to check on Nakata. As before, the AC was roaring full blast, blowing cold air into the room. And in the midst of that chilled room, Nakata was still dead. Compared to the night before, death seemed to have a tighter grip on him. His skin had grown ashen, his closed eyes more fixed and solemn. He wasn't about to come back to life, suddenly sit up, and say, *My apologies, Mr. Hoshino. Nakata just fell asleep. I'm sorry. No need to worry, I'll take it from here*—and then deal with the stone. That was never going to happen. Nakata's checked out for good, Hoshino thought, and that's a fact.

He started shivering from the cold, so he stepped out and shut the door, then went into the kitchen, brewed some coffee in the coffeemaker and drank two cups, made some toast and ate it with butter and jam. After eating he sat in the kitchen, smoked a couple of cigarettes, and gazed out the window. The clouds had blown away sometime during the night, leaving an unbroken sunny summer sky. The stone was in its customary spot next to the sofa. It didn't sleep a wink, didn't wake up, just crouched there, unmoving, the entire night. He tried picking it up and easily lifted it.

"Hey there," Hoshino said in a cheerful voice, "it's me. Your old pal Hoshino, remember? Looks like it's just you and me today."

The stone was—not unexpectedly—speechless.

"Ah, that's okay. Doesn't matter if you don't remember. We have lots of time to get to know each other—no need to rush."

He sat down beside the stone, started rubbing it, and wondered what sort of things you might talk about with a stone. Having a conversation with a stone was a first and he couldn't think of any appropriate topics. Best to avoid anything difficult this early in the morning, he figured. The day was long, and whatever popped into his head would be fine.

He gave it some thought and chose a favorite subject: girls. He reviewed each and every girl he'd ever slept with. If he stuck to the ones whose names he remembered, it didn't add up to all that many. He counted them off on his fingers. Six, all told. If I add the ones whose names I don't know, he thought, there'd be a lot more, but we'll put those on hold.

"I guess it's pretty pointless talking to a stone about girls I've slept with," he said. "And I suppose you aren't exactly thrilled to hear all about my exploits first thing in the morning. But I can't think of anything else, okay? Who knows, maybe some lighter topic'll do you some good for a change. FYI and all that."

Hoshino related some episodes in as much detail as he could recall. The first was when he was in high school, back when he was into motorcycles and getting into trouble. The girl was three years older than him and worked in a little bar in Gifu City. They pretty much lived together for a while. The girl was serious about the relationship, said she couldn't live without him. She phoned my parents, he remembered, but they were none too happy about it, and the whole thing was getting too intense, so once I graduated from high school I joined the Self-Defense Force. Right after I joined up I got stationed at a base in Yamanashi Prefecture, and the relationship fizzled out. I never saw her again.

"I guess lazy's my middle name," Hoshino explained to the stone. "And when things get sticky I tend to head for the door. Not to brag or anything, but I'm pretty quick on my feet. I've never followed anything to the bitter end. Which is sort of a problem, I suppose."

The second girl he met near the base in Yamanashi. He was off duty one day and helped her fix a flat on her Suzuki Alto. She was a year older than him and attending nursing school.

"She was a nice kid," Hoshino said to the stone. "Big breasts, a very warm person. And man, did she like to get it on! I was only nineteen, and we used to spend every day between the sheets. Problem was, she was jealous like you wouldn't believe. If I didn't see her on my days off she'd give me the third degree, ask where I went, what I did, who I was with. I told her the truth, but that didn't satisfy her. That's why we broke up. We were together for about a year, I guess. . . . I don't know how you are, but I can't stand anyone getting on my case. I feel like I can't breathe, and it makes me depressed. So I ran away. The cool thing about the SDF is you can always hole up on base till the whole thing blows over. And there's nothing anybody can do about it. If you want to dump a girl with no problems, going into the SDF's your ticket. Good thing to remember. But it's not all roses—not with digging foxholes and piling up sandbags and crap."

The more he talked, the more Hoshino realized how pointless his life had been. Four of the six girls he'd gone out with had been nice. (The other two, if you looked at it objectively, had personality problems, he decided.) Most of them had treated him pretty well. No drop-dead beauties among them, though each was cute in her own way, and let him have sex whenever he felt like it. Never complained if he skipped foreplay and went straight to the main course. They fixed meals for him on his days off, bought him presents on his birthday, lent him money when he was a little short before payday—not that he ever remembered paying them back—and they never demanded anything in return. All this, and I was an ungrateful bastard, he concluded. I took everything for granted.

To his credit, he'd never cheated on any of them. But let them complain a little, try to win an argument, show a bit of jealousy, urge him to save some money, get a little overwrought, or express even a hint of worry about the future, and he was out of there. He always figured the most important thing about girls was to avoid any sticky situations, so all it took was one tiny wave to rock the boat and he was gone. He'd find a new girl and start over. He was sure most people did the same.

"If I were a girl," he said to the stone, "and was going out with a self-centered bastard like me, I'd blow my stack. I'm sure of it, now that I look back on it. I don't know how they all put up with me for so long. It's amazing." He lit a Marlboro and, slowly exhaling smoke, rubbed the stone with one hand. "Am I right or what? I'm not so good-looking, no great shakes in bed. Don't have much money. Not such a great personality, not too bright. A lot of negatives here. Son of a poor farmer from the sticks, a no-good ex-soldier-turned-truck-driver. When I think back on it, though, I was really lucky when it came to girls. I wasn't very popular, but I always had a girlfriend. Someone who let me sleep with her, who fed me, lent me money. But you know something? Good things don't last forever. I feel that more and more as time goes by. It's like somebody's saying, *Hey, Hoshino, someday you're gonna have to pay up.*"

He rubbed the stone while relating his amorous adventures. He'd gotten so used to rubbing it that he didn't want to stop. At noon a school chime rang out, and he went to the kitchen to make a bowl of udon, adding some scallions along with a raw egg. After lunch he listened again to the *Archduke* Trio.

"Hey, stone," he called out right after the first movement ended. "Pretty nice music, huh? Really makes you feel like your heart's opening up, don't you think?"

The stone was silent.

He had no idea if the stone was listening, to the music or to him, but he forged ahead anyway. "Like I was saying this morning, I've done some awful things in my life. I was pretty self-centered. And it's too late to erase it all now, you know? But when I listen to this music it's like Beethoven's right here talking to me, telling me something like, *It's okay, Hoshino, don't worry about it. That's life. I've done some pretty awful things in my life too. Not much you can do about it. Things happen. You just got to hang in there.* Beethoven being the guy he was, he's not about to say anything like that. But I'm still picking up that vibe from his music, like that's what it's saying to me. Can you feel it?"

The stone was mute.

"Whatever," Hoshino said. "That's just my opinion. I'll shut up so we can listen."

When he looked outside at two, a fat black cat was sitting on the railing on the veranda, gazing in at the apartment. Bored, Hoshino opened the window and called out, "Hey there, kitty. Nice day, isn't it?"

"Yes, indeed, it *is* a fine day, Mr. Hoshino," the cat replied.

"Gimme a break," Hoshino said, shaking his head.

The Boy Named Crow

The boy named Crow flew in large, languid circles above the forest. After inscribing one, he'd fly off to another spot and carefully begin another, identical circle, each invisible circle following another in the air only to vanish. Like a reconnaissance plane, he scanned the forest below him, looking for someone he couldn't seem to locate. Like a huge ocean, the forest undulated beneath him and spread to the horizon in a thick, anonymous cloak of interlaced branches. The sky was covered with gray clouds, and there was neither wind nor sunlight. At this point the boy named Crow had to be the loneliest bird in the world, but he was too busy to think about that now.

He finally spotted an opening in the sea of trees below and shot straight down through it to an open piece of ground. The light shone on a small patch of ground that was marked with grass. In one corner of the clearing was a large round rock and a man in a bright red sweat suit and a black silk hat was sitting on it. He wore thick-soled hiking boots, and a khaki-colored bag lay on the ground beside him. A strange getup, though the boy named Crow didn't mind. This was who he was after. What the man had on was of little consequence.

The man looked up at the sudden flapping of wings and saw Crow land on a large branch. "Hey," he said cheerfully.

The boy named Crow didn't make any reply. Resting on the branch, he gazed, unblinking, expressionless, at the man. Occasionally he'd incline his head to one side.

"I know who you are," the man said. He doffed his hat and put it back on. "I had a feeling you'd be coming here before long." He cleared his throat, frowned, and spat on the ground, then stamped the spit into the dirt with his boot.

"I was just resting, and feeling a bit bored with no one to talk to. How about coming over here? We can have a nice little talk. What do you say? I've never seen you before, but that doesn't mean we're total strangers."

The boy named Crow kept his mouth shut, holding his wings close in against himself.

The man in the silk hat lightly shook his head. "Ah, I see. You can't speak, can you? No matter. I'll do the talking, if you don't mind. I know what you're going to do, even if you don't say a word. You don't want me to go any further, do you? It's so obvious I can predict what'll happen. You don't want me to go any further, but that's exactly what I want to do. Because it's a golden opportunity I can't let slip through my fingers—a once-in-a-lifetime opportunity."

He gave the ankle of his hiking boots a good slap. "To leap to the conclusion here, you won't be able to stop me. You aren't qualified. Let's say I play my flute, what's going to happen? You won't be able to come any closer to me. That's the power of my flute. You might not know this, but it's a unique kind of flute, not just some ordinary, every-day instrument. And actually I've got quite a few here in my bag."

The man reached out and carefully patted the bag, then looked up again at the boy named Crow perched on his branch. "I made this flute out of the souls of cats I've collected. Cut out the souls of cats while they were still alive and made them into this flute. I felt sorry for the cats, of course, cutting them up like that, but I couldn't help it. This flute is beyond any world's standards of good and evil, love or hatred. Making these flutes has been my longtime calling, and I've always done a decent job of fulfilling my role and doing my bit. Nothing to be ashamed of. I got married, had children, and made more than enough flutes. So I'm not going to make any more. Just between you and me, I'm thinking of taking all the flutes I've made and creating a much larger, far more powerful flute out of them—a supersize flute that becomes a system unto itself. Right now I'm heading to a place where I can construct that kind of flute. I'm not the one who decides whether that flute turns out to be good or evil, and neither are you. It all depends on when and where I am. In that sense I'm a man totally without prejudices, like history or the weather—completely unbiased. And since I am, I can transform into a kind of system."

He removed his silk hat, rubbed the thinning hair on top of his head, put the hat back on, and quickly adjusted the brim. "Once I play this flute, getting rid of you will be a snap. The thing is, I don't feel like playing it right now. It takes a lot out of me, and I don't want to waste any strength. I'll need all of it later on. But whether I play the flute or not, you can't stop me. That should be obvious."

The man cleared his throat once more, and rubbed the slight swell of his belly. "Do you know what limbo is? It's the neutral point between life and death. A kind of sad, gloomy place. Where I am now, in other words—this forest. I died, at my own bidding, but haven't gone on to the next world. I'm a soul in transition, and a soul in transition is formless. I've merely adopted this form for the time being. That's why you can't hurt me. You follow me? Even if I were to bleed all over the place, it's not real blood. Even if I were to suffer horribly, it's not real suffering. The only one who could wipe me out right now is someone who's qualified to do so. And—sad to say—you don't fit the bill. You're nothing more than an immature, mediocre illusion. No matter how determined you may be, eliminating me's impossible for the likes of you." The man looked at the boy named Crow and beamed. "How 'bout it? Want to give it a try?"

As if that was the signal he'd been waiting for, the boy named Crow spread his wings wide, leaped off the branch, and darted straight at him. He seized the man's chest with both talons, drew his head back, and brought his beak down on the man's right eye, pecking away fiendishly like he was hacking away with a pickax, his jet black wings flapping noisily all the while. The man put up no resistance, didn't lift a finger to protect himself. He didn't cry out, either. Instead, he laughed out loud. His hat fell to the ground, and his eyeball was soon shredded and hanging from its socket. The boy named Crow tenaciously attacked the other eye now. Once both eyes were replaced by vacant cavities, he turned immediately to the man's face, pecking away, slashing it all over. His face was soon cut to ribbons, pieces of skin flying off, blood spurting out, nothing more than a lump of reddish flesh. Crow next attacked the top of his head, where the hair was thinnest, and still the man kept on laughing. The more vicious the attack became, the louder he laughed, as if the whole situation was so hilarious he couldn't control himself.

The man never took his eyes—now vacant sockets—off Crow, and in between laughs managed to choke out a few words. "See, what'd I tell you? Don't make me laugh. You can try all you want, but it's not going to hurt me. You're not qualified to do that. You're just a flimsy illusion, a cheap echo. It's useless, no matter what you do. Don't you get it?"

The boy named Crow stabbed at the mouth these words had come from. His huge wings ceaselessly beat at the air, a few shiny black feathers coming loose, swirling in the air like fragments of a soul. Crow tore at the man's tongue, grabbed it with his beak, and yanked with all his might. It was long and hugely thick, and once it was pulled out from deep within the man's throat, it squirmed like a gigantic mollusk, forming dark words. Without a tongue, however, not even this man could laugh anymore. He looked like he couldn't breathe, either, but still he held his sides and shook with soundless laughter. The boy named Crow listened, and this unheard laughter—as vacant and ominous as wind blowing over a far-off desert—never ceased. It sounded, in fact, very much like an otherworldly flute.

Chapter 47

I wake up just after dawn, boil water on the electric hot plate, and make some tea. I sit down beside the window to see what, if anything, is going on outside. Everything is dead quiet, with no sign of anybody on the street. Even the birds seem reluctant to launch into their usual morning chorus. The hills to the east are barely edged in a faint light. The place is surrounded by high hills, which explains why dawn comes so late and twilight so early. I go over to the nightstand where my watch is to check the time, but the digital screen's a complete blank. When I push a few buttons at random, nothing happens. The batteries should still be good, but for some unfathomable reason the thing stopped while I was sleeping. I put the watch back on top of my pillow and rub my left wrist, where I normally wear it, with my right. *Not that time's much of a factor here.*

As I gaze at the vacant, birdless scene outside, I suddenly want to read a book—*any* book. As long as it's shaped like a book and has printing, it's fine by me. I just want to hold a book in my hands, turn the pages, scan the words with my eyes. Only one problem—there isn't a book in sight. In fact, it's like printing hasn't been invented here. I quickly look around the room, and sure enough, there's nothing at all with any writing on it.

I open the chest of drawers in the bedroom to see what kind of clothes are inside. Everything's neatly folded. None of the clothes are new. The colors are faded, the material soft from countless washings. Still, they look clean. There's round-neck shirts, underwear, socks, cotton shirts with collars, and cotton trousers. Not a perfect fit, but pretty much my size. All the clothes are perfectly plain and design-free, like the whole idea of clothes with patterns never existed. None of them have any makers' labels—so much for any writing there. I exchange my smelly T-shirt for a gray one from the drawer that smells like sunlight and soap.

A while later—how much later I couldn't say—the girl arrives. She taps lightly on the door and, without waiting for an answer, opens it. The door doesn't have any kind of lock. Her canvas bag is slung over her shoulder. The sky behind her is already light.

She goes straight to the kitchen and cooks some eggs in a small black frying pan. There's a pleasant sizzle as the eggs hit the hot oil, and the fresh cooking smells waft through the room. Meanwhile, she toasts some bread in a squat little toaster that looks like a prop from an old movie. Her clothes and hair are the same as the night before—a light blue dress, hair pinned back. Her skin is so smooth and beautiful, and her slim, porcelain-like arms glisten in the morning sun. Through the open window a tiny bee buzzes in, as if to make the world a little more complete. The girl carries the food over to the table, sits in a chair, and watches me eat the vegetable omelette and buttered toast and drink some herb tea. She doesn't eat or drink anything. The whole thing's a repeat of last night.

"Don't people here cook their own meals?" I ask her. "I was wondering because you're making meals for me."

"Some people make their own, others have somebody make meals for them," she replies. "Mostly, though, people here don't eat very much."

"Really?"

She nods. "*Sometimes* they eat. When they want to."

"You mean no one else eats as much as I do?"

"Can you get by without eating for one whole day?"

I shake my head.

"Folks here often go a whole day without eating, no problem. They actually forget to eat, sometimes for days at a time."

"I'm not used to things here yet, so I have to eat."

"I suppose so," she says. "That's why I'm cooking for you."

I look in her face. "How long will it take for me to get used to this place?"

"How long?" she parrots, and slowly shakes her head. "I have no idea. It's not a question of time. When that time comes, you'll already be used to it."

We're sitting across from each other, her hands neatly lined up on the table, palms down. Her ten little resolute fingers are there, real objects before me. Directly across from her, I catch each tiny flutter of her eyelashes, count each blink of her eyes, watch the strands of hair swaying over her forehead. I can't take my eyes off her.

"*That time?*" I say.

"It isn't like you'll cut something out of yourself and throw it away," she says. "We don't throw it away—we accept it, inside us."

"And I'll accept this inside of me?"

"That's right."

"And then?" I ask. "After I accept it, then what happens?"

She inclines her head slightly as she thinks, an utterly natural gesture. The strands of hair sway again. "Then you'll become completely yourself," she says.

"So you mean up till now I haven't been completely me?"

"You are totally yourself even now," she says, then thinks it over. "What I mean is a little different. But I can't explain it well."

"You can't understand until it actually happens?"

She nods.

When it gets too painful to watch her anymore, I close my eyes. Then I open them right away, to make sure she's still there. "Is it sort of a communal lifestyle here?"

She considers this. "Everyone does live together, and share certain things. Like the shower rooms, the electrical station, the market. There are certain simple, unspoken agreements in place, but nothing complicated. Nothing you need to think about, or even put into words. So there isn't anything I need to teach you about how things are done. The most important thing about life here is that people let themselves be absorbed into things. As long as you do that, there won't be any problems."

"What do you mean by absorbed?"

"It's like when you're in the forest, you become a seamless part of it. When you're in the rain, you're a part of the rain. When you're in the morning, you're a seamless part of the morning. When you're with me, you become a part of me."

"When you're with me, then, you're a seamless part of me?"

"That's true."

"What does it feel like? To be yourself and part of me at the same time?"

She looks straight at me and touches her hairpin. "It's very natural. Once you're used to it, it's quite simple. Like flying."

"You can fly?"

"Just an *example*," she says, and smiles. It's a smile without any deep or hidden meaning, a smile for the sake of smiling. "You can't know what flying feels like until you actually do it. It's the same."

"So it's a natural thing you don't even have to think about?"

She nods. "Yes, it's quite natural, calm, quiet, something you don't have to think about. It's seamless."

"Am I asking too many questions?"

"Not at all," she replies. "I only wish I could explain things better."

"Do you have memories?"

Again she shakes her head and rests her hands on the table, this time with the palms faceup. She glances at them expressionlessly.

"No, I don't. In a place where time isn't important, neither is memory. Of course I remember last night, coming here and making vegetable stew. And you ate it all, didn't you? The day before that I remember a bit of. But anything before that, I don't know. Time has been absorbed inside me, and I can't distinguish between one object and whatever's beside it."

"So memory isn't so important here?"

She beams. "That's right. Memory isn't so important here. The library handles memories."

After the girl leaves, I sit by the window holding my hand out in the morning sun, its shadow falling on the windowsill, a distinct five-finger outline. The bee stops buzzing around and quietly lands above the windowpane. It seems to have some serious thinking to do. And so do I.

When the sun is a little bit past its highest point, *she* comes to where I'm staying, knocks lightly, and opens the door. For a moment I can't tell who I'm looking at—the young girl or *her*. A slight shift in light, or the way the wind blows, is all it takes for her to change completely. It's like in one instant she transforms into the young girl, a moment later changing back into Miss Saeki. Not that this really takes place. The person in front of me is, without a doubt, Miss Saeki and no other.

"Hello," she says in a natural tone of voice, just like when we passed in the corridor of the library. She's wearing a long-sleeved navy blue blouse and a matching knee-length skirt, a thin silver necklace, and small pearl earrings—exactly as I'm used to seeing her. Her high heels make short, dry clicks as she steps onto the porch, a sound that's slightly out of place here. She stands gazing at me from the doorway, as if she's checking to see whether it's the real me or not. Of course it's the real me. Just like she's the real Miss Saeki.

"How about coming in for a cup of tea?" I say.

"I'd like that," she says. And, like she's finally worked up the nerve, she steps inside.

I go to the kitchen and turn on the stove to boil water, trying to get my breathing back to normal.

She sits down at the dining table in the same chair the girl had just been sitting in. "It feels like we're back in the library, doesn't it?" she says.

"Sure does," I agree. "Except for no coffee, and no Oshima."

"And not a book in sight," she says.

I make two cups of herbal tea and carry them out to the table, sitting across from her. Birds chirp outside the open window. The bee's still napping above the windowpane.

Miss Saeki's the first one to speak. "I want you to know it wasn't easy for me to come here. But I had to see you, and talk with you."

I nod. "I'm glad you came."

Her trademark smile plays around her lips. "There's something I have to tell you." Her smile's nearly identical to the young girl's, though with a bit more depth, a slight nuance that moves me.

She wraps her hands around the teacup. I'm gazing at the tiny pearl piercings in her ears. She's thinking, and it's taking her longer than usual.

"I burned up all my memories," she says, deliberately choosing her words. "They went up in smoke and disappeared into the air. So I won't be able to remember things for very long. All sorts of things—including my time with you. That's why I wanted to see you and talk with you as soon as I could. While I can still remember."

I crane my neck and look up at the bee above the window, its little black shadow a single dot on the sill.

"The most important thing," she says quietly, "is you've got to get out of here. As fast as you can. Leave here, go through the woods, and back to the life you left. The entrance is going to close soon. Promise me you will."

I shake my head. "You don't understand this, Miss Saeki, but I don't have any world to go back to. No one's ever really loved me, or wanted me, my entire life. I don't know who to count on other than myself. For me, the idea of a *life I left* is meaningless."

"But you still have to go back."

"Even if there's nothing there? Even if nobody cares if I'm there or not?"

"That's not why," she says. "It's what *I* want. For you to be there."

"But *you're* not there, are you?"

She looks down at her hands clasping the teacup. "No, I'm not. I'm not there anymore."

"What do you want from me if I do go back?"

"Just one thing," she says, raising her head and looking me straight in the eye. "I want you to remember me. If you remember me, then I don't care if everybody else forgets."

Silence descends on us for a time. A profound silence. A question wells up inside me, a question so big it plugs up my throat and makes it hard to breathe. I somehow swallow it back, finally choosing another. "Are memories such an important thing?"

"It depends," she replies, and lightly closes her eyes. "In some cases they're the most important thing there is."

"Yet you burned yours up."

"I had no use for them anymore." Miss Saeki brings her hands together on the table, her palms down the way the young girl's were the first time. "Kafka? I have a favor to ask. I want you to take that painting with you."

"You mean the one in my room in the library? The painting of the shore?"

Miss Saeki nods. "Yes, *Kafka on the Shore*. I want you to take it. Where, I don't care. Wherever you're going."

"But doesn't it belong to somebody?"

She shakes her head. "It's mine. He gave it to me as a present when he went away to college in Tokyo. Ever since then I've had it with me. Wherever I lived, I always hung it on the wall in my room. When I started working at the Komura Library I put it back in that room, where it first hung, but that was just temporary. I left a letter for Oshima in my desk in the library telling him I wanted you to have the painting. After all, the painting is originally *yours*."

"Mine?"

She nods. "You were there. And I was there beside you, watching you. On the shore, a long time ago. The wind was blowing, there were white puffy clouds, and it was always summer."

I close my eyes. I'm at the beach and it's summer. I'm lying back on a deck chair. I can feel the roughness of its canvas on my skin. I breathe in deeply the smell of the sea and the tide. Even with my eyes closed, the sun is glaring. I can hear the sound of the waves lapping at the shore. The sound recedes, then draws closer, as if time is making it quiver. Nearby, someone is painting a picture of me. And beside him sits a young girl in a short-sleeved light blue dress, gazing in my direction. She has straight hair, a straw hat with a white ribbon, and she's scooping up the sand. Steady, long fingers—the fingers of a pianist. Her smooth-as-porcelain arms glisten in the sunlight. A natural-looking smile plays at her lips. I'm in love with her. And she's in love with me.

That's the memory.

"I want you to have that painting with you forever," Miss Saeki says. She stands up, goes to the window, and looks outside. The sun's still high in the sky. The bee's still asleep. Miss Saeki holds up a hand to shield her eyes and looks at something far off, then turns to face me. "You have to go," she says.

I go over to her. Her ear brushes against my neck, the earring hard against my skin. I rest both palms on her back like I'm deciphering some sign there. Her hair brushes my cheek. She holds me tight, her fingers digging hard into my back. Fingers clinging to the wall that's time. The smell of the sea, the sound of waves breaking on the shore. Someone calling my name from far, far away.

"Are you my mother?" I'm finally able to ask.

"You already know the answer to that," Miss Saeki says.

She's right—I do know the answer. But neither one of us can put it into words. Putting it into words will destroy any meaning.

"A long time ago I abandoned someone I shouldn't have," she says. "Someone I loved more than anything else. I was afraid someday I'd lose this person. So I had to let go myself. If he was going to be stolen away from me, or I was going to lose him by accident, I decided it was better to discard him myself. Of course I felt anger that didn't fade, that was part of it. But the whole thing was a huge mistake. It was someone I should never have abandoned."

I listen in silence.

"You were discarded by the one person who never should have done that," Miss Saeki says. "Kafka—do you forgive me?"

"Do I have the right to?"

She looks at my shoulder and nods several times. "As long as anger and fear don't prevent you."

"Miss Saeki, if I really do have the right to, then yes—I do forgive you," I tell her.

Mother, you say. I forgive you. And with those words, audibly, the frozen part of your heart crumbles.

Silently, she lets go of me. She takes the hairpin out of her hair and without a moment's hesitation stabs the sharp tip into the inner flesh of her left arm, hard. With her right hand she presses down tightly on a vein, and blood begins to seep out. The first drop plops audibly to the floor. Without a word she holds her arm out toward me. Another drop of blood falls to the floor.

I bend over and put my lips on the small wound, lick her blood with my tongue, close my eyes, and savor the taste. I hold the blood in my mouth and slowly swallow it. Her blood goes down, deep in my throat. It's quietly absorbed by the dry outer layer of my heart. Only now do I understand how much I've wanted that blood. My mind is someplace far away, though my body is still right here—just like a living spirit. I feel like sucking down every last drop of blood from her, but I can't. I take my lips off her arm and look into her face.

"Farewell, Kafka Tamura," Miss Saeki says. "Go back to where you belong, and live."

"Miss Saeki?" I ask.

"Yes?"

"I don't know what it means to live."

She lets me go and looks up at me. She reaches out and touches my lips. "Look at the painting," she says quietly. "Keep looking at the painting, just like I did."

And she leaves. She opens the door and, without glancing back, steps outside and closes the door. I stand at the window and watch her go. Quickly she vanishes in the shadow of a building. Hands resting on the sill, I gaze for the longest time at where she disappeared. Maybe she forgot to say something and will come back. But she never does. All that's left is an absence, like a hollow.

The dozing bee wakes up and buzzes around me for a while.

Then, as if finally remembering what it's supposed to be doing, it flies out the open window. The sun shines down. I go back to the table and sit down. Her cup is sitting there, with a bit of tea left in it. I leave it where it is, without touching it. The cup looks like a metaphor. A metaphor of memories that, before long, will be lost.

I take off my shirt and change back into my sweaty, smelly T-shirt. I put the dead watch back on my left wrist. Then I put the ball cap Oshima gave me on backward, and the pair of sky blue sunglasses. Finally I tug on my long-sleeved shirt. I walk into the kitchen and drink a glass of tap water, put the glass in the sink, and take a final look around the room. At the dining table, the chairs. The chair the girl and Miss Saeki sat on. The teacup on top of the table. I close my eyes and take a deep breath. *You already know the answer to that.*

I open the door, go outside, and close the door. I walk down the porch steps, my shadow falling distinct and clear on the ground. It looks like it's clinging to my feet. The sun's still high in the sky.

At the entrance to the forest the two soldiers are leaning against a tree trunk like they've been waiting for me. When they see me they don't ask a single question. It's as if they already know what I'm thinking. Their rifles are slung over their shoulders.

The tall soldier is chewing on a stalk of grass. "The entrance is still open," he says. "At least it was when I checked a minute ago."

"You don't mind if we keep the same pace as before?" the brawny one asks. "You can keep up?"

"No problem. I can keep up."

"It'll be a problem, though, if we get there and the entrance is already shut," the tall one comments.

"Then you're stuck here," his companion adds.

"I know," I say.

"No regrets at having to leave?" the tall one asks.

"None."

"Then let's get going."

"Better not look behind you," the brawny one says.

"Yeah, that's a good idea," the tall one says.

And once again I set off through the forest.

Once, as we're hurrying up a slope, I do glance back. The soldiers warned me not to, but I couldn't help it. This is the last spot you can see the town from. Beyond it we'll be cut off by a wall of trees, and that world will vanish from my sight forever.

There still isn't a soul on the street. A beautiful stream runs through the hollow, small buildings line the street, the electric poles casting dark shadows on the ground. For a moment I'm frozen to the spot. I have to go back, no matter what. I could at least stay there until evening, when the young girl with the canvas bag will visit me. *If you need me, I'll be there.* I get a hot lump in my chest and a powerful magnet's pulling me back toward the town. My feet are buried in lead and won't budge. If I go on I'll never see her again. I come to a halt. I've lost all sense of time. I want to call out to the soldiers in front of me, *I'm not going back, I'm staying.* But no voice comes out. Words have no life in them.

I'm caught between one void and another. I have no idea what's right, what's wrong. I don't even know what I want anymore. I'm standing alone in the middle of a horrific sandstorm. I can't move, and can't even see my fingertips anymore. Sand as white as pulverized bones wraps me in its grip. But I hear her—Miss Saeki—speaking to me. "No matter what, you have to go back," she says decisively. "It's what *I* want. For you to be there."

The spell is broken, and I'm in one piece again. Warm blood returns to my body. The blood she gave me, the last drops of blood she had. The next instant I'm facing forward and following the soldiers. I turn a corner and that little world in the hills vanishes, swallowed up in dreams. Now I just focus on making it through the forest without getting lost. Not wandering from the path. That's what's important now, what I have to do.

The entrance is still open. There's still time until evening. I thank the two soldiers. They lay down their rifles and, like before, sit down on the large flat rock. The tall soldier's still chewing on a bit of grass. They're not out of breath at all after our breathless rush through the woods.

"Don't forget what I told you about bayonets," the tall soldier says. "When you stab the enemy, you've got to twist and slash, to cut his guts open. Otherwise he'll do it to you. That's the way the world is outside."

"That's not all there is, though," the brawny one says.

"No, of course not," the tall one replies, and clears his throat. "I'm just talking about the dark side of things."

"It's also real hard to tell right from wrong," the brawny one says.

"But it's something you've got to do," the tall one adds.

"Most likely," the brawny one says.

"One more thing," the tall one says. "Once you leave here, don't ever look back until you reach your destination. Not even once, do you understand?"

"This is important," the brawny one adds.

"Somehow you made it through back there," the tall one says, "but this time it's serious. Until you get to where you're going, don't *ever* look back."

"Ever," the brawny one says.

"I understand," I tell them. I thank them again and say good-bye.

The two of them come to attention and salute. I'll never see them again. I know that. And they know that. And knowing this, we say farewell.

I don't recall much of how I got back to Oshima's cabin after leaving the soldiers. As I made my way through the thick forest my mind must have been elsewhere. Amazingly, I didn't get lost. I have a vague memory of spotting the daypack I'd thrown away and, without thinking, picking it up. Same with the compass, the hatchet, the can of spray paint. I remember seeing the yellow marks I'd sprayed on tree trunks, like scales left behind by some giant moth.

I stand in the clearing in front of the cabin and gaze up at the sky. The world around me is suddenly filled with brilliant sounds—birds chirping, water gurgling down the stream, wind rustling the leaves. All faint, but to me it's like corks have been pulled from my ears and now everything sounds so alive, so warm, so close. Everything's mixed together, but still I can make out each individual sound. I look down at the watch on my wrist, and it's working again. Digital numbers flash on the green screen, changing each minute like nothing had ever happened. It's 4:16.

I go into the cabin and lie down on the bed in my clothes. I'm exhausted. I lie there on my back and close my eyes. A bee is resting above the window. The girl's arms glisten in the sunlight like porcelain. "An example," she says.

"Look at the painting," Miss Saeki says. "Just like I did."

White sands of time slip through the girl's slim fingers. Waves crash softly against the shore. They rise up, fall, and break. Rise up, fall, and break. And my consciousness is sucked into a dim, dark corridor.

Chapter 48

"Gimme a break," Hoshino repeated.

"Nothing's about to break here, Mr. Hoshino," the black cat said wearily. The cat had a large face and looked old. "I figured you were bored all by yourself. Talking to a stone all day."

"But how can you speak human language?"

"I can't."

"I don't get it. How are we able to carry on a conversation like this? A human and a cat?"

"We're on the border of this world, speaking a common language. That's all."

Hoshino gave this some thought. "The border of the world? A common language?"

"It's all right if you don't understand. I could explain, but it's a long story," the cat said, giving a couple of short, dismissive flips of its tail.

"Wait a sec!" Hoshino said. "You're Colonel Sanders, aren't you?"

"Colonel *who*?" the cat said sullenly. "I don't know who you're talking about. I'm me, and nobody else. Just your friendly neighborhood cat."

"Do you have a name?"

"Sure I do."

"What is it?"

"Toro," the cat replied hesitantly.

"Toro?" Hoshino repeated. "Like the real expensive part of tuna, you mean?"

"Correct," the cat replied. "The local sushi chef owns me. They have a dog, too. They call him Tekka. *Tuna Roll*."

"Do you know my name, then?"

"You're pretty famous, Mr. Hoshino," Toro replied, and smiled.

446

Hoshino had never seen a cat smile before. The smile quickly faded, though, and the cat went back to its usual docile expression.

"Cats know everything," Toro said. "I know that Mr. Nakata died yesterday, and that there's a valuable stone over there. I've lived a long life and know everything that's happened around here."

"Hmm," Hoshino murmured, impressed. "Hey, instead of us just shooting the breeze out here, why don't you come inside, Toro?"

Lying on the railing, the cat shook its head. "No, I'm fine here. I wouldn't be able to relax inside. Besides, it's a nice day out, so why don't we just talk here?"

"Fine by me," Hoshino said. "Say, are you hungry? I'm sure we have something to eat."

Again the cat shook his head. "Thanks, but I'm all set for food. In fact, keeping my weight down's more of a problem. If your owner runs a sushi shop, you tend to have a bit of a cholesterol problem. Jumping up and down's not easy when you're carrying some excess pounds."

"Well, tell me then, Toro, is there some reason you're here?"

"There is," the black cat said. "I thought you might be having a hard time dealing with that stone all alone."

"You got that right. Definitely. I'm in kind of a bind here."

"I thought I'd lend you a hand."

"That would be great," Hoshino said. "Take a *paws* in your schedule, huh?"

"The stone's the problem," Toro said, shaking his head to get rid of a buzzing fly. "Once you get the stone back the way it belongs, your job's over. You can go wherever you want after that. Do I have that right?"

"Yup, you got it. Once I get the stone closed that's all she wrote. Like Mr. Nakata said, once you open something up you got to close it. That's the rule."

"That's why I thought I'd show you what to do."

"You know what I should do?" Hoshino asked, excited.

"Of course," the cat said. "What'd I tell you? Cats know *everything*. Not like dogs."

"So what should I do?"

"You have to kill it," the cat said soberly.

"Kill it?" Hoshino said.

"That's right. You've got to kill it."

"Who is this *it* you're talking about?"

"You'll know it when you see it," the black cat explained. "Until you actually see it, though, you won't understand what I mean. It doesn't have any real form to begin with. It changes shape, depending on the situation."

"Is this a person we're talking about?"

"No, it's no person. That's for certain."

"So what does it look like?"

"You got me," Toro said. "Didn't I just explain? That you'll know it when you see it, and if you don't you won't? What about that don't you understand?"

Hoshino sighed. "So what is this thing's real identity?"

"You don't need to know that," the cat said. "It's hard to explain. Or maybe I should say you're better off not knowing. Anyhow, right now it's biding its time. Lying in some dark place, breathing quietly, watching and waiting. But it's not going to wait forever. Sooner or later it'll make its move. I'm figuring today is the day. And it will most definitely pass in front of you. It's an opportune moment."

"*Opportune?*"

"A one-in-a-million chance," the black cat said. "All you have to do is wait and kill it. That will put an end to it. Then you're free to go wherever you like."

"Isn't that against the law?"

"I wouldn't know about the law," Toro said, "being a cat and all. Since it's not a person, though, I doubt the law has anything to do with it. Anyhow, it's got to be killed. Even your typical cat next door like me can see that."

"Okay, say I want to kill it—how am I supposed to do it? I don't have any idea how big it is or what it looks like. Hard to plan a murder when you don't know the basic facts about the victim."

"It's up to you. Smash it with a hammer if you like. Stab it with a carving knife. Strangle it. Burn it. Bite it to death. Whatever works for you—but the main thing is you've *got to kill it*. Liquidate it with extreme prejudice. You were in the Self-Defense Force, am I right? Used taxpayers' money to learn how to shoot a rifle? How to sharpen a bayonet? You're a soldier, so use your head and figure out the best way to kill it."

"What I learned in the SDF was what to do in a war," Hoshino protested weakly. "They never trained me to ambush and kill something whose size and shape I don't even know—with a hammer, no less."

"It'll be trying to get in through the entrance," Toro went on, ignoring Hoshino's protests. "But you can't let it—no matter what. You've got to make sure you kill it before it gets inside the entrance. Got it? Let it slip by you, and that's the end."

"A one-in-a-million chance."

"Exactly," Toro said. "Though that's just a figure of speech."

"But isn't this thing pretty dangerous?" Hoshino asked fearfully. "It might turn the tables on me."

"It's probably not all that dangerous when it's on the move," the cat said. "Once it stops moving, though, watch out. That's when it's dangerous. So when it's on the move, don't let it get away. That's when you've got to finish it off."

"*Probably?*" Hoshino said.

The black cat didn't reply to that. He narrowed his eyes, stretched on the guardrail, and slowly got to his feet. "I'll be seeing you, Mr. Hoshino. Remember to kill it. If you don't do that, Mr. Nakata will never rest in peace. You liked the old man, didn't you?"

"Yeah. He was a good man."

"So you've got to kill it. Liquidate it with extreme prejudice, as I said. Mr. Nakata would've wanted you to. So do it for him. You've taken on his role now. You've always been a happy-go-lucky type, never taking responsibility for anything, right? Now's the chance to make up for that. Don't blow it, okay? I'll be rooting for you."

"That's encouraging," Hoshino said. "Oh, hey—I just thought of something."

"What?"

"Maybe the entrance stone is still open to lure it in?"

"Could be," Toro said diffidently. "One more thing. It only makes a move very late at night. So you should sleep during the day to make sure you don't fall asleep late and let it get away. That would be a catastrophe."

The black cat leaped nimbly onto the roof next door, straightened his tail, and walked away. For such a huge cat he was light on his feet. Hoshino watched from the veranda as the cat disappeared. Toro didn't look back even once.

"Man alive," Hoshino said, then went back into the kitchen to scout around for potential weapons. He found an extremely sharp kitchen knife, plus another heavy knife shaped like a hatchet. The kitchen had only a rudimentary assortment of pots and pans, but quite a collection of knives. In addition he selected a large, hefty hammer and some nylon rope. An ice pick rounded out his arsenal.

Here's where a nice automatic rifle would come in handy, he thought as he rummaged around the kitchen. He had been trained to shoot automatic rifles in the SDF, and was a decent marksman. Not that he expected to find a rifle in a cupboard somewhere. If anybody ever shot off an automatic rifle in a quiet neighborhood like this, there'd be hell to pay.

He laid all his weapons down on the living-room table—the two knives, ice pick, hammer, and rope. He put a flashlight beside them, then sat down next to the stone and began rubbing it.

"Jeez," Hoshino said to the stone. "A hammer and knives to fight something, and I don't even know what it is? With a black cat from the neighborhood calling the shots? What the hell kind of deal is *this*?"

The stone, of course, withheld comment.

"Toro said it *probably* wasn't dangerous. *Probably*? But what if something out of *Jurassic Park* springs up? What the hell am I sup-posed to do then, huh? I'd be a goner."

No response.

Hoshino grabbed the hammer and swung it around a few times.

"If you think about it, it's all fate. From the time I picked up Mr. Nakata at the rest area till now, it's like fate decided everything. The only one who hasn't had a clue has been *me*. Fate is one strange thing, man," Hoshino said. "Right? What's your take on it?"

The stone maintained its stony silence.

"Well, what can you do, right? I'm the one who chose this path, and I've got to see it through to the end. Kind of hard to imagine what repulsive thing's gonna pop out—but I'm okay with that. Got to give it my best shot. Life's short, and I've had some good times. Toro said this is a one-in-a-million chance. Maybe it wouldn't be so bad to go out in a blaze of glory. At least try to win one for the old guy. For Mr. Nakata."

The stone's silent vigil continued.

Hoshino did as the cat had told him and took a nap on the sofa in preparation for the night. It felt strange to follow a cat's instructions, but once he did lie down he was able to sleep soundly for an hour. In the evening he went into the kitchen, defrosted some shrimp curry, and had it over rice. As it started to get dark, he sat down next to the stone, knives and hammer in easy reach.

He turned off all the lights except for a small table lamp. That's best, he figured. It only makes a move at night, he thought, so I might as well make it as dark as possible. I want to wind this up soon, too—so if you're out there, show your face! Let's get it over with, okay? Once we're finished here I'm going back to Nagoya, to my apartment, and call up some girl and get it on.

He no longer talked to the stone. He just waited there silently, glancing every so often at the clock. When he got bored he'd swing the knife and hammer around. If anything happens, he thought, it's got to be the middle of the night. Though of course it might take place before that, and he wanted to make sure he didn't miss his chance—his one-in-a-million chance. Now wasn't the time to slack off. Every once in a while he took a bite of cracker and a sip of mineral water.

"Hey, stone," Hoshino whispered. "It's past midnight now—the time the demons come out. The moment of truth. Let's you and me find out what's gonna happen, what d'ya say?" He reached out to touch the stone. Maybe it was just his imagination, but the surface seemed slightly warmer than usual. He rubbed it over and over, to buck up his courage. "I want you to root for me too, okay?" he said to the stone. "I could do with a little emotional support here."

It was a little after three a.m. when a faint rustling noise started to come from the room where Nakata's body lay. A sound like something crawling along tatami. But there weren't any tatami, because that room was carpeted.

Hoshino looked up and listened closely. No mistake about it, he thought, I don't know what it is, but something's happening in there. His heart started to pound. He stuck the hammer in his belt, grabbed the sharpest knife in his right hand, the flashlight in his left, and stood up.

"Here we go . . . ," he said to no one in particular.

He crept silently to the door to Nakata's room and opened it. He switched on the flashlight and played it quickly around the body. That's definitely where the rustling had come from. The beam illuminated a long, pale, thin object that was squirming out of Nakata's mouth. The object reminded Hoshino of a gourd. It was as thick as a man's arm, and though he couldn't tell how long it was, Hoshino guessed that about half of it was out. Its wet body glistened like mucus. Nakata's mouth was stretched wide open like a snake's, to let the thing out. His jaw must have been unhinged, it was so wide open.

Hoshino gulped loudly. His hand holding the flashlight was trembling a little, the light wavering. Jeez, now how am I supposed to kill this thing? he wondered. It didn't seem to have any arms or legs, eyes or nose. So slimy you can't even get a good grip. So how am I supposed to *liquidate* it? And what the hell kind of creature *is* it, anyway?

Was it a kind of parasite that had been hiding inside Nakata all this time? Or was it the old man's soul? No, that can't be it. His intuition told him that kind of creepy thing couldn't have been inside Nakata. Even *I* know that much. It had to come from somewhere else, and it's going through Mr. Nakata just to get inside the entrance. It showed up when it wanted to, using Mr. Nakata as a kind of passageway for its own purposes. And I can't let that happen. That's why I've got to kill it. Like the cat said, *liquidate it with extreme prejudice.*

Hoshino went over to Nakata and quickly stabbed his knife into what seemed to be the head of the thing. He pulled out the knife and stabbed again, over and over. But there was little resistance to the knife, just the crisp feel you get when you plunge a knife into a soft vegetable. Below the slimy exterior there was no flesh, no bones. No organs, no brain. Once he pulled the blade out, the mucus covered up the wound right away. No blood or liquid oozed out. It doesn't feel a thing, Hoshino thought. No matter how fiercely he attacked it, the thing kept on creeping out of Nakata's mouth, nonplussed.

Hoshino tossed the knife to the floor and went back to the living room and picked up the heavy hatchet-shaped knife. He swung it down on the white thing over and over, splitting the head open, but just as he thought, there was nothing inside—just the same mushy white as the outer skin. He slashed at it a few times, finally severing part of the head, which squirmed like a slug on the floor for a moment, then stopped moving like it was dead. This had no effect on the rest of the body, which continued to ooze forward. Mucus soon covered up the wound, swelling up so the thing looked the same as before. None of this slowed it down as it wiggled on out of the old man's mouth.

Finally, the whole object was out, revealing its entire form. The creature was about a yard long, with a tail, which finally allowed

Hoshino to figure out for sure which end was which. The tail was like a salamander's, short and thick, the tip abruptly tapering down to a thin point. It had no legs, no eyes, no mouth or nose. But it most definitely had a will of its own. No, Hoshino thought, it's more like a will is *all* it has. He didn't need to figure that out logically, he just knew it. When it's on the move, he thought, it just happens to take on this shape. A chill ran up his spine. Anyway, he concluded, I've got to kill it.

He tried the hammer next, but it didn't do any good. He'd pound one part of the creature only to see the surrounding flesh and mucus fill in the depression he'd made. He carried over a small table and started bashing the thing with one of the legs, but nothing slowed down its inexorable advance. Like some clumsy snake it slowly, steadily crawled toward the next room and the entrance stone.

This isn't like any other living creature I've ever seen, Hoshino thought. No weapon has any effect on it. There's no heart you can stab, no throat you can throttle. So what the hell can I do? This thing is *evil*, and no matter what I've got to keep it from getting into the entrance. Toro said I'd know it when I saw it, and damn if he isn't right. I can't let this thing live.

Hoshino went back to the kitchen to look for something else to use as a weapon, but couldn't find anything. Suddenly he looked down at the stone at his feet. The entrance stone. That's it! I can use the stone to smash the thing. In the dim light the stone had a more reddish cast to it than usual. He bent down and tried to lift it. It was terribly heavy, and he couldn't budge it an inch. "I see—you're back to being the entrance stone," he said. "So if I close you up before that thing gets here, it won't be able to go inside."

Hoshino struggled with all his might to lift the stone, but couldn't.

"You're not moving," he said to the stone, gulping down big breaths. "I think you're even heavier than before. You're a real ball-buster, you know that?"

Behind him the rustling sound continued. The white thing was steadily getting closer and closer. He didn't have much time.

"One more try," Hoshino said. He rested his hands on the stone, took a huge breath, filling his lungs, and held the air in. He focused all his energy on one spot and put both hands on one side of the stone. If he couldn't lift it this time, he wouldn't have a second chance. *This is it, Hoshino!* Now or never. I'm gonna do this if it kills me! With all the strength he could muster he gave a groan and lifted. The stone raised up slightly. He put his last ounce of energy into it and managed—like he was stripping the stone off the floor—to lift it up.

His head felt faint and the muscles in his arms were screaming with pain. His balls felt like they'd long since been busted. Still, he couldn't raise it any higher. Hoshino thought of Nakata, how the old man had given his life to open and close the stone. Somehow, some way, he had to see it through to the bitter end. Toro told him he had to take over from the old man. His muscles were aching for fresh blood, his lungs dying for air to make that blood, but he couldn't breathe. He knew he was about as close to death as you can get, the abyss of nothingness gaping open right before his eyes. But he ignored this, focused all his strength one last time, and pulled the stone toward him. It lifted up and, with a massive thud, flipped over and fell to the floor. The floor shook with the shock, the glass door rattling. The stone was tremendously, profoundly heavy.

Hoshino sat there gasping for air. "You did good," he told himself a few moments later, once he finally caught his breath.

Once he'd closed the entrance, taking care of the white object was surprisingly simple. It was shut out of where it was headed, and it knew it. It stopped its forward advance and started crawling around the room looking for a place to hide, perhaps hoping to crawl back inside Nakata's mouth. But it didn't have the strength to escape. Hoshino went right after it, chopping it to pieces with his cleaver. Those pieces he chopped into even tinier ones. These little bits writhed for a while on the floor, but soon lost strength and stopped moving. They curled up into tight little balls and died, the carpet glistening with their slime. Hoshino gathered all the pieces with a dustpan, dumped them in a garbage bag that he tied closed with string, then put this bag inside another that he also tied up tight. This he put inside a thick cloth bag he found in the closet.

Completely drained, he squatted on the floor, his shoulders heaving as he took deep breaths. His hands were shaking. He wanted to say something, but couldn't form the words. "You did a good job, Hoshino," he managed to say a few moments later.

With all the noise he'd made attacking that white creature and flipping the stone over, he was worried that people in the apartment building had woken up and were even now dialing 911. Fortunately, nothing happened. No police sirens, no one pounding on the door. The last thing he needed was for the police to come barging in.

Hoshino knew the bits and pieces of the white thing stuffed tightly in the bags weren't about to come back to life. There's no place left for them to go, he thought. But it was a good idea just to make sure, so he decided that as soon as it was light he'd go to the beach and burn them all up. Turn them into ash.

And once that was over he'd head back to Nagoya. Back home.

It was nearly four by this time, and getting light out. Time to get going. Hoshino stuffed his clothes into his bag, including—just to be on the safe side—his sunglasses and Chunichi Dragons ball cap. Getting snagged by the police before he could finish would mess up the whole thing. He took along a bottle of cooking oil to use to light the fire. He remembered his CD of the *Archduke* Trio and tossed it in his bag as well.

Finally, he went into the room where Nakata lay in bed. The AC was still on full blast, and the room was freezing. "Hey there, Mr. Nakata," he said, "I'm about ready to take off. Sorry, but I can't stay here forever. I'll call the cops from the station so they can come take care of your body. We'll just have to leave the rest up to some kind patrolmen, okay? We'll never see each other again, but I'll never forget you. Even if I tried to, I don't think I could."

With a loud rattle the air conditioner shut off.

"You know what, Gramps?" he went on. "I think that whenever something happens in the future I'll always wonder—*What would Mr. Nakata say about this? What would Mr. Nakata do?* I'll always have someone I can turn to. And that's kind of a big deal, if you think about it. It's like part of you will always live inside me. Not that I'm the best container you could find, but better than nothing, huh?"

But the person he was addressing was nothing more than a shell of Mr. Nakata. The most important part of him had long since left for another place. And Hoshino understood this.

"Hey there," he said to the stone, and reached out to touch its surface. It was back to being just an ordinary stone, cool and rough to the touch. "I'm heading out. Going back home to Nagoya. I'll have to let the cops take care of you too. I know I should take you back to the shrine where you came from, but my memory isn't so good and I don't have any idea which shrine it is. You'll have to forgive me. Don't put a curse on me or anything, okay? I only did what Colonel Sanders told me to. So if you're gonna put a curse on anybody, he's your guy. Anyhow, I'm happy I could meet you. I'll never forget you, either."

Hoshino put on his thick-soled Nike sneakers and walked out of the apartment, leaving the door unlocked. In one hand he held his bag with all his things, in the other the bag with that white *thing's* corpse.

"Gentlemen," he said, gazing up at the dawn rising in the east, "it's time to light my fire!"

Chapter 49

Just after nine the next morning, I hear the sound of a car approaching and go outside. It's a small four-wheel-drive Datsun truck, the kind with massive tires and the body jacked up high. It looks like it hasn't been washed in at least a half a year. In the bed are two long, well-used surfboards. The truck grinds to a stop in front of the cabin. When the engine cuts off silence returns. The door opens and a tall young man climbs out, wearing an oversize white T-shirt, an oil-stained No Fear shirt, khaki shorts, and sneakers that have seen better days. The guy looks around thirty, with wide shoulders. He's tanned all over and has three days' worth of stubble on his face. His hair's long enough to hide his ears. I'm guessing this must be Oshima's older brother, the one who runs a surf shop in Kochi.

"Hey," he says.

"Morning," I reply.

He sticks out his hand, and we shake hands on the porch. He has a strong grip. I guessed right. He does turn out to be Oshima's older brother.

"Everybody calls me Sada," he tells me. He talks slowly, choosing his words deliberately, like he's in no hurry. Like he has all the time in the world. "I got a call from Takamatsu to come pick you up and take you back," he explains. "Sounds like some urgent business came up."

"Urgent business?"

"Yeah. I don't know what, though."

"Sorry you had to go to all this trouble," I tell him.

"No need to apologize," he says. "Can you get ready to leave soon?"

"Give me five minutes."

While I'm stuffing my things in my backpack, he helps me close up the place, whistling all the while. He shuts the window, pulls the curtains, checks that the gas is off, gathers up the remaining food, does a quick scrub of the sink. I can tell from watching him that he feels like the cabin's an extension of himself.

"Seems like my brother likes you," Sada says. "He doesn't like all that many people. He's sort of a difficult person."

"He's been really kind to me."

Sada nods. "He can be pretty nice when he wants to be."

I climb into the passenger seat of the truck and toss my backpack at my feet.

Sada turns on the ignition, shifts into gear, leans out the window to check out the cabin one more time, then steps on the gas. "This cabin is one of the few things the two of us share as brothers," he says as he expertly maneuvers down the mountain road. "When the mood hits us, we sometimes come here and spend a few days alone." He mulls this over for a while, then goes on. "This was always an important place for the two of us, and still is. It's like there's a power here that recharges us. A quiet sort of power. You know what I mean?"

"I think so," I tell him.

"My brother said you would," Sada says. "People that don't get it never will."

The faded cloth seats are covered with white dog hair. The dog smell mixes with that of the sea, plus the scent of surfboard wax and cigarettes. The knob for the AC is broken off. The ashtray's full of butts, the side pocket stuffed full of random cassette tapes, minus their boxes.

"I went into the woods a few times," I say.

"Deep in there?"

"Yes," I reply. "Oshima warned me not to."

"But you went in anyway."

"Yeah," I say.

"I did the same once. Must be like ten years ago." He's silent for a time, concentrating on his driving. We're on a long curve, the thick tires spraying pebbles as we go. Every so often there're crows beside the road. They don't try to fly away, just watch intently, with curious eyes, as we pass by.

"Did you run across the soldiers?" Sada asks as casually as if he'd asked me what time it was.

"You mean those two soldiers?"

"Right," Sada responds, glancing at me. "You went in that far, huh?"

"Yeah, I did," I reply.

His hands lightly gripping the wheel as he maneuvers it, he doesn't respond, and his expression doesn't tell me anything.

"Sada?" I ask.

"Hm?" he says.

"When you met those soldiers ten years ago, what did you do?"

"What did I do when I met those soldiers?" he repeats.

I nod and wait for his answer.

He glances in the rearview mirror, then looks in front again. "I've never talked about that to anyone," he says. "Not even to my brother. Brother, sister—whatever you want to call him. Brother works for me. He doesn't know anything about those soldiers."

I nod silently.

"And I doubt I'll ever tell anybody about it. Even you. And I don't think you'll ever talk about it to anyone, either. Even to me. You know what I'm trying to say?"

"I think so," I tell him.

"What is it?"

"It's not something you can get across in words. The real response is something words can't express."

"There you go," Sada replies. "Exactly. If you can't get it across in words then it's better not to try."

"Even to yourself?" I ask.

"Yeah, even to yourself," Sada says. "Better not to try to explain it, even to yourself."

He offers me a stick of Cool Mint gum. I take one and start chewing.

"You ever try surfing?" he asks.

"No."

"If you have the chance I'll teach you," he says. "If you'd like to learn, I mean. The waves are pretty decent along the Kochi shore, and there aren't so many surfers. Surfing's a more profound kind of sport than it looks. When you surf you learn not to fight the power of nature, even if it gets violent."

He takes out a cigarette from the pocket of his T-shirt, sticks it in his mouth, and lights it up with the dashboard lighter. "That's another thing that words can't explain. One of those things that's neither a yes or a no answer." He narrows his eyes and blows smoke out the window. "In Hawaii," he goes on, "there's a spot they call the Toilet Bowl.

459

There're these huge whirlpools because it's where the incoming and outgoing tides meet and crash into each other. It goes around and around like when you flush a toilet. If you wipe out there, you get pulled underwater and it's hard to float up again. Depending on the waves you might never make it back to the surface. So there you are, underwater, pounded by waves, and there's nothing you can do. Flailing around's not gonna get you anywhere. You'll just use up your energy. You've never been so scared in your life. But unless you get over that fear you'll never be a real surfer. You have to face death, get to really know it, then overcome it. When you're down in that whirlpool you start thinking about all kinds of things. It's like you get to be friends with death, have a heart-to-heart talk with it."

At the gate he gets out of the truck and locks it back up, jiggling the chain a couple of times to make sure it'll hold.

After this we don't talk much. He leaves an FM station on as he drives, but I can tell he's not really listening to it. Having the radio on's just a token gesture. Even when we go into a tunnel and all we hear is static, he doesn't mind. With the AC broken, we leave the windows open when we get on the highway.

"If you ever feel like learning how to surf, stop by and see me," Sada says as the Inland Sea comes into view. "I have an extra room, and you can stay as long as you like."

"Thanks," I say. "I'll take you up on that. I don't know when, though."

"You pretty busy?"

"I have a couple of things I have to take care of."

"Same with me," Sada says.

We don't say anything for a long time. He's thinking over his problems, I'm thinking over mine. He keeps his eyes on the road, left hand on top of the steering wheel, and smokes an occasional cigarette. Unlike Oshima, he doesn't speed. With his elbow propped on the open window, he drives down the highway at a leisurely pace. The only time he passes other cars is when they're going way too slow. Then he reluctantly steps on the gas, goes around, then slips right back into his lane.

"Have you been surfing for a long time?" I ask him.

"Hmm," he says, and then there's silence. Finally, when I've almost forgotten the question, he answers.

"I've been surfing since high school. Then it was just for fun.

Didn't really get serious about it till six years ago. I was working at a big ad agency in Tokyo. I couldn't stand it so I quit, moved back here, and started surfing. I took out a loan, borrowed some money from my folks, and opened a surf shop. I run it alone, so I can pretty much do whatever I want."

"Did you want to come back to Shikoku?"

"That was part of it," he says. "I don't know, I don't feel right unless I've got the sea and mountains nearby. People are mostly a product of where they were born and raised. How you think and feel's always linked to the lay of the land, the temperature. The prevailing winds, even. Where were you born?"

"Tokyo. In Nogata, in Nakano Ward."

"Do you want to go back there?"

I shake my head. "No."

"Why not?"

"There's no reason for me to go back."

"Okay," he says.

"I'm not very connected to the lay of the land, the prevailing winds and all that," I say.

"Yeah?" he says.

We're silent again. Silence doesn't seem to bother him a bit. Or me either. I just sit there, my mind a blank, listening to the music on the radio. He's staring at the road straight ahead. Eventually we exit the highway, turn north, and come into the Takamatsu city limits.

It's a little before one p.m. when we arrive at the Komura Library. Sada drops me off in front but doesn't get out himself. The engine's still on, and he's heading right back to Kochi.

"Thanks," I say.

"Hope we can see each other soon," he says. He sticks his hand out the window, gives a short wave, then peels out on his thick tires. Heading back to catch some big waves, to his own world, his own issues.

I put on my backpack and pass through the gate. I catch a whiff of the freshly mown lawn in the garden. It feels like I've been away for months, but it's only been four days.

Oshima's at the counter, wearing a tie, something I've never seen before. A white button-down shirt, and a mustard-yellow-and-green-striped tie. He's rolled the sleeves up to his elbows and doesn't have a jacket on. In front of him, predictably, there's a coffee cup and two neatly sharpened pencils.

"Hey," he greets me, adding his usual smile.

"Hi," I say back.

"Guess you caught a ride with my brother?"

"That's right."

"Bet he didn't talk much," Oshima says.

"Actually, we did talk a little."

"You're lucky. Depending on who he's with, sometimes he won't say a word."

"Did something happen here?" I ask. "He told me there was some-thing urgent."

Oshima nods. "There are a couple of things you need to know about. First of all, Miss Saeki passed away. She had a heart attack. I found her collapsed facedown on her desk upstairs on Tuesday after-noon. It happened all of a sudden, and it doesn't seem like she suf-fered."

I set my pack on the floor and sit down in a chair. "Tuesday after-noon?" I ask. "Today's Friday, right?"

"Yes, that's right. She died after the regular Tuesday tour. I proba-bly should've gotten in touch with you sooner, but I couldn't think straight."

Sunk back in the chair, I find I can't move. The two of us sit there in silence for a long time. I can see the stairs leading to the second floor, the well-polished black banister, the stained glass on the landing. Those stairs always held a special significance for me, because they led to her, to Miss Saeki. But now they're just empty stairs, with no mean-ing at all. She's no longer there.

"As I mentioned before, I think this was all predestined," Oshima says. "I knew it, and so did she. Though when it actually happens, of course, it's pretty hard to take."

When he pauses, I feel like I should say something, but the words won't come.

"According to her wishes, there won't be a funeral," Oshima con-tinues. "She was quietly cremated. She left a will in a drawer in her desk upstairs. She left her entire estate to the foundation that runs the library. She left me her Mont Blanc pen as a keepsake. And a painting for you. The one of the boy on the shore. You'll take it, won't you?"

I nod.

"It's all wrapped up over there, ready to go."

"Thanks," I say, finally able to speak.

"Tell me something, Kafka Tamura," Oshima says. He picks up a pencil and gives it his usual twirl. "Is it okay if I ask you a question?"

I nod.

"I didn't need to tell you she died, did I? You already knew."

Again I nod. "I think I did."

"I thought so," Oshima says, and draws a deep breath. "Would you like some water or something? To tell you the truth, you look as parched as a desert."

"Thanks, I could use some." I am pretty thirsty, but hadn't realized it until he mentioned it.

I down the ice water he brings me in a single gulp, so fast my head starts to ache. I put the empty glass back on the table.

"Care for some more?"

I shake my head.

"What are your plans now?" Oshima asks.

"I'm going to go back to Tokyo," I reply.

"What are you going to do there?"

"Go to the police, first of all, and tell them what I know. If I don't, they'll be after me the rest of my life. And then I'll most likely go back to school. Not that I want to, but I have to at least finish junior high. If I just put up with it for a few months and graduate, then I can do whatever I want."

"Makes sense," Oshima says. He narrows his eyes and looks at me. "That sounds like the best plan."

"More and more I've been thinking that's the way to go."

"You can run but you can't hide?"

"Yeah, I guess so," I say.

"You've grown up."

I shake my head. I can't say a thing.

Oshima lightly taps the eraser end of a pencil against his temple a couple of times. The phone rings, but he ignores it.

"Every one of us is losing something precious to us," he says after the phone stops ringing. "Lost opportunities, lost possibilities, feelings we can never get back again. That's part of what it means to be alive. But inside our heads—at least that's where I imagine it—there's a little room where we store those memories. A room like the stacks in this library. And to understand the workings of our own heart we have to keep on making new reference cards. We have to dust things off every once in a while, let in fresh air, change the water in the flower vases. In other words, you'll live forever in your own private library."

I stare at the pencil in his hand. It pains me to look at it, but I have to be the world's toughest fifteen-year-old, at least for a while longer. Or pretend to be. I take a deep breath, fill my lungs with air, and manage to inhale that lump of emotion. "Is it all right if I come back here someday?" I ask.

"Of course," Oshima says, and lays his pencil back on the counter. He links his hands behind his head and looks straight at me. "The word is that I'll be in charge of the library for a while. And I imagine I'll need an assistant. Once you're free of the police, school, what have you—and provided you want to, of course—I'd love to have you back. The town and I aren't going anywhere, not for the time being. People need a place they can belong."

"Thanks," I tell him.

"You're quite welcome," he says.

"Your brother said he'd teach me how to surf."

"That's great. He doesn't take to most people," he says. "He's a bit of a difficult person."

I nod, and smile. They really are quite alike, these two brothers.

"Kafka," Oshima says, looking deep into my eyes. "I could be wrong, but I think that's the first time I've ever seen you smile."

"You could be right," I say. I most definitely am smiling. And blushing.

"When are you going back to Tokyo?"

"Right now, I think."

"Can't you wait till evening? I can drive you to the station after we close up."

I consider this, then shake my head. "Thanks. But I think it's best if I leave right away."

Oshima nods. He goes into a back room and brings out the neatly wrapped painting. He also puts a single copy of the record "Kafka on the Shore" in a bag and hands it to me. "A little present from me."

"Thanks," I say. "Is it okay if I go up and see Miss Saeki's room one more time?"

"Go right ahead."

"Would you come with me?"

"Of course."

We go upstairs to her room. I stand in front of her desk, lightly touch its surface, and think over all the things it has absorbed. I picture her slumped facedown on the desk. How she always sat there, the window behind her, busily writing away. How I brought her coffee, when she'd glance up as I opened the door and came inside. How she always smiled at me.

"What was it she was writing here?" I ask.

"I don't know," Oshima replies. "One thing I *do* know for sure is she took a lot of secrets with her when she left this world."

A lot of *theories* as well, I silently think.

The window's open, the June breeze gently rustling the hem of the white lace curtains. A faint scent of the sea is in the air. I remember feeling the sand in my hand at the beach. I walk away from the desk and over to Oshima, and hold him tight. His slim body calls up all sorts of nostalgic memories.

He gently rubs my hair. "The world is a metaphor, Kafka Tamura," he says into my ear. "But for you and me this library alone is no metaphor. It's always just this library. I want to make sure we understand that."

"Of course," I say.

"It's a unique, special library. And nothing else can ever take its place."

I nod.

"Good-bye, Kafka," Oshima says.

"Good-bye, Oshima," I say. "You know, you look good in that necktie."

He lets go of me, looks me in the face, and smiles. "I've been waiting for you to say that."

Shouldering my backpack, I walk to the local station and take the train back to Takamatsu Station. I buy a ticket to Tokyo at the counter. The train will get in to Tokyo late at night, so the first thing I'll have to do is find a place to stay for the night, then head over to my house in Nogata the next day. I'll be all alone in that huge, vacant house. Nobody's waiting for me to come home. But I have no other place to go back to.

I use a public phone at the station and call Sakura's cell phone. She's in the middle of work but says she can spare a couple minutes. That's fine, I tell her.

"I'm going back to Tokyo now," I tell her. "I'm at Takamatsu Station. I just wanted to tell you."

"You're finished running away from home?"

"I guess so."

"Fifteen's a little early to run away, anyway," she says. "But what are you going to do back in Tokyo?"

"Go back to school."

"That's probably a good idea," she says.

"You're going back to Tokyo too, aren't you?"

"Yeah, probably in September. I might go on a trip somewhere in the summer."

"Can I see you in Tokyo?"

"Yeah, of course," she says. "Can you tell me your number?"

I give her the number at my house, and she writes it down.

"I had a dream about you the other day," she says.

"I had one about you too."

"A pretty raunchy one, I bet?"

"Could be," I admit. "But it was just a dream. What about yours?"

"Mine wasn't raunchy. You were in this huge house that was like a maze, walking around, searching for some special room, but you couldn't find it. There was somebody else in the house, looking for you. I tried to yell a warning, but you couldn't hear me. A pretty scary dream. When I woke up I was exhausted from all that yelling. I've been worried about you ever since."

"I appreciate it," I say. "But that's just a dream too."

"Nothing bad happened to you?"

"No, nothing bad." *No, nothing bad*, I tell myself.

"Good-bye, Kafka," she says. "I have to get back to work, but if you ever want to talk, just call me, okay?"

"Good-bye," I say. "Sister," I add.

Over the bridge and across the water we go, and I transfer to the bullet train at Okayama Station. I sink back in my seat and close my eyes. My body gradually adjusts to the train's vibration. The tightly wrapped painting of *Kafka on the Shore* is at my feet. I can feel it there.

"I want you to remember me," Miss Saeki says, and looks right into my eyes.

"If you remember me, then I don't care if everyone else forgets."

Time weighs down on you like an old, ambiguous dream. You keep on moving, trying to slip through it. But even if you go to the ends of the earth, you won't be able to escape it. Still, you have to go there—to the edge of the world. There's something you can't do unless you get there.

It starts to rain just after we pass Nagoya. I stare at the drops streaking the dark window. It was raining the day I left Tokyo, too. I picture rain falling in all sorts of places—in a forest, on the sea, a highway, a library. Rain falling at the edge of the world.

I close my eyes and relax, letting my tense muscles go loose. I listen to the steady hum of the train. And then, without warning, a warm tear spills from my eye, runs down my cheek to my mouth, and, after a while, dries up. No matter, I tell myself. It's just one tear. It doesn't even feel like it's mine, more like part of the rain outside.

Did I do the right thing?

"You did the right thing," the boy named Crow says. "You did what was best. No one else could have done as well as you did. After all, you're the genuine article: the toughest fifteen-year-old in the world."

"But I still don't know anything about life," I protest.

"Look at the painting," he says. "And listen to the wind."

I nod.

"I know you can do it."

I nod again.

"You'd better get some sleep," the boy named Crow says. "When you wake up, you'll be part of a brand-new world."

You finally fall asleep. And when you wake up, it's true.

You are part of a brand-new world.

The year is 1984 and the city is Tokyo. A young woman named Aomame follows a taxi driver's enigmatic suggestion and begins to notice puzzling discrepancies in the world around her. She has entered, she realizes, a parallel existence, which she calls 1Q84—"Q is for 'question mark.' A world that bears a question." Meanwhile, an aspiring writer named Tengo takes on a suspect ghostwriting project. He becomes so wrapped up with the work and its unusual author that, soon, his previously placid life begins to come unraveled. As Aomame's and Tengo's narratives converge over the course of this single year, we learn of the profound and tangled connections that bind them ever closer.

Fiction

ALSO AVAILABLE

After Dark

After the Quake

Blind Willow, Sleeping Woman

Dance Dance Dance

The Elephant Vanishes

Hard-Boiled Wonderland and the End of the World

Kafka on the Shore

Men Without Women

Norwegian Wood

South of the Border, West of the Sun

Sputnik Sweetheart

Underground

What I Talk About When I Talk About Running

The Wind-Up Bird Chronicle

Wind/Pinball

VINTAGE INTERNATIONAL
Available wherever books are sold.
www.vintagebooks.com

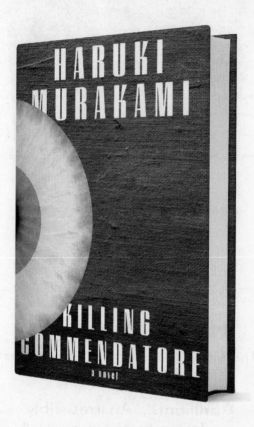

1Q84
Haruki Murakami
The complete novel in a 3-volume boxed set

"Brilliant.... An irresistibly
engaging literary fantasy."
— *The Washington Post*

978-0-345-80293-4

Also find other works at HarukiMurakami.com

Vintage International